hand his

stran s a

"What's the matter?" Tam growled without slowing his progress.

"I just wanted you to know that we've finished checking the astronomical instruments that were malfunctioning."

Tam turned to face the scientist.

"Were malfunctioning? Just what do you mean by that? Has it put the ship in danger? My God, why didn't you tell me about this earlier?"

Gull held up his hands in protest. "No, the malfunction wasn't that serious, I assure you. Nothing that directly affected the ship's performance. No, Hadir Polat, this was more subtle than that."

"Well, what is it then?" Tam said impatiently. "Come on, you don't bring something to my attention and then dismiss it as trivial. I know you better than that. Hell, I chose you myself for that very trait! Now, tell me."

"It was the long-range astronomical instruments," Gull explained quietly. "Apparently, the systemic noise in them was enough to indicate that there were five major satellites orbiting Thetti and two smaller moons. We've checked and rechecked the original readings and can only locate six of them now. One of the smaller ones seems to have, uh, disappeared . . ."

VIXEN

BUD SPARHAWK

VIXEN

Published by
Dorchester Publishing Co., Inc.
200 Madison Ave.
New York, NY 10016
in collaboration with Wildside Press LLC

ISBN-10: 0-8439-5945-2
ISBN-13: 978-0-8439-5945-1

The name "Cosmos Books" and the Cosmos logo are the property of Wildside Press, LLC.

Printed in the United States of America.

ARRIVAL

Covenant, the great, silent fish of a ship, swam silvery and smooth, slick as light, through the cold, empty dark. The dormant ship slept, but it would briefly wake to peer about to ensure that it had not deviated from its preordained path or to avoid some bit of cosmic flotsam — perhaps a vagrant comet sweeping across the arc of stars — before returning to a restless slumber. But mostly it slept through the light years as it followed the unique signature of one specific, distant star.

*

Cold.

That was the first thing the Hadir, Tam Polat, became aware of: the intense cold that permeated every cell of his body, a cold that so deep that he felt as though the core of his heart was a frozen pellet, barely able to pump the slush-filled blood through his frigid veins. He strained to open his eyes, worked hard to force his eyelids to break free of their coating of ice. The shivering started long before he succeeded.

Where was he? He could barely recall something about a trip and something he had to do at the end of it, he was so cold. Oh yes, he had to remember to pick up some drinks for the people who were coming over tonight to help celebrate Solstice Day. That must be why he was so cold — winter had started and the temperature was dropping. But why did he have to pick up the drinks? He worried at the lost memory until he recalled that Larisha was bringing some new team members to see him. But what was he supposed to get? For the life of him, he couldn't remember.

God, it was cold!

Tam's shivering became more intense. Must have fallen through the ice, he thought. Wasn't there a pond or stream he had to cross to get home? A fall into winter waters would be a shock to his body. Perhaps he was in the hospital and they were trying to bring him back to life. Would

Doctor Chen be there, hovering over him, coaxing him back from the brink?

No, Chen wouldn't be in the emergency ward of the local hospital. He was on the departure team. Why had he thought that Doctor Chen should be here, wherever here was?

The ice that held his eyelids tight finally gave way, and he blinked at the bright lights shining down on him, on his steaming, naked body. Why had they left him lying here without clothing or even a decent blanket to warm him? Didn't anybody in this hospital care about . . .

But the ceiling wasn't that of any hospital he'd ever seen. Too close, too blue, too slick and shining, it looked like nothing more than the inside lid of a food container.

Something clicked, as if a floe had broken loose, releasing his memories. Sudden clarity flooded his mind with certain knowledge of this place, this time, and the critical rôle he was destined to play upon revival.

This was no hospital. There had been no accident, no fall into icy waters. The Solstice Day he'd remembered was years, perhaps centuries in the past. No, this chill awakening had nothing to do with an accident, but Doctor Chen had most definitely been involved. Doctor Chen had put Tam into this chamber. Doctor Chen had frozen him for the long one-way trip.

A few moments more and his eyes finally adjusted to the lights . . . the radiant lamps warming his body, bringing him back up to normal temperature. He could feel the warmth seeping into his bones, thawing the core of ice at his center, melting the years of stasis away, drop by drop; a snowflake of months here, a snowbank of frozen years there, and a century's icicle, all flowing away as life returned and the flurry of pelting minutes began.

The shivering finally ceased, his fingers and toes stopped tingling, and he became aware of a great thirst. His throat was parched. Something insistently prodded his right cheek. He turned his head and noticed a thin tube at mouth level moving back and forth. As he opened his lips, the tube slid smoothly forward, and a trickle of warm broth ran over his tongue and down his throat. He gagged for a second and then remembered to swallow. The hot fluid coursed through him, warming his insides and restoring his strength.

"Take it slowly," he recalled Doctor Chen cautioning during the indoctrination sessions. "You must work your way back to life with great care. One does not abuse the body after so long a sleep." Good advice. If the trip had gone according to profile, he would have been in stasis for, at a minimum, nearly two hundred years.

Two hundred years! My God, Doctor Chen would probably be dead by now, as would most of those who had prepared the crew for the voyage. He wished he could thank them for the excellent job they'd done to ensure his survival, but that would be impossible, given the exigencies of interstellar travel. No, they would have already gotten whatever rewards they'd deserved, died, and been forgotten, along with everything else he had known. All that was calendar and light years in the past. None of them were any longer his concern.

When the radiant lamps clicked off, Tam slid the cover away with stiff and aching arms before drifting across the cold chamber to the lockers. He struggled to straighten himself, his muscles protesting their long disuse. Finally, with an effort of will, he reached a locker, opened it, and pulled out a thick coverall. After struggling for agonizing moments with stiffened fingers, he got himself dressed. With still greater effort, he put warm stockings on his feet to protect them from the chill of the deck.

His glandular balancing was still going on. He simultaneously felt joy and sorrow, lassitude and exhilaration, always out of step with his raging emotions. Manic energy fought against a crushing depression for a few seconds while, a heartbeat later, beaming optimism battled lassitude.

"Wait the emotional storm out," Chen had cautioned. "It will pass."

He made a half turn and lowered himself into his seat, pressed two buttons, and waited as the unit heated three steaming mugs to restore the nutrients that his body had lost. Chen's insistent protocol demanded that he down them all before starting work.

"It will do the others no good if you, uh, expire before you can attend to their needs."

Doctor Chen had sounded as though he were lecturing on manners instead of a life-saving, life-restoring procedure. But he would follow the old doctor's advice. He would do as he was taught. One did not lightly ignore the advice of the wise. One did not ignore the orders of the Hand of God's chief scientist.

The liquid in the first mug tasted salty. Tam suspected that it was designed to restore his electrolyte balance. The second was so sweet that he could barely get it down — sugar for quick energy, he thought, as his brain began to function normally.

The contents of the third mug were a surprise — warm, dark chocolate, just the way he liked it. He savored the taste. It might be the last chocolate he'd have for years. Good old Chen, ever the considerate one.

Memory returned with a rush. He was the Hadir, Tam Polat, in command of the Hand of God's own ship — *Covenant* — on its voyage from Heaven to Meridian. He was to prepare the way for the wave of settlers who would arrive fifty years behind him. His mission was to survive, to exploit whatever resources he found, and to have this system ready for colonization. He had the authority and means to do anything and everything necessary to that end.

Within an hour, Tam felt much stronger and, with the strengthening nourishment inside him, he began the arduous process of bringing the Raggi, Bul Larisha, his second in command, out of stasis. He unpacked blankets to wrap her in when she awoke.

"Best that the people not face the indignity of waking naked," Doctor Chen had said. The psychological support provided by the thick warm blankets was as important as the physical benefit, he'd insisted.

But Tam didn't care about that. All he really cared about at the moment was that the blankets would help Larisha revive faster so she could de-ice enough of the crew to warm this ship and rid it of the stink of too many years, too many chemicals, and too few human activities.

After he had started the restoration process for Larisha, he wormed his way to the command module through the tightly-packed bags, boxes, and containers of supplies that filled every compartment and corridor. The module was cold as the grave, still recovering from the near-absolute-zero of the emptiness between the stars. He touched the toggle that would open the observation port's cover, but did not flip it on.

This was an historic moment, one that no one in this system would experience for another thousand years, when the next wave of the expansion left. He wanted to savor it, to burn it into his mind forever.

But there was something else staying his hand. He felt as if he were under observation. He felt as if God Himself were watching his actions — as if he were being weighed by something far beyond his ken.

"Emerging God, I am Your faithful servant," he intoned. "I will justify Your trust in me. I will do the work of the Hand as You directed." The simple declaration of faith gave him comfort. He would have been remiss had he allowed his hubris to make him forget his rôle, his humble place in God's plan. He flipped the cold toggle, hardly breathing, as the cover began to withdraw.

His first impression was of a huge expanse of blinding white. Then he noticed the other colors, the full spectrum of subtle shades. The complexity of form, the infinite depths.

He screamed in fright. His worse fears had been realized. God was watching him.

When Tam Polat recovered from shock, only bright stars sparked on the deep velvet field of the heavens. None of the configurations was familiar. A single star, brighter than all the rest, blazed off to one side. It had to be their target. They had arrived.

He shivered. Had the apparition been a transient effect of the drugs, or had he actually been blessed to see the true face of God? He recalled the apparition with such intensity, such clarity, that he knew it could not have been a figment of his imagination. No, his perceptions, his memories of that sight, were too vivid. It must have happened. He was blessed indeed.

He was still trembling from that awesome feeling of being examined, weighed, and then discarded as if unworthy of notice. He prayed that the other Men would be spared such a degrading experience.

But why had he been so blessed? Perhaps he, as leader of their enterprise, as the Hadir of Heaven's mission, had been granted the boon of seeing a tiny piece of God's greater glory. Perhaps it had been a reward, an affirmation of his historic rôle.

Yes, that was the only explanation. Heaven's Hand had chosen well. He *was* truly blessed.

With renewed strength, he turned to continue his work.

ONE

A full week after emerging from the long freeze, Tam was still amazed at how easily he tired after such a long and peaceful sleep. Of course, it was very easy to tire in the chill air of the ship — air that still stank of machine sterility and dust too-long undisturbed. He shivered once more and rubbed his arms to help his circulation. Surely time would cure him of this weakness.

According to the schedule, Larisha's Halfings, the maintenance crew in particular, were supposed to have the environmental units operating by now. That should have produced a little heat and provided some relief. So why couldn't he detect any warm air coming through the vents in the command module? How long must he wait before he felt a change in the temperature?

But that was a foolish question. For two hundred years or more the ship had been a hairsbreadth above the ambient temperature of interstellar space. Even with the ship's heaters going full blast, it would take a long, long time before these cold walls and decks grew warm. With a sigh over matters even he, as the mission's supreme ruler — Hadir — could not control, he pulled his heavy parka around him and turned his attention to other matters.

Thus far, things had gone according to plan, with no more crises than expected: A few systems had failed over their long years of disuse; some of the crew members hadn't survived stasis; and the hull had suffered minor damage from debris encountered during the long voyage. But all of these events had been anticipated, and contingency plans had been made. Repairs, replacements, and disposal were quickly accomplished.

Larisha had already de-iced more of the Halfing technicals and had them preparing the living quarters for the others who would soon be revived. Preparing the spartan quarters took time; time to find the necessary connections, determine the proper fittings, and locate the appropriate tools.

The Halfings's stumbling confusion and their initially slow progress had been expected. The lower orders didn't have the same constitution as the Men. It would be a while before they recovered from their long sleep. Give them time to adjust and grow strong and things would become normal, Larisha insisted.

Once Larisha's Halfings had the ship more liveable, he could bring his trusted Outriders and their Scouts out of deep freeze. He always intended to have enough of Men to control Larisha's Halfings and their mongrels. It wouldn't do to let the ship's population get too much out of balance.

Tam had been working hard since his shivering arousal from the long, sleepless night. He'd spent most of his time since awakening in revising the de-icing schedules and going over the ship's data about this star system with Outrider Gull Tamat, his science advisor. He had to learn as much as possible before he acted. He wasn't going to select which of the several mission options he was going to implement until he knew more about this system.

Tamat, the head of the science team, had already charted three gas giants in the system. One of them — which Gull had named Thetti, after the Prophet's mother — was visible from the ship. It was the sixth from the primary, which had been named Hannah.

Heaven's astronomers had been quite correct in their long range appraisal of this system: Meridian, the name chosen for their destination, was the only habitable planet. At present that destination was on the other side of Hannah. Meridian had been briefly visible to the ship's sensors as they approached from galactic west, perpendicular to this system's ecliptic. They were now, according to the ship's records, running parallel to the orbit of Meridian and already slowing to match its pace and begin their descent to its orbit.

Tam watched the bright, ruddy globe of Thetti and its constellation of seven satellites swim across the command module's observation port. Thetti would be rich in resources they could exploit to supplement their diminishing stores.

But mining the gas giant was only one of several supporting options to prepare the way for settlers. He could, as one option, build a space habitat — the beginnings of a base from which the settlers could exploit this system's resources. A habitat would have been his choice had Heaven's astronomers proven incorrect. But, since Meridian appeared to be a habitable planet, he could exercise his second option: bypass the gas giants and make a direct approach. It was his choice alone, although, for form's sake, he would seek the support of the Men's Council — his trusted lieutenants — and, he added ruefully — that of Dalgrun Wofat, Palm of the Hand of God, ship's religious leader, and a huge pain in the ass.

But the support of those Men would only be a formality. As the ship's Hadir, as its absolute leader, he could and would select whichever option he felt would best serve God's plan, with or without their permission. Such was the authority given directly to him by the Hand of Heaven, practically directly from God. No one could dispute his decisions. His encounter with God himself only reënforced his certainty. He could not choose wrong.

He continued watching the bright dot of Thetti and the lights closest to it. Some of those lights were moons and some were stars, but which were which? He could not tell without a telescope or Gull's expert assistance. One of the points of light sparkled with a spectrum of color and reminded him of his vision. God as a crystal being — what a strange form for him to have taken.

As he stared, the sparkling star began to move. He jerked to full alert, wondering what it might be; there were no shuttles or scoops deployed as yet. Had one of the Halfings working outside the hull drifted loose? Could it be some hapless worker's suit lights? There were few referents to gauge distances in the starry sky.

The dot swiftly brightened and faded. In less than a second, it was completely gone.

Tam let out his breath, his heart racing, his mind awhirl. How could the light simply disappear? Where could it have gone? What had it been? He tried to recall some details of what he had seen in that fraction of a second, but could not make sense of that all-to-brief glimpse.

"What the hell happened?" he demanded as he slapped the communications console's TRANSMIT button. "That crystal light — did anyone else see where it went? Report!"

At that moment, Gull Tamat pulled himself into Tam's cramped command center. Gull was a swarthy Man, the same height as Tam, although with longer legs. Gull's dark hair was nearly black, and he tied it back in a knot typical of the fashion of Man's cadre. He differed from Tam and the rest of the Men in only a few details: His bright brown eyes always held a hint of hidden amusement, with a smile lurking about their corners. It was as if he alone held the punch line of some amusing joke.

"What's happening, Hadir?" he said. "What's the matter?"

"There was a light that just disappeared," Tam said. He stared down at the indicators from the ship's sensors. "It was there one minute ago. Right near the edge of the planet, damn it!"

"Hmmm, I don't see anything out of the ordinary." Gull leaned over Tam and peered out. "Did you say this thing passed out of sight behind Thetti?"

"Damn it, it didn't pass out of sight. It disappeared! Check and see if you can find something that would confirm what I saw. The sensors must have captured a record of its disappearance. There was no way an event like that could have evaded detection."

The responses to Tam's panicked cross-ship transmission started to come in. Station after station reported nothing out of the ordinary.

"That may not be indicative," Gull Tamat said dryly.

"All of the people working on the hull were on the side facing away from Thetti."

"Then they wouldn't have seen it," Tam said at once.

Gull listened to the reports, nodding. "I agree. It looks as if you were the only observer, Hadir Polat." Then curiosity got the better of him. "But you said 'crystal.' Why did you mean by that?"

Tam hesitated, trying to sort out the confusing image, "Did I say that? How strange." He let the comment hang. On reflection, he doubted if he could really say it was a crystal with any degree of certainty. "I believe I was thinking that the light was sparkling — crystal-like. Perhaps that is why I said it."

"Perhaps something reflected off the hull in the glass." Gull continued to peer through the observation port.

Tam nodded slowly. "Yes, perhaps." Still, the instruments and the outside observers hadn't reported anything. "I guess we can't deny the evidence, can we?"

The scientist checked the instruments once more, just to make sure. "Yes, it must have been a reflection. I wouldn't worry about it."

Then Gull looked closely at Tam. "On the other hand, your strong reaction to something so trivial could be a sign that you are overly tired. Perhaps that is why you were so easily mistaken. I suggest that you get some sleep. You've been pushing yourself far too much."

When Tam didn't change his expression, Gull continued.

"Hadir Polat, listen to me. Everything appears to be well in hand at the moment. Larisha and the others have the Halfings working hard. We're starting to de-ice some Folk, and their help will help us restore the ship to full operation. Please take it easier on yourself. Some rest would give you a clear head."

Tam slowly nodded. "You may be right, Gull. I haven't been sleeping that well lately." He forced a laugh. "It's probably because of the damn cold. All right, I will do just as you advise, old friend. We can discuss what you have learned of this system later, after I get some of your suggested rest." With those words, he waved Gull away.

But the memory of the light nagged him as he transferred temporary command to the Raggi. Had it only been a reflection, or had it been real? Should he believe his own senses, should he honor his own memory, or should he accept the solid evidence of the sensors, not to mention the reports from the crew?

The question vexed him until he fell into an uneasy sleep.

Gull Tamat looked completely confident as he stood before Tam and the Men's council.

"I have perused the ship's records in great depth and conclude that this is a very rich system," he announced. "Our people should be able to exploit its resources for centuries to come.

"First, Meridian is exactly what our astronomers predicted. It has an atmosphere that is nearly Earth-normal, so we'll only have to make a few adjustments, perhaps do some atmospheric seeding to adjust the mix of gases, so that, by the time the settlers arrive, we'll have a decent planet waiting for them."

"You said this is a rich system. What are its resources?" Tam interrupted.

Gull pursed his lips. "The three gas giants are useful. Thetti, the nearest one, has the greatest potential. Its atmosphere is rich in gases we can use to fabricate the materials we'll need. It also has a large amount of particulate matter suspended in its clouds. If I were to choose which of the three gas giants we should mine, I would strongly recommend Thetti."

Tam considered that assessment. "I would have thought the distribution of resources would be a little more equitable."

Gull hesitated. "The others are good candidates, but they are pretty far out from the primary and are rather cold.

I would say that we'd have to work much harder to extract anything of value from them. No, Hadir Polat, Thetti is our best bet." He hesitated for a moment and then added. "That is, if you decide to use it to build up our store of resources before heading to Meridian."

"I have not yet decided," Tam said curtly. "For the moment, I am considering all options equally. Now, tell us more about Thetti. I want to know about those seven moons. Are they of any use to us?"

"Um . . ." Gull shifted uncomfortably. He was clearly nervous and ill-at-ease over this question.

"Well," Tam said, "surely you've collected *some* information on the Prophet's mother's sisters, haven't you?"

A few of the Men laughed at Tam's joke.

"Six moons, Hadir Polat," Gull Tamat said slowly. "There are only six moons around Thetti."

Tam frowned. "You initially reported seven moons. Were you mistaken?"

Gull coughed, a nervous little explosion that was clearly forced. "I suspect that there was some error in the astronomical instruments. A bit of noise introduced during our long passage, perhaps. We are searching for the reason."

Tam sensed something amiss. He had known Gull too long. The Man was never uncertain. And he seldom, if ever, made a mistake of this magnitude. Best to pursue this matter later, in private. No point in embarrassing the scientist before this crowd.

"Fine, so we now have doubtful data," Tam said irritably. "Please recheck all other readings, so we can be sure of what is really out there." He settled back. "Now, why don't you tell us what information you *think* you know."

Gull continued, clearly stung by the mild rebuke.

Three days later, Gull approached Tam with a sheaf of reports in his hands. "Do you have a moment?" he asked, a strange note in his voice.

"What's the matter?" Tam growled without slowing his

progress. "Tell me on the way to the engine compartment. There's some sort of difficulty with the mains I have to look into."

"Nothing serious, I hope," Gull replied as he tagged along.

"Bringing the ship up to livable conditions isn't proceeding according to plan. Larisha told me there's some glitch in expanding the ring around the center of the ship." Tam threaded his way through a hatch. "The ship's slow rotation is making some of the crew sick."

"I know what you mean," Gull said. "This gravitational differential between head and feet would make anyone ill." He rubbed his belly to indicate the area of distress.

Tam paused. "Really? It doesn't bother me all that much. But that doesn't matter. The inadequate rotation is slowing the pace of getting the ship completed and therefore has to be fixed."

Through the morning he'd worked with Larisha to decide on which experts they had to de-ice to supplement the Halfings technicians she already had on hand. Somehow the Man who had been trained for this complicated task hadn't been placed high enough on the revival list — another stupid manifest mistake some witless clerk back on Heaven had made. He wished that he could have that clerk here now, freezing his ass off and throwing up on a regular basis. Regardless, those without his iron belly would have to suffer another day or two until the expert was up and about.

"What was it you wanted to talk about?" he asked the scientist as they squeezed between the sacks of supplies that had been stuffed into every available space on the ship. Once they had the ship expanded there would be more room — if the ship ever was expanded, he added pessimistically.

The ship's belly was a ring of compressed foil which, when forced out by the ship's rapid rotation, would expand into a ring nearly half a kilometer in diameter. At the same time the forward and aft sections would be moved slowly apart. This move would form the expanding ring into a fat disk. It was tedious and precise work fraught with risk, which was why they needed the Man who had been trained for this.

Once the ring was formed the workers would divide the disk's interior into corridors, compartments, work rooms, laboratories, and mechanical rooms. The ship would become, if everything went right, a small city.

"I just wanted you to know that we've finished checking the astronomical instruments that were malfunctioning." Gull squeezed past bulging sacks of vacuum-dried fruits.

Tam arrested his forward motion by placing one hand against a container of figs. He turned to face the scientist.

"*Were* malfunctioning? Just what do you mean by that? Has it put the ship in danger? My God, why didn't you tell me about this earlier?"

Gull held up his hands in protest. "No, the malfunction wasn't that serious, I assure you. Nothing that directly affected the ship's performance. No, Hadir Polat, this was more subtle than that."

"Well, what is it, then?" Tam demanded. "Come on, you don't bring something to my attention and then dismiss it as trivial. I know you better than that. Hell, I chose you myself for that very trait! Now, tell me."

"It was the long-range astronomical instruments," Gull explained quietly. "Apparently, the systemic noise in them was enough to indicate that there were five major satellites orbiting Thetti and two smaller moons. We've checked and rechecked the original readings and can only locate six of them now. One of the smaller ones seems to have, uh, disappeared."

Tam pursed his lips in thought. "That is very strange. I can't believe that you've lost an entire moon."

The scientist looked embarrassed. "I didn't say that we lost it. As I said before, it must have been some noise in the system, some bright blips that we interpreted as a minor satellite. It isn't as if we actually lost it," he concluded plaintively.

Tam laughed at the Man's fallen face. "Don't be so upset, Gull. I was just joking. It's not your fault that one of the moons disappeared." He smiled to show that this too was a joke, but Gull Tamat interpreted it differently.

"It wasn't a moon," he repeated angrily. "I told you that it was an anomaly — some bad data, was all."

"So why are you concerned enough to come to me?" Tam asked. "If it was an error that no longer exists why should it concern me?"

Gull rattled his papers again. "It seems that the last mistaken record was made just a few days ago.

"So?" Tam smiled politely. He was growing weary of the scientist's inability to come to the point.

"It seems that the malfunctioning instrument stopped malfunctioning around the same time you reported seeing that disappearing star."

Tam stopped immediately. "Are you saying that the two events are related? What I saw was a reflection of something near the ship. It must have been something small and close, not a damn moon, for God's sake!"

Gull grinned. "You have a good grasp of reality, Hadir Polat. All right, so the two events aren't related. It would be impossible for the moon to have been what you say you saw. Quite impossible."

"A coincidence, that's all it was, Outrider. A silly, chance coincidence."

Gull nodded in agreement. "Yes, you must certainly be right, Hadir Polat. I stand corrected. I am sorry to have troubled you."

Tam slapped the scientist on the shoulder. "No trouble, old friend. But keep your crew looking for that malfunction just the same. I want absolute assurance that our instruments are doing what they're supposed to. Absolute assurance!"

"As you wish Hadir Tam Polat," Gull bowed obedience. "As you instruct."

Tam tried to think no more of the matter for the rest of the day. But Gull's lost moon came to mind later, as he was resting in the quiet of his bunk. He thought about the bright crystal essence of God that he'd seen through the port. He thought about the tiny disappearing star, the one that all of the instruments and all of the possible observers had said hadn't happened. Had it really been something near Thetti? Could that have been the missing "moon" despite the obvious impossibility of it all?

He played with that thought. Was such a thing just too fantastic to believe? Wouldn't Gull Tamat's instruments detect something moon-sized if it disappeared? He'd supposed it to be a small object, as Gull had insisted at the time, but it could have been farther away — it could have been a moon-sized item circling Thetti!

Then he shook himself. A moon, even a small one, could not break the laws of physics. God did not play kick-ball with astronomy, at least not in real time! No, if the moon had existed at all, then it would surely have registered on the instruments. The disappearance of anything that size would probably have perturbed the ship's path a measurable degree as well.

He'd only had that briefest of glimpses and still wasn't sure of the memory. Gull must have been correct; it had been nothing more than a chance reflection, a trick of the eye, a phantasm. And a coincidence as well.

Besides, a moon would not resemble a crystal.

The repairs to the main engines required nothing more than replacement of a minor part that had frozen sometime during the cold years and someone who could authorize the work. He cursed. For that they'd had to lose three days of progress. Briefly, Tam wished that they had enough leisure time that he could apply some much needed discipline to the workers. Nothing motivated the Halfings like a good public whipping. By God, if he were back on Heaven with a squad of good horse behind him, they'd not dare . . .

But they were not on Heaven. His beloved grassy plains were far behind them, and enough horses for a squad could not be bred in this system for years. Until then, his Men had to walk about like common people, like the damned mongrels.

Thanks to the repair job, the ship's revolution gradually stabilized so that the ring could be extended from where it had laid collapsed, like a thick belt, around the mid-line of the ship. The crew immediately began filling the newly created space with supplies and machinery from the storage spaces in the main ship. This shifted considerable mass from the ship's center and gradually slowed the speed of the ship's revolution.

Finally, a decent degree of artificial gravity was achieved at the rim. Work on the ship proceeded without further incident.

The ship's engines remained still as the crew waited for their Hadir to tell them which option he would choose. Everyone knew that there was sufficient fuel remaining in the tanks to reach and orbit Meridian. The need to reach their destination, to walk on the surface of a planet once again, to start to build for the future, was palpable throughout the ship.

Yet, they also knew that prudence argued mightily for orbiting Thetti and mining its depths. That would ensure them of enough reserves to handle any contingency. Hadn't the Hadir publicly stated that replenishing their fuel before proceeding would be the wisest choice?

There was also a third option: to build a habitat, an orbiting refuge, just in case something untoward should occur as they tried to conquer Meridian. Perhaps, some mused as they awaited the Hadir's decision, he would choose a combination of the three.

Tam was still uneasy in dealing with Bul Larisha: his Raggi, leader of the Halfings, his former lover, his official wife. The presence of Larisha on the ship was something that he regretted. At one time, she had seemed such a perfect candidate. Not only was she a loyal follower of the Hand of God, but was an excellent Man in other respects. Brilliant and witty, with excellent technical, academic, and political credentials, Larisha had passed every test and met every criteria the Hand had set for those in command positions. Of her capability for the rôle, there was no doubt. She had also declared to Heaven's Hand her warmest desire to spread the seed of Man throughout the universe. He himself, the Hadir of the Meridian *Covenant*, had endorsed her inclusion vigorously, declaring her the best stock that Men had to offer.

Which was perfectly understandable. At that time, he had been deeply in love with her. At that time, he had not yet asked her to marry him. At that time, he had thought that they were going to ride together in God's great plan to extend Man's dominion over the universe. At that time, he'd not known her failings.

Or his own.

Palm Dalgrun staggered into Tam's cramped quarters barely a day after she'd been de-iced. She wore the formal robes of her station instead of the quilted parkas the rest of the crew had donned.

"I'm too damned old for this," she said as she dropped heavily into the single chair. "Chen didn't tell me that I would ache so much."

Tam smiled. "What do you expect after a two hundred year sleep? That you could jump up from the chamber and ride a horse as well as you did back on Heaven? Trust me, give it another day or two, and you'll feel almost like your old self."

Dalgrun shivered and folded her arms across her chest. "And it is so cold, too. I would think that you would have brought the ship at least up to a decent temperature before you started waking us."

"Warmer for you than it was for us. Why don't you talk to Raggi Larisha about that? I've been asking her about the heat for weeks now," Tam suggested. "But," he said with a dismissing wave of his hand, "that is not why you came to see me, is it? What can I do for you?"

Dalgrun settled back in a rustle of fabric. "I feel that our relationship got off to a bad start, Hadir Tam Polat. Since we are now hundreds of years and God alone knows how far from our dear Heaven, we should at least try to become more favorably disposed toward each other."

"Fine. Can you lead an engine team or supervise welding operations on the hull? Can you calculate orbital mechanics, program the instruments, prepare food, erect bedding and tables, or any of the other ten thousand tasks that still remain to be done by our working crew? Tell me, dear Palm, what can you do for me?" There was no mistaking the animosity in his voice.

Dalgrun bristled. "While it is true that I am not useful in the trivial tasks you describe, I nevertheless have skills that can serve the ship."

Tam barely concealed his sneer at this declaration. "Hadir Tam Polat," she continued. "You are so focused on the mundane, on the temporal matters of the ship and crew, that you ignore their spiritual needs. They must be starved to hear the words of the Prophet, they must thirst to hear the Revelations once again. After all, it has been over two hundred long years since they last heard the words of God."

Tam snorted. "As far as anyone in the crew are concerned, it was only a week or two since they last attended services. Nobody has been conscious during our long passage, so the actual years are of no consequence."

"Nevertheless," Dalgrun continued as if she were not convinced, "they are in serious need of spiritual guidance. I think that holding services would calm them and renew their dedication to the mission."

Tam rubbed his chin in thought. "There is a way that you could help me, dear Palm. I have been concerned that the Men and the Halfings are becoming too friendly, too companionable. The lines between them often becomes blurred under our rather arduous workload. Perhaps you could reenforce the lessons of the Prophet by reminding the Men of their sacred duties toward the race."

Dalgrun clapped her hands. "That is an excellent thought, Hadir Tam Polat. I will make that the homily for my first service next week. Of course, you will make arrangements for all to attend, won't you?"

Tam smiled, surprised that the Palm was so quickly agreeable to his suggestion. Maybe she would be of some use in keeping the crew in line. It would be useful to have the spiritual leader of the mission on his side. He could use her moral authority to supplement his own.

"I understand, Palm Dalgrun Wofat," Tam said carefully. "So long as we keep the mundane and spiritual domains separate, we will have no conflict. Do we understand each other, dear Palm?"

"Yes. Excellent." Dalgrun beamed as she squirmed in her chair and rubbed her hands together. "Now, about my quarters. They are much too small. Why, I hardly have enough space to have more than a few people visit at once. Surely someone with my prestige and authority should have better quarters than that. Don't you agree?"

Tam became instantly furious. He had the mongrels sleeping in the de-icing chamber, the Halfings sharing beds, and the Men bunking two to the berth. How dare this, this pompous, useless Palm demand that he grant her special favors. He would . . .

"You know," the Palm said matter-of-factly as she examined her nails. "I wanted to complement you on your fine bloodline. You are quite pious, I understand, so much so that you wanted to command both the mundane and the spiritual aspects of the mission."

"It was not such a secret," he replied bitterly.

"I know, yet I took the opportunity to study your background in depth long before we left Heaven. You have quite a heritage, Hadir Polat."

Tam seethed at the implication that she had known more about him than he did of her. Apparently, everyone had conspired to keep her assignment to the ship from him. The memory of her sudden appearance, just before launch, completely eradicated his earlier, friendly expectation that they could get along.

Dalgrun continued. "But your family is no longer with us. You are now the sole repository of the fine genes that have been placed in your trust. It is important that you ensure that they are perpetuated, that they do not end with you."

"You can take that up with my wife," Tam said sharply.

"Don't insult me, Hadir Tam Polat," Dalgrun snapped back. "I am well aware of the difficulties between you and the Raggi."

At Tam's start of surprise she continued, "Oh, don't worry about it. I won't denounce your failure to preserve your marriage or anything so barbaric. After all, we are on our own out here. We are now the Hand of Meridian — the final authority for all human matters in the system. I feel sure that we can be permitted to bend the rules a little to make our lives somewhat easier. Rest easy, Hadir Tam Polat, I leave the matter of your marriage difficulties for you and Raggi Bul Larisha to resolve."

Tam struggled to follow her conversation. "If you are going to remain quiet, then why did you bring it up? Are you suggesting that Larisha and I . . ."

"No, not at all," Dalgrun replied, settling back. "I merely use it as an example to remind you of our spiritual situation and of the power that I hold. Do not forget, Hadir Tam Polat, that you are merely the Arm of the Hand. You are merely the tool who is to deliver the seeds of the Hand of God to Meridian.

"As to myself," she placed a hand on her breast. "I am the Palm, the holder of the soul that the Arm conveys.

Through me and my ministers, we will ensure that God's plan survives in this new place. Here we will continue to build for the glory of the Emerging God. I trust that this system will be a pious and just place, in accordance with the laws of the Hand." The threat that she would use his failed marriage against him in some way was not very subtle.

"As I said before, dear Palm," Tam spat out, "I think we understand each other now. I will tell them to provide larger accommodations for you."

Dalgrun got to her feet and straightened her robes. "I thank you, Hadir Tam Polat. Isn't it wonderful what a little spiritual guidance can do for the soul? Good day."

And with that, she left.

TWO

"We are the hands of God," Dalgrun pronounced to open the service a few days later. Only those Men and Halfings not essential elsewhere were present.

"In each of us is the seed of our priceless inheritance, the gift that our ancestors learned directly from God during at the time of the Revelation. Of all God's creations, we alone — we Men — have received God's compact to dominate and fill the universe!"

"This is what makes us truly human," all of the Men replied in unison.

"That is what makes us human," Dalgrun, the Palm intoned. "This holy compact is what differentiates Man from the lesser orders."

"We are the fingers of the Hand," the Halfings said in unison. "We exist only to serve the Hand of Man."

"Amen," Dalgrun said and made the sign. "Listen to the words of God, as revealed to the Prophet, Let Hartsa, aeons ago: I am the true and only God and I give to Men this charge; that you be fruitful and multiply, that you hold dominion over all of the universe and all that is within. You will have mastery over the lower orders. You will do this to prepare the way for the emerging God. You will do this for me, for from you will come the Emerging God."

"Thus speaks the words of the Prophet," she concluded. "This is the word of God."

"We understand and obey the order of the revelation," everyone responded and regained their places on the deck.

Tam stirred restlessly as Dalgrun droned through the prayers and other routine portions of the service. He was satisfied that the Palm's homily was on the proper order in society, as he had asked. She made it amply clear that everyone, Men and Halfing, should know their place and hold true to their own kind. "Only through strict adherence to our social order," Dalgrun insisted, "can the Emerging God be achieved. Only through your individual righteous conduct can you perfect your soul."

Tam was dissatisfied with the homily, which dwelt too much on the spiritual and not enough on the day-to-day. The message he'd asked her to inject about the crew's behavior toward the "lesser orders" might have been lost on the Halfings. They were such simple people, hardly capable of understanding such sophisticated reasoning. Why hadn't she just come out and said that Men were flirting with sin whenever they treated the Halfings as anything other than failed humans? It was too subtle for such a critical message. Too damn subtle by half!

"We lost three more of the Folk," Jas reported to Larisha. She and Tam had been huddled in the command capsule over a particularly vexing air purifier problem for several hours when the veterinarian showed up.

"Who were they?" she snapped. She was in no mood for bad news.

"My best breeder and two of her mates," Jas said, with much wringing of his hands. "I knew that they shouldn't have iced them in groups. It was damn stupid to scrimp on funds when it didn't really matter. I hate losing her."

"So that's what that damned sniveling and yammering is all about," Tam snarled without looking up from his console. "We can't concentrate on bringing the ship back on line with all that noise. It's very disturbing. Would it be so terribly hard for you to make them shut the hell up?"

Jas shrugged. "Not much, Hadir Polat. But I felt that it would be best to let them cry until they get over the deaths. Crying relieves the pain of the loss, you know. Huh, I feel like joining them — she was a good girl."

"I hope you aren't taking more than a professional interest in your charges," Tam said without looking up. There was always trouble when the Halfings started treating the mongrels as if they were humans. That was why he wanted Dalgrun Wofat to stress the lesson so hard.

"Raggi Bul wouldn't have selected me if she suspected that I was less than completely professional," Jas shot back instantly. "Don't worry about me, Hadir Tam Polat. I can be depended upon to do my job properly."

Tam nodded. "I would hope so. But lets get back to the dead mongrels — were any of them on our essential list?"

Larisha glared at him. "That's a pretty cold thing to say, Tam! Don't you feel anything about their deaths? You make it sound as if we just lost some damn engine part."

Tam threw a cold glance over at the veterinarian before replying and then turned back to her. "Damn it, Larisha, it isn't as if we lost some of the crew, for God's sake. They're only mongrels."

"Only mongrels? Tam, the Folk are vital members of our mission. They're just as important to our success as the rest of the crew. I know how you objected to bringing so many of them along, how you feel about the lesser orders. But I would think that you could at least try to show a little bit of concern. After all, they are living, breathing, feeling people."

Tam slammed the panel. "Oh hell. All right; I am sorry that we lost three productive working mongrels right at the beginning of our mission. I'm sorry that the rest of them now have to pick up the load. I'm sorry that we'll probably have to waste more time and resources training some other of the Folk to do their jobs. Damn it; yes, yes, I am sorry about the whole mess. Does that satisfy you?" He glared at her.

Before Larisha could reply, Jas cleared his throat. "None of the three that died were at the top of the priority list, Hadir Polat. All of them were strongbacks. Those were the only losses to report. I now have twenty-two priority one Folk de-iced." He looked away from Tam and addressed Larisha. "The new ones will be ready for work in two days, at most. Where do you want them to report, Raggi Bul?"

The veterinarian's slight was subtle, but telling. Tam continued to stare coldly and impassively at Jas. To acknowledge such disrespect would be to show that he had noticed.

"Put them on clean-up detail until we get Master Blum de-iced," Larisha said calmly with a quick glance at Tam. "He'll inform you when and where they are needed."

Tam ran his finger down the purifier checklist, made a clucking noise of affirmation, adjusted a control, and then looked up. "You'll need to de-ice some replacements for those three you lost. Get another batch thawed as quickly as possible."

Jas looked at Larisha as if seeking support. "I will get these Folk stabilized first. Once that's done, I'll see about de-icing the rest."

"That will be fine," Larisha replied, supporting the impertinent vet and continuing to aggravate Tam.

"Hate to wait with so much to do," Tam muttered. "Well, I guess Blum will have to work the rest of them all the harder. All right, do it," he ordered with a wave of dismissal. "You can go now," Tam said, reasserting his command over the conversation. "And shut them up! I don't want all that infernal racket while I'm trying to concentrate!"

Jas tugged on his forelock as a sign of respect and departed.

"You didn't need to be so abrupt with him," Larisha said as soon as her veterinarian was out of earshot. "He's just trying to do his job. You know how Jas loves taking care of the Folk. That's why I chose him, if you will recall. He has a way with them."

"Pfaugh! I can just imagine the kind of person who loves those damned, filthy mongrels. What a nauseating thought — just make sure he doesn't carry that 'love' of his too far." Tam made clucking noises. "Most people would think that sort of thing is disgusting, you know."

"You are the one who is absolutely disgusting," Larisha said haughtily. "You know what I meant. Jas really is concerned about our Folk — both personally and professionally — and you should respect that."

When Tam didn't immediately reply, she continued. "But let's get back to the point. I'd appreciate it if you could treat my veterinarian with a little more respect. There was no reason to be so rude."

"I haven't the luxury or time to be polite to everybody in the damned ship, not while there's so much work to be done! Get that across to your people — if they do their jobs I won't be rude, otherwise I'll ride them so hard they'll think I was one of our ancestor's hell-horses!"

Larisha sniffed. "I also would like it if you would stop calling our Folk mongrels! That's what is really disgusting. They are still people. The Halfings and the Folk both deserve a little respect from us."

"Respect?" Tam sneered. "Oh come off of it, Larisha. The Halfings don't expect respect from us. All they want is for us to tell them what to do, provide work, food, and shelter. Trust me; the Halfings are happiest when they know their place. The next thing, you'll want me to treat the damn mongrels as if they were human!"

"I wouldn't go quite that far," Larisha laughed. "But do try to be civil, please. I do depend on Jas."

"Oh, very well. I'll try," Tam mumbled, half in apology, half in anger. "But don't you let him forget his place!"

It wasn't easy for Tam to understand his wife's feelings for the mongrels and the Halfings. She had been born to wealthy farmers who had an extensive estate on the sultry coast of Heaven's equatorial continent. From her earliest days Larisha, had been trained to run the estate, manage the assets — fifty Halfings and over one hundred mongrels — and husband the seed crops that were the basis of the family's wealth.

Larisha's parents had died in a freak accident when she was about thirteen. This left her in complete control of the estate, since there was no living relative willing to take on the somewhat arduous responsibilities of the large Bul holding. Most of her close relatives had settled comfortably elsewhere. They, and especially their pampered children, were far removed from grubbing in the soil. Most considered such toil beneath them.

It therefore became Larisha's duty to assume the management of the estate. The four Men who had worked with her parents tried as best they could to educate her about the intricacies of running the enterprise and managing the assets. The exposure to so much commerce broadened her understanding of the world she inhabited, and she matured far beyond her years.

By the age of eighteen, she had travelled extensively as a result of conducting the farm's business and dealing with her customers both far and near. Not only had she been successful in managing the estate but had also enlarged its acreage considerably, mostly through canny trading with the adjacent farms. It appeared that she had a definite talent for the farming business.

Larisha's parents had been Empathists, who believed that Men owed kindness and compassion to both the Halfings and the Folk. They forbade the use of the term 'mongrel' by any of the family or staff and even went so far as to politely inform visitors that such vulgar words were not acceptable. Insofar as possible, given the realities of the society in which she lived, Larisha accepted her parents' credo. She was a kind and benevolent steward of her assets, providing far more comforts to the Folk than most of the other estate owners.

All of which must explain her insane attitude toward the Folk, Tam thought, bringing his reflections back to the present. The difference of their views had come up many times before.

Unlike Larisha, he had been raised more traditionally in Sached, a strict and restricted Separatist community. There were no Halfings allowed into the tightly policed compound, even to do the menial chores of household maintenance.

Tam was ten before he saw one of the Folk. "Mongrels," that's what his father had emphatically called them at the time. The disdain and disgust in his voice was evident to Tam's impressionable young ear. He never heard them referred to otherwise by his family or friends.

Many of the good people of Sachet were in favor of eliminating the mongrels completely, since they were of no further use to Man's eventual evolution to Godhood. But complete elimination of the genetically flawed would be impossible economically. So much of the backbreaking work on Heaven was accomplished with mongrel labor. Nearly all of the food was raised and harvested by the estate mongrels. Mongrels worked the infrastructure, repaired the roads, built the cities, and worked on all of the factory production lines. In short, the mongrels did work that was too boring, too strenuous, or too demeaning for Men.

How little that difference in viewpoints had seemed to matter when he'd first met Larisha. How little their differences had seemed as they courted and wed. How trivial those differences between them had seemed in those joyful days before they set forth from Heaven to this new system.

Tam sighed. Would things have been different had he known? It was a question that bothered him more than he would admit.

The ship still wasn't warm enough when Larisha reported: "We have most of the Men and Halfings awake now. Half of the Folk have been de-iced, and the ship is marginally operational."

"Why hasn't Jas gotten the rest of the damn mongrels out of the freezer?" Tam growled. "We'll need all the help we can get for the next phase of work."

"Give him time, Tam. He's thawing them at a reasonable pace. If he proceeds any faster, it'll imperil their health. They're not some disposable resource you can call up as you please."

Tam felt the heat rise. "Come off of it, Larisha! You aren't getting soft on the mongrels, are you? Worse thing that could happen is for you to become attached to the damn things. Need I remind you that they are here to be worked, just like the Halfings, until we get this ship stabilized and secure. In case you forgot, that is why we came here, not to start some damn softhearted kennel in the sky."

Larisha said nothing. She continued moving her finger down the checklist until she found the item she wanted. "Let's talk about getting the ship's greenhouse operational. I've got six dozen types of plants rooted and ready for planting, plus the insects and invertebrates we'll need for ecological balance. Can you tell me when we'll have enough power for the lighting I'll need?"

"Soon!" Tam snorted and then chuckled. "I hope that you're not going to get as attached to the greenhouse bugs as you seem to be to those mongrels."

"You know, I wonder why I was ever so attracted to you." Larisha swung her head so that her black hair whipped across her face. "Perhaps it was because I thought you had a heart under that cold exterior of yours!"

She shot out of the command module and headed toward the solarium.

"I did have a heart," Tam muttered to her departing back, "but that was before you broke it."

Win accompanied his boss, Fren Bulgat, as they unpacked the suits for the engine crew. He'd been awake for three weeks now and had been working nearly every waking hour. Being among the first of Blum's Folk to be de-iced was an honor, he'd thought at assignment time back on Heaven, but the reality of the 'honor' turned out to be nothing more than hours of cold, hard, unremitting labor and too little sleep.

He hadn't realized that restoring the ship's life after its long voyage between the stars involved so much work. The very first to awaken had to bring the life support systems back on line. Hadir Polat, Raggi Bul, and the Halfings had done that. They'd also gotten the power plant working and energized the great empty parts of the ship in preparation for the awakening crew and their Folk. Those critical steps completed, they then began de-icing quads of the Folk, four at a time. Win had been one of the tough young Folk in the second quad to be de-iced.

Win's first job had been to get the Worker's dormitory ready. This involved checking the waiting cabins, bringing their temperature up to standard, and flushing water into the sanitation systems. The occupants, after they had been de-iced, would take care of actually outfitting the compartments and turning them into livable quarters.

Win had to sleep cheek by jowl with the rest of the Folk for the first month after they had awakened. They slept in the same chamber where they had been de-iced and had done the warm bed rotation, eight hours on and eight off, each Worker rolling out of one side of his bunk as someone else rolled in behind. At least it kept the bunks warm.

Hadir Polat and the Men occupied the first set of quarters once they were completed. The rest of the cramped spaces within the expanding ship were doled out as appropriate to rank and station as more of the crew awakened. The Men got private quarters, the Halfings shared ones, and Folk clustered in the dormitory. Despite some crowding, things had progressed to the point where none of the Folk had to share a bunk, which was a blessing, Win thought as he headed to his newly assigned room.

When he'd arrived he'd discovered that the room was a four-by; he had to share his portion of the dormitory with three other Folk — a girl about his own age, an older woman, and a worker on the engine crew. Given the hectic pace of the work schedule, it was seldom that more than two of them were using the beds.

"Check that suit carefully, lad," Fren warned him. "We can't trust that the fabric's any good after all this time."

Win examined the surface of the suit with great care, looking for any wrinkle or tear that might betray decay from the long years in storage. "Looks all right to me," he reported.

"We'll see. Put it over here and we'll put a little pressure in her — see if she holds true." Boss Fren matched action to word, and the suit expanded as the air hissed into it. Win swabbed each of the seals with water to see if any bubbles formed. He was especially careful around the elbow and knee joints.

"That's four atmospheres and she's holding pressure," Fren said when the suit ballooned up and bounced against the deck as if alive. "I guess this one's all right, Win. Let the air out and bring another one over."

For the next two days Win and the boss checked the full complement of suits, subsystem by subsystem — everything from pressure to electronics to motility. They were very careful with each, knowing full well that the crew's lives depended upon their suits being in absolutely perfect condition. This far from Heaven, there were no second chances in case of a failure or accident. Should a suit fail to protect its owner, there could be no hope of restoration or revival. Death would be final and absolute.

Win took his responsibilities very seriously.

Tam straightened his tunic and admired the trim line of his dress uniform in the mirror. One good thing about the freezing and the spartan rations was that he'd lost the beginning of the paunch he'd acquired that last year on Heaven. Damn, he hadn't looked this good in years. He turned around to see how he looked from another angle. He hadn't been this trim since he'd married Larisha. He winked at his image in the mirror and headed toward the ceremony.

When he arrived on the mess deck, he saw that most of the Men had arrived before him. They were seated along the benches the Halfings had set up in the center of the large chamber.

Most of the Men had adorned their utilitarian work

clothing with some article they'd brought with them — a bright red scarf here, a few scraps to ribbon there. Four or five of them had put on full dress uniforms. Unfortunately none of them were alike, rendering the term 'uniform' moot.

One of the Men had put on a gold and red skirt. The flash of bare legs was a shock after so many months of seeing everyone in trousers. "Well done," he said admiringly. She had nice legs, too.

Against the back wall sat those Halfings who were off duty. Larisha had insisted that they be included, and Tam had grudgingly acceded to her wishes — it was easier than arguing over such a trivial matter.

He noticed a few mongrels among the Halfings and wondered why they had come — of what possible interest would a marriage ceremony be to them? The damned mongrels probably coupled without formalities — their morals as absent as their souls.

"Well, let them see how true Men behave," he muttered under his breath. Perhaps it would have a beneficial effect on them to see that the higher orders respected their joining.

Dalgrun pulled herself from her seat when she saw the Hadir enter. Moving at a dignified pace, she took her place facing the Men. A couple stood and walked to face her, turning their backs to the seated Men.

Tam quietly took his place next to Dalgrun. A few last-minute stragglers filtered in from the passageways, whispering, "Excuse me" as they found their places. They settled quickly when Tam glowered in their direction.

When everyone was quiet, Tam cleared his throat and announced, "Welcome to this, *Covenant*'s first marriage ceremony. These two Men," he indicated the man and woman before him, "requested that their marriage be postponed until they were de-iced so they could have the honor of being the first married in this system." Tam grinned at the crowd. "Well, I think this is a wonderful idea. Maybe tonight they'll generate more heat than our engineers seem able to provide for the rest of us."

The audience grinned at his joke while the two before him shuffled in embarrassment. Out of the corner of his eye, he saw that Larisha was not amused.

"Anyway, I just want to say that this is a wonderful way to start the mission. I wish the two of you the greatest joy. May the God emerge from your loins," he added ceremoniously.

Dalgrun cleared her throat. "Dearly beloved of God, we are gathered this day to celebrate the joining of Laun and Jut Bulgat."

As she continued with the ritual words, Tam took his seat beside Larisha. He tried to look attentive as the ceremony continued. The words brought back a flood of memories of his own marriage.

He'd met Larisha in the early years of training for this trip to a world they would later call Meridian. She had been identified as a possible candidate to lead the planetary survey and development team. Her abilities in managing large groups, her knowledge of farming and business, not to mention her age, made her an outstanding pick. Tam, the SubHadir Tam Polat at the time, had gone to interview her, declared her the best candidate he had ever interviewed, and immediately set about convincing her to join the team, to travel with them to settle yet another world for the Hand, for humanity, for God.

They had a brief courtship, a formal marriage that symbolically sealed the bond between shipboard and planet command, between Hadir and Raggi, by welding the two rôles.

If only he had known of her failings, then he could have spared himself years of arguments and disappointments. A year before the launch of the *Covenant*, Tam decided that he could no longer abide Larisha's subterfuges and plots. Why, he asked her, couldn't she just come out and tell him what she wanted to do instead of making it always look like some chance occurrence? He hated being manipulated and detested her denials that she had not planned events to bend him to her way. Still, they held the fantasy of their marriage together, for the ship, for the mission, and simply for appearance's sake.

Had they done otherwise, they would have lost this chance. They would have lost Meridian.

Larisha was also thinking about their courtship as the ceremony continued. How could she have known the bounds that marriage would place on her? She had been an innocent fool, a rustic farmer unschooled in the sea of subtle plots that the city-bound seemed to swim among without thinking.

On her first trip to Burlingshorn, the capital city, she had been flattered by the dashing young officer's attention. After all, she had been invited by the Hand to become a candidate for the holy mission, not only as a deputy to the mission, but in command of the key settlement team.

The knowledge of her prospective responsibilities had both flattered and frightened her. The honor of the offer battled with her desire to remain in the comfortable farming niche she had created for herself. She had been quite unsettled by it all.

Through the many days of interviews and testing, Tam had shown her the delights and secrets of Burlingshorn, including some not normally seen by visiting farmers. She had discovered that he was not only a handsome devil, but witty and daring, and absolutely in control of himself. He was, to her naïve eye, a true leader — the best of the best. To her he had seemed a demi-god, able to do no wrong.

Naturally, she fell deeply in love; and, when he asked her to Sachet to visit his parents, she knew that he must feel the same. A pity that her love for Tam blinded her to the obvious. How could she not have known how poor his attitude toward the Folk and the Halfings would be when she saw the Separatist church, the walled compound, and the restriction signs on the gates?

But she hadn't noticed or didn't let it bother her. Weeks later, when the Hand formally offered her the position, she invited Tam, along with several other members of the preparation team, to visit her estate and discuss the possibilities.

Doctor Chen complimented her on her well-planned gardens and fields, admired what she had done with the infrastructure of buildings and systems, and was intensely interested in the methods she used to manage her assets. "Excellent skills, excellent!" he had remarked and rubbed his hands in pleasure.

The rest of the team enjoyed the bucolic luxury of her estate and their pleasant vacation from the hectic pace they had been working. Only occasionally did they speak with her about her rôle, her position, her responsibilities.

Tam ignored all discussion of mission and rôles. Instead, he focused entirely on her as a person, giving her his undivided attention, or at least whatever could be spared when Doctor Chen wasn't discussing some aspect of the mission with him. One evening, long after the others were asleep, they first made love. It was in the flowered garden bower that she had built as a place of quiet refuge. It was the one place she always longed to return to during her travels. It was the place that, more than any other, meant home. Tam proposed a few weeks later, and she'd accepted.

Doctor Chen thought that her skills were far greater than she imagined. To her surprise, Chen suggested that she become the Hadir Tam Polat's deputy — the leader of the planetary exploitation crew, the people who would prepare the way for the settlers who would follow.

Larisha accepted and threw all of her energies into learning her new rôle. She very quickly, by virtue of her experience with managing the Halfings and the Folk, became an important and integral part of the command crew. The rôle of Raggi fit her comfortably, like a well-worn glove.

It had taken nearly two years before she discovered that the Hadir Tam Polat's virtues were actually flaws in his character, flaws that she could no longer abide. She disliked the way he manipulated her and insisted on planning everything to the tiniest detail. While she could accept that his wish to live a life that spontaneity and chance, she could not bear to live such a life.

At the same time Tam refused to accept that she did not plan every single action. Whenever some chance happening occurred that threw him off the track, he insisted that she had deliberately planned it.

Finally, she could stand it no longer and told him so. A separation at this late stage of preparations was impossible. She was fully committed to the mission. She had sold her estate and invested all of her assets into the seed and plant stock she would take with them on the ship. Further, the Hand would be extremely displeased, and their displeasure was not something to be ignored.

Tam agreed that they should, for the good of the mission and the ship, remain married, but it would be in name only. They would say nothing to the Hand. They would reveal nothing of their enmity to anyone. On the day of the launch, they had joined the ship as Hadir and Raggi, the happily married couple everyone thought they were.

"And so I pronounce you as one in God's eyes. Go forth and be fruitful. Fill the firmament with God's own people, hold dominion over all creatures great and small, for in you is the Emerging God. From your loins will come the destiny of the race, from you will come the future." She made the sign of the Revelation, a circle of her right hand over their heads, and signalled for everyone to rise as she cast God's blessing over them to sanctify the union. Dalgrun's words brought Larisha's thoughts back to the present.

Far in the back, unnoticed by Men or Halfings, eight Folk, four couples, knelt before Rex, the Folk Administer. As Dalgrun made her motion, so too did Rex.

"And to you a life of pleasure and fulfillment," he whispered. Then the three of them rose to receive God's blessing on their union from the Palm.

"So!" Tam shouted at the top of his voice as soon as the final words were spoken by the Palm. He stood and waved a small stick he'd pulled from the side of his boot. Ten of the Men lined up behind and slightly to each side of him. Tam lowered the stick and pointed it at the couple.

At once the ten swiftly moved forward and separated the couple. Five of the Men surrounded Laun and the other five circled Jut. Tam moved quickly to the group holding the woman and led them out of the chamber.

Down the corridor they raced, ignoring the faint cries of protest from the new bride, until they came to a room with an open hatch. "In here," Tam said as they pushed the bride inside.

The five then lined up in the corridor, facing back the way they had come. Tam stood before them, waiting.

A few minutes later the remainder of the Men came charging up the corridor, the groom at their head. Without pause he ran up and grabbed at Tam's stick.

But Tam was ready for the move and snatched it away. He danced backwards, holding the stick out of reach as the five Outriders closed on each side. The groom made another move, a feint to the right, and then grabbed the stick with his left hand. They tugged for a few moments, and then Tam released it.

No sooner than he did so but the crowd advanced on the five and pushed them back down the corridor, forcing them past the open doorway, inside of which the bride awaited.

With a whoop, the groom threw his arm around her waist, pulled her into the corridor, and escorted her through the crowd who had followed him, waving the stick victoriously overhead. They headed back to the chamber while the crowd guarded their backs.

"Sort of lacks something without the horses," Blum

said as they walked behind the crowd. "He never would have gotten close, had you been riding."

Tam nodded. "Yes, but I would have let him claim his bride anyway — after he proved his leadership and desire!" He grinned. "But don't worry. We'll ride the high plains on Meridian within a decade. Once we're on the plains, we'll be able to have a proper ceremony!"

THREE

Work was constant, with breaks for sleep and eating the only respite from the unending tasks of awakening the ship. Win's companions in his compartment were Gold and Dagger — who worked opposite shifts — and a girl. They had such diverse schedules that only two were ever awake at the same time. Most of the time either Gold or Dagger were abed when he entered. On occasion, he had an opportunity to briefly speak to them before dropping off into his much needed sleep.

The girl, whose name he hadn't learned, hadn't spoken to Win in all of the time since he'd been assigned. At first, he thought it was because they never seemed to occupy the compartment at the same time. But perhaps he'd been sleeping whenever she was there. He had noticed her resting form in the bunk once, when he stumbled in off mid-watch, but hadn't the nerve or inclination to wake her.

There came a moment when the girl and Win arrived at the same time. Win didn't know what to say and was embarrassed by his timidity. He ignored her and busied himself with straightening his bunk, arranging his few possession in the single drawer provided for him to give himself time to think of what he could say. Behind him, on the opposite side of the room, he could hear her performing the same inconsequential tasks.

Then he was done and the silence loomed like a large vulture on his shoulders, growing more hungry by the moment. Win knew that if he turned he would have to speak to the girl. But he had nothing else to do, nothing to waste the moments. Then he spied his towel, grabbed it, and raced for the communal shower.

Win cursed himself vigorously for being such a fool as the thin trickle of tepid water ran over him. Here he'd had the opportunity to speak to her, to become acquainted with what appeared to be an attractive girl, and what did he do but run out like some awkward adolescent (which, he remembered instantly, he most certainly was!). *Damn, damn, damn.* He struck the shower's wall repeatedly. *How can I be so stupid, so immature?*

The girl was sitting on her bunk when he returned. She gave him a little smile as he sat down. Their knees were barely a half meter apart.

"My name is Amber," she said timidly and hesitated. "I'm in the reserve," she added. Win noted how her face lit up with a shy smile when she spoke.

"My name's Win," he replied, jumping up from the bunk and extending his hand to her. The towel started to slip, so he withdrew his proffered hand to hold it in place. "Blum's contingent," he added quickly to hide his embarrassment.

"I knew you were one of Blum's." Another little smile played on her lips for the briefest of instants. She tilted her head to one side. "When I asked Gold about you, she told me that you were one of the first Folk to be de-iced. She said you helped revive the ship and that you work directly with the boss almost every day." There was no doubting the admiration in her voice.

Win couldn't imagine how Gold had managed to find out so much about him. Most likely she'd gathered her information from other Folk, although he couldn't understand why she would have any curiosity about him.

"I didn't realize that they had called out the reserve," he replied to her comment. "They still haven't gotten all of Blum's Folk de-iced. Still," he added with a shy smile. "I'm glad that they did."

Amber returned his smile, and hers did not instantly disappear this time. It transformed her face into a thing of radiant beauty. Win had never seen such a change come over someone's face and, now that the smile had faded, he discovered that Amber's beauty remained. For a second, he lost track of the conversation, so bemused by this amazing transformation.

"They told me that there were some losses and they

needed replacements. That was why some of us reserves were de-iced ahead of schedule."

Win thought hard, trying to bring his thoughts back to whatever had been said before. "Losses?" *What she was talking about?*

"Oh yes, there weren't enough Folk to cover all of the work that needed to be done, so they had to de-ice more of us."

"That's strange. Blum's contingent is only sixty percent effective so far and, according to Boss Fren, we're right on schedule. I haven't heard him say anything about needing additional Folk." Of course, with the crew and Folk spread over the entire, expanding ship, he could have easily missed such news.

"I've been working with the doctors," Amber said. "Helping them in the thawing chambers. I don't really have much to do except carry blankets and stuff."

"That's very strange. I would think that you'd be working the life support or something more critical. What is your specialty?

"I was trained as a nurse. Maybe that's why they brought me out — just in case there's an accident and they need someone to care for the victim."

"Sure, that must be it," he said. With all of the activity going on in bringing the ship up to full activation, there was always the chance for an accident.

An awkward pausecame, during which he continued to stare at Amber. She had the most lovely blond hair and the largest blue eyes he had ever seen. Now that he had a chance to examine her at close range, he realized she was quite the prettiest girl he had ever seen.

Suddenly he noticed that she was staring back at him with equal intensity. "Do I have something on my face?" he asked self-consciously, fingers leaping to his cheek and wiping furiously.

Amber laughed, a delightful lilt that sent shivers along Win's backbone. "Oh no, I was just thinking that you are

even nicer than Gold said. I was so worried that you would-
n't talk to me. You've ignored me up until now, you know."

Win stuttered. "I . . . I didn't want to wake you, didn't
want to bother you. Not that I didn't want to, you understand. Oh, I'm sorry, I didn't mean that. Well, yes, I guess I
did — mean that I meant that. Oh darn, am I making a mess
of this?"

Amber giggled, a sweet trill that ran up and down the
scales. "No more than I am. Can we start over again?" She
put out her hand. "I am very glad to meet you, Win."

"And I you," Win replied as he extended his right hand
to take hers, holding firmly onto the towel with his left.
When he relaxed his grip, she held on. He did not pull back
but left his hand in her pleasantly warm and soft grip.

"What do you remember about Heaven?" he asked casually as he moved to sit beside her.

"Oh, everything," she said quickly. "But I'm afraid I
might start to miss some things. What do you think you will
miss the most?"

It was a good question, and Win pondered for several
moments before answering. The next few hours were spent
exchanging memories of the homes they'd left so many light
years behind, so many centuries in the past.

Win learned that, while he had grown up in the mountains
of Heaven, Amber had been raised on coastal plains — one
of the new cities along the edge of Heaven's western ocean.
From her earliest childhood, she had known that she would
be among those being taken to the stars on the Hand's next
expedition. Her whole life had been leading to this trip.

As had Win's.

Amber was the most fascinating creature he'd ever met;
attractive, intelligent, witty, and wise. Where he was a fumbling, stumbling fool, she was graceful and sophisticated.
She had learned and done things beyond his imagining.
He could not believe her descriptions of the Sweet Ocean,
a body of water that she declared was so vast that one

could not see the other side. He marvelled when she told him that she frequently swam, immersing herself completely in those dark waters, possibly exposing herself to the unknown denizens who lurked in its depths. He thought it most daring of her.

He laughed at Amber's surprise when he told her of his love of climbing mountains, scooting up the hillsides with line and piton, hanging by a hand-jam from a crevice, or descending in a rapid rappel to rest safely on a narrow ledge. Sore hands and rope-burned palms were the worse dangers, he assured her, provided one was careful and, he added with a smile, you couldn't drown on a mountain.

And so the evening went with each revelation from Win being matched by another from Amber. By the time Win finally crawled into bed for some much-needed rest, he knew that he was hopelessly in love.

He hoped Amber felt the same way about him.

One hundred and eighty days later, the last of the Men was de-iced and fit for duty. Tam looked over the crew list with some satisfaction. Of the eighty Men who had set out from Heaven all — every single one of them — had survived their cold sleep. Of the two hundred Halfings only five had been lost. Luckily none had been in the critical skill categories.

Half of the two hundred mongrel Folk had been de-iced so far. Most had fared the trip pretty well, with a loss of only six quads — twenty-four of the damned things. He wished that he'd not let Larisha and Chen talk him into bringing them along. The space would have been better used to transport another fifty Men or the same number of Halfings. Then this system would be rid of the useless baggage of their primitive genetic past.

Pfaugh, what use was it to debate the Folk's value at this juncture? They were here, and he had to deal with the situation. Well, he'd let Larisha take care of them — maybe she could take all of the mongrels with her when she led the team down to the surface of Meridian. For his own part, he'd just as soon stay on the ship, where he wouldn't have to see their disgusting forms.

Larisha took that moment to bustle in with an armload of schedules, which she dumped onto an empty spot among his mess. Her hair was in disarray; obviously, she was too rushed to even brush it back. When he'd first met her, it was long and held on top her head with silver combs. He loved taking the combs out and running his fingers through her hair as they made love. He'd thought it her best feature.

But that was the past. Now her hair had just recovered enough from the freeze to need some slight management.

"You need to work with your hair," Tam said as she sat down.

"What the devil are you talking about? Fix my hair? Do you have time for such vanities, Tam?" She ran her fingers through her hair and worried at a tangle her fingers encountered for a moment. That taken care of, she jumped right into her reason for coming to him.

"When are you going to get enough power for the lighting so I can finish my greenhouse?" she demanded. "I need to start producing some fresh vegetables and fruit, not to mention adding some fresh air to the ship's atmosphere."

"Don't be in such a hurry," Tam snapped back. "We have nearly two years of supplies in storage that we can live on, if need be. And the ship's scrubbers are doing a fine job of keeping the air circulated, thank you. Your greenhouse can wait while we get more important things done."

"Dry rations and reconstituted paste won't be enough for most of the Men," Larisha replied. "They keep asking if we could just have some lettuce, a few greens . . ."

"Just tell them that fresh vegetables aren't exactly high on my list of mission priorities!"

Larisha sighed and pulled a few sheets from the pile on the chair. She waved them in front of Tam's face.

"These reports tell me that we already know everything we need to about this system; eight planets with three of them gas giants, four arid rocks, and confirmation that our target planet, Meridian, is hospitable. What more do you need to know? Let's get on with the mission. Let's get the greenhouse started so we have stocks to plant when we land."

Tam looked up from his board. For the first time, Larisha noticed the thin fatigue lines around his eyes, the sagging folds of skin that told her of his lack of sleep and worry.

"Is there something you aren't telling me?" she asked, suddenly concerned. Since awakening, they both had been so busy that she had little knowledge of what he was doing except where their schedules and tasks intersected.

Tam waved a hand. "It's nothing serious, nothing to bother about. Gull still hasn't determined how the astronomical instruments malfunctioned. He still can't explain why that moon disappeared, for one." He paused. "I've told the science crew to continue looking into it."

"Tam Polat, I know you too well to believe that. You think this 'malfunction' business is more than some mistake in the instruments, don't you? You look really concerned about it."

Tam sighed and sagged in his chair. "I knew I couldn't hide anything from you, damn it. Okay, but this goes no further, understand?"

When he got Larisha's agreement, he continued. "Remember that moon, the little one that we thought was orbiting Thetti, the one Gull said was just a blip on the records?"

Larisha nodded. "Of course. I was at the briefing, if you will recall."

"So you were. Well, at first I believed that Gull was correct when he said that there might have been some sort of systemic error. But later I discovered that closer examination revealed that the moon had been orbiting, revolving around Thetti just like the other satellites."

"Orbiting, you say?" Larisha repeated. "How could that be if it was an instrumentation error?"

Tam shrugged. "That is what we need to find out. I don't like mysteries."

"Perhaps it was just a reflection — an optical illusion," Larisha suggested. "Some trick of refraction, perhaps?"

Tam shook his head. "Gull's science crew say they can't explain how such a thing would happen. If we are to believe the records, there is no way that it could be anything but a moon, a damn Thetti satellite! That's what worries me."

"But, even if it was there, what has a disappearing satellite to do with us? It might be scientifically interesting for Gull, but that's no reason to let it stop us from heading for Meridian and proceeding with the landing option." She paused and looked at Tam. "We are going straight to Meridian, aren't we?"

Tam shook his head slowly. "I haven't decided which option I'll use, Larisha. One option that is certain is to mine the gas giants and replenish our ship. Before we rush to Meridian, we must build up our ability to deal with whatever other mysteries we might discover in this system."

Larisha was appalled. "You can't do that! You are supposed to deliver us directly to Meridian, not wait around trying to solve astronomical puzzles."

Tam crossed his arms. "The Hand gave me the authority to do what I deemed best for the mission, you know. Well, I've elected to mine Thetti first, and if we can uncover the answer to this damn missing moon mystery while we're doing it, the better I'll like it!"

Larisha was about to reply when she realized Tam was lying. She noticed that he'd started speaking out of the corner of his mouth — a sure indication that he wasn't telling her everything. She'd learned that little indicator during their long relationship. Lying!

But she hesitated challenging him on it. She was Raggi, his second in command. She had a right to know everything that might affect the settlement. Did he think this little astronomical mystery had something to do with them? For the life of her, she could think of no logical reason.

On the other hand, if Tam was breaking down under the stress of command, she would need some support, just in case she had to take over. Perhaps she should discuss the matter with Dalgrun, who, as Palm of the Hand, was equal to Tam in authority, if only on religious matters.

Larisha looked at Tam's lying face for a moment and then decided: *Yes, I will do just that. I will speak to Palm Dalgrun at the first opportunity.*

"The first colonist's ship will arrive in fifty years," she said softly, returning to the subject she'd come to discuss, and one more dear to her heart. "We'll need to have Meridian ready for them. I really need to get my plants going. I need those lights in the greenhouse."

Tam grumbled and surrendered easily. It was another sign of his weariness.

"I'll instruct Blum to send you some mongrels. Just don't mention this little scientific mystery to anyone, all right? Wouldn't want our people upset over something that will probably turn out to be nothing at all. No need for them to be distracted from their work to talk about a possibly missing moon."

Larisha nodded as if she were agreeing, but thought that Tam would see that she hadn't been taken in by his facile explanation. He could read her well. Maybe that had been the problem — he had come to know her far too intimately for comfort . . . much as a parasite gets to know its host, she added venomously to herself.

She also knew that his authorization for the greenhouse lights was a bribe for her silence, a bribe that she would accept, for the moment.

Tam thought a party would be a good idea now that all of his Men were out of the freezers. The quarters were ill-equipped to be sure, but most of the heavy work had been completed, and they could finally be occupied. He doubted any of the Men would object to finally having some privacy after having to share space as if they were Halfings.

He'd had a crew clear out one of the storage bays — the one that held the materials they used to outfit the expanded habitation disk. The storage space was tight, but adequate for the crowd. He only expected one third of the crew to be there at any one time. That was why the party was to go on for four shifts — to allow everyone to attend.

Tam was momentarily puzzled by the colorful panels that decorated the storage space's walls before he recognized them as the color coded pallet lids. He next realized that somewhere in the cargo hold there had to be a lot of open containers. He made a mental note to commend whoever'd thought of it They did add something to the otherwise utilitarian space, however. He made another mental note to remind Blum to have someone put them back in place when this was over.

The table was a bright surprise. The cooks had managed to make standard rations look appetizing by cutting them into imaginative shapes and adding a little color here and there. But the greatest surprise came when he bit into one. The chefs must have brought a little of Heaven's spices along with them. After so many days of bland rations, these tangy morsels were a delightful change.

"Enjoying yourself, Hadir Tam Polat?" Dalgrun asked as she approached. "Have you tried this wonderful drink they've created for the party?" She thrust her cup toward him.

Tam took a tiny sip, then a deeper drink. "Fruit, and not a little alcohol, unless I am mistaken," he said with satisfaction.

Dalgrun grinned. "Two hundred year old brandy, Hadir! I had the foresight to use some of my personal cargo allowance to bring on a few cases. I swear it turned out even better than I expected! By God and the Prophet this is wonderful."

"I take it that this isn't your first cup," Tam said dryly. "I'd be cautious if I were you, dear Palm. Decorum is very important."

But Dalgrun wasn't to be discouraged. "I have more decorum in my arm than any twenty men. Don't worry about me, Hadir Tam Polat. I know my limits. Say, do you know how to dance?"

Tam became aware of the lively rhythm a dozen Halflings were playing at the far end of the room. He vaguely recalled the tune, something that had been going around just before launch time. He'd been too busy to learn the steps at the time.

"I'm afraid not," he said. "But I'm sure Blum will be more than willing to escort you through the figures." He grabbed Blum by the elbow and pushed him into the Palm's arms. With a whirl of her skirts, Dalgrun led his hapless Outrider into the swirling dance.

Tam carefully made a complete counterclockwise circuit of the room, pausing a moment to talk with each of the groups of Men. Someone had prepared a stiff punch of reconstituted fruit juice. Judging by its potency and the burning sensation that put fire in his belly, he suspected they had used some extract from the fuel tanks. Still, he had to admit, it did loosen and relax one. After another two drinks, he was so loose that he even had a word or two with the Halfing musicians.

An hour later the party was in full swing. Everyone was dancing to the wild playing of the Halfing band, whether they knew the steps or not. Dalgrun even managed to drive him around the floor for another set, her breath indicating that she had made at least one more trip to her secret store of brandy.

Finally, during a lull in the music, Tam was able to stagger away and find a chair where he could rest. "How that woman manages to keep going is beyond me," he said.

"She was quite an athlete back on Heaven," Larisha said as she slid into the chair next to his. "Just because she's the Palm doesn't mean that she shouldn't be in good shape."

"True, but not quite that good a shape. God, I feel like I've just broken a new stallion!"

"Speaking of stallions, it looks as if the Palm has more

than dancing on her mind at the moment." Larisha pointed at the far side, where Dalgrun had a young Man pinned between the food table and the wall. The youngster looked increasingly uncomfortable as the Palm pressed against him. "Let me rescue him."

"Yes, see if you can get our Palm out of the way. She is too full of the spirit at the moment for her own good."

When Larisha raised an eyebrow inquiringly, Tam explained about Dalgrun's store of ancient brandy and its disposition. "So it would be helpful were she to be discreetly taken away." He stopped abruptly.

"What is it?" Larisha asked. She turned to look in the direction where Tam was staring.

There was nothing untoward. No fights, no outrageous behavior. The dance floor had a few couples dancing, one of the new group dances consisting of intertwining loops and circles, occasional pairings and separations. She wondered what Tam had seen to produce such a black look.

"I am going to put a stop to this!" he said angrily and took a step forward.

Then Larisha saw the problem, at least what Tam must think was a problem. Two of the people in the circle of dancers were Halfings while the rest were Men.

"Tam, wait!" she said and took him by the arm. "Let them be. If the people want to have fun then let them. It won't hurt anyone to let the social barriers down for a few hours. Come on, dance with me."

Tam softened. It wasn't as if they were actually dancing as couples, not really. The figure just called for a little handholding. Yes, he would let it go, but only for the moment.

And only because Larisha felt so damn good in his arms.

He managed to reappear at the party during each shift. It was partly to let the crew know that he was interested in their welfare, and partly to make certain that this dancing business wasn't getting out of hand. He also wanted to make sure that the Palm wasn't embarrassing herself further.

The next day there were a few hangovers, some sore muscles from too much dancing, several new liaisons, and one more marriage to arrange. The fancy rations were exhausted, the punch completely consumed, and the crew in a generally relaxed mood.

It was, by any measure he could think of, a most successful party.

Larisha was preparing seedlings for planting when she heard someone walking down the aisle between the long troughs of the greenhouse. The footsteps stopped just behind her. It could only be the worker Tam had promised he would send. What was his name? Win?

"About time you got here," Larisha said. "I need those pots moved over there." She pointed to the row of containers and waved her hand in the general direction of the long troughs that had been set up directly beneath the new bank of lights.

"Do you want me to put them all together or space them out under the lights?" Win asked as he slipped on his gloves. "And is there any special order you want them to have?"

"That's a very good question," Larisha replied, looking up from her work for the first time. "As a matter of fact, that's a very intelligent question. Have you worked with plants before, perhaps on one of the farms back on Heaven?" She looked closely at him. *Can he be one of my own Folk?*

Win smiled at her. "No, mistress. It's just that, since everything on the ship seems to have a specific place, I figured that these pots wouldn't be any different."

"Nevertheless, I wouldn't have expected such an observation from a . . ." she coughed nervously into her fist and then shook her head. "Never mind. Here, take this first one," she indicated a large container near her foot. The tips of a few bright green shoots were just emerging from the dark, moist soil, "Take this one down to the far end and then space the rest of them evenly along this line." She indicated the spacing with a spread of her hands. "Be very careful that you don't touch the shoots."

As Win started to lift the heavy container, Larisha hesitated, wondering if he could handle such a load by himself. He appeared to be so young, an adolescent in fact. She noted the way his muscles stood out on his lithe body as he lifted the heavy pot. The boy was quite strong for his frame, having musculature more in keeping with someone older and more mature.

In some ways, his slim physique reminded her of Tam's when they had first met, years and years before. God, how she had loved to run her hands over his chest and back in those days. How she had enjoyed the feel of his strong, wiry arms around her. Well, she had quickly learned what a cold, hollow cavity that handsome body surrounded and how lacking in passion it could become; much to her regret. Best that those times were behind her. She shook her head to clear it of those memories.

As the shift progressed, she found herself watching Win more and more as they worked together to get the greenhouse set up the way she wanted. There was something appealing about the youngster, some indefinable quality that she couldn't quite place. Certainly it was more than his physical appearance. Perhaps it was the discovery that there was an alert and inquiring intellect in such a young Folk that piqued her curiosity.

Win had inquired into everything she ordered him to do with a probing curiosity. Normally, she would find this sort of drilling from a worker offensive. It was not ordinarily a worker's privilege to question her orders. However, in this case she found his curiosity appealing. In fact, he learned so quickly that, by the end of the day, he was starting to make some very good suggestions, sometimes even for improvements on her own ideas. Several times she caught herself thinking of him as one of the Halfings, almost a peer, but each time she caught herself before crossing that line. Respect, but not equality was what was needed from him. She should never let one of the Folk forget that, and especially not this one.

"I am going to tell Blum that you are to work in my greenhouse for the duration," she said to Win at the end of the shift. "There's a lot to be done here, and I need to have someone with a genuine feel for the place, such as yourself, to work with me. That will allow us to progress faster and maybe even get the greenhouse completed ahead of schedule."

"Yes ma'am," Win replied. "But I'm scheduled to help Boss Fren unpack the scoops tomorrow. I work right with him, you know."

Larisha brushed his protest away with a shrug. "There are a dozen other Folk who can do that, I am sure. No, I'll make it a point to speak to Blum this very evening. I'll simply tell him that you are needed here. You will report here in the morning. Is that clear?"

Win nodded. "Yes ma'am. But the boss doesn't pay much mind to what the supervisors want. He gets his orders right from command, you know. Sorry, ma'am, but I need to hear that from him."

Larisha smiled. "You really don't know who I am, do you?" Command, indeed! Well, it was nice to know that the boy was obedient as well. This would make their working relationship so much the better. "Don't worry about that. I'll take care of it. Now, run along. I'll expect you here first thing at the start of day shift." God, he was a good-looking youngster, she thought as he walked away from her. He moves like a cat, silky smooth. There must have been some damned good genes in there somewhere.

It was such a pity he was just Folk.

FOUR

As the ship slowly matched orbits with Thetti, Larisha discovered that Gull Tamat had still not provided a rational explanation for the disappearance of Tam's moon, as she had come to think of it. Apparently Tam was still intrigued by that stupid, irrelevant mystery. *Why can't he accept that it was just a blip on the record, another one-time event in a mysterious universe that defies explanation? Well, if Gull's inquiry proves to be nothing more than a fruitless pursuit of a phantom it will certainly weaken Tam's command position.* She was certain that most of the crew wanted to get on with the settlement of Meridian, not hang about in space building a store of resources on the slim chance that Meridian might prove inhospitable.

But she would honor Tam's request for silence. She would bide her time.

Over the next few weeks, Tam added additional Folk to the greenhouse crew. She had given Win authority over some of them. The boy had shown that not only did he fully understand her immediate objectives, but grasped the essence of her long-range plans as well. He'd proven himself creative enough to deal with the many unforeseen problems that invariably cropped up in such a project. Although her other duties kept her extremely busy, she always managed to find time to drop by to see the greenhouse.

"Nearly finished with the first set of plantings, mistress," Win informed her one evening when she asked about their progress.

Larisha looked down the long rows of rapidly growing vines and emerging trees, most of which were responding admirably to the growth-accelerating hormones metered into the steady flow of nutrients to their roots.

Most of the current vegetation within the greenhouse had been selected for rapid growth, targeted to get the ship's oxygen production up as well as provide an environment in which the longer-lived, and slower-growing plants could live. Some of her fast-growth, oxygen-producing selections had been engineered to grow at meters per day, adding leaves so fast that their expansion could be observed with the naked eye. However, their lush, dense vegetation was an illusion, a temporary jungle that would vanish in a few months as more permanent species replaced them.

The heavy, damp atmosphere of the place made her homesick for the tropical estate she'd left behind on Heaven. But, if she squinted her eyes, she could easily imagine this greenhouse to be one of her gardens in the back lot, where she'd experimented with her stock. A surge of homesickness overcame her, and she wondered, for the twentieth time, if she'd been right to accept this mission, to dedicate the rest of her life to the expansion of God's dominion in this foreign realm. The rich smells of moist soil, the rustle of explosive growth awoke her suppressed doubts and made her wish that she could once again sit in her bower and enjoy the warmth of a summer's evening.

"Mistress." Win interrupted her thoughts and brought her attention back to the chill reality of the greenhouse. "Do you have anything else for me to do today?"

Larisha had quite lost track of the time. She glanced around and noted that the other Folk had departed. The lights were starting to dim for the night cycle.

"Walk with me," she said to Win as the artificial dusk deepened, hiding the struts and ribs of distant walls in shadow, making the verdant growth embrace her. "Show me what we've accomplished this week. I want to get a better feel for where we are."

Win hesitated. "The shift is over, mistress. I, uh, I have something to do." He scuffled his feet in a nervous little dance.

"Nonsense," Larisha said, dismissing the boy's weak objection. "The greenhouse is one of the more critical projects I have. Nothing you have to do could be more important than that." She turned her back on him and began to move away. "Come along now. Show me what you've done with my plants."

Win hesitated, but had no choice except to follow. As they walked along, he described the culture and preparation of each of the several species his Folk had brought to fullness. He told Larisha of the difficulties they'd had with the greenhouse's stubborn plumbing and the solutions he'd crafted.

"I found some manuals that had this, uh, misting system," he explained. "So I rigged it to ensure the proper humidity for your kudzu. Here, mistress, if you'll look up there," he pointed through the maze of tightly wound vines at a bright, partially concealed object, "you can see how we arranged the nozzles to maximize the dispersion."

Larisha placed her foot on the edge of the trough and began to step up. "Let me get a closer look. Some of these vines can't tolerate too much moisture. It might cause them to rot."

With one foot on the sill of the slippery trough, she leaned forward and pulled the leaves apart so she could examine the misting nozzles better. A vine blocked her view, so she reached over to move it. As she did so she felt her foot slip. As she fell backwards, she grabbed at the vines to recover her balance, took hold, and felt them break loose.

Then she felt Win's arms catch her, softening her fall as they tumbled onto the floor, a cascade of vine falling over them, wrapping them in a mass of slick, damp leaves.

"Are you all right?" Win asked breathlessly.

Larisha found herself pressed tightly against him. One of his arms encircled her waist; and their legs were entwined, tied together by the tangled vine. His mouth was so close to hers that she felt his breath on her lips as he spoke.

Larisha felt a rush of emotion that took her by surprise. She didn't respond to his question for a long moment, trying to understand why this boy, this Folk, should awake such strong feelings in her. It would be so easy to . . .

"I'm fine," she replied, placed one hand on his chest,

and pushed herself away. "Help me get these damned vines untangled, would you?"

Win struggled to move away from her, slipping his arm free of her waist and tugging the vines away from his legs and hers. The vegetation seemed to have a mind of its own, despite his valiant efforts. Finally, he prevailed, stood, put out his hand, and pulled Larisha to her feet.

Larisha stood before him silently, holding onto his hand and looking into his deep blue eyes. "Thank you for catching me," she said softly. "I could have been seriously hurt if you hadn't been there." She made no effort to release his hand. She stroked the fine hairs on his cheek with her free hand.

Win shrugged. "Mistress, it was my fault for letting you climb up there. I should have told you that the edges of those troughs are slippery when they're wet. Besides, Boss Fren would have my butt if I let anything happen to the greenhouse supervisor."

Larisha laughed. This boy was so refreshing, so naïve to think that she was just a "greenhouse supervisor." Was this precious boy so innocent that he didn't realize the privilege she had granted him?

"You really don't know who I am, do you?" she asked.

"You're one of the supervisors, aren't you?"

Win looked so puzzled that she laughed again.

"You are such a dear. How could you not know? My name is Bul Larisha. I'm the leader of the Halfings. I am the mission's Raggi. All this," she waved her hand, "comes under my command."

Win's mouth gaped in surprise. "More than the greenhouse?" he asked incredulously.

"Yes, more than the greenhouse!" she repeated wickedly. "I am second in command over the whole damn ship." The expression on Win's face when he realized who she was seemed so priceless that she nearly laughed aloud. He was such a naïve dear that she knew that she just had to find something else for him to do. There was no way she would let such an amusing, valuable Worker become a common laborer.

"Didn't Larisha tell you to accelerate the de-icing program?" Tam demanded of Jas Bulgat. "Didn't you hear me say the same thing?"

"Hadir Polat, I've had my hands full since you started moving the ship toward Thetti," the veterinarian said apologetically. "I've got one hundred and seventy-two Folk operational so far, and that's almost more than the Halfing supervisors can handle at present, according to Raggi Larisha. I don't think we should revive any more until you have enough people to supervise them."

Tam brushed Jas's words aside with a sweep of his hand. "We have enough supervisors. We've de-iced all of the Halfing technicians and engineers, and they are all ready to go to work as soon as they get the arms and legs they need. That's your job — Larisha needs those mongrels working now, not later! I'd advise you to get moving if you want to stay on her good side."

"I've heard that she's already got some Folk working directly for her in the greenhouse. They've nearly gotten it into operation. Bets are that they'll bring in a crop before we reach Meridian."

Tam glared angrily at him. "That supposed to be a joke? I don't like to hear people second-guessing my decisions." The ice in his voice was evident.

Jas held his hands before his face and bowed his head. "I meant no offense, Hadir Tam Polat," he whined. "But why did you think I was making a joke? Aren't we on schedule?"

Tam examined the vet's face for a long while, trying to decide if this pathetic example of a Halfing was as much a fool as he appeared. Perhaps, he thought — giving Larisha the benefit of the doubt — she and the others had erred in selecting Jas for such a responsible position. Perhaps on closer examination they'd discover that his genes didn't even qualify him for being among the Halfings. Wasn't there a trace of blue in his eyes? He decided to mention this to Larisha to see what her reaction might be.

Finally he spoke. "Since you ask, I will tell you of my plans. I have directed the ship to head for Thetti, the nearest planet. I have decided that we need to replenish our resources before we attempt to settle Meridian. I am surprised that someone hasn't told you about this. I understand that the selection of the mission option has been quite the topic of conversation whenever I am not around."

The acid in Tam's voice gave the vet pause.

"I swear that I've heard not a word of this, Hadir Polat," he replied. "As you know, I spend most of my time in the dormitories, looking after the Folk. Doesn't leave a lot of time to socialize with the rest of the crew."

"Well, you should socialize more," Tam said. "Isn't right, even for you, to have nothing but mongrels to talk to. Might start thinking you understand them if you do that for long. You might even start thinking of them as something more than tools, and I won't tolerate that," he snapped. "Do you understand me, Jas Bulgat? We have to keep the lower orders in their place!" His voice barked out the last as a command.

"I agree, Hadir Polat," Jas replied tentatively, and then continued. "But someone needs to talk to the rest of the crew about this besides me. I think that some of the people are getting too attached to their Folk, no matter how much I caution them." Then he added, as if in apology; "I mean, it's hard not to like some of them, working so close day after day. It's easy to forget that they're not Halfings, not real people."

Tam made a rude noise in the back of his throat. "The damned mongrels are just tools, damn it! Everybody ought to understand that!" Flecks of spittle formed at the corners of his mouth.

Jas backed away. "Hadir Polat, it isn't the Folk's fault. They like the people they work with, too. I can tell they hate to return to the dormitories. Most of them can't wait to get out to work with the crew. It's hard to discipline them. They are such simple things. They mean no harm."

"I'd better not hear about anyone making pets of our working stock," Tam snarled. "Worst thing to happen was bringing so many of those damn beasts along on this mission. I argued against it from the beginning, wanted to increase both Men and Halfings instead, but nobody would listen to me. Now we're stuck with them."

"But," Jas said, "if the Folk weren't along, then there would be no use for me, would there?"

Tam stared at the vet for a long time, letting the uneasy silence out drag out until Jas hung his head in shame. It was clear what the Hadir thought without another word being said.

"I've got to get back to the dormitory," Jas mumbled apologetically as he touched his forelock. "It's getting close to their dinner time."

"Yes, take care of your mongrels. I am sure they are just dying for your devoted, loving attention." The way Tam said it made Jas's concern over his charges sound as if it were something dirty and vile.

Over the next few months, the ship matched orbits with Thetti, approaching in an extended hyperbolic orbit. Tam had insisted that the approach path be calculated with great care. If anything unexpected occurred, he wanted the option of using the planet's massive gravity well to slingshot them away from danger. If nothing unexpected happened, they could use Thetti's mass as a gravity brake that would, with a little help from their engines, put them into a nice circular orbit, safely outside the zone where the missing moon had been orbiting.

The crew's efforts had finally expanded the ship to its full capacity; now it had become a huge cylinder. The giant engines projected to the rear, while the spindly command pod rode out in front, a tiny spike rising above the main body. A sprinkling of scoop ships and shuttles were berthed along the outer edges of the cylinder. Tam intended to launch them into Thetti's atmosphere once the ship became stabilized in orbit.

By the time they reached Thetti, every one of the Folk had been de-iced, with only a few more deaths to reduce their numbers. The Folk were providing the crew with muscle and spare hands for heavy and tedious tasks. It was work well-suited to their brutish natures, Tam mused.

Under his insistence, Gull's science crew had been maintaining a constant vigil on Thetti and its environs. They were under orders to be alert for any further sign of the missing moon. At the same time, Gull was still trying to determine if there had been a recording error or, worse yet in his orderly mind, the moon had really disappeared.

Despite Tam's constant prodding and prompting, Gull could find no reason for the astronomic instrument's systemic errors. Neither could his team come up with a reason, even a half-assed theory, on how an entire satellite large enough to appear on the ship's automatic long-range scans could suddenly vanish without a trace. Neither could Gull's team find anything near the location that could have been mistaken for the missing moon.

It was all very puzzling, everyone in the science crew concluded, and very mysterious. It had to be an error in the instruments, they insisted with declining conviction.

The longer that the mystery remained, the stronger Tam's recollection of that crystalline God grew. While he'd initially thought it had been a blessed vision, now he suspected that he had seen something quite real, quite significant, and quite impossible. But there was no other explanation — so long as Gull could find no "systemic error," his vision must remain valid.

Why had he been the only one to see it?

"When will you give up this wild goose chase for this moon of yours and put us down on Meridian," Larisha demanded. "There is nothing to be gained by hanging around Thetti. Whatever Gull Tamat though he detected isn't here, if it ever was to begin with. It is senseless to delay reaching our primary objective just because of a stupid recording error. You yourself suggested such a possibility in the beginning, didn't you, Tam?"

Tam nodded, but said nothing. How could he explain why he had chosen this particular option? What if he told Larisha what he had seen with his own eyes? If he also declared that he had actually seen a moon disappear, she would have him removed from command. The last thing the mission needed was a Hadir subject to hallucinations.

But it hadn't been a hallucination; he knew that to the core of his being. The crystalline observer had been as real to him as Thetti, which glowed ruddily outside of the glass, just as Larisha glowered darkly inside, he thought with wry comparison.

He recalled analyzing what he had seen, what he thought he'd seen in those few horrifying seconds after awakening. He could remember every facet of the brilliant, sparkling crystal structure. It had such complexity that he couldn't recall but a few of its myriad details, such as the symmetrical projections to either side and the cluster of rubies at the forward end. Neither of these were repeated elsewhere on the object's surface, as they would have been had this been a natural crystal. It was either a creature like none they had ever imagined or something completely artificial — an artifact of intelligent life.

No, it couldn't be! That such a possibility should exist at all would be a repudiation of everything Men believed, everything God had told them, everything the human race understood about its place in the universe.

Either it was God, or Men had been following a false doctrine for centuries.

That thought took his breath away. Through all of history, Men had never doubted that no one was their equal. They had dominated every alien race they had encountered. But none of those had presented much of a challenge. All had submitted to Man's dominance.

Until now.

Had he been blessed by God to be the first to test Man's dominion against aliens who were capable of space flight? Had he been chosen to prove God's Revelation of Man's dominion? Surely the crystalline object could not be an inhuman intelligence, despite his memories that contradicted this view.

But the idea that it could be an alien artifact shook him to the very center of his belief. To imagine that it was not God, that the huge, beautiful object might be some hateful alien, had shaken his faith. Hadn't God revealed to the Prophet that there were no alien races superior to Man? Hadn't the most preëminent of scientists, scholars, and religious for the last ten centuries agreed that the universe belonged to Man alone. Hadn't God given Man special dominion? Why else had God permitted humanity to spread its seed to the stars if not to be fruitful and multiply in compliance with His covenant? The core of Tam's faith, the very foundations that he had accepted for his entire life had been thrown in doubt by the sight of that vast object.

Gull's recorders had shown only the fuzzy dot of a tiny moon, even at the highest resolution. Tam could find no indications of crystalline structure, no bright facets, nor indication of anything out of the ordinary in any of the images he was shown.

To tell the Palm, Dalgrun Wofat, or any of the people, for that matter, that their Hadir had seen an artifact of an alien civilization would be to overthrow the ship's entire culture. Such a statement would challenge all their beliefs, deny the purpose of their holy mission, their very lives. No one would believe him. No one!

To overcome their objections, he must have concrete evidence, positive proof that could not be denied by even the most severe of skeptics. Until Gull Tamat and his technicians found such evidence, Tam knew that he must keep his thoughts to himself.

*   *   *

"You have not given adequate justification for this delay of our settlement," Palm Dalgrun chided him. "Why we are not heading directly for our destination is a question on everyone's lips."

Tam did not trust Dalgrun. She had been assigned only a short time before launch. All of the other members of the crew had been personally cleared by either himself or Larisha, but Dalgrun had materialized, seemingly out of thin air just before the final round of icing, just before the last of the crew underwent treatment.

Doctor Chen had escorted Dalgrun into the ship, introduced her as the chosen representative of the Hand of Heaven, and departed.

Dalgrun hadn't waited for Tam or Larisha to question her about her abrupt intrusion into their well-planned expedition. "I have been given the duty to accompany you on this blessed journey," she announced cheerfully. "My rôle will be to ensure that the Hand's policies are followed to the letter. I am to help you make the kinds of decisions that will enrich and expand humanity among the distant stars."

When neither Tam nor Larisha responded, she continued: "I am to be your religious mentor and guide. I am to serve the ship in any way that I may." She bowed gracefully and offered her hand.

Tam was stunned. At no time had anyone connected to the mission mentioned any dissatisfaction with his decisions or his ability to command. At no time in his career leading up to this final, glorious assignment had anyone so much as hinted that he was not a completely obedient pious servant of the Hand. To discover at this late date that the leadership of the Hand felt it expedient to extend their direct influence so far into the future, to send someone to second-guess their Hadir's future decisions, was beyond his understanding. How long had they known of this? How long had Chen plotted to keep knowledge of this person, this religious leader, from him? He drew in a breath to tell this woman what he thought of the idea.

"We are very glad to have you accompany us," Larisha interrupted while Tam was still assembling the explosive words in his mind. "I often wonder if my decisions would be the ones that God would want me to make. I welcome the idea of an advisor who will counsel me and ease my doubts."

Dalgrun smiled amicably, obviously pleased by the Raggi's smooth words. "I would not want you to feel otherwise, my dear. I am an expert on the policies and philosophies of the Hand and have been an advisor to the highest councils for several years. I must admit," she continued with a depreciating gesture, "that I did not know the destiny for which I was being prepared until recently." She threw a worried look about the small confines of the command cabin. "Frankly, the thought of going on such a long journey frightens me immensely." She shivered. "The idea that I will not be able to return, never to see Heaven again . . . Well."

"I know what you are feeling," Larisha said sympathetically. "It is hard to leave one's home."

"This will be a trying mission," Tam said harshly, angry at this apparent amiability of his nominative wife toward this religious intruder. "My crew are all experts. They have all of the skills we'll need to survive and prepare the way for the settlers. *Covenant* will only have enough resources to survive for two years, perhaps less, after we arrive. It will take everyone working long and hard to gather what we need, to survive whatever may await us! Anyone who can't contribute some vital skill or talent will be a drain on valuable resources. A drain we could better do without!" He stared hard at the woman to drive home his point.

"I believe ministering to and caring for the souls of our crew to be as important as seeing to their physical needs." Dalgrun replied quickly. "I am a certified Palm. I know enough psychology to deal with any interpersonal problems that can arise among your crew. Believe me, Hadir Tam Polat, I will pull my own weight even as I help you with your decisions. You will find that we will work very well together."

"Come, let me show you around the ship," Larisha said, acting to forestall another outburst. She led the Palm away before he could say another harsh word. No doubt, she'd noted his frown and read the signs of an imminent explosion.

As she led Dalgrun, away she glared over her shoulder. Tam knew from experience that was his signal to back down and let her handle the situation. Well, she'd better, he thought. In the meantime he was going to take this matter up with Chen and the others. Help him with decisions — Ha! He'd see about that!

But, in the end, the will of the Hand's leadership had prevailed. Chen ever so politely informed him that he would either accept their gracious offer of Dalgrun Wofat or be removed from command. They were certain that he could do a very good job under Raggi Larisha, Chen added cruelly. It was obvious that the good Doctor understood quite well the pact that Tam and Larisha had formed between them. Tam was certain that the Doctor would use that bit of nasty information to displace both of them if necessary.

With no apparent choice in the matter, he had bitterly acceded to the Hand's wishes. As a result, this Palm of God, this woman, was now questioning his judgement about a mission option he had chosen! How dare she intrude on his command judgement. How dare she! Tam seethed with anger at the effrontery.

"I repeat, what is the justification for this alteration of mission?" Dalgrun said impatiently.

Tam fought to contain his sudden burst of anger, to hide his desire to grab her by the scruff of her neck and wring her throat. Instead he took a deep breath, paused, and then said, as calmly and evenly as he could manage, "I have elected to go with an alternative option. I believe it will be prudent to build a habitat before we proceed to Meridian.

The presence of a habitat will give us a wider range of options should we encounter —" He hesitated for the briefest millisecond. "— difficulties."

Dalgrun raised an eyebrow as she seized on that momentary hesitation. "Difficulties? Of what sort? I've looked at Gull's profiles of Meridian and see no problems that we cannot not overcome with our current resources. The planet is within acceptable parameters for settlement. We should get on with the prime mission and start preparing for the coming settlers."

"I realize that," Tam said stiffly. "Nevertheless, prudence dictates that we be prepared."

Dalgrun stared at Tam for a long time. "No, that's not all. Am I right to suspect that this has more to do with your concern over that anomaly of Gull Tamat's? This choice of options is more than simple prudence, isn't it, Hadir Tam Polat?"

When Tam did not immediately reply, she continued. "What is it about that supposedly missing satellite that so intrigues you? Is there something that you are not telling me?"

Damn, Tam wondered, could the woman see right through him? She sounded just like Larisha.

"Not at all," he answered dismissively. "I simply think that the best course is to be cautious when we encounter something we can't explain. This missing moon could be the result of some force that represents a danger to us. The better part of wisdom says that the matter should be investigated fully before proceeding. Besides, we can use the time to mine Thetti for additional resources needed to build the habitat."

"As I said before, the crew is very concerned about the change in plans," Dalgrun said calmly. "None of them are happy about being required to stay in this ship when there's a decent planet waiting near at hand. Hadir Tam Polat, you must understand how many of the crew want to feel solid ground under their feet. They want to see the sun overhead.

This empty, dark space is depressing to everyone, like this chill that pervades the ship," she shivered as if to illustrate her point. "The sooner we get down onto the surface of Meridian, the better I'll like it."

Tam raised an eyebrow. "The better *you'll* like it? I thought we were talking about the crew's feelings."

"I think most of the crew feel as I do," Dalgrun replied haughtily. "Only some of your Men were trained for ship duty. The rest do it only of necessity." She paused. "I am going to defer judgement on this mission change for a while to see what develops. So long as your decisions don't affect the long-term plans of the Hand, I will say nothing more."

She turned to go and then stopped and slowly turned around to face Tam. She raised a finger and shook it as if correcting an wayward child. "Just make certain that you always keep our overriding purpose clearly in mind. It is never wise to confuse one's personal interests with those of the Hand." With those closing words, she left.

Had her words been empty threats, or did she have some power to back them? She was far too discerning, too suspicious of his motives, for his liking. He'd have to be very careful from now on; careful not to do anything that would raise further questions about his capability to command.

What a problem. How could he make not only Dalgrun, but the others, realize how important it was to understand what he had seen without making them think he was insane?

And probably a blasphemer as well.

Tam found Larisha in her greenhouse, sitting in a small space beneath the spreading limbs of a fast-growing catalpa tree. "I come here often," she said casually as he sat beside her. "Whenever things get too difficult, I come here. I look at the plants flourishing in this place and remember Heaven. It clears my mind and refreshes me so that I am able to deal with all of my other problems again."

He nodded.

"See that space over there?" She pointed at a tiny enclave at the end of one of the rows of plants. "I think I will put a bower there. It would be a place to sit and reflect. It would be a refuge from the day's concerns."

"Just like the one you had at your farm," Tam guessed. "I remember that bower well. We sat there often." He smiled and then stopped — damn, he'd thought that memory long submerged. Why did he bring it up now?

"Maybe I should think about using it when you finish," he continued, hoping Larisha hadn't noticed his lapse. "Lord knows but I need someplace to sit and figure out what I need to do next. There's always so much to do, so much to plan."

Larisha looked at him with a knowing smile. "That was our problem; you always were too calculating for your own good, always trying to 'figure out' things. I think that is why you got this command — because of your pathological planning." She considered for a moment. "But plans don't always work out, Hadir. Sometimes things just happen."

Tam was about to say something when she put up a hand to silence him.

"You are the only one I know who has to plan his entire life to the last detail. Don't you realize that the universe doesn't always follow a rational pattern, that spontaneous events can disrupt the most careful of plans?"

Tam started at her words; did she suspect anything? Larisha was never one for subterfuge or subtlety where he was concerned. Perhaps he had trained her in that — always forcing her to state outright what she expected in clear terms instead of hinting and hinting until he thought he would go mad trying to outguess her. Then he realized that, perhaps, she had been discussing his mission decisions with Dalgrun. It was too much of a coincidence that the two of them should say such similar things.

"Are you talking about my choice of options?" he asked. "I've already told you my reasons. This investigation of that missing moon is just an incidental interest. It doesn't divert any serious resources from our efforts."

Larisha smiled and plucked a leaf from the branch nearest her head. She stripped the stem, bent it into a loop, stuck it on her finger, and admired it as if it were some precious ring.

"My, aren't we getting defensive," she said slyly. "I assume that Dalgrun has been questioning you over your selection of options. She told me the crew are more upset than they let on."

So they had been talking about him. "More likely the Palm's been projecting her own feelings," he suggested cautiously. "Why they ever put someone who has such an aversion to space on board this ship is beyond me."

Larisha touched his arm ever so gently. "Be very careful, Tam. Dalgrun Wofat has acquired more power than you realize. All of the crew respects her rôle as the Palm of the Hand. What's more, they respect her as a person with deep and sincere concerns for their welfare. They all know she has only their best interests at heart."

Tam was stunned. How had this damned Palm, this late-comer, this intrusive addition to his ship, managed to subvert his handpicked crew? He'd been assuming that she had confined her attentions to religious matters, only to realize that she'd been fostering something close to mutiny among his own people. He felt the heat of anger growing in his breast.

"Her guidance on worship days is very comforting to the crew," Larisha continued, not noticing the expression on Tam's face. "She is our anchor to Heaven, the Palm of the Hand of God sent to guide and support us so far from everything we knew and loved. I think it wonderful that most of the crew have accepted her as their spiritual leader. Just as I have."

"So they trust her and not me?" Tam spat out angrily. "Damn it, Larisha, I am the Hadir of this mission. It is my responsibility to see that it succeeds!"

"Oh, everyone respects you, Hadir Tam Polat. It's just that, well, you are rather cold and calculating. You've kept so distant that we all feel that we've lost touch with you."

There was a strange note in her voice. Tam wondered about that. Was this another of her damned subtle hints, something that he had to agonize and analyze for hours before he began to understand what she meant?

"How can that be?" he said, responding to her words alone. "I've had staff meetings nearly every day. I'm out there dealing with the problems throughout the ship. How can you say that I am being distant?"

"Working with people and socializing are two different things." Larisha shot back. "You never were one for being warm and friendly."

There, now that was a not-too-subtle dig at him. Well — the hell with her!

"Yeah, that's what you always said," he replied to show her that he understood the subtext. "Well, that's the way I am, the way I've always been. That's how I got command of this mission, and how I am going to make certain we are ready for the settlers when they arrive. Everybody should be able to see that!"

"Investigating some stupid moon is not a way to restore confidence in your judgement!" Larisha said in exasperation. "There are those who think you have lost sight of the reason we were sent here. Tam, listen to me. Everyone is talking about this preoccupation of yours. It just isn't worth wasting time on." She clutched at his arm, taking hold of the material on his sleeve and gripping it tightly "You may be in more trouble than you realize."

He shook her hand away. "Perhaps if everyone were a little more attentive to their jobs instead of wasting time trying to understand my motivations we'd all be better off!" he barked. "Which brings me to the reason I came to see you. I understand that you have diverted some of Blum's mongrels to work in your greenhouse."

When Larisha nodded, he continued. "I thought that the greenhouse was finished." He looked around them. "It certainly looks that way to me. Listen, if you needed additional resources, you should have cleared it with me. I could have assigned some of the mongrels from reserve if you'd asked. Blum's Folk are too good to waste on tending your plants."

"I am the Raggi, your deputy, and leader of Halfings, which, in case you've forgotten, includes all of the technicians and engineers," Larisha shot back. "I don't need your damned permission to accomplish tasks within my purview. I'm not just your damned wife, Hadir! I have command authority!"

Tam rocked back at the vehemence in her voice. Damn, he had thought that she, of all people, would have faith in his judgement. "Listen to your own words, Tam; you're losing control! You didn't really hear a thing I said. I really *am* starting to wonder if you are fit for command."

Angrily, he rose from the bench and stalked off, pushing through the jungle like a wounded lion.

The interior portions of the ship's expanded disk were nearly finished. As Tam toured the outer ring of the torus the Folk had erected about the mid-ship line, he noted the care with which the fittings had been secured. Not only were they properly latched down, but each clinch pin was welded solidly in place. It would have been enough just to ram the pins into position and lock them down with a spot weld, but apparently Blum had wanted to make them neatly finished as well.

"Good work here," he congratulated Blum as he admired the smooth welds. "You've a good respect for detail."

Blum grunted. He was slightly shorter than Tam and, like most of the people in Man's cadre, had a thick shock of tangled black hair. Blum was broad across the shoulders, with bowed, massive arms and rough, callused hands. Despite his bulk, he moved with mincing steps that were not without a measure of grace.

Perhaps, Tam thought, Blum had been a dancer before becoming Master of the Kennels. Dancing wouldn't have been in his portfolio. Or maybe that gracefulness was some ability ingrained in his genetic heritage — a holdover from a more primitive time when coördination was a survival characteristic. He'd noted that a few of the Men moved the same way. Perhaps it was a genetic trait the Hand was fostering. Time — God's time — would tell which. For now, nothing would be gained by wondering.

"The finish wasn't my idea," Blum admitted. He rubbed one blunt finger along the smooth weld. "One of the Folk said they'd be better finished off like this. Less chance for them to snag on something."

"One of the mongrels suggested this? Really?" Tam was incredulous. Perhaps the Hand had trained them better than he thought. "A mongrel, you say. That is interesting."

"Most of 'em had to be smart to be brought along," Blum said. "We got the best of the lot, I'd say. Most of them are right clever."

Tam clucked his disapproval. "Well, perhaps they are, but they're still inferior stock. I'm sure we'd have done better with fewer of them and more of the Halfings. Can't trust the mongrels the way we can the Halfings."

Blum grunted again. Whether he intended it as agreement or simply grudging acknowledgement Tam had no way of telling. He continued his inspection tour without further mention of the mongrels.

While they were checking the circulation system, Blum mumbled something Tam didn't catch. The Man had been acting as if there were something on his mind the whole time they had been inspecting the torus. Several times he'd opened his mouth as if he were going to speak and then had stopped, shaking his head as if thinking better of it. Finally, Tam could stand it no longer.

"Is there something you want to speak to me about?" he demanded. "Come on, man. Spit it out!"

Blum mumbled something quickly, but his words were

so indistinct that Tam couldn't make them out. "What was that?"

"Problems with some of the mongrels," Blum finally said. "People getting too close, you know. It's not a good thing." He kept looking away as he said these words, as if afraid to meet Tam's eyes directly.

"What do you mean?" Tam laughed. "Are some of the crew making pets of the mongrels?" Then he recalled Jas Bulgat's idle comment about the relationships between the mongrels and some of their supervisors and scowled. "Damn it, Man, you know better than to allow that. We brought the mongrels along to be worked, and that's all they're for! You're the blasted Master, so it's your responsibility to keep them in line and —" He paused. "— discipline the crew as well, if need be. You have the authority to do so and I'll back you up."

Blum shifted his feet and looked even more uncomfortable. "Can't do much about what's happening, mostly. Valid reasons, most of them have. Can't violate direct orders," he said with a sudden glance at Tam. "Besides, I don't really know that's what's happening."

Tam considered: Was Blum being overly sensitive about the situation, or was there something more specific that he was hinting around?

"If you find out anything, let me know," he ordered. "We can't let that sort of thing happen. Next thing you know, some pervert will take advantage if we let it continue."

"Still have to follow direct orders," Blum repeated with emphasis as he turned away. "I've got to send them where somebody needs them." He turned his head and looked directly at Tam, as if hoping to convey some hidden message through the crevices of his lined face.

"Just let me know if you find out anything more certain," Tam repeated and wondered why Blum didn't just come out and say whatever he thought. Why bother him with idle rumors and suppositions? He had more serious things to worry about. He had no time to play guessing games.

There was no more said about the matter the rest of the tour. It was not like Blum to be so circumspect, so guarded, Tam reflected afterwards. Well, there was another damn puzzle. Maybe Larisha had been right, maybe he wasn't having enough contact with the crew.

Later, in the quiet of his room, Tam thought about what the Master had implied about the crew getting too friendly with the mongrels. First thing you knew, they'd be making friends of them and ruining them as tools. Well, he'd been against bringing the mongrels along to begin with, and now the very problem he'd foreseen was popping up.

FIVE

"I want you to make sure the mongrels understand their place," he told Jas the next day. "I want you to enforce discipline at every opportunity. We need to put a stop to this — this *fraternization* before it becomes a serious problem that I will have to address!"

"I've seen no indication of a breach of discipline," the vet replied cautiously. "I have all of the Folk reporting back to the dormitory at the end of their shifts. I've checked with Master Blum, and he informs me that every one of them reports to their assigned work places as instructed. Nor," he continued with embarrassment obvious in his voice, "have I heard of any crew wanting to take them to their quarters, if that is what you are worried about."

Tam was shocked to hear the vet voice the very thing that he feared the most. The idea of one of the crew stooping to roll about with one of the mongrels, to sully the pure blood of Man, was more than he could bear.

"Lord, I hope not!" he spat out. "I fail to see how any self-respecting Man would choose to . . ."

Jas grinned at Tam's obvious distress, but quickly wiped the smile from his face when the Hadir glanced his way. To cover his gaffe, he said, "You'd be surprised at the way I've seen a few people look at them. Sometimes it's hard for someone working beside them to remember that the Folk aren't Men or Halfings and start treating them as equals. Crew needs to remember that the Folk have feelings, just like the rest of us. It's really sad; the Folk are the ones who always get hurt when crew makes a mistake." The passion in the Man's voice was unmistakable.

"You sound just like the Palm," Tam sneered. "Another bleeding heart. Listen, I don't give a damn about how your stupid mongrels feel. It's crew discipline that I worry about. Maybe I should speak to Dalgrun. Perhaps she can give our crew members the right kind of guidance at worship.

Maybe she can pass the word for people to keep their humanity in mind when they're around the mongrels. Yes, I'll ask Dalgrun to remind everyone of the meaning of racial purity during the next worship service."

"Personally, Hadir Polat, I think your concerns are over nothing," Jas said. "I spend enough time in the dormitory to know the Folk pretty well. If anyone would understand what was going on, it would be me.

"It's true that the mongrels love being worked, and probably some of them even have grown attached to crew members. But that's normal — happens all the time back home, and nothing comes of it. I think your concerns are groundless, Hadir Polat. There is no strong evidence of any untoward relationships forming between the crew and their Folk, and much less any fraternization."

Tam hesitated and wondered how much credence he could put in the vet's words. He already had doubts about the Man and his relationships with his charges.

"Maybe you are right and I am letting rumors and innuendo influence me. But, just the same, keep your ears and eyes open. I want you to put a stop to anything like this at the first sign of trouble. Report directly to me about it when you do!"

As Jas pulled his forelock and departed, Tam wondered if he could trust the veterinarian's judgement. The Man hadn't shown much sign of intelligence so far. For one thing, it was clear that he was too emotionally involved with the mongrels to be objective. That was probably because he spent more time in the dormitories than among the Halfings. A person could easily get a biased view if he did too much of that. Jas probably believed everything his mongrels told him. It was a dangerous situation for someone in his profession.

Hmmm, I'll definitely have a word with Dalgrun about stressing proper behavior. Always best to be safe in these matters. The crew would listen to her, and, if he did find some evidence that one of the Halfings had fraternized with a mongrel, he'd make a bloody-by-damned example of them. A harsh punishment might be just the thing to take everyone's mind off of his decisions and focus them on their real task.

Gull Tamat notified him that the examination of Thetti was proceeding normally. The exploration crews were probing the atmosphere to determine the mix of gasses and availability of resources. That information was necessary before the ship could determine what they needed to process whatever they recovered from the vast planet's depths.

"There's a high degree of warm particulate matter in the upper levels of the clouds," Gull reported. "I would speculate that there's considerable volcanic activity further down. We're trying to identify the main sources now, mostly by looking for heat signatures."

"Anything useful?" Tam asked.

"We already know that we can produce some good quality plastics. Lots of methane and water for building blocks. We'll have to break down the latter for oxygen and hydrogen. There's darn little of that free in that atmosphere, even at the top layer, because there's so little radiation at this distance from the primary."

"When can we start sending scoops down to begin mining operations?" Tam fired back. "I want to start replenishing our resources as soon as possible."

"I've already passed my findings along to the scoop pilots," Gull Tamat assured him. "We've identified two reasonably clear layers that hold the greatest promise and minimize the danger from the heavier dust layers."

Tam raised an eyebrow. "Why do you think there is danger that high? I can't see how a little air-borne dust could affect the scoops."

Gull Tamat coughed. "We are having some more problems with the instruments," he said apologetically. "For some reason, they keep telling us that there are some rather large fragments within the cloud formations."

"Large fragments? Particles, pebbles, stones, boulders, or what? I thought the scoops were hardened against most of the grit they'd encounter."

"These particular fragments aren't grit," Gull said with another apologetic cough. "They're more like, ahem, mountains."

"Mountains?" Tam repeated.

Gull nodded. "Yes. These things look to be about ten times the size of one of our scoops."

Tam felt a chill wash over him. "Perhaps they're merely fragments of that moon that disappeared," he suggested.

"Even so, fragments of this size should have been too heavy to float in Thetti's upper atmosphere," Gull said, "and would have fallen to the surface months ago, in any case. Nor would they move contrariwise to the prevailing winds," he continued. "That is why I suspect that we have a problem with the analysis equipment. These putative fragments might simply be another manifestation of the same problem as that phantom satellite."

"Send someone down to take a look," Tam ordered. "I want to know what the hell is going on in this system. I want some answers that make sense."

"But I want to make certain that the instruments . . ." Gull began.

"Damn your instruments! Get a pilot on a scoop and send him down in the atmosphere to see if those damned 'glitches' of yours are real or not!"

As soon as Gull Tamat left Tam sat back and chewed on his thumb. God on Heaven, he thought, what have we uncovered?

Since their first hesitant conversation, Win and Amber had become more than just friends. Every moment they could share, they spent talking about their lives; happenings on the ship; rumors they'd heard; and, in general, each other, their feelings, and their dreams.

But the opportunities to be together were few, what

with the working schedules each had to meet, and often either Gold or Rex were present in the room, affording little opportunity for intimacy. Whenever their schedules made it impossible to be alone the two of them sat in the dining area and talked the time away, robbing their much needed sleep for the pleasure, the sheer joy of being with each other a few moments more.

The services that Rex conducted in the weeks between the Palm's scheduled ceremonies were another opportunity for them to be together. Win always sat beside her on the hard floor as Rex went through the litany. He responded at the appropriate places, followed the rituals, and listened with half an ear to the words of comfort and praise to the demi-gods they served. But it was Amber who was the focus of his mind, the single thing that drew him.

It was a blissful time. Win could hardly wait to return to the dormitory each evening, hoping scheduling had once again permitted Amber and him to have time together.

But it was Gold sitting on his bunk when Win returned from work. She was carefully knitting something that was either a scarf — an item much in demand within the still cool ship — or something else entirely. She put the needles aside as he entered and folded her hands in her lap.

"What is it?" Win asked, suddenly fearful. Had something had happened to Amber? The expression on Gold's face told him that whatever she had to say was not going to be pleasant.

"Sit here," she said and patted the spot beside her. "I've been meaning to talk to you for several weeks. It's about this relationship between you and Amber."

"Is she all right?" Win blurted out, hoping that his fears were baseless. Had something happened to her? "What . . . ?"

"Oh, dear me," Gold said and patted Win on the shoulder. "No, nothing has happened to Amber. At least, not yet. And certainly not at all if you two change your ways."

Win was confused. What was so wrong with them being

friends. What concern was it of Gold, or anyone else for that matter?

"What do you mean?" he asked. "We've done nothing wrong."

The older woman clucked her tongue. "That's not what I'm seeing. Others have noticed as well and started to talk. It's only a matter of time before Jas or the boss finds out that there's a budding romance between you two. If that happens, we'll all suffer."

"What have the Men to do with anything Amber and I do? We're just Folk. What we do on our free time is our own business!"

"Amber is reserve," Gold said sadly. "She is part of the breeding stock the Men brought along. I suspect that each of her matings have already been planned." She paused and looked sympathetically at Win. She placed one hand on his shoulder and shook her head sadly. "Her future mate is someone else in reserve, not you. After all, that's what she's for."

Win choked. "No, that can't be. They wouldn't have put her here if that were true." He waved his arm to encompass their small room. "She's was de-iced because she's a nurse," he protested desperately, reaching for an excuse, something to prove that what Gold had said wasn't true — couldn't be true! "Amber was de-iced to care for those who are either sick or injured."

Gold squeezed his arm again. "She is a nurse, but think about it, Win. What better training for a mother-to-be than nursing? No, I assure you; the only reason Amber is temporarily staying with us is because there were no other bunks available. As soon as the breeding dormitories are ready for occupancy, she'll be moved over."

"No," Win said, springing to his feet and turning on her, wrenching his arm from her grip. "You must be mistaken! What you say can't be true. Nobody can take Amber away from me. Nobody!" The last was a shout that brought some others racing into the room. Two burly Folk, older and more heavily muscled than Win, moved to grab him.

"No problem," Gold told them. She spun Win about to face her so that the others could not see his tear-stained face, the look of utter despair that etched his features. Almost, the crushed soul of the young Folk showed in his eyes. "Win just had some bad news," she told them. "Go on back to your rooms. I can handle this by myself."

She turned back to him. "Lie down for a while," she suggested with a kindly voice after the others had left. "You need to think about what I said for a while. You are a good boy. I'd hate to see you get into trouble."

"But . . ." Win started, but Gold put her fingers over his lips.

"Rest and think. I will take care of things. You just think about your proper place, and Amber's. You wouldn't want to cause any trouble, would you?"

Win started and sat up on the bed. Someone, something had brushed his cheek and awakened him. He blinked and looked around in the dim light of the room. In the background, he could hear Rex snoring softly.

Amber sat on the edge of his bunk, her hands on her knees. "Did I wake you?" she whispered quietly. "I didn't mean to. I just wanted to be close to you for a little while longer before I leave. Gold wants me to move in with some other people."

Win reached out and took her hand in his. "You don't have to leave. I need you here, with me."

Amber took the proffered hand and clasped it in her own. "I know, and I need you, my love. But after Gold explained things to me, I understood what might happen to you if we . . . kept on. Oh Win, I thought that reserve was what I wanted when I left Heaven, but after meeting you it all changed. I want to be yours."

With those words, she threw herself into his arms. Win held her tight as she cried, her sobs muffled by the thick covers. Tears rolled down his face and dampened her hair. He brushed the moisture away with one hand, feeling the silky smoothness of her blonde hair beneath his fingers and the curve of her skull beneath. The thought that someone else, someone neither of them had ever met, would some day hold her close and do the same was a burning, aching agony in his breast.

Finally her sobbing stopped and she withdrew from his arms. "I will never stop loving you," she said. "Never!"

And then she was gone.

The next few weeks were misery for Win. He could scarcely find a moment when he did not think of Amber. Each such thought was an stabbing, agonizing torment. He tried not to recall the way she looked, tried not to think of the warmth of her kisses, tried not to think of her body against his own, but it was impossible. There were too many reminders of the times they had spent together. He could not look at her bunk without remembering the hours they had spent lying together, talking of home and the future they expected to share on Meridian. He could not eat without remembering the meals they'd shared, the precious moments alone among the dining crowd.

Fren noted his changed behavior immediately. "Raggi Larisha being mean to you?" he'd asked one morning as he checked in.

"No," Win replied. "This is something personal."

"Won't have crew mistreating my charges," Fren continued as if he hadn't heard. "I want you to tell me if she does anything out of line. You hear me?"

"Yes, boss," Win replied. "But that isn't it. Bul Larisha treats me fine; very well, in fact. I enjoy working for her." He tried to smile to show that he really meant what he said, and realized, as he did so, that he did indeed like working for the Raggi. She always gave him interesting assignments, listened to his suggestions, and seemed to go out of her way to teach him something new. "I like her."

Boss Fren frowned. "Don't get too attached, now. Pay attention to your work and leave it at that. Make sure you don't overstep your place, you hear? Men and Folk shouldn't get too friendly. You've heard the Palm's cautions in services, haven't you?"

Win nodded. "Yes, boss, I understand."

Amber was waiting in the greenhouse elevator when he entered at the end of the workday. Her hand was holding the door open. "I saw you coming," she said with a smirk she let the doors slide shut and seal the two of them inside. The car started the slow trip to the dormitories on the outer ring.

Win didn't hesitate. He stepped forward and embraced Amber, pulling her body close to his. In a second, his lips found hers; and then he felt her tongue on his, her lips pressing against his own, their warm breath combining, intermingling as they tried to meld into a single entity.

"Oh God, I miss you," she said when their lips parted for a moment. "I forgot how wonderful you taste."

Win grunted and pressed his lips to hers once more. There were only a few minutes before the door would open, only a few precious moments into which they had to pour weeks of sorrow and longing. Only a few scant instants until they started the agony of separation all over again.

The chime sounded and Amber moved to the other side of the car. She wiped her mouth and grinned at him. "I love you," she whispered before the door opened.

Win had no chance to reply as other passengers pushed into the car and Amber departed. The ride to the dormitories seemed to take forever, but all the while he savored the lingering feeling of holding her close, feeling her lips on his once again.

He wondered when they could do it again.

Their meetings after that were few and furtive. One time

out of three they would have the elevator to themselves. Twice they saw each other in the dining area and lingered at their serving table, acting as if they were just good friends chatting amiably over a meal. This was far less than satisfactory as far as he was concerned. To be so near to her and not be able to touch, to embrace, was difficult. Still, it was better than the alternative.

"I've met some of the reserve," she told him one evening. "They seem very nice."

Win grunted. "Yeah, they would," he said grudgingly.

"Really, they're very nice. I talked to them for quite a while. They tell me that I come from good stock, highly intelligent and beautiful."

Win felt a pang of jealousy. "You are," he said with a forced smile. "Very beautiful."

Amber blushed, her cheeks burning bright red against her pale skin. "Am not. My nose is too long and my mouth is too wide. Besides, I have all of this colorless hair. I wish it was darker."

"So you could look like a Man?" Gold said as she plopped down beside them. "People would get very upset if they heard you say that. Trying to pass for a true Man is punishable by death. You don't see any of the Halfings doing that, do you?"

"Halfings?" Win asked, curious at the term. "I thought all of the crew were Men."

Gold laughed at his question. "Dear me, no. Oh Win, you are so innocent. Listen; the crew is made up of two types of people — Men and Halfings."

"Like Bul Larisha," Win said. "She's a Raggi."

"No, Larisha is *the* Raggi. She's one of the Men herself, even though she leads everyone in the Halfings."

"I am confused," Win admitted.

"And me, too," Amber added. "How can there be two kinds of humans?"

Gold considered. "Didn't they teach you children anything? No, I guess both of you were special cases, raised exclusively for this mission of ours. Well," she went on, "let me see if I can keep this straight. The Men are the true humans. They're the ones with the straight black hair and brown eyes."

"Fren has brown eyes," Win said.

"Fren's a Halfing. You can tell by that little lock of hair he wears at the back."

"But if he has to do that, then what is the difference?" Win prodded. "I can see the differences between us mongrels and the others; our hair colors are all shades and types, our eyes are every color you can imagine, and we're all different sizes. All of the others look the same, more or less."

"True, but the real differences aren't something you can see," Gold went on. "Long ago the Men had a visit from God. I don't know which planet it happened on, or exactly when — ten, twenty centuries back, I've heard. Anyhow, God touched the Men and declared them to be the inheritors of the universe. They were his children, the ones who would perfect his image, the ones from whose line the Emerging God would arise.

"Since then the Men have been trying to achieve their ultimate form, trying to perfect their stock and evolve. They desperately want to be worthy of the God who lies ahead of them, somewhere in their future."

Win thought about what she had said. "But why are there any Halfings?"

"A good question," Gold replied. "The Halfings are those whose genetic makeup failed to meet the exacting criteria that God set forth. They are considered less than human, even though they may appear to be the same. The preservation of the purity of God's bloodline is why Halfings wear the lock, and why we mongrels must never cross the line. We are the genetic backwater that the true humans are trying to breed away from. If we weren't needed to labor for them, we would not exist."

"But why bring us along, if we are so unworthy?" Amber asked.

Gold frowned to indicate what she thought of that question. "Someone has to do the work in the fields and factories. I can't imagine a Man doing such manual labor, could you?" The way she said it was less a question than a bitter observation.

"So you think I shouldn't want to be as beautiful as the crew," Amber said, bringing the conversation full circle. "I guess I'll never look like them. I'm not anything special."

Gold said between her teeth, as if biting the words off of something too tough to chew. "Oh, you are very special, my dear. Why, you are probably the best girl on the ship. All of us are going to be very proud of your children some day."

With those words, Win fell into a black pit of despair. For a while, he had managed to suppress the reason for Amber's separation, the reason for her presence on this ship. For a while, he had imagined that their separation was a temporary situation, one that eventually would end and bring them together again. But Gold's words burst the brief bubble of happiness that had surrounded him for the past hour. He could tell from the expression on Amber's face that she felt the same. The rest of their meal was eaten in silence.

It was the end of the shift, nearly the start of the night cycle. Win made certain that all of the automatics were functioning correctly, that the feed containers were filled with nutrient solution, and that the drains in the troughs were clear so that the excess water and nutrients could run back into the recycling vats instead of overflowing into the aisles. Only after he secured the greenhouse did he turn to leave.

Amber was waiting at the entrance to the elevator. "I wanted to see these wonderful plants you keep talking about," she said with a smile.

Win quickly looked around to see if anyone had observed Amber's arrival. The passageway was empty for a change. All of the humans, Halfings, and Folk had left for the evening. Quickly he pulled her out of sight, just in case someone remained.

"What are you doing here?" he demanded even as he pulled her close and smothered her face with kisses.

"I had to see you again," Amber replied breathlessly. "I wanted to see what you've created. Come on, show me what you've done." She she stepped forward and gazed around. "Oh, this is so beautiful. I had no idea there was so many plants. It's a jungle in here." She squealed in delight. "This looks just like home!"

"Not so much as it will be when we get finished," Win said proudly. "We have most of the root stock in place and several varieties of fruit trees. Over here are the vegetable bins — we'll have a fresh crop coming out every six weeks from now on." He raced down another aisle, pulling her along. "Come here, see what Larisha had us put in a few weeks ago. You'll love this!"

Amber followed him down the narrow passage between the towering masses of vines and tree limbs that stretched toward the lighted panels overhead. They were dimming into the night cycle. Finally, they turned a corner.

Amber stopped and looked upward in amazement. "It . . . it's beautiful," she exclaimed breathlessly. Before her was a small terraced garden with a small bench that was surrounded on three sides by vegetation. The bench faced the end of the blind alley. To anyone sitting there, no other part of the greenhouse could be seen.

On each of the enclosed garden's terraces grew a profusion of flowering plants of every shade and hue. To Amber's immediate right was a swath of huge, bell-shaped violets, their soft, velvety, purple petals in stark contrast to the stiff orange stamens. Above these were erect, flaring trumpets of yellow, striped with gold, on deep green stems. The flourish of trumpets were bracketed by cascades of multicolored blossoms so tightly wound on their stiff stems that they seemed to be solid columns of color.

As Amber's gaze roamed the terraces she realized that

the seeming confusion of flowers was quite deliberate, an orderly design that had been set up to please the eye.

"Step over here." Win indicated a place near the small bench. As Amber moved to where, he pointed he told her, "Take a deep breath."

Puzzled as to what he wanted, Amber inhaled. She let the delicious scent of the flowers fill her nose, surround her with the aroma of Heaven, of home. The heavy perfume of the assembled blossoms wafted to the bench by a slight downdraft across the face of the terraces. "Oh, it smells so wonderful!" she said.

"And so do you," Win said and drew her close.

She came easily into his arms, fitting her body to his as if they were a perfectly matched set. They embraced for a long while, allowing the scent of the flowers to mingle with their own as they tried to remove the memories of their long separation.

Later, Win found a tarpaulin for them to lie upon as the lights above them dimmed deeper into the night cycle and dropped a blanket of darkness onto them.

SIX

Larisha was feeling very restless. It wasn't enough that Tam had this preoccupation with that damned anomaly, but now he was sending scoops to pursue new phantoms that the ghost in Gull's machines had produced. Where would it all end?

Dalgrun seemed to think that Tam's preoccupation was nothing much to worry about, at least not for the moment. Until the scoops came back empty, they had to believe what Gull's probes told them, she'd said.

On the matter of the optional mission plan, Tam was, Dalgrun had keenly observed, well within his authority to establish a spatial habitat prior to exploring Meridian if he deemed it necessary. That much had been set out in the mission protocols.

Legally, only if he diverted the ship from the ultimate goal of preparing the system for the settlers could she, as Palm of the Hand, using all of her moral authority, usurp him and appoint another as their leader.

Patience and legalities weren't good enough for Larisha, however. Dalgrun didn't know Tam the way she did. After all, living through four years of hell with his compulsive planning of every damn detail told her that he left nothing to chance. That relationship had given her a unique perspective on him that others, no matter what their training and insights, could never match.

She knew with absolute certainty that Tam was hiding something behind that facade of excuses about prudence and caution, regardless of what he had supposedly shared with her. She didn't for one moment believe that this preoccupation that something was amiss with Thetti was merely of passing interest to him. From the look in Tam's eyes when he spoke of it, she knew that it was the main reason for this foolish wait around the gas giant. Something had seriously derailed his otherwise good judgement. Either that, or this was another of his intolerable, complex, long-range plans being put into action.

But what could he be planning? That was the question. What was it about Thetti that had Tam so focused that he would risk his position as Hadir? What could motivate someone as cautious as Tam to act so, so . . . unlike himself?

Then there was Win. The boy was a wonder with her plants. He seemed to have a natural bent in working with the stock she had brought from Heaven, adjusting their delicate stems with those long-fingered hands of his. What, she mused, would it be like to have those fingers caressing her body? She recalled the strength of his arms from that day he had caught her. She could remember how the hard muscles of his body had felt as she pressed against him.

Larisha jerked with surprise. What could she be thinking about? The boy was Folk, Folk! God, how could she even consider having that boy touch her, let alone . . . .

Well, best to leave that train of thought alone, she concluded, rubbing her hands with disgust, as if to cleanse them of her impure, unholy thoughts. She must really be tired if adolescent fantasies were creeping into her otherwise mature thought processes. What could she have been thinking of?

Still, Win was a handsome boy, like some of the purebreds they'd raised back on her estate. Perhaps that was where these indecent stirring had come from, simply nostalgia playing on her emotions.

The thought of home reminded her of the bower she'd had Win construct, the one that Tam had threatened to sully with his presence. She'd copied it from the one she had in her garden down to the detail of the tiny bench she used to sit upon. The original bower was where she and Tam had first made love. Momentarily, she wondered if she had unconsciously built it to remind Tam of what they'd had, or was it what it seemed, a copy of a setting she'd loved?

She shook her head to clear it. One could go crazy if one started to analyze every little thing one did. Who knew what motivations sparked anything, and who cared in the end? The bower was beautiful, and nearing its peak, with the orchids on the lower tier almost ready to bloom.

Larisha decided to visit the greenhouse to see what the bower looked like at night. She'd often sat in the one at home to think things out when she was troubled. Perhaps it would ease her mind, settle this vague uneasiness that she felt, if she sat there surrounded by reminders of happier, more innocent times. Yes, and maybe she'd be lucky enough to be there when the orchids bloomed and released their nocturnal perfume.

The dim greenhouse light turned the plants into dark masses of ambiguous forms, lurking towers of dark vegetation, tall skeletons waiting to pounce, and rustling sounds as if wicked creatures were astir. Almost, she could imagine herself in some deep wood, with the unknown just on the other side of that copse, or perhaps a little gully hidden behind that bush. She'd liked exploring the woods as a child, although her parents never let her go there alone. No, there were always a couple of the family's Folk along to insure her safety.

As Larisha walked along the aisles, she was impressed by the organic sounds of the greenhouse. Elsewhere, throughout the ship was the constant bustle of the crew and Folk, the cry of machines, the clamor of transports, the clatter of tools, and the numerous sounds of the construction as the ship prepared to process the riches of Thetti.

Here in her greenhouse refuge, however, there was only the rustle of the leaves, the gurgling of the pumps and circulators, and the steady ticking of the timers as the canisters metered their rations of nutrients into the troughs. It was a pleasant symphony of sibilant noise, just barely above the lower level of hearing.

Wait! What was that noise? Larisha stopped and listened again. For a moment it sounded as if she had heard two people talking; but now, try as she might, she could only hear the sounds of the greenhouse, as familiar as her own voice. She continued walking.

There they were again; she was certain this time! She crept forward, trying to be as quiet as she could. Since the voices sounded as if they were coming from the bower, she moved in that direction, her curiosity growing by the moment at who could be using her most private, most personal place.

Could Tam have followed up on his threat of using her sanctuary to collect his thoughts? It would be very unlike him to do so, but if not him, then who? She continued moving forward as quietly as she could, not wishing to disturb whoever it was — providing that they were doing no harm. After all, she couldn't deny a crew member access to something so lovely, could she?

The two forms on the tarpaulin were obviously making love. Larisha smiled. What a delightful compliment to her creation, that two people should chose to creep up here and use it in this way.

She recalled how she and Tam had once done that, and then the smile faded when she also remembered that he had planned the seduction long ahead of time, even though he had tried to make her believe it was spontaneous.

She'd hated him when she'd learned the truth of his deception. She'd felt used when she'd glanced in his appointment book and saw that "make love to Larisha" was neatly sandwiched between entries for dinner and a meeting with Doctor Chen. True to his plan he'd had her right on schedule, not missing a minute.

But she did not draw back from the view of the couple. Who they could be? Was this some illicit liaison or merely a couple who wanted a brief moment of romance in the otherwise stark and utilitarian ship? If only one of them would move their head into the light a little more she could . . .

The sudden appearance of the female's head was a shock. Larisha felt disbelief as Amber's blond hair was illuminated by the shaft of light. My God, thought Larisha, someone is having sex with a Folk! She felt her gorge rising. How a Man or a Halfing could even think of doing such a thing was beyond the pale. She rushed forward, now anxious to discover who this pervert might be.

"Larisha?" Win exclaimed, rising naked out of the darkness as the wraith descended upon them. In one awkward movement, he gathered his clothing and sputtered; "I didn't know . . ." he began.

"How could you!" Larisha screamed, shocked beyond her wildest imaginings. "After all that I've done for you, this is how you repay me? Get out! Get out, both of you! Get away from my flowers! Get out of my garden! Go! Go! Go!"

She beat on Win's shoulders and head with her fists, striking repeated blows, driving him before her, driving him out of her life. He was just like Tam, just like every Man she had ever loved, damn it! It was just like them to take your heart and break it. How could she have ever trusted this, this, *mongrel!*

The blond-haired bitch was staring at her in open-mouthed wonder as she hurled invective upon the fumbling, stumbling Win. "How could you do this to him?" Larisha screamed at her. "How could you!" She reached out, her fingers like the claws of some avenging angel, seeking to grab handfuls of that filthy, pale blond mane.

Amber sprinted away before Larisha could reach her and, when Larisha turned, she found that Win had escaped as well.

Good riddance to trash, she thought. That would teach her to try to treat the damned Folk fairly. Tam had been right; the mongrels were just tools, just implements to be used. It was a mistake to think of them otherwise.

A pink blossom brushed the back of her hand. Larisha

looked at it. She recalled when she and Win had set that particular plant in place and how she had described its ancestry to him. It was cloned from a cutting of the one in the original bower.

She plucked the blossom, lifted it to her nose, and smelled it, the heavy fragrance reminding her again of home and loves lost. She pulled another blossom free, and then one more, and another.

Suddenly all of the anger and torment spilled out. She grasped the plant's stem and pulled it free, its roots dribbling soil and dampness onto the tarpaulin where Win had been making love to another . . . another mongrel! She grabbed a second plant, pulled it loose and tossed it beside the first.

Then she flew into motion, ripping, pulling, throwing, tearing, shredding everything in the bower, working her way up the terraces until the tarpaulin was covered with a carpet of vegetation and the air heavy with the perfume of crushed leaves and blossoms.

"This will make a nice place to put the compost heap," she said when she was finished and her anger had played itself out. She climbed back down from the destroyed terraces and then, calmly, turned her back on the residue of her anger and kicked the bench over, shattering its fragile boards.

The next morning sanity returned. She never should have allowed her emotions to overcome her. It was quite uncharacteristic and unbecoming for a Man, especially one with her rank and position, to lose control to such an extent, even under that justifiably severe provocation.

Try as she might, there was no memory of why the sight of those two Folk having sex was so disturbing. Most likely, she believed, was her liking for Win. The boy was so young, so innocent and intelligent, that to do something like this would be unlike him, especially when he knew the value she'd placed on that bower.

More likely the little blond vixen had seduced him with her wiles. She'd heard that the reserve were deliberately oversexed, the better to produce additional quality Folk. That being so, the vixen probably took advantage of Win in a weak moment, wiggling her skinny body before the boy, teasing him to the point that his animal nature overcame good judgement. Yes, that must be what had happened, she concluded.

In that case, it was lucky that she had come along when she did, else some other crew member might have discovered them and gotten both into trouble.

Larisha started. When had she decided to protect Win? Somehow, at some time during the restless night, her unconscious must have determined Win's innocence long before her rational mind came to the same conclusion. Yes, she would have to find some way to prevent Win from getting into trouble, and that meant keeping that vixen away from him. But how?

She recalled that Jas kept a close eye on his charges, making sure that the ordinary Folk stayed away from the reserve stock. Perhaps a word or two would keep that blond bitch in her place, somewhere that she would have no opportunity to further tempt Win.

Yes, that would be just the solution. Of course, she would have to keep a close eye on Win herself. There would have to be a task that would keep him close to her.

Putting down the mongrel Chat had been a tough decision for Tam, but given the situation, it was necessary. Jas had pleaded for mercy for his charge, Master Blum had recommended simple, direct punishment — a good whipping — while Larisha had said that Tam should do nothing. She placed most of the blame for the incident on the Halfing supervisor. He should never have let things get so out of hand.

It was bad enough finding that the mongrel was out of the dormitory without supervision, but to find it rooting through one of the crew's quarters was intolerable. They'd found a set of codes for the scoops and a copy of the Book of Revelation in the mongrel's pockets. The Book!

Possession of the Book by a Folk was enough to merit death: No mongrel had the right to read the words of God for themselves. That was why Dalgrun held services for them; to explain God's plan in a way their simple minds could grasp. Who knew how, left to their own devices, they would misinterpret the words of the Book?

The codes were a more serious matter. With them, the mongrel could have easily stolen one of the scoops, although for what purpose Tam couldn't grasp. Stealing a scoop and escaping couldn't have been its plan; there was simply no place the scoop could have gone. Meridian, the only planet that could marginally support life, was so far away from the ship's present location that the scoop would run out of air months before it approached the planet.

Even if the mongrel somehow managed to overcome that little problem, the scoop couldn't possibly have landed. A scoop was only minimally aerodynamic. They'd been designed to fly in the thick atmospheres of gas giants, not the weak atmosphere of an Earth-like planet such as Meridian.

If the scoop had attempted to enter Meridian's atmosphere and land, the delta vee would be so high that the scoop would have burned up or, failing that incendiary end, smashed on the surface.

Why had the mongrel stolen the codes? It was a mystery nearly as puzzling as the missing moon.

Tam ordered the mongrel to be put down where the rest of the Folk would see. He wanted to illustrate what happened when one of them stepped out of line. It was a good object lesson for the rest of the crew as well.

In private, away from the Folk, Tam had the supervisor whipped so hard that the blood flowed from her back. That little exhibit of his authority had probably given the crew something to talk about. Perhaps, he hoped, it would also stop the endless second-guessing about his actions.

He made certain that Dalgrun made a point of the Hadir's rightful anger at this serious breach of the social fabric. He made certain that she told them that he, the Hadir Tam Polat, had the backing of the Hand and God in this matter.

Win found that the services were to be held that night instead of on ten-day eve, the usual time. The Folk waited until Jas left for his evening's visit with his friends before they convened.

"We are here to pray for Chat's soul," Rex intoned over the sobbing of Chat's mate and several of Chat's close friends. Win himself felt like crying before the service was over. He had been horrified when the Master had put the garotte around Chat's throat and tightened it. Win had nearly thrown up when Chat's face turned red, then purple with congealed blood. His eyes looked like they were going to pop out of his head from the pressure. Win had actually felt relief when Chat had slumped to the deck. He was glad when, after almost five minutes he had died and ended his suffering. Now Win felt remorse over having such selfish feelings. He felt shamed.

After the service a few of the others gathered around him. "A terrible thing, this death," one of them said.

"Taking a life as if it were nothing," another said quietly.

"That's what you get when you let one of them get friendly with you," the first one spat.

"Damn shame, Chat was a fine worker."

"One of the best."

Over in one corner, Win noticed a group that was discussing something that must have been very serious. A couple of them were talking and making angry gestures to punctuate whatever they were saying. He had to pass by them on his way back to his cabin and couldn't help overhearing a few words.

". . . own stupid fault for getting caught. Should have had

someone else . . ." The speaker stopped when he noticed Win's presence. The group was silent until Win was out of earshot. He glanced back from the doorway and saw that they had resumed their discussion now that he couldn't overhear.

How could someone say that it was Chat's fault for what happened? Had they no sensitivity to the pain his death had caused? Had they no sympathy for the Worker's friends and family? He was amazed that someone could be so insensitive.

SEVEN

Tam was disappointed that none of the scoops they'd sent into the clouds had sighted one of Gull's floating mountains. The pilots complained of limited visibility, of their radars becoming confused by the floating dust, and of having to fight the fierce crosswinds. All these, Tam suspected, were excuses for their inability to bring him confirmation of these objects.

Gull's team suggested once again that a better reason was that these objects were no more than some error in the ship's instruments. "Perhaps they were right," he'd explained to Tam. "Certainly the lack of evidence seems to point in that direction."

So lacking any reason not to do otherwise, Tam had given the order to commence mining operations. Immediately the ship began sending scoops on a regular sweeping pattern that would maximize the amount of material they collected while minimizing the expenditure of fuel and time.

This use of the scoops was routine, a method that had been perfected over the ten centuries since Heaven had been settled. The scoops regularly returned to the ship, relieved themselves of their loads, and once more descended into the howling maelstrom in the upper atmosphere of Thetti. It was routine. There were no surprises as, around the clock, the line of scoops dipped into the atmosphere and returned.

Nor were there any further revelations regarding the missing satellite. Despite everything Gull Tamat could dream up to test the premise that there had not been a satellite in orbit about Thetti, he could discover nothing more than was already known. Their astronomical instrumentation was in order, the images were unequivocal, the moon had been there, where now there was nothing.

No, not simply nothing — there was not even the absence of something. The volume near the orbit where the moon had been sighted was as undifferentiated in every respect from the space about it. Neither had the other satellites perturbed as a result of the missing moon. This latter fact was even more puzzling than if the moon had actually been lost.

Meanwhile, the early samples from Thetti's atmosphere indicated that they would be able to refine sufficient amounts of carbon, hydrogen, and nitrogen to produce the high-density plastics they needed. There were also sufficient materials they could use to build the polymers for the skin of the habitat. The first scoops had already brought up enough material to begin construction.

The plan was to construct a huge plastic sphere, tight enough to hold a decent atmosphere, and then use its skin as the matrix for constructing the habitat. By the time the sphere was filled out, the manufacturing sections would have turned out kilometers of structural members needed to reënforce the sphere's skin. Construction would be difficult and dangerous work, maneuvering so much building material in orbit, but the crew had been well trained back at Heaven. There should be no unforeseen problems.

Once the internal structure of the habitat was in place, the ship would recover rocky material from one of the smaller moons. By smelting and then foaming the rocky materials, they would produce slabs of rock-crete that would be used to make the habitat's internal structure. The inevitable metallic byproducts of the smelting operation would be used to forge the habitat's heavy machinery, engines, and hatches.

Construction of the habitat would take considerable time, Tam reminded himself. Even if the scoops came back with the purest of elements, even if the manufacturing and smelting operations proceeded without problems, and even if the crew and Folk were able to maintain a frenetic building schedule, it would still take a year or more to bring the habitat to the point where it would be self-sufficient.

That gave him a year in which Gull could discover the truth behind that damned crystalline object he'd encountered. Certainly within a year the science team ought to be able to discover something.

Despite the delay in reaching Meridian, the habitat was the prudent option to select, he rationalized. Just the same, he would keep everyone on an accelerated schedule. Perhaps by doing that he could get the habitat liveable earlier, which would give them a refuge in case anything happened to the ship.

And that definitely was prudent!

He told Blum to put all the people he could on the habitat construction. "Put everyone you can spare and the best mongrels on the job," he'd said. "I want that hab finished as quickly as possible."

"I'll use the best Folk I got available," Blum muttered in response to the order. "Not the best there are."

Tam had heard the same complaint several times before. Something had been eating at Blum for weeks now. Was he dissatisfied with his rôle as Master, or was there some deeper problem, something personal, affecting him? Perhaps he was still smarting from Tam's decision to put that mongrel down instead of giving it a good whipping, as if he had felt the Man to be responsible?

"I thought all of your mongrels were operational," he replied. By God, if the veterinarian had been misleading Larisha and him, despite his direct orders to report everything, he'd have the Halfing pushed out the airlock. "Well," Tam demanded, "can you or can't you get all of the hands you'll need?"

Blum nodded, but reluctantly. "More than enough, Hadir Polat. The problem is not numbers, it's the way the Folk are being used. Isn't right that we should waste utility Folk doing God-knows-what. Isn't right that they should be so close to people."

"Have you been having trouble with discipline again?" Tam demanded. "I thought putting that one down would be a lesson to everyone. Maybe I should have done a few more, just for show — maybe we'd have fewer potential problems."

Blum frowned and examined the access panel on the nearest hatch as if he had never seen one before. "Problem wasn't the worker, Hadir Polat. Problem was the way the Man treated it, letting it in quarters and all. Killing Folk won't put a stop to it, not by any means. Crew follows examples, you know."

One name leaped immediately to Tam's mind — Jas Bulgat! Damn the Man; he was right to worry that the veterinarian spent too much time in the dormitory. He'd suspected that the Man was getting too damn familiar with his charges. Sure, it was evident in the way he'd tearfully pleaded for mercy when they'd been forced to put the thieving mongrel down. He must be the one that Master Blum was hinting about.

Now that he thought about it, it was logical that the veterinarian would be the only one who could be making pets of the mongrels. "Who?" he asked, seeking confirmation of his suspicions.

Blum looked even more uncomfortable than before, squirming and looking closer at the panel he found so fascinating. He wouldn't look up to meet Tam's direct gaze.

"Not my place to say, Hadir," he said.

Tam slammed his fist against the wall. "Don't be coy with me, Master! I want to know which crew members are giving you problems with the mongrels. By God, I want names!"

"Not having problems with the mongrels," Blum said with obvious hesitation. "Just saying that there might be problems down the line if the crew gets the idea that its all right to be too friendly with Folk." He looked longingly at Tam, eyes begging for the questions to stop.

Tam was getting increasingly frustrated with all this dancing about. "So you have no specifics, no names, no events, nothing to back up your assertions. Is that correct?"

Master Blum mumbled something indistinct.

Tam took Blum's answer and hanging head for agreement, but he didn't believe that for an instant. The Master was protecting someone, someone that he wouldn't, or couldn't criticize. Well, he didn't need to; Blum's interests were close to the veterinarian's, which was probably why the Master wanted to protect him. Yes, indeed, the fingers of Jas's behavior fit neatly into that particular glove.

But instead of saying so outright, Tam said; "If you have nothing specific, then don't bother me. Give me something that I can act upon." He paused and then said confidently; "I think I know who you suspect, even if you won't come right out and say so."

The expression on Blum's face was a study in agony as he struggled with a suitable answer. "Not my place to say," he finally spat out. "Don't question my superiors."

"Nor should you," Tam replied, pleased to have confirmation of his suspicions. So the Man imagined that he was protecting Larisha by not identifying Jas. It was typical of Blum not to cross the lines of command. Most likely the Master had thought the problem was Larisha's to solve instead of the Hadir's.

"Well, I need no further information from you," Tam said with a wave of dismissal. "I can proceed independently from here. Thank you for bringing the matter to my attention."

Blum exited quickly, moving in that unique, graceful, bow-legged gait.

Jas! He was pleased that his initial appraisal of the Man had finally proven correct, despite Larisha's continual support of him. Now he had only to find specific evidence of misbehavior, and he could take care of two problems at once.

There was a possible bright side to this discovery. Perhaps another, harsher application of discipline would finally bring the lower orders into line. And it would humble Larisha and show her the error of treating the mongrels as if they were real people.

Larisha glanced up as Jas approached. The vet looked

apprehensive, as if being called to her cabin was something to be feared. Insofar as she knew he had no reason to be apprehensive, unless he were guilty of something she did not know about.

Perhaps his apprehension surrounded suspicion on his part that she might have discovered some dark secret. Now there was a thought: what could such a secret be? Perhaps there was some aspect of this Halfing that she should learn more about.

Ever since they'd been de-iced there had been friction between the veterinarian and Tam, who obviously could not tolerate Jas. Recently, he had grown even more critical of him. She recalled Tam's complaints about the time Jas spent in the dormitory instead of working with the crew. Could that lack of contact with the Men and the Halfings be the source of Jas's guilt?

On the other hand, perhaps Jas had befriended some of his charges, going beyond the somewhat loose bounds permitted for one of his vocation. Had her precious Jas, this frail Man, become a little too enamored of his Folk? It was not unheard of: Back on the estate, it happened quite frequently, but was usually stopped after a few words of warning.

Of course it was quite easy to form a relationship with some of the Folk. One could easily forget the religious, social, and genetic differences that separated them from Men and Halfings, she mused. She had become very dependent upon her own dear Win. Sometimes she felt as if he were a member of her own household instead of merely another one of Blum's workers. Well, in time she would change that; Win was much too intelligent and creative to waste at some menial task. She could always make a place for those who were useful to her regardless of whether they were Men, Halfings, or even Folk, if it came to that.

But Win's utility wasn't all there was to it. At times she'd think of him simply as another person, another Man. Of course, she'd never admitted that lapse to anyone else, nor did she really believe that he was anything other than Folk for more than an instant. Her morals were too high for that sort of adolescent fantasy.

"You wanted to see me?" Jas said with a catch in his voice. He pulled his forelock and shuffled his feet as he waited for her answer.

Larisha smiled at his obvious discomfort. "Do be seated, Jas." When he perched on the edge of the single chair opposite her she continued. "I was just recalling the early days, when there were only a few of us de-iced in our freezing ship. I recall the excellent work you did with the Folk, de-icing them single-handedly and getting them settled. You practically did the whole thing yourself until Blum was up and about." She paused, "I don't think Hadir Polat ever fully appreciated the valuable services you performed."

Jas looked down at the deck. A flush of embarrassment was visible on the back of his neck. He said nothing in response to her praise.

How charming, Larisha thought. *The poor soul is embarrassed by a little praise! How little appreciation he must get to have that sort of reaction. Well, perhaps I can use that weakness to my advantage as well.*

"I just wanted you to know that I, for one, wanted to thank you for your work then. And now, as well."

"Just doing the work I signed on to do," Jas replied depreciatingly. "Responsibility for the health and welfare of the Folk is on my back. You wouldn't believe the lengths I have to go to insulate my children from the crew."

"Did you say 'children?'" Larisha replied, raising an eyebrow.

Jas coughed. "I used the term to let you know how I feel about them. I've heard you talking to the Hadir about how he should treat them like people instead of just assets to be worked." He looked pleadingly at Larisha, an expression that was so vulnerable and open that it was pathetic. "I figured that you'd understand how I felt."

"Of course I do," she purred at once. "Your 'children' are such wonderful creatures; so loving and helpful. Why, one could almost think of them as real people. Is that what you mean?"

Jas smiled, his face opening in a broad grin. "I knew you'd understand, Raggi Bul. I've seen how decently you've treated Win, pulling him out from under that Fren brute who was working him so hard. I've been meaning to thank you for that for a long time, but never felt it was my place to do so."

"Yes, I found Win to be a real prize, quite a cut above the average Folk," Larisha answered cautiously. *How easily this Man is led,* she thought. *The next move, however, will require some delicacy.* She proceeded cautiously.

"Yes, Win is certainly special. Which is why I continue to let him work with me. Have you seen the wonderful work he's done with the greenhouse project, by the way? My estate gardener couldn't have done more. I just wish . . ." She let her voice trail off, her gaze prompting Jas into a reply.

"I am glad his services have been satisfactory," Jas said, on cue. "Is there something else that I could help you with?"

Larisha hesitated, drawing the moment out for a long while as Jas danced about, shifting his weight from one side to the other. "There is a small favor that you could do for me," she hinted. "It isn't something I'd normally ask, but it would help my work go much more efficiently."

"Whatever you want."

Excellent, she thought. The Man was practically fawning, he was so eager to please. Larisha sighed to indicate how her many responsibilities weighed so heavily on her shoulders.

"As you well know, my duties require me to be available at all times. Sometimes I get called away in the middle of the night to attend to some matter or other. Of late," she continued, "I have been using Win as my assistant, giving him duties beyond those the greenhouse project requires. I've discovered that he has quite a knack with technical matters concerning the ship and schedules. Really, I am quite lost when he is not around."

"I see," Jas said slowly as he struggled to decipher her request. "Are you saying that you want me to change Win's schedule to the evening shift?"

Larisha looked up suddenly. "Oh no! That would not do! I need him during the day shift as well. He is still responsible for supervising the greenhouse Folk, you know."

Jas looked even more confused than before. "Well, what do you want me to do, then?" His face screwed up in thought as he worked his way through the puzzle. Finally a solution must have dawned for he looked up with a surprised expression. "Raggi Bul, are you asking me to, to assign Win to you exclusively?"

Larisha smiled and clapped her hands. "Why, that is an excellent suggestion, Jas. I don't know why that didn't occur to me. Would you do that? I assure you that it would not reflect on either you or Master Blum. After all, I am Raggi." Perhaps she was overstating her case to remind him of her position in the command structure, but it wouldn't hurt either.

Now for the difficult part, the words that were most dangerous to both of them. "Perhaps you could occasionally let Win stay in my quarters instead of the dormitory. I have a small room where he could sleep when he isn't working."

Jas hesitated and shifted nervously. "That might be a problem, Raggi Bul. Folk's not supposed to do that." The veterinarian had clearly become upset by the sudden turn in the conversation. "There's a reason we keep the Folk in the dormitory when they aren't working. Hadir Polat says it's bad for discipline for them to have such freedom." He thought for a moment and then added: "You see, it doesn't keep them socialized properly if we don't keep them separate when they aren't working. They might forget their place."

"Neither of which will happen here," Larisha assured

him. "Win has considerable contact with the other Folk during the day. Why, he supervises a number of them to keep the greenhouse maintained. Besides, I think you can trust me to keep him in line if he forgets his place." She let just the slightest edge of anger appear in her voice. "After all, I have managed far larger groups of Folk than the few we have with us."

"I meant no insult," Jas protested, holding up his hands in supplication. "It's just that letting Win stay with you would set a bad precedent. Lots of the crew want to make friends of the Folk as well."

"Friends!" Larisha spat out, rising to her feet and leaning forward over the desk, her face darkening in anger. "Listen to me, Jas. I do not intend on making this Folk boy a . . . friend! Quite the contrary. There are very practical reasons for my request, as I took pains to point out earlier." She sniffed and sat back down.

Jas practically quivered in his seat. Lord, she could see him shaking from here.

When he did not respond to that outburst, she sighed. The Man was so obtuse, just like Tam in some respects. Were all Men so dense that they did not understand simple conversational gambits?

"It has come to my attention that Win has been bothered by one of the reserve bitches — Amber; I think her name was Amber. I understand that she's been pestering him for some time. To my mind, she presents too much of a distraction for someone as young and innocent as Win. I need my assistant's mind clear and sharp, not mooning on about some bitch who wiggles her behind at him at every opportunity."

"I had no idea this was going on," Jas replied slowly, as if amazed that such behavior could have escaped his attention. "I knew that they were friendly," he offered. "I recall seeing them talking in the dining hall sometimes, but attached no special meaning to it. Lots of the Folk form strong friendships. The two of them shared a room, you know. That's how they came to know each other."

If he only knew how far that friendship had progressed, Larisha thought. But no, she couldn't admit that or it would get Win in trouble as well.

"I understand that she is quite promiscuous," Larisha said quietly. "Win tells me that if he doesn't give her what she wants, she'll just go after some other worker. This probably wouldn't be a problem had you followed Hadir Polat's instructions more carefully." Larisha noticed Jas wince and knew that her barb had struck its target.

"I — I was holding her back from breeding for the time being. There are already four of the other Folk pregnant, you know," he added quickly, as if he had the excuse ready at hand. "I didn't think letting her wait would be a problem. The reserve were all selected because of their affinity for each other, as well as their superior bloodlines. For one of the reserve to seek another, outside of her group, would be quite unusual. Nevertheless, it is possible," he admitted grudgingly. "Yes, entirely possible."

So Jas believes me. Excellent!

"I've a better idea," Larisha suggested. "Why don't we move Win to my quarters. That will remove the temptation for the time being. Once we do that, you can take this Amber creature under your immediate supervision. Perhaps you should keep a constant eye on her for me."

Jas rubbed his chin in thought. "Hmmm, that might work. Certainly would keep your boy out of trouble until I get Amber paired. Hadir Polat still wants me to accelerate our mating schedule, you know." His eyes glistened as if he'd a new thought, but he didn't disclose whatever had occurred to him.

"Well?" she prommpted him.

"Yes, Raggi Bul, I'll do as you say. Matter of fact, I think I might do the same with her as you suggest for Win. Neither of them could get into trouble if we keep our eyes on them all the time, right?" He winked at her with a twinkle in his eye.

That wink indicated that the veterinarian was more perceptive than she liked. It was clear how he intended to use Amber. Well, that was no concern of hers so long as it kept the little bitch away from her Win.

But if she had read his motive correctly, eventually, she would have to do something about it. But not for a while. Not while Jas was still of use to her.

"Right," she replied as straight-faced as she could to his leering face.

Gull Tamat was excited when he had called for Tam to join him in Bay Five, one of the berthing slips for the scoops. But he hadn't said what had so excited him, what demanded the attention of the Hadir. Tam wondered as he hurried to the bay?

Gull didn't say anything when Tam entered. He just pointed at the recently berthed scoop that towered above him.

Tam gazed along the sharp planes of the scoop's fuselage. Frost sparkled across the vessel's surface as the moist air of the ship met its cold metal. Here and there the skin of the scoop looked as if it had been touched by an artist's brush, with filigrees of ice swirling and touching across its dark surface. One long sweep of sparkling frost stood out in particular. It stretched from near the nose almost to the stern of the scoop.

Strange, Tam thought, that it should be so much brighter than the rest. Then he started. That was no frost-touched fan of ice, no accident of condensation; it was a scar on the metal itself, a gouge in the nearly impervious, dark surface of the scoop!

"The pilot didn't see the object until an instant before they made contact," Gull explained as he led Tam closer. "As it was, he barely got a glimpse before he became — ah — preoccupied with getting the scoop back under control."

Tam reached out to touch the scar.

"Don't touch that!" Polat grabbed Tam's arm. "We

haven't had a chance to take a sample yet. I want to see if it left any residue we can analyze."

Tam continued to stare at the long scar. Whatever had hit the scoop had to be pretty massive and moving at a fair relational speed to do this sort of damage. Who would have thought that a rock that massive would be found that high in the atmosphere?

"What do you think it was," he asked idly. "Meteorite, some fragment thrown high by an eruption, or what?"

Gull looked as if he were surprised at the question. "Oh, didn't I tell you? Thought that I had, Hadir Polat. Sorry." He looked off into the distance, as if seeing something beyond the surface scar on the scoop.

When he maddeningly said nothing further, Tam demanded. "So, what was it then?"

Gull now looked even more confused than before. "The object that hit the scoop, you mean? I thought that you understood already. I mean, why else would I have asked you down here? The pilot said he saw something at least ten times the size of the scoop! He said he saw a large crystal-like object just before impact!"

PART TWO

EIGHT

Bul Larisha found herself increasingly preoccupied with the work on the habitat. Tam had been driving the entire crew to meet his accelerated schedules for completion ever since that chance encounter with the bit of flying rock down in the clouds.

Tam's Men had mobilized nearly all of the Halfings to work on the habitat, which left only a skeleton crew to manage things on the ship. As a consequence, she was continually on the habitat dealing with one crisis after another.

Her absence put Win under a lot of stress, for she left him to take care of the numerous things that she didn't have time to do herself. The boy was starting to show the strain of her demands, working late into the night and then looking hollow-eyed most mornings.

When the crew finally got the habitat's outer decks completed, Larisha was ready to establish the habitat's newly constructed greenhouse. Win was the logical choice to manage the transfer. He already knew most of the ship's management systems and was familiar with her plants' unique requirements and knew her preferences for their handling. Reluctantly, she relieved him of other duties so he could make the habitat's greenhouse his sole focus.

She still had not moved Win into her quarters. Jas had repeatedly assured her that the Amber bitch was being kept safely away from him in the dormitory. In addition, Jas assured her that he had set Amber's schedule so that she was on the opposite sleeping cycle and, when awake, was working far from wherever Larisha had assigned Win.

She wondered how Jas could be so assured that the two of them never met. Movement among the Folk in the dormitory was unfettered during their off-duty time, so he must be applying some additional restrictions to keep Amber close. Nothing about Win's behavior indicated that anything had changed.

Whenever Larisha finished her other work, she looked

into the habitat's greenhouse to check on progress. Usually this was near the end of the day cycle, when most of the Win's Folk had departed. She enjoyed the quiet as they strolled along the rows, observing the emerging stalks of vegetation, smelling the rich aroma of damp soil, and tasting the bite of nutrients that permeated the air. Here and there one of the rapid-growth vines was shooting up a wire frame, reaching for the lighted panels far above, trying to fill the space with its spreading leaves.

Win hadn't yet installed the misting nozzles that had proven so effective back on the ship. He was probably waiting for the vines to proliferate further. Idly, she thought about how she'd foolishly slipped on the edge of the trough. God, she could still recall the feel of Win's arms as he caught her, remember his sweet breath on her lips, the hard feel of his muscular body against hers as they tumbled to the deck.

Damn! She shook her head to halt that line of thought. A grown woman had no right to let such impure thoughts come into her head. Win was Folk, a worker to be used and nothing more. No matter how attractive he might be, there would be no excuse for her to consider him as anything else.

Still, she remembered . . .

Win was perplexed. He had not seen Amber for months. The ache in his heart was so heavy that he thought at times he would just die. He often lingered in the ship's dining room, waiting to catch a glimpse of her, hoping to see that mane of blond hair bobbing among the crowd. He just wanted to speak to her, to touch her, to hold her in his arms one more time . . .

But he never did. Neither did she surprise him in the elevator. Each time the doors opened, he felt a rise of excited expectation that made his heart momentarily race. Eagerly he would look inside, hoping against hope that he would see her face, the impish grin that told him that they would have a precious few minutes, a few priceless seconds alone.

But he was always disappointed, seeing only the familiar faces of the crew or other Folk. Sometimes his heart would stop when he glimpsed a thatch of blond hair peeking over the shoulders of the people in the elevator or spot such among the crowded passageways. But he was always disappointed. His heart would sink when the realization that some handsome boy, another reserve, a stranger, might someday know Amber more intimately than he.

Gold gave him no clues to where she had gone and averted her eyes whenever he asked. "Best you forgot her, as I advised," she'd say. "Best you forget about her."

Nor would anyone else reveal her whereabouts, or even admit that they knew her. It was as if all of the Folk were conspiring to hide something from him.

Win debated asking Larisha to find out what had happened to Amber. After all, since Jas Bulgat worked for her, he should know the location of all the Folk. But Win did not ask. The Men, friendly as they might seem, were always reluctant to discuss Folk matters. The few tentative inquiries he'd made were dismissed summarily, usually by Larisha changing the subject to some aspect of his work or, more often, her own concerns.

Larisha had become increasingly preoccupied with the activities of the science team. He'd overheard her talking to Dalgrun, the Palm, about it one evening as he pored over the arrangements she'd wanted him to make to the habitat's crop rotations. As Win debated the choices between brachiated and stemmed, he overheard them discussing the latest discovery by the scoops.

"It appears that Gull Tamat's original guess — that the objects are merely observational errors — was a mistake," Dalgrun told Larisha.

"Yes," Larisha replied. "Didn't Tam order the science team to capture one of the crystal things in the planet's atmosphere? I know he wants to examine one in detail."

"For the past week he's sent squadrons of scoops, equipped with all kinds of detectors, into the clouds. But no one found a thing. They all came back empty-handed," said Dalgrun.

"Any hint of these flying crystals?"

"Nothing at all," said Dalgrun.

"I don't understand what is so important about them," Larisha complained. "Certainly the scoops need to be more careful with those — those things, but that is no reason to waste time on a massive search effort. Why should it take so much time to find something this big?"

The Palm smiled. "Thetti is a very big planet, my dear. Since the scoops can only operate for a brief time before they must return from each mission, it might take months to examine the entire planet. Also, the dynamic nature of the atmosphere makes the search doubly difficult."

"So we have to sit here while Tam wastes time searching for something that we might only discover by chance?" Larisha had replied hotly. "Listen, they ran more than one hundred scoop missions before they hit something. There is no reason to suspend mining operations for this senseless search. The risk can't be that great!"

The Palm cocked her head to the side. "I suspect your concern over this has less to do with the Hadir's command decisions than you let on. Are we running low on materials because of the delay?"

Larisha shifted uncomfortably. "No, we have enough reserves to keep construction of the habitat going for several more weeks. Resupply from Thetti is far from critical. No, my concerns stem from my feeling that there is something more to Tam's fascination about these objects than he is telling. Ever since we entered this system, he has had this fixation on Thetti and that missing moon. Every time I talk to him about the subject, I have the feeling that he is not being candid, that he knows something he isn't revealing. I feel that he is holding back the single vital piece of information that is the key to these mission changes; our failure to proceed directly to Meridian; and this foolish, foolish search for these damn crystal fantasies."

Fantasies? Win's ears perked up at that. He had heard about the sudden cessation of mining from the Folk who worked down in smelting, refining, and manufacturing, but no one seemed to know the reason. What sort of alien thing was hidden in the howling maelstrom within the clouds of Thetti? Or was it a fantasy of Tam Polat's

For a moment, he wished that he could be one of those crystals. How wonderful it would be to drift loose and free, tacking this way and that through the atmosphere, unbound by gravity, unrestricted by mountain or stream, free to go wherever and whenever one wished. What would he do if he were one with them, exploring, seeking, finding the Amber crystal and flitting higher and higher with her, sharing the delights and pleasures of a life without bounds?

"Pay attention to your work," Larisha chided him when she noticed his absent stare. "We need to get those plans done so your crew can start on them in the morning."

Win started at her rebuke and, with some reluctance, brought his thoughts back to the task at hand. Yes, he would put the trees there and the crops over here. And tonight he would dream of crystals.

But Larisha's review of his work took longer than he thought, and he ended up sleeping in a small room, hardly bigger than a locker, in Larisha's quarters. He fell asleep the instant his head hit the rolled-up blanket that served as a pillow.

The next morning he accompanied Larisha to the habitat and began working on the changes that she'd dictated. They had the elevator to themselves, so Win stood well away from the Raggi; she at the door and he in the back corner. He thought of Amber the entire trip.

Gull could not explain his lack of success in capturing whatever had impacted the scoop.

"Most likely the impact destroyed the object," he'd said patiently. "For an object of that size to be so high in the atmosphere, it would have to be mostly empty space, a balloon, and a fragile one at that. I would guess that the impact completely destroyed it."

"That isn't reasonable," Tam shot back. "First, there couldn't be just one of these things. Nature doesn't work that way; a balloon indicates some form of life; and where there is life, there are usually several copies of nearly everything!"

"Not necessarily," Gull replied after considering Tam's words. "I, for one, do not believe that this is necessarily an alien life form. It could be a bubble ejected by some exotic volcanic action. Were that bubble to trap some heated gas, the object might easily float away."

"Did you find evidence of that from the samples you scraped from the scoop?"

Gull shifted his feet uncomfortably. "I, uh, we didn't find anything. The bits of material from the scoop were all hull metal — scratches from the scoop itself."

Tam snorted. "Let me get your argument straight: This fragile balloon that you contend some volcano kicked out, this chance, ephemeral bit of Thetti, was completely destroyed by its brush with the scoop. Am I correct so far?"

Gull nodded. "Yes," he said tentatively.

"Fine. Now you also say that this fragile balloon was nevertheless substantial enough to put a ten-meter scratch in the nearly impervious metal of a scoop's hull without leaving a trace of itself behind. Where is the logic in that, Gull?" he asked incredulously. "How can it be light and fragile, yet strong enough to damage a scoop's hull?"

The chief scientist grinned. "You have me there, Hadir Polat. I'm just as puzzled over the discrepancy as you. Anything that tough has to be too heavy to float, but it did."

"I take it the scoop pilot had no warning from his instruments."

Gull grimaced. "Radar's useless down there. There's too much white noise from the lightning storms. We use lidar to keep the ships aware of each other's positions. Collisions are one of the worries in this sort of operation."

"The lidar didn't give him any warning either, I suppose."

"Not a peep. If we want to capture one of these things we're going to have to find some detection method that works." He paused as if thinking hard and then his face lit up. "The original analyses we thought were anomalies came from the infrared viewers. We haven't used them since. We were worried that they might give more erroneous readings."

He raced from the room, shouting for his crew as he went.

Tam smiled. Maybe now they would get some results.

They lost one of the scoops when it closed on a crystal balloon. They had detected dozens ofthem. True to Gull's perception, the objects put out considerable infrared signature, allowing detection at a distance. Tam examined the ghostly images with wonder and rising excitement.

These were no bubbles from Thetti's volcanic belches. Although a gas-filled balloon would be roughly spherical, these objects were angular appeared to be symmetric in the longitudinal and horizontal axes, with clusters of projections fore and aft. Their shape was too regular, too smooth for some accidental creation.

He could scarcely believe the science team's estimates of their density. For objects of that size to float in the atmosphere, they would have to be lighter than the surrounding air. Even if they consisted of the lightest materials they could think of, the objects' skin' could scarcely be more than a few millimeters thick, hardly substantial enough to withstand the rigors of Thetti's howling winds. Hardly substantial enough to tear a forty meter scar along the side of a hardened scoop hull!

There was another puzzle. One object had been sighted moving against the wind, and at a speed much lower than the stall speed of the scoops. For the entire period of observation it held its altitude steady.

"It is," Gull contended, "simply impossible for something so fragile, so light, to hold its improbable shape while fighting the fierce winds. All of which means," he surmised, "that there must be some sort of strengthening mechanism beneath that thin skin. Such knowledge could be very useful, Hadir. We must capture one for examination."

Tam agreed at once. The next squadron deployed a tetrahedral flight pattern. This formation was designed to enclose the object and force it up, out of the atmosphere if possible. Gull Tamat was concerned that it might explode when if it left the atmosphere. Decompression, he insisted, would render examination difficult.

"Perhaps you want to ride it back here like a horse?" Tam had suggested sarcastically.

Tam discovered the vet's new living arrangements almost by accident. He'd stopped by Jas's quarters one night to find out why there were so few of the reserve pregnant. If the veterinarian didn't start the Folk producing more babies now, then the settlers wouldn't have the work force they'd need fifty years hence. He was also worried that his schedule would fall behind if the vet coddled the mongrels too long. Jas had been heard to complain that the Folk were being forced beyond reasonable limits.

He got some stares from the mongrels as he took a shortcut through the dormitories to get to Jas's quarters. He could have come the other way, through the crew section, but this was faster. No sense taking the long way around when he was so close.

He'd never been in the dormitory before, hadn't realized how barren and bare it was. But clean, he noted with approval. He'd half expected to find shit in the hallways and the pervasive smell of the tightly packed mongrels hanging over the area like a fog.

He glanced into a few rooms as he passed. He couldn't understand how they could stand being packed so closely, but he had been told that this is what the Folk preferred. Personally, he thought it aberrant to live four to a room.

The mongrels all got out of his way, fading into the shadows. None spoke, but he heard whispers behind his back as he passed. He wondered what they were saying, not that it mattered in the slightest.

He finally came to Jas's quarters. He rapped and heard someone stir inside.

He was shocked when a blonde mongrel opened the door. She was dressed in a short shift that revealed most of her pasty pale skin. Her long, pale hair hung long down her back and looked so tangled that she must have just gotten out of bed. She jumped back when she saw him and raised her hand to her mouth.

"Who is it?" Jas shouted from somewhere behind her. "Who the hell is coming to see me at this time of the night?" He walked into the room while rubbing sleep from his eyes.

"Oh my God!" he exclaimed when he saw Tam and pulled his tunic closed. Quickly he walked to the door and pushed Amber out of the way. "This isn't what you think," he said nervously.

Tam glared accusingly as the nearly naked blonde hid behind Jas. Had Jas no shame, no sense of morality, no sense of his proper place? Just because he was Halfing did not mean that he was not bound by the mores and sense of decency of civilized society.

"This is not what it looks like," Jas said into the lengthening silence. "This is not what you must be imagining!"

Without waiting for an explanation, Tam turned and stamped away. He did not trust himself to speak to the pervert. How could the Man abuse his position so flagrantly?

"Hadir Tam Polat, wait!" Jas pleaded behind him. "Please listen to me!"

"I cannot denounce him without evidence," Dalgrun protested when Tam told her of what he had discovered. "Just because the Man had a worker in his quarters doesn't mean he was doing anything immoral. Even Larisha keeps one of them with her occasionally."

"That is completely different," Tam argued. "Larisha has perfectly valid reasons for letting the mongrel stay with her. I gave her permission, and so did Jas. I did not," he emphasized, "authorize him to use the mongrels to satisfy his perverted appetites."

"So you say, Hadir Tam Polat," the Palm said sternly. "However, I do not think it abnormal for the veterinarian to have one of the Folk in his quarters. He is within easy access of the dormitories, and he cares greatly for them. Perhaps she was merely seeking his help on some matter. Perhaps he was examining her for some medical problem we know nothing about."

Tam snorted. "Listen to me; the bitch was wearing practically nothing, both had clearly been in his bed. It takes no imagination at all to determine what they had been doing. Come on, Dalgrun Wofat, even you must admit he has no justification for having a female mongrel in his bedroom."

"Allegedly in his bedroom," Dalgrun interjected. "You have no proof there was anything untoward."

"Perhaps we should have the bitch examined," Tam suggested. "I checked to see if she had been bred as yet and discovered that Jas has been holding her, and a few others, back from the breeding program." He paused, as if a new thought had come to mind. "A harem, do you suppose?"

When Dalgrun did not respond, he continued, "I will have her checked by our doctors. If she is still a virgin, then I will believe in Jas Bulgat's innocence, although I would still question his judgement. Otherwise, we have the evidence of my eyes and the physical examination. That should put a close to the matter."

Dalgrun put her fingers together to form a tent. She peered across the steeple at Tam. "Should I ask what action you will take should the examination prove your suspicions?"

Tam stalked to the viewport and stared out at the habitat. It hung like a ruined balloon, back-lit by reflected rose light from Thetti. The giant planet was a ruddy color, striped by bands of darker brown. Both were nearly the same apparent size.

"If the tests are positive, I will have the bitch put down," he said slowly. "That should send a message to the mongrels and the crew that I will not tolerate any more of this supposed friendliness. The Halfings are still humans, even if deficient, but the mongrels are, are . . . animals!"

Dalgrun nodded slowly.

"As to Jas," he continued. "Well, we really have little need for a vet now that the mongrels are all de-iced and the dormitory is completed. Maybe one of our doctors can be recruited to fill the void. It can't be too difficult to treat a mongrel's medical problems."

"Would you really put Jas Bulgat down as if he were a common worker?" Dalgrun asked. Surprise was evident in her voice. "That would send quite a message to the Halfings — a very unsettling message," she added. It was obvious that she did not think this was a good idea.

"The Halfings must be made to understand that I will rigorously enforce civilized behavior on this ship. We cannot allow such perversions or they will eventually destroy the fragile moral fabric of our crew. Do I need to remind you that the knowledge of this perversion violates every rule of the Hand?"

"It is not necessary to remind me," Dalgrun said firmly. "I am quite aware of the list of sins the Prophet handed down. Still, I do not think a death sentence would be a good decision, although it speaks well to your commitment to uphold the policies of the Hand. Perhaps a more suitable punishment would send a more pointed message."

Tam scratched his chin in thought. "Are you suggesting a punishment that will serve to reinforce the Halfings's core beliefs? Yes, having Jas around as a constant reminder of my resolve might work out better."

"I commend you for your perception, Hadir Tam Polat. Perhaps I misjudged you." Dalgrun smiled as she rose to leave.

Tam nodded. "And I misjudged you, Palm Dalgrun Wofat. You are a good advisor. I thank you for your support. Now, let me make arrangements to have the bitch examined."

A squadron of the scoops finally managed to surround one of the objects. They forced it higher and higher until it emerged from the top of the cloud layers, where they could image it. Unfortunately the object escaped and plunged back into the clouds. Its movements were so purposeful that there was no longer any doubt that it was a living creature.

The clear and well-defined images that the scoops obtained from that attempt awakened Tam's memories of the immense crystalline structure he had glimpsed upon awakening. Were these cloud-crystals connected to that awesome being? Could one of these things have been attracted by his approaching ship? The thought was terribly frightening.

Gull Tamat theorized that these crystals had been created deep in the atmosphere and gradually gained altitude as they grew. If that was so, could they mature into space-faring beings? Could the depths of this huge planet produce a life form unlike anything humanity had ever encountered? Such a find would be exciting, especially if they could tame the creatures and harness them to the greater advance of humanity. If true, it would still the voice of his internal doubt about Man's supremacy, about his lapse in faith. Only time would tell. The scoops would eventually capture one for examination.

Until they did so, he had a ship to command. And a sinner to cleanse.

Dalgrun supported him down the line when Amber's examination was completed. Quite obviously the bitch had been sexually active, and recently too.

Jas denied the entire thing, protesting that he was trying to protect the other mongrels, trying to protect his prime breeding stock, trying to do his best for the mission's greater good.

"Don't lie to me," Tam snarled with barely concealed fury. "Don't continue this farce of denying your immoral, bestial relationship with this bitch. At least preserve enough of your dignity to feel shame. Or perhaps you are so far into your perversion that you no longer have the capacity to do so."

"Listen to me," Jas protested. "I only brought the girl into my quarters because the Raggi recommended it. I was just trying to keep her away from another boy and the others. It was for the good of the mission that I did this. You have to believe me."

Tam turned to Larisha.

"I admit that I asked Jas to help me shield Win from the aggressive nature of the bitch," Larisha admitted.

The veterinarian's face lit up with relief, but fell as Larisha continued without pause. "But I certainly did not suggest that Jas Bulgat do so by satisfying the female's animal cravings himself. That," she'd declared with scorn evident in her voice, "must have been his own idea." Her voice then softened. "I think this might have started as an outgrowth of his sympathetic feelings toward his charges."

"What will happen to Amber," Jas asked during a break in Tam's insistent questioning. "Who will take care of her?"

Larisha moved away and stood at Dalgrun's side, leaving Tam alone to face the veterinarian.

"That is not your concern," Tam said simply. "I wanted to put the bitch down. Both the Raggi and I felt that allowing a mongrel who had sex with a Halfing to remain where she could speak of it would be asking for trouble. But Dalgrun felt the measure was too harsh. We are going to put her back into the freeze until we reach Meridian."

"You bastards! That will kill her!" Jas lunged forward. Tam easily blocked the smaller Man's wild swings. Guards took his arms.

"How can you destroy the best damn female we had in reserve? Oh God, poor Amber. How can you even think of doing this?" Jas sobbed. "I love her." He began to cry.

"I could have you executed for this," Tam said with loathing. "Bestiality is a crime against humanity, against the Hand, and against the Emerging God in all of us. It is a sin that cannot be tolerated in any measure."

"Amen," said Dalgrun. "We Men are superior beings born to rule over the lesser creatures. The Halfings exist only to serve our needs, and the Folk to bear the burdens of both. So it is ordained."

Tam acknowledged her brief homily with a nod. "But I will be merciful to you, Jas Bulgat. The Palm insists that we need your skills and your knowledge too much to sacrifice you."

A look of relief passed over Jas's face when Tam said that. *Well, that relief will be short-lived.*

"Instead, I am going to send you to live among the mongrels you love so much. I will give you the opportunity you deserve." He drew in a breath and pronounced his sentence. "On this day I dismiss you from the crew. You are no longer under my command. You are no longer a Man!"

"But what does that mean?" Jas wondered out loud with a puzzled look on his face. "There are only the Folk and the Halfings in the crew. Where else can I go?"

Dalgrun cleared her throat and returned to Tam's side. "I renounce your humanity," she intoned. "I curse you and lift the protection that the Hand gives to all Men. Is it clear what I am saying?" she demanded.

"I am to become one of the Folk," Jas croaked, his face at first a study in disbelief.

"There is one small detail I omitted," Tam added. "A brief operation that you'll hardly notice. After all, it would be a terrible sin to allow the seed of the Halfings to mingle with the mongrel's bloodlines, wouldn't it? Besides, we can't have the mongrel bitches take advantage of you any more. Trust me, this is for your benefit."

The import of Tam's words had an immediate effect. Jas knees buckled. The crewmen carried him away.

"Pervert," Tam spat.

NINE

Larisha was with the Palm when the news came.

Dalgrun took another sip of her brandy and then straightened the table. She gathered the mats, placed the dishes on the tray, scraped away the few crumbs from their dinner into her palm and deposited them in one of the cups. She brushed her hands vigorously.

"I did not expect Tam to take such pleasure in his administration of justice," she said to Larisha as she continued to rub her hands, her long fingers interlacing and twisting. "The way he acted was . . ." she picked up a napkin and dabbed at a tiny spot on her palm, "inappropriate. I can still see the Hadir's smile. I wouldn't be surprised to hear that he will attend the operation. As for the female, well, we can't let her spread tales about having relations with Men, can we?"

Larisha agreed. "Just the same, I hate to see good stock go to waste. But you are right; it would be bad for discipline if she were left awake."

"I don't see how someone with your tender feelings could have lived with him." Dalgrun toyed with her brandy. "The Hadir seems so cold and dispassionate in comparison."

"His lack of obvious passion was one of the qualities that endeared Tam Polat to the Hand," Larisha said. "Didn't you yourself declare that the Hadir must rule the crew with an iron fist? Well, Tam can certainly do that — I doubt that he has an ounce of empathy. There was no reason to pass such a brutal sentence on poor Jas."

"I don't see a conflict between his feelings and justice, my dear. Hadir Tam Polat exercised his best judgement on the matter of the veterinarian. I fully support him. Only . . ." Her voice trailed off as she looked wistfully away.

"Only what? What else were you going to say, dear Dalgrun?" Larisha prompted.

"As I said before, you are too compassionate." Dalgrun placed her hand over Larisha's and squeezed gently. "You need to develop a more objective view if you are ever to command."

Larisha's heart jumped. Could Dalgrun's remark imply that she too had doubts about Tam's ability to lead them? Had his amusement and joy at inflicting Jas's punishment tipped the scales in her favor? Perhaps, if he persisted with this preoccupation with Thetti, Dalgrun would finally see the folly of his actions and act to remove him.

"I will work on distancing myself from my charges," she promised and returned the reassuring clasp. "Now, let us return to the Halfings over at the habitat. They need some sort of spiritual guidance. Look here. . . ."

The link chimed and Dalgrun answered. She threw a sharp glance at Larisha, then a look of concern crossed her face as she listened to whoever was on the other end.

"Both of them?" she asked. "Are you quite certain?"

She returned to the table and downed the remainder of the brandy. "That was the medical crew. Jas is dead."

Larisha looked up from her papers. "What? How . . . ?"

"Gave himself a quick slice across the throat with a scalpel. Killed the female worker as well. God help his soul. I suppose I must have services for him, now."

Larisha sighed. "Poor Jas. But perhaps it is better this way. The girl might not have survived the freeze anyhow." She stood. "Excuse me, dear Palm. I had no idea of how late it had become and have some matters I must take care of. Please notify me of when the services will be conducted."

She left the Palm's quarters and headed for her own.

"Win?" Larisha said as she peered into his tiny room. "Ah, you are still awake. Good."

Win looked up from the text he was studying. "What? Is there something you need me to do?"

"Oh no, I just received some bad news and thought it best that I come and tell you myself."

Win jumped with alarm and took a step toward the doorway. "Has something happened to the gardens? I knew that the nutrient flow wasn't being adjusted properly! Or is it the bean vines? The trees? Do you want me to go up and help fix things?"

"This has nothing to do with the greenhouse." Larisha motioned him back into his cubby. "This involves some trouble in the dormitory. Do you remember that friend of yours — Amber? Was that her name?"

Win nodded. He hadn't seen Amber for weeks. Gold had been strangely silent when he inquired about Amber's whereabouts, as had everyone else he asked. They didn't need to explain. He finally realized that she had joined the rest of the reserve. Gold and the rest were trying to protect him from that news, damn them! And now Amber was in some sort of trouble, something serious enough to come to the attention of the Raggi herself.

"Wha— what is it?" he choked out, hoping that whatever had occurred, it could be overcome by a little discipline, a change of quarters, such as Gold had arranged for them, to keep her out of trouble. "Please, tell me," he begged.

"You'd better sit down," Larisha sat beside him on the little bunk. She patted his hand, letting her fingers linger for a moment. "I know you were Amber's friend, weren't you? It's always hard to hear bad news about one's friends." She took his and held on tight. "You know how everyone must keep to their place? Win?"

When he nodded, she continued, "The Men — the Hand — are the leaders and the seed of humanity, the vehicle of the Emerging God. Every one of the Men has a pure bloodline going back centuries, to the very founding of Heaven."

What has religion to do with Amber? Win stirred with impatience, but did not say anything. Larisha would get to the point in her own time.

"You do know the differences between Men and Half-ings, Halfings and Folk, don't you?"

Win recalled Gold's explanation and, although he didn't completely understand, replied, "Yes, someone told me about that. What does this have to do with Amber?"

"No decent Man would have relations with a Halfing," Larisha continued earnestly. "It's not only a matter of law, but one of taste, of morality. A Man just doesn't lay with an inferior, regardless of the circumstances. Men who would dare do that with a Halfing are scorned because it calls their very humanity into question. It is a sin for Men and Halfings to mix. You do understand, don't you, Win?"

"Men don't breed with anyone but their own. Just like the Folk breed only with Folk," he answered directly. Why was she treating him as a child? Why was she going over things that everyone knew? Didn't the Palm preach this same thing every service?

When Larisha patted his hand to show that she understood, Win finally asked. "Are you going to tell me that Amber has," he hesitated, as if saying it aloud would make it true, "has she mated with someone else? Is that the bad news you have?"

"There is a greater sin for Men and the Halfings," Larisha continued as if she hadn't heard his question. "Sometimes people act in improper ways; they give in to their fantasies, or worse. Their perversions make them do things that no rational Man or Halfing would ever even consider. Sometimes people step outside the bounds that decent society has established. People sometimes do heinous, sinful things."

"What did Amber do?" Win shook, unable to contain himself any longer. "Please, you have to tell me!" He held her hands tight, hoping that she could feel his burning need to know.

"Oh, Win," Larisha said plaintively, returning his clasping grip. "I am trying to make you understand. This Amber, well, she consorted with one of the Men, and," she hesitated for a heartbeat and then finished the sentence, "she was killed as a result."

"Killed?" Win didn't understand the meaning of the word. "Killed?" he repeated, dumbstruck as the meaning of the term began to become too frighteningly clear in his mind.

"She was discovered to be consorting with that pervert Jas. No," she shook her head, "he is dead as well, by his own hand. He killed your friend before he took his own life."

Win felt an emptiness inside, and in that void a fire began to flare, its flames licking emotions held too long in check. His heart felt as if it would swell and burst. A numbness began at the back of his neck and gradually engulfed his entire being. Something nameless grew from the burning emptiness and grew larger with each passing instant. He took a deep breath and tried to release it, but the emptiness grasped it, twisted, and turned it into a long wail of pain, of longing unfulfilled, of something beyond description.

He started to speak and choked, coughed. His cough became a sigh, a sob, then a torrent of heaving waves of grief that built on themselves. Wave after wave of emotion washed over him as his sobs built in intensity.

He wanted to curl into a ball around this burning torment and sink into oblivion. *No Amber, no Amber, no Amber,* his mind kept repeating, as if the repetition could undo the fact of her death. He reached out his arms in supplication and felt Larisha's arms about him, pulling him close. He felt her hands on his back, patting him gently while she whispered a steady stream of comforting words into his ear.

"Lie down," she said and, as he did so, found that she followed, keeping him in her comforting embrace.

"Why? Why?" he repeated, as if there could be some reason that would make Amber's death make sense to him. There had to be some purpose in it, some reason that made sense.

"Shush," Larisha whispered as she held him close and continued ministering to his needs. He buried his face against her shoulder and felt his tears soak her clothing.

Larisha gently pushed him back and wiped at his wet cheeks with her fingers. "I had no idea you felt so strongly about her," she said. "I am so sorry I had to tell you this, but I thought it would be better than hearing it from someone else."

"Thank you," Win replied through his sobs. "You are very good to me."

Larisha brushed the words aside. "I look after my own. Now come here; let me hold you some more."

She pulled him to her and placed her arms about him. She stroked his hair.

Win allowed himself to be held. For a moment, in Larisha's arms, he recalled the way that Amber had held him, and then the grief resumed and threatened to overwhelm him. He clung tightly to Larisha, as if her warmth would keep the sorrow at bay.

Larisha awoke with a start, staring up at the strange, close walls, momentarily disoriented in the darkness. In the murky haze of semi-wakefulness she rolled over and snuggled against the warm body beside her.

Then she came wide awake, remembering where she was and who this was beside her. She lifted her head and looked at the sleeping Win. His face was puffy from crying, his eyes red where he had repeatedly rubbed them. His youthful face looked so innocent, so vulnerable. She reached out and tenderly brushed a strand of hair away from his eyes.

Win stirred at her touch and threw an arm across her breast. Such a beautiful body, Larisha mused, making no effort to disturb him by moving his arm. She had no idea that he would feel the loss of his friend so deeply. Why, she realized with dawning amazement, his grief had been nearly Man-like in its intensity. In the semi-darkness, she could almost ignore his colorless hair and pale skin. In this dim light, she could almost believe he was one of the handsome lovers she'd had during her wild youth, when the embers of desire still burned hot and deep. Something stirred within her as she remembered those torrid adolescent nights on Heaven when her fantasies were sometimes made real.

Win moved against her. "Amber?" he mumbled sleepily.

"There, there," Larisha said quietly and put her arm around his shoulders. He moved against her.

God, but his body feels so good. Win pressed tightly closer. *Oh my,* she thought as she felt his response against her hip. Curious, she reached down to examine this event. How would it compare to Tam's, she wondered with a barely suppressed giggle and loosened the cord binding his tunic.

Win was definitely excited. He was so hard. Larisha let her hand stroke the velvety smoothness, her fingers lingering at the head for a few seconds before she withdrew her hand in embarrassment. She felt shamed that she had taken such liberties with the sleeping, defenseless boy.

"Amber," Win whispered again and pressed close once again.

"I'm sorry," Larisha whispered into his ear. "I didn't mean to wake you." But, unbidden, her hand returned to him as if it had a mind of its own.

What am I doing? It was as if her body had taken control over her brain. *I shouldn't be doing this.* But the boy's need for comfort was so great, she reasoned. There would be no harm in letting him hold her if it would help ease his pain. There could be no shame in comforting such an obviously wounded youngster, would there?

Win continued to press insistently against her, quite obviously aroused. The poor boy, Larisha thought and loosened her gown. She was curious to discover what his pale skin would feel like against her own, but only for a moment, she promised herself.

The contact with Win's skin made her nipples become hard and erect. God, but his skin felt so good, so warm. She could feel herself become damp as she inhaled the warm maleness of him.

Then he was on her, kissing her, caressing her, pressing her back against the bed. She ran her hands over the smooth, hard muscles of his back. She could feel the strength of his young body and let the sheer sensuous pleasure of skin against skin take over, letting the demands of her body block out all other thoughts except the satisfaction of its insistent desire.

She knew that she was damned even as she reveled in Win's passionate embrace. Was that wicked knowledge what made the act so damned intense? But her needs were not subject to rational analysis, not now. She pulled him tightly to her, wrapping her legs around him, guiding him into her, feeling the pleasure build and build until there was nothing else in the universe except the pounding, rising excitement of making love.

"This never happened," she warned Win when he awoke the next morning. She grabbed her gown and pulled it on. What could she have been thinking of to try to comfort the boy — one of the Folk? How had she let her good judgement and compassion become seduced by the boy's animal desires? Well, emotions had been high, and Win's needs so great, that it had overcome them both. It would never happen again. *No,* she thought angrily, *to do that would be perverted, twisted, sick!*

"You are never to speak of what happened last night to anyone," she repeated. "If you do, it will mean your death. Do you understand? Do you know what would happen?"

"They would kill me just like they killed Amber." Win looked up at her. "Would that be so bad?"

"They would do harm to me as well," Larisha said. "Grievous harm. You wouldn't want that, would you?"

Win started with alarm. "No! You have been so good to me, to all of the Folk. I would never do anything that would bring you harm."

"Good. So long as last night never happened, the two of us are perfectly safe." She paused. "I think it would be best if you continued to stay here for a few more days. Yes, you can use the time to compose yourself and get over your grief. I doubt that you would be able to concentrate on your work anyway."

"Thank you," Win said.

Throughout the day, try as she might, Larisha could not drive thoughts of Win from her mind. At the most awkward moments, memories of the feel of his lips on her breasts, the way the boy used his tongue to circle their tips, came unbidden from the depths. In the middle of scheduling the recycling facilities for the habitat, she recalled how it had felt when he'd entered her. During the meal break, she found herself caressing the sides of her cup and comparing the smoothness of its surface with the feel of his skin under her hands. How hard, how vital he had been. God, she hadn't felt this way in years!

No, it was impossible. She was behaving just as she had when she'd fallen in love with Tam and turned into a fluttering fool who couldn't concentrate, couldn't do anything without thoughts of him intruding.

But Win was a damned Folk, not the handsome, forceful, dashing Hadir Polat! Win wasn't even a Man, for the Prophet's sake! Had she no shame, no dignity, no disgust at her abominable behavior? She was Raggi, a true human in all respects — how could she have fallen so low as to cavort with one of the lower orders? It simply wasn't rational to feel this way, not rational at all. She must have been out of her mind.

But Win was so beautiful, the other half of her mind argued. He was so compliant, so exciting. She paused at that last thought. Perhaps that was the attraction. Maybe the intense pleasure from their night together was simply the excitement of crossing a forbidden line. Could it be the delicious idea of stealing sinful pleasure that had made the experience so incredibly sensuous? Or had it been her more altruistic, sympathetic side that allowed the boy to do what he wished? Was it her inherent desire to comfort a creature crying in pain that had driven her to allow it to happen? Well, it would not happen again.

Still, she found herself rushing to return to her quarters at the end of the day, anxious to see Win. Her Win.

In the middle of the next night, Larisha heard Win crying softly in his cubby. "Damn him," she muttered. "How long is this bawling going to go on?" She climbed out of bed and made her way down the hall.

"Are you all right?" she asked. She stood by his bed and looked down at him in the dim light from the hall.

Win had thrown the cover back to expose his torso, One of his legs was on top of the covers. One arm was thrown across his face, hiding his eyes. From the way his chest was heaving Larisha knew he was trying hard to suppress his sobbing. A pang of sympathy shot through her.

"I know how difficult it must be for you, losing your friend like that." She sat on the edge of the bed. When she reached out to pat him on the shoulder, she found her hand running down his chest. The small hairs tickled the tips of her fingers. She let her hand linger on his slowly rising and falling abdomen for a long moment. Unbidden, her fingers explored the thin line of curling hairs that cushioned her travels from his navel to groin.

Win took his arm from his face and stared up at her. *His expression is so desolate, so sad.* She reached out to wipe his wet cheeks.

"Don't be sad," she said. "I know what you need."

Her hand resumed its exploration, and Win's body responded immediately. He turned on one hip to make a space for her.

Larisha hesitated, as if there were something she had resolved, something that she had promised herself, but she could not remember it as the blood hammered in her head and the patch between her legs grew moist and warm. Without another thought, she threw caution to the wind and let herself be pulled into the hurricane of passion that swept all other thoughts, all sadness, all shame away.

At Larisha's invitation and encouragement, Dalgrun Wofat had become a frequent visitor to Larisha's quarters. The two were becoming good friends and, in time, Larisha hoped, co-conspirators in ousting Tam from his position as Hadir.

Larisha also hoped that Dalgrun's frequent visits would provide a cover for her. So long as the Palm was frequenting the Raggi's quarters, no one would suspect the depths of sin into which she had descended.

At least three nights a week, Dalgrun would stay over, usually at Larisha's insistence following one of their late night discussions. That move, she thought, was an even better cover even if it did prevent her from visiting Win's cubby.

She was very pleased to see how Dalgrun had taken to Win as well. Once the Palm had discovered how intelligent and creative the boy was, she asked to use him on some of her own work. Win, for example, showed a remarkable affinity for organizing the dossiers that Dalgrun maintained on the Halfings. On those evenings when Larisha didn't have anything for Win to do, she would let him work on Dalgrun's files.

Larisha thought that it was a cozy arrangement. It protected her darkest of secrets, her most heinous of crimes. Best of all, Dalgrun seemed to suspect nothing. Win was ever the proper Worker when she was around.

And whenever the Palm was not there, she had Win, her Win.

Larisha was still fuming after another of her shouting sessions with Tam about his intransigence over the move to Meridian. She didn't waste time on preliminaries as Dalgrun entered the cabin, but began speaking immediately.

"I tell you, the Man is unbalanced," she declared. "He is wasting more of our valuable resources."

Dalgrun sighed. "I notice that you only became this incensed when it involves Hadir Tam Polat. What has he done now?"

Larisha began pacing, working off frustration. "He's having the scoop ships try to bring one of these balloons out of Thetti's atmosphere. Why he is wasting time on that, I have no idea; it certainly won't provide any more resources for the habitat nor move us one meter closer to settling Meridian." Larisha turned to face the Palm. "This is just like that fixation he had on the missing moon — the moon that Gull Tamat doubts was even there! Listen, Dalgrun, if I were in command, I'd be doing everything I could to get our people down on Meridian. I would be putting all of our resources toward preparing for the settlers. I wouldn't waste time and energy on gathering useless knowledge and chasing by-God-damned, stupid balloons!"

"But you are not the Hadir," Dalgrun observed dryly, "and so long as Tam does nothing to endanger the mission he can dictate how the ship's assets are to be used." She settled herself into the comfortable chair, folded the red fabric of her skirt about her legs, and crossed her hands in her lap.

"The Hadir honestly believes that these objects represent either an opportunity or a threat and is acting accordingly. He assures me that he is simply being prudent by ensuring that the scoops are not endangered by these things, whatever they are. He insists that the habitat must be finished before we can attempt Meridian." She smiled at Larisha. "I know you won't like this, but I must say that I agree with him."

Larisha snorted. "Easy for you to agree, dear Palm. You don't know Tam as well as I do! Everything he does has a reason, a reason that fits one way or another into his damned plans. I believe he is deliberately misleading you, me, us, the entire crew, by pursuing these phantasms. They are just a way to justify some other action he's planning. I don't trust him or his words. The Hadir is subtle and cunning, on that you may trust me."

"Suppose that you are right. Have you proof that he is

working against the best interests of the Hand? Can you state even one possible reason he might have?"

When Larisha didn't respond, Dalgrun continued. "I can see no opportunity for him to vary from the mission set by the Hand, no way he could profit from some rogue action on his part." She shook her head. "You must be wrong, my dear. Perhaps you are letting your past experience influence your thinking. Perhaps you are letting your personal feeling interfere with your judgement."

Larisha didn't try to hide her reaction. It had been no secret that their marriage was a thing of the past. Dalgrun had indicated that she knew about that little falsehood a mere two days after she was de-iced. The woman had an uncanny ability to pick up on tiny clues about people, their thoughts, their behavior. Fortunately, the Palm had not chosen to chastise her on it; instead she had encouraged Larisha to unload her frustrations and feelings about Tam's failings, just as she was no doubt doing right now.

Larisha fumed. "Why is it so hard for you to believe what I tell you? Tam has a reason for these diversions of his, and when I discover what it is . . ." She left the threat unfinished.

"If it is against the Hand, then I will act as well," Dalgrun finished the sentence. "Until then, I must give him the benefit of the doubt. Really, Larisha, I have been listening to you for months now and, frankly, I am growing weary of your complaints. Bring me proof that Hadir Tam Polat is acting against the wishes of the Hand, something that I can use, and I will act."

"Then you'd better get ready," Larisha shot back. "Tam told me not an hour ago that one of the squadrons has finally captured one of those balloons. Tam is bringing it aboard the ship."

Dalgrun sprang to her feet in an instant, her robes rustling around her. "He's going to do what? That is a very dangerous thing to do. He had no discussion with me on this."

"Nor with me, the Raggi," Larisha said. "Neither has he consulted his immediate staff. The only one he has taken into his confidence is Gull Tamat. Both of them are so focused on finding out more about these things that they ignore the danger."

Dalgrun was already on her way out of the door. "We cannot allow him to place the ship at risk."

Larisha smiled wickedly. "No need to hasten, Dalgrun. I have taken some precautions. I have done what I could with my limited resources."

TEN

"What do you suppose it could be?" Dalgrun peered through the port at the angular, crystalline object floating a few kilometers away. The object glistened rose-hued in reflected Thetti-light as it slowly rotated.

"No telling." Tam folded his arms and glared. "We won't find out unless we examine it."

"It is prudent that we not risk the Men when dealing with the unknown," Dalgrun sniffed.

"Your advice sounded more like a threat to my crew," Tam growled. "I have to find out what these things are. The only way I can do that is to bring it on board where we have the proper tools!"

Dalgrun pointed to a bright light now approaching the object. It was one of the shuttle craft. "What is that? Have your Men decided to disobey my instruction, Hadir?"

Tam cursed and spun around. "What do you know about this, Larisha? That's one of your craft."

Larisha shrugged. "Rather than risk any of the Men, I thought it would be better if some of my Halfings dismantled it. That should make it easier for Gull to examine."

Dalgrun said nothing as Tam activated the link and told his crew to order the shuttle away.

Bright sparks began to appear near the surface of the object — torches! Tam couldn't discern the individual figures from this distance.

"You don't know what you are risking," he muttered, half to himself. "You just don't know."

"Do you still think it is some natural alien life?" Dalgrun idly watched the sparks of the torches. "Don't those look like facets on a crystal?" She pointed. "Your object appears to be something precipitated out of a solution."

"Gull and I don't think that's what it is. It moved purposefully, away from the scoops," Tam replied. "No simple mineral formation would do that. If it's smart enough to evade us then it must have at least the rudiments of intelligence. It could even be a machine!" He laughed at his last remark, a forced laugh that rang hollowly in the chamber.

"Perhaps you are right," Dalgrun said with pursed lips. Obviously she had not found the remark so amusing. "We shall discover which is correct after the Raggi's Halfings take it apart." She hesitated. "Gull insists that this thing can fly, does he? Well, wouldn't an airborne creature be more, ah, *organic* in appearance?" Dalgrun asked. "I would never have imagined that something so angular could fly."

"I was not joking when I said they might be machines," Tam said flatly. "Perhaps some alien civilization built them and left them here."

Dalgrun laughed and slapped his arm. "Some alien intelligence? Is that what you are suggesting? Oh, Hadir, you are so amusing!"

When Tam did not respond, her laughter stopped and a stern look crossed her face. "I would be very careful about voicing such thoughts, Hadir Tam Polat. Your statements border on heresy. There can be no alien civilizations, no intelligent creatures, to leave artifacts behind. You will find no evidence that God gave another race dominion over the universe as he did to Man."

Tam smiled grimly. "Of course, what a foolish thought on my part. That object must be some obscene alien life form native to Thetti. You must be right." Sarcasm dripped from his words.

"At most, we will find it is nothing more than a simple animal," Dalgrun continued confidently. "One that grew deep down, near the planet's crust, and rose into the clouds to graze."

"Where there are cattle there are predators," Tam said. "What is taking them so long to move away?"

"Aren't you two pushing your imaginations beyond the evidence?" Larisha laughed. "Let's just wait to see what the . . . God of the Prophet, what was *that?*"

Several bright flashes came from the object. "Get away

from the port!" Tam said.

A bright flash nearly blinded him. He shoved Dalgrun one way and pulled Larisha to the other. He slapped at the release to lower the shield over the port.

In seconds, pieces from an expanding wave of debris rattled against the ship's hull. Tam held his breath, waiting for any signs of decompression, hoping that the port would not shatter. Only when the sound of the many impacts stopped did he lift the shield.

Where the object and its dismantlers had been was a growing ball of sparks from the debris hurtling away. He estimated that some of the residue would hit the habitat in another hour or so.

"Warn the hab," he yelled over the ringing alarms and confused shouts of the crew.

He noted that several rescue ships were already heading toward the site, but he doubted there could be any survivors.

"I see that we were correct about exercising caution, wouldn't you say, Hadir Polat?" Dalgrun struggled to her feet and brushed her robes. "If that explosion had taken place on board our ship . . ."

"I never would have done something as stupid as putting torches to something full of methane and oxygen," Tam shouted angrily. Then he noticed that his arm was still around Larisha's waist. He let go and pushed her away. "Consider yourself admonished for near-terminal stupidity, Raggi," he snarled. "The next object we capture will be examined my way! I will allow no interference from either of you — spiritual or mundane. Understood?" His tone made it clear that he expected no answer, only compliance.

"If there is a next one," Dalgrun interjected. "I think it would be foolhardy to attempt to capture any more. If they pose no potential harm, then let them be. We have better things to do with our assets and our time than chase balloons."

"There were sixteen people in that crew," Larisha said

as she stared at the fading glow. "Sixteen Halfings and some Folk."

"Are you certain there were only your people on board?" Tam asked. "Thank God you didn't put any of my Men at risk. I'd never forgive you if you'd done that."

Larisha stared at him with of loathing. "Sixteen of our crew members just died. Sixteen! Doesn't that bother you?"

Tam shrugged. "Of course it does. Now the rest of your Halfings will have to take up the slack, and you've probably done considerable damage to their morale, besides scaring the pilots and everyone else to Hell and back. Now we have to waste more time cleaning up, which will further disrupt the schedule."

Larisha let her anger show. "Is that all you can think of, your precious schedule?"

"How do you expect me to react?" Tam shook his finger in her face. "What you did was stupid as hell, and a handful of your Halfings are dead as a result. Don't you try to make me feel guilty over a few words when there is nothing to excuse your ignorant, unthinking interference!"

"We gain nothing by arguing over what is past," Dalgrun interrupted smoothly. "Let us see what we can learn from this terrible event and go on with the mission. It is the will of the Hand that is important, not our feelings."

"I will examine another of these objects," Tam promised. "It is imperative that we understand them so they do not imperil our scoops when they are mining the atmosphere."

Dalgrun paused at the doorway. "That is a good reason, one that I can support. But be certain that is your only reason, Hadir Tam Polat. We cannot afford any further mistakes."

She took the still fuming Larisha by the arm and led her away.

The weeks had gone by in a blur for Win. The ache in his breast from the loss of Amber had started to fade to a dull pain, never forgotten ache, always lying just beneath his thoughts, ready to spring forward and bring a rush of sorrow to his life.

The nights with Larisha helped relieve his loneliness. She was so good to him that he had no choice but to give her what she obviously needed from him. He still did not understand why she continued to deny her part in their liaisons, nor why she continued to admonish him on the mornings after. There were some things about Men's behavior that he simply did not understand.

He dug a spoon into the bowl of fortified porridge. He chewed the tasteless paste and recalled breakfasts he'd had with Amber in the dining hall. This brought back memories of their joyful conversations and her loving glances. Larisha never ate meals with him, never had conversations regarding anything except work, and never spoke during their bouts of fierce lovemaking.

"Good morning, Win," Dalgrun yawned widely. "What are you eating? It looks, uh, nourishing." She made an expression of distaste. "Is there any fruit?"

Win nodded toward the bowl on the counter. "I brought some over from the habitat's garden yesterday. The apples should be ripe but the peaches are still a little tart."

Dalgrun picked up the apple near Win's bowl and sniffed. "Excellent," she declared after taking a healthy bite. "These are quite good. I seem to recall this variety from Heaven. Are these the same or a derivative?"

"Larisha brought some of her own apple clones," Win admitted. "That's from a graft. She says they taste exactly like the ones she grew. They'd taste even better if we hadn't forced them to grow so fast."

Dalgrun chewed on the apple for a moment in silence. "You really like working for Larisha, don't you?" As she sat on the chair next to his her robe fell open and exposed her legs.

Win glanced away. "She is quite good to me. I am proud to work for someone as important as her."

"And are you good to her?" Dalgrun leaned closer and took another bite of his apple. "Do you do everything she tells you to?"

Win nodded. "Yes, that is my job — to provide what she needs. I really try hard to satisfy her."

"I'll bet that you do," Dalgrun moved closer. She ran a finger over Win's forearm. "You have such nice arms," she said as she rubbed his biceps. Her hand moved to his shoulder and caressed the short hairs on the back of his neck. "Do you like me, Win?"

Win shifted uncomfortably in his seat, wishing that the Palm would remove her hand, but unwilling to offend her.

"You are Larisha's friend," he replied.

"Larisha's good friend. Probably her best friend in the entire ship, after you."

"I'm just her helper, not her friend," Win protested, recalling Larisha's warning about admitting to any relationship outside of work.

Dalgrun laughed, but did not remove her hand.

"Oh, I think you are more than just a helper, Win. Tell me, does she have you service her on occasion? Do you do a good job for her?" The Palm's hand was now fumbling with the fastenings of his tunic.

What does she suspect? Win thought furiously. Had he said something to give rise to the Palm's suspicions. Oh God, what if he had? Would he be killed and Larisha shamed? What had he done to make the Palm think that there was something going on? What could he have done to betray them?

"I don't know what you mean," He tried to keep his voice as steady as possible as Dalgrun fumbled the fastenings loose.

Dalgrun laughed. "Oh, come now. You can't really expect me to believe that Larisha has something like you around at night and isn't tempted. I might be slow, but I'm no fool. You do sleep with her, don't you?"

Win shook his head violently from side to side. "No. No!" What was he to do? How could he protect Larisha?

Dalgrun was running her hand up and down his back, pushing his shirt down with each repetition until it fell around his waist. She tilted her head to one side and looked admiringly at his chest. "Don't get me wrong, Win. I can certainly understand the temptation you offer. God, but you are gorgeous."

"I . . . I have to go," Win tried to push himself back from the table. He had to get away before she made him reveal something about Larisha.

"Don't be silly. I need you to go over some reports with me. They're in my room. Come along now. I have a job for you."

Win debated fleeing or doing as she instructed. Would there be some opportunity to save himself and Larisha if he fled, or would it be a better idea were he to stay and allay her suspicions? He decided to do as she asked.

As soon as he entered Dalgrun's, room she pushed him onto the bed and began to remove her robe. "Get undressed," she demanded. "I want you to service me."

Win was so shocked that he couldn't move. "You are the Palm of the Hand of God," he said incredulously. "You cannot want me to do this!" *It must be a test. She is testing me to see if I have the strength of will to resist.*

"Don't be stupid. I can do anything I want. Nobody can question the Palm." By this time she'd removed all of her clothing. She leaned over him and reached down to pull off his pants. "Come on, help me, damn it!"

"But, but . . ." Win continued to protest. He couldn't believe what was happening. "I can't do this. It isn't proper. It is a sin!"

Dalgrun laughed. "Don't take me for a fool, you filthy boy. Listen, if you don't do as I tell you, I will accuse Larisha and you of what you most certainly have been doing down here when I am not around. You wouldn't want anything to happen to her, would you?"

Win shook his head quickly. "N-no," he said and reached to help her slip the pants over his hips. This was the price of her silence, he realized. The irony of it all dawned on him; to save Larisha from being accused of a sin born of love and compassion he would have to commit one of simple lust.

"Oh my, I can understand why she keeps you around," Dalgrun said breathlessly and pounced astride him. "Now, let me tell you what I want you to do."

As she directed him to give her pleasure Win wondered about the situation and the Palm's lack of concern for this sin. A question that had never occurred to him before rose unbidden in his mind: What were these Men to use him so? Had similar pressures been put on his Amber by Jas Bulgat, forcing her to go against the Hand, deeper and deeper into sin, leading her to her doom?

As Dalgrun approached her climax under Win's mechanical ministrations, he wondered why Dalgrun would go unpunished when innocent Amber had been killed. Was it a typical Man's action, no different from using Folk to do all of the ship's unpleasant or dangerous tasks? What were these Men to use their Folk so?

Dalgrun groaned and arched her back, pulling him more deeply into her as she clawed at his hips. The pain of her nails biting into his flesh sent him unbidden into eruption, a ripping wave of relief that was sensation without content, a loveless contribution on his part.

"You are very, very good," Dalgrun complimented him afterwards. The sheen of sweat glistened on her bare body. "Now, just lie still and hold me for a while until I calm down."

He did as she asked. As they lay there, side by side, he realized that he would be called upon to do this again and again. He would be called on to 'service' her and Larisha. That was his job, his function. The rest of his work was merely cover to hide his real purpose. How could he have not understood, how could he not have known?

Beside him, Dalgrun sighed and patted his leg. "You are a very good boy, Win. Very good."

"You are driving everyone too hard with this insane schedule of yours, Tam" Larisha complained. "You should give everyone a breather, give them a chance to relax a bit. Work on the habitat is progressing much faster than anyone ever expected. According to my estimates it will be completely ready for occupation within two months."

"We could have done it sooner if you were a bit more coöperative instead of criticizing me," Tam bit back. "It's your foot-dragging, your initial reluctance to support the habitat option that delayed things."

"Maybe it was your draconian discipline of the Folk that made the work go slower," she replied with malice evident in her voice. "The crew is so preoccupied, with those two executions and your hideous sentence on Jas, that they aren't doing their best. You should have shown a little more compassion."

"I have an objective to achieve, and damn little time to waste worrying about other people's feelings," he said bitterly. "If you have something constructive to contribute, I will listen. If you don't, then stay out of my way. I am not going to accept any more delays or excuses from you. I want that habitat worked on as fast as the crew can move, faster if possible."

"Very well, Hadir Tam Polat," Larisha hesitated only long enough on his formal title to irritate him; but, when he did not remark on her tone, she continued. "We've got most of the greenhouse organized, the hull is holding a decent atmospheric pressure, and we've collected plenty of ice for water. Given that living conditions would be pretty rough for a while, the habitat could be occupied in its present state. But you already know that from my reports."

Tam studied his schedules for a moment more. "What if we moved the mongrels and most of the Halfings over there immediately? Couldn't we finish the habitat faster if the

Halfings and their helpers didn't waste time flitting back and forth?"

Larisha paused. "Yes, I suppose that would create some efficiencies. But the living quarters over there are minimal — bare decks and no walls as yet. It's pretty grim."

"They can do without creature comforts. Surely you haven't forgotten the conditions we lived in for the first six months after we were de-iced." She grimaced; she had not. "Now, I repeat; can you assure me that the habitat can support all those Halfings and mongrels? That's all I need to know."

"I could make the arrangements to move as many over there as the systems will support, but it's so unnecessary," she protested. "Most of them should stay here, in the ship."

Tam scowled. "Are you saying that you won't support my orders? My Men can do most of the ship's tasks. Just because they're Men doesn't mean they can't do the hard work as well as your Halfings. Now, are you going to do as I requested or not?"

"I will give the orders," Larisha said reluctantly. "Do you want me to accompany them?"

For the briefest of instants, Tam appeared to soften. "No — no sense for you to go over there, as yet. I'm sure that you can oversee matters from this end. Once we get the habitat finished and have an alternative base for the settlers, we can start planning our assault on Meridian. I'd like to send the first group down to the surface within the year."

Larisha stared in astonishment. "You finally think we should explore Meridian? Well, it's about time! I thought you were going to keep us out here, screwing around with Thetti and the habitat, forever."

"It was never my plan to ignore Meridian. That is the long term objective of our mission, after all. I simply didn't think it prudent to explore the planet immediately. Best, I thought, to have a back-up station prepared."

"So you'll lead the group on Meridian while I manage the habitat. Is that your plan?"

"No, your place is on Meridian. Your knowledge of farming and estate management will help the work go faster there. They need you, an experienced leader."

"So who will command the habitat? I hardly think that you can manage both."

Tam laughed. "Don't be ridiculous. I'll put Dalgrun Wofat on the habitat as its leader. She's very qualified and that will get her out of our way." He observed the puzzled look on her face. "To answer your obvious question; I intend to continue examining whatever is going on here at Thetti. I am still not satisfied that these objects aren't a threat."

"So you persist in this idiocy," Larisha fired back. "This search for something that has nothing to do with us! Why are you doing this? Whatever is driving you, Tam?"

"Call it curiosity."

"You are insane," she said in parting.

"Is this wise?" Larisha asked when Dalgrun proposed that they share her quarters. "With all of the Halfings moving to the habitat, there'll be plenty of room. What excuse could you have for doubling up with me? Consider, what will people think of your objectivity if you as the Palm and I as the Raggi are living together?"

Dalgrun waved to encompass the ship around them. "There are a number of people who are starting to question your relationship with the boy you keep here. If I move in with you, it will allay those nasty rumors. 'What could Larisha be doing while the Hand of God's Palm is present?' they will ask themselves. Obviously, the answer is that nothing untoward can possibly occur. Trust me, moving in with you is for your own good. You are too valuable as Raggi to be burdened by ugly rumors."

"Rumors?" Larisha repeated. She had been so careful to say nothing of the way she felt about Win in public that she could not imagine rumors circulating. She was certain that Win hadn't revealed anything either — he was too intelligent to risk his own life by talking about what they did in private. She had warned him many times that to do so was certain death.

"There is nothing going on between Win and myself," she protested hotly. "Why, I am shocked — shocked — that anyone could question my behavior, that anyone would doubt my morals. I would have thought that my position, my behavior would be above reproach." She hoped that she had injected the right note of indignation and anger into her voice.

Dalgrun smirked and prodded her shoulder. "Oh come off of it, my dear. We both know what how you've been using Win and, I must admit, I don't blame you at all. I am sure that he's a very warm comfort on this chill ship."

Larisha was shocked to her core. For a moment, she wondered if she had heard the Palm correctly. Had Dalgrun actually stated that she was aware of her nocturnal activities? That, in itself, was revealing enough, but to hear the implication that she approved was beyond belief.

"Pardon me, what did you say?" she gasped.

Dalgrun's smile grew. "You heard me right, my dear. I said he's very good in bed. That's why I want to move in here, better to share him with you. I'm a little tired of making excuses to be here when you aren't around."

"You've been having sex with Win," Larisha choked out woodenly. Had she been so blind that she hadn't suspected that other women might be as attracted to Win as she had been? But she would never in her wildest imagination have thought that the Palm of the Hand of God herself harbored such thoughts. This was incredible, impossible. It was beyond belief!

Then a suspicion dawned. Perhaps the Palm's statements were a trap. Maybe this admission was something the Palm had devised to trick her into an outright confession. Were she to confirm what Dalgrun accused her of doing, it would doom both Win and her.

Instead of admitting it, Larisha touched on the other side of the equation. "You've been sleeping with Win."

"Of course I have," Dalgrun laughed out loud. "Did you think that you could keep a boy that sweet all to yourself? Don't be silly."

Larisha felt her face redden.

"Now, let's take care of the details," Dalgrun continued matter-of-factly. "I'll have my things brought down here. We'll convert the office space to my bedroom. I'll have Win start on that right away and, while he is doing that, perhaps we could discuss a schedule." She smiled again. Larisha thought it was a wicked, crooked smile that turned Dalgrun's pleasant face into something obscene and horrid.

"Schedule," she repeated. She was beyond shock, beyond any further surprise. "You want us to schedule our sinning?"

"Shush. Don't give me any of those silly children's sermons about sins of the flesh. We're both adults here, Larisha, capable of keeping things within bounds. You know as well as I that both of us have to consider our positions. We are responsible for the lives and souls of those embarked on this journey. We cannot allow ourselves to form close friendships within the other Men, to open ourselves to those we command. No, we must stand above them, apart from them — object lessons as those dedicated to serving the greater glory of the Hand of God! No, my dear, we cannot afford affairs, not when we might have to send our lovers off on some risky venture. Don't you agree?"

Larisha nodded, not knowing what else to say. She was still numbed by the revelations of the last few moments.

The Palm continued. "Consider: Don't we deserve some respite, some degree of comfort? After all, we are women with ordinary appetites, wouldn't you say? Using Win this way is quite logical, particularly when we can handle the situation so neatly. Besides, this sort of thing will probably keep Win docile while it provides the both of us with relief."

"But it is a sin!" Larisha protested vehemently, ashamed that she should even be listening to these horrible words spilling from the Palm's mouth. "It is a sin for humans to lay with their Folk."

Even as she protested what Dalgrun suggested, her mind was already considering it, rationally weighing the pros and cons of such an bizarre arrangement. Were Dalgrun to live here, the small voice of her emotional side seemed to be saying, suspicion would be averted for certain. Even better, that lack of criticism would give her much more freedom with Win than she would otherwise have.

The voice of reason, the tiny cry that she was complicit in admitting her sins, faded away until it could scarcely be heard at all.

At the same time, her rational mind calculated, she didn't like the idea of sharing Win with another woman, not even the holy Palm of God herself. What sort of relationship would that be, the three of them sharing a bed, albeit at different times?

Wait a moment. Hadn't Dalgrun said that the two of them were doing it already? That meant that Win had been deceiving her for weeks and weeks, maybe even months!

Sharing him with the Palm was therefore, her logical mind continued triumphantly, simply ratifying what was already a bitter fact. Perhaps the arrangements she suggested wouldn't be so bad after all.

"Sin is merely a matter of definition," Dalgrun said, as if delivering a sermon to some docile Halfings. "A sin violates the social order when it is observed by society and acknowledged as being against the common good. If we accept this definition then, so long as no one is aware of the act, there can be no sin — no act against the social fabric has been done. Besides," she added with a broad wink, "Am I not the interpreter of the Word of God and the divine

Revelation for the Hand? Therefore, if I declare that this is no sin, who will dispute me? I bless you, my dear. You are free of sin."

She waved a benediction in Larisha's direction.

"There, you see, we are quite within the limits of my authority. Now, come along, Larisha, and help me decide on how we shall arrange my things." She put her arm across Larisha's shoulder and hugged her. "Trust me, this will work out just fine."

Larisha was at a loss. What else could she do but agree? Win was too innocent to have been the one to start anything, too loving to prey on Dalgrun's charity. It must have been something that Dalgrun Wofat had initiated. Larisha was determined to find out what the Palm could have used to force Win into this.

ELEVEN

Win never knew when one of the two Men would come to him, rouse him from sleep, rouse him in other ways with practiced moves and warm, seeking hands and moist lips.

He had no voice in the timing or the choice of when or who came to his bed. The two Men were fully in control over him, holding the power of life and death in their hands.

Win's resentment of their use grew with each nightly session even as, more disturbing still, he found himself enjoying their visits, anticipating their attentions despite his smoldering anger. The two were so different from Amber; neither brought the gentle love or attention to his needs to his bed. Their couplings were uniformly vigorous, dispassionate, and frequently brief. Never once were any of the couplings anything that could be considered loving. He found the comparison between the sexually authoritative Dalgrun and the passive, submissive Larisha interesting. What he learned from the one could be used with great effect on the other.

Occasionally, Win fantasized what it would be like to have both of them with him at once, but said nothing of his imaginings for fear of the reaction it might bring. Still, he sometimes amused himself with the wicked, wicked thought of a passive Dalgrun and an aggressive Larisha, as if his thoughts were paying them both back for the resentment he felt.

Any mention of the nightly visits were taboo, he learned. Neither of the women ever spoke of their play with him afterwards, nor did he ever hear them discuss it between themselves. They behaved as if what each knew was happening were not taking place, denying the fact while participating in the acts. This self-deceit, he thought, appeared to be a very Mannish trait. It was also one he detested.

Would he ever accuse the two of them and bring the approbation of the ship down upon them? He doubted it. No one would place any credence on the word of a Folk over that of the Raggi and the Palm.

And so he continued to do his duty.

"I can't believe it!" Larisha threw her papers across the room as soon as the call was finished. "Tam found another of those damned things and is having it brought up here. Didn't the fool learn his lesson the first time? Why is he endangering the ship?"

"As he has said on numerous occasions, he wishes to discover if it represents a threat to our mining operations," Dalgrun reminded her. "He is within his authority to do this."

Win's ears perked up. They were talking about finding some more of the crystal balloons, and Larisha sounded as if they were some sort of threat. Perhaps these Men were not so all-knowing as they acted. He busied himself with some papers as he tried to learn more.

"He won't listen," Larisha said. "You heard what he said. Damn, you'd think that explosion was my fault! Wasn't he the one who brought it here? How could he blame it on me?"

Dalgrun ignored the rhetorical question. "There is risk, as I cautioned. Perhaps I should remind the Hadir of the very real possibility that I might find this at odds with the objectives of the Hand."

"No chance. Once Tam makes his mind up, nothing you say will change it. But you are welcome to try; you might enjoy his reasoning. He has a way of rationalizing everything he does."

"Then I will not bother to argue," Dalgrun said quietly. "I will simply insist that he perform his examination with great care and in a way that doesn't put the ship at risk."

"And if your gentle persuasion fails, will you help me remove him from command?" Larisha asked. "We cannot let his insane behavior damage our mission. We cannot let him continue to subvert the directions we must follow."

"We will bide our time and see what happens," Dalgrun equivocated. She left it at that.

Win tried to understand what they were planning, but couldn't quite grasp it.

"Damn the woman," Tam cursed to himself as he watched the shuttles position the second object they had brought up from the depths into place midway between the habitat and the ship. How dare the Palm question his judgement. Couldn't she see how much the objects needed to be examined, how much they needed to be understood? Or maybe his facile explanations of that were as transparent to her as they had apparently been to Larisha. Was he such a fool that women could see through his lies, or was that simply his doubting nature making him suspect as much?

He was certain that Larisha had expressed her suspicions to the Palm. It would be hard for her to resist doing so, living as they were and probably sharing confidences. He was just as certain that the Palm had been given every little detail about their brief relationship. No doubt it would have been a very biased depiction: Larisha's own self-protective interpretation, warped by a bitter memory and lasting enmity.

Well, no matter. He shrugged the thoughts away. Any attempt by him to set the story straight about the breakup would be interpreted as an excuse, an apology for whatever actions Larisha had lied about.

It was curious that the Palm had moved in with Larisha. At first he'd thought it a good idea, a way of putting to rest those nasty, whispered rumors about that mongrel she kept in her quarters. After the affair with that pervert, Jas, everyone was sensitive about relationships with the lower orders. But he expected that Larisha, as well as the Men in general, would naturally be above suspicion — there were some things a Man just would not do!

Still, he knew how needy Larisha could be; and, as far as he could discover, she'd no affairs since arriving. No! He shook his head to empty it of the most wicked of thoughts. Now he was being as filthy in his thoughts as the ones he despised. Was it his imagination's way of striking back by imagining Larisha engaged in bestiality? These hideous, dirty, filthy thoughts had no place in his mind. He took a deep breath and tried to cleanse his thoughts and erase the evil suspicion. There could be nothing going on with the boy, he repeated. Why, he finally added, with a amusement, if there were then the Palm herself would have to know about it as well.

And that was simply ridiculous.

There was a flurry of activity as the shuttles arranged themselves behind the object and fired their engines. Billows of evaporating steam formed into icy frost and the sublimated immediately into component molecules in the vacuum. Tam grew alarmed as they found it hard to stop the object's rotation.

From this angle the object appeared even more regular in shape than the other one they had captured. He had expected this one to look more crystalline, with more evidence of that than its vaguely crystal-like, rhombic regularity. If its shape had arisen naturally, he mused as he recalled Dalgrun's words, wouldn't it have a more organic appearance? Wouldn't it be more flexible, more like a bird or insect — a creature molded by its airy habitat?

On the other hand, this might indeed be an artifact, a machine, a made object. Although it lacked the appearance of a living creature, neither did it have the characteristics of a machine. He could see no machined parts, no pieces independent of the body, nothing one could clearly point at and say "This was made by alien hands." No: it looked like something one dug out of the ground, deposited on some cave floor, or precipitated from solution.

Now there was a thought. Suppose there had been an alien technology based on chemical processes. Suppose these machines were built from layers of different materials.

Excitement seized him. Deep in the atmosphere of Thetti the pressures and temperatures could be such that the fire-based technologies that seemed so natural to humankind would be impossible. He stared at the ruddy, opaque atmosphere of Thetti, and tried to imagine a civilization in its depths, of a society of creatures so unlike humans as to be unrecognizable. That civilization would be inferior to his own, of course. After all, hadn't God given Men dominion over all the universe?

Still, the image of that crystal ship flying through space to greet them haunted him. Wouldn't it imply that these creatures had been touched by God as well if they had achieved space flight?

Careful, he cautioned himself. Such thoughts came close to blasphemy, as the Palm had sternly reminded him earlier. *I am tired, and the mind sometimes wanders into strange pathways from fatigue. None of this: Larisha, aliens, Dalgrun, God, would have occurred to me if I had been rested and in a proper state of mind.* He quickly said a prayer to the Emerging God for forgiveness.

With one last look at the crew's delicate maneuvering of the object, he turned and headed to bed for some much-needed sleep. Tomorrow Gull Tamat and his team would tell him what they had discovered. He needed to be well-rested to deal with that, and to make some decisions based on their findings. Sleep came surprisingly swiftly, hardly allowing him to dwell on any of the matters that had so troubled him earlier.

"This appears to be a solid object," Gull Tamat said confidently. "Further, it appears to have lost its ability to maneuver once out of the atmosphere. It is also considerably more massive than the other. We had to add two more scoops to move it up to orbit."

"Massive?" Tam queried with a glance out the port. "It doesn't look that much larger."

Gull Tamat smiled. "Excuse me, I used the term in its

strictest sense. This object is quite dense, far too dense to float in Thetti's atmosphere, I should add. I cannot determine how this is accomplished, but I am certain it is only a matter of time before we find this out.

"It also has an interesting internal structure," Gull Tamat continued. "There are regions of denser materials within it. We've done some probing and found that these pockets are discretely separated pockets of specific materials."

Tam recalled his earlier thoughts about chemical technologies and shivered. "How could that happen?"

Gull leaned forward. "A most interesting question. There are pores along the edges of the object — near those things that look like spears. These pores are specifically sized to permit the passage of certain molecules. In my opinion this is nothing more than a huge filtering machine. It separates the heavier elements into the fore-pockets and the lighter ones further aft."

Tam started at Gull's use of the term 'machine' but then realized with relief that Gull must be using the term in its generic sense. He wasn't actually declaring this to be an artifact. "So this object is nothing more than a huge vacuum cleaner?"

Gull Tamat jumped up and began to pace the room. "At first that's what I thought. But then I wondered how, with so much mass, could it provide enough lift to keep itself aloft. It has no wings and certainly is anything but aerodynamic. Neither is there a mountain high enough for it to glide from."

The scientists's momentary pause gave Tam time to reflect on what he had just learned. The implication that this was indeed an alien creature from Thetti was interesting, not to mention being a great relief. It showed how being tired had fueled his overactive imagination. He was chagrined that he should have had such wild imaginings the previous night and grinned at his own foolishness.

Gull looked up "Did I say something amusing, Hadir?"

When Tam shook his head. Gull continued: "I must admit that I cannot answer that question. We still don't understand how these objects propel themselves, but I have my team working to find out. Give us a few days."

"Was there something else?" Tam asked. "Something I should know."

Gull Tamat paused, then said, "There is something that puzzles me. As I said earlier, we are drilling a sample bore through the object to analyze the composition of the various pockets. As we do so we're running a continuous spectrographic analysis at the drill site. Thus far, this shows us that the outer layers are mostly carbon — a compressed diamond coating that seems to absorb most of the radio spectrum. That is why we had such difficulty finding these objects with radar."

"Where would it get so much carbon?" Tam asked. "And how would it build a layer that dense?"

"We've discovered that every layer of the object contains the same percentage of iridium. Not a huge amount, but more than is present in the atmosphere of Thetti. We are wondering where the object could have acquired this."

"Meteors, perhaps comets. Or there might be an abundance of iridium down on the surface of Thetti where the thing originated. Likely the same place it got the carbon."

Polat looked doubtful. "That would not explain the amounts we've found. It appears that the element is distributed evenly throughout the object. No, iridium is very heavily present wherever this thing arose."

A cold chill ran down Tam's backbone. "What," he asked in a voice drained of emotion, "are you saying?"

"I do not think these objects are native to Thetti," Gull Tamat replied as he stared directly into Tam's eyes. "It is my belief that they must come from elsewhere. Possibly the cometary belt around this system."

The scientist's words struck Tam like a lightning bolt. "Say nothing of this to the rest of the crew," he said harshly. "Put as many people as you can on studying this object;

and, damn it, be careful. I don't want another accident."

Gull Tamat smiled. "My people are quite intelligent, Hadir. We won't use torches on something we know nothing about! We're being very careful to avoid the gas pockets."

"I want a complete run-down on everything you discover," Tam ordered. "Two days! Get whatever you can and brief me again in two days."

It was only after Gull Tamat had left that Tam allowed himself to feel fear. A cold, penetrating shaft of panic seemed to grow with each passing moment. That object he had seen when he had awakened had been no hallucination.

It was not his own God that he had seen.

The briefing room was filled with the members of Gull's science team. Gull sat at the foot of the long table while Tam sat at the head.

"You are certain of your findings, then," Tam said hollowly. For the past four hours he had the science team go over every finding, every detail, every test they had performed on the object. He'd forced them to analyze every aspect of their work over and over, probing for some systemic error that might suggest a different result, a different interpretation, a different conclusion than the one he most feared.

But none of their findings could be denied, nothing of what he suspected could be refuted. Gull Tamat had been quite thorough, leaving nothing to chance, no avenue unexplored. With centuries of scientific knowledge behind his analyses, no one could dispute the facts.

"Your conclusions are that these are created objects," Tam said at the end of the discussion. "You are certain that they are not naturally occurring, nor are they living creatures, and certainly not the result of any conceivable geologic processes."

"None of those possibilities exist," Gull Tamat replied.

"After a detailed examination of the structures within these machines — Yes, Hadir, I said machines, although how they were constructed is beyond us. Perhaps we can discover that after we take them apart, layer by layer. Oh, don't worry," he added, "we will be very cautious. There will be no explosions."

"What could have created them?" Tam's voice cracked despite his attempt to hold it steady. "Could their creators be in the cometary belt?"

Gull Tamat cleared his throat. "I seriously doubt that, Hadir Tam Polat. A better question might be, *when* they were created."

At Tam's raised eyebrow he continued. "Based on the emission studies we've done, we have decided that these objects are incredibly ancient — on the order of millions and millions of years, possibly dating as far back to the formation of Thetti itself. It is highly unlikely that their creators could still exist after all this time. If they had, wouldn't we see the evidence of their civilization all around us?" He smiled at the agreeing nods of the rest of his team. "No, I think that we can confidently conclude that whoever built these machines is long gone, forgotten by all but God."

"I pray that you are correct," Tam replied dryly. He wished that he shared the scientist's confidence. "However, my concern is not with your conclusions, but with practical results of such an announcement to the crew. I am considering whom we should tell, whom we can warn that other technologically advanced races exist in the universe. I am considering sending word back to Heaven."

"But the creators of these objects must be dead," Gull said emphatically. "I doubt that God would allow any rivals to Man. How can the Emerging God be created if there exists a race greater than ours?"

"It is not that I doubt Man's dominion," Tam said cautiously. Who would have expected that the head of the science team would be so religious that he was blinded to the possibilities of a rival? "It is just that certain members of our crew, and certainly any settlers, need to know that something potentially dangerous might be out there. Who knows what else these 'long-dead' aliens might have left behind?"

Gull Tamat made a tent of his fingers. "I will instruct my team to remain quiet if that is what you wish. We have no wish to disturb the crew unnecessarily."

"And I will speak to the Palm about this," Tam promised. "Perhaps she can give us the necessary religious guidance to deal with this issue. I am not unaware of the chaos such an announcement would cause both here and on Heaven." He smiled as he considered what effect this evidence would have on the rigid Palm. Perhaps she would not be so powerful once she was humbled.

"An excellent idea, Hadir," Gull Tamat agreed. "Meanwhile we will continue to explore this fascinating artifact."

Something awoke Tam around mid-watch. He sat straight up in his bed, jolted awake by what he imagined was a very human scream. Now that he was awake he realized that the fading scream was the dregs of a dream, a phantom of something buried too deep within the confines of his mind to recall. He got out of bed to check the status of the ship. What had triggered this sudden nervousness he was feeling?

There were no reported problems within the ship. All systems were fine, and the habitat reported the same. As he was turning away the link called. It was Gull Tamat. He looked haggard, his eyes were pools of pain. "We've had a little problem," he gasped. "Something is happening to the object, I'm not sure what."

"What did you do?" Tam demanded. "What do you mean — something happening?"

Gull Tamat screwed his face tight. "We were drilling to examine a mass near the core of the object, trying to extract a sample for testing. It looks as if it is more dense than the other parts. There's a line of such masses along one of the object's axes.

"As soon as the bit touched the mass the whole object started oscillating — very low frequency — and heating a few degrees above ambient. I don't know what is going on, but it appears that the entire object is consuming itself from the inside at a rapid rate. We are observing a rapid loss of mass."

"Where is all that mass going then?" Tam demanded. "A little heat and some shaking shouldn't consume that much energy."

"I know, I know," Gull Tamat responded. "All mass, all energy is going somewhere. It is definitely doing something we don't understand. Listen, I'm getting everyone away. Three of us will try to move the object further away from the ship."

"Just strap a shuttle on it and get the hell out of there yourself!" Tam ordered. "This is no time for heroics. You're too important for that."

"There, that's the last load," Gull reported as the last of his crew left the object. "All right, we're firing the engines now to move the object. We'll need to guide it to make certain that it moves away from the ship and the habitat."

He paused for several minutes. "That's strange; we're accelerating far more rapidly than we should. The object must be losing mass at an increasing rate, but there isn't any change in heat emission. Strange — it's absolutely quiet in the radio frequencies as well. I wonder where all of that energy is going?"

"Figure that out later," Tam fought to keep his voice calm. "Just get the hell away from it!"

"I believe that the object's mass is decreasing at a geometric rate, Hadir. But I can't see wha—" The transmission cut off abruptly.

Tam raced to the nearest port and looked out. From this angle he saw a bright flare illuminate the face of the habitat. "No!" Tam screamed, but the pinpoint of light grew before his eyes as the ship rotated to bring it into view. It was clear that the shuttles had been consumed by an intense burst of energy from the object.

What had been the purpose of that incredible expenditure of mass and energy, Tam wondered as he quickly threw on some clothing and raced for the command module. Had Gull Tamat's team accidentally tripped some protective measure?

Or, he thought with a feeling of dread, thinking of the other ship he had seen disappearing into the stars, had the object sent out a cry for help with that blast of energy?

"I warned you about bringing another one of those damned, dangerous balloons up here!" she reminded him viciously as Tam and Larisha reached the command pod. He ignored her biting comment as he began checking the status of the ship. Larisha was doing the same for the habitat. Hardly anyone not looking in the direction of the blast had noticed anything amiss. There had been no damage to either ship or habitat.

"We could have lost everything," Larisha continued chiding him as the last of the status reports rolled in. "Damn it, Tam, why do you persist? Leave Thetti for the settlers to deal with and concentrate on getting us down on Meridian. It isn't our mission to solve this system's scientific mysteries."

But Tam paid her no mind. He was busy monitoring the ships that were rushing into the area to see if there were any survivors. With Gull gone, he would be lost. The scientist had been his most faithful Outrider since the Meridian project began.

"Hadir, we've spotted something. I think it's the hull of a shuttle. Damn, it's pretty scorched. Can't see any holes in it, though. There might be somebody left alive inside."

"Bring them in," Tam ordered at once. He dispatched a medical team to the docks for any survivors who might be on board as he prayed to the Emerging God that there were survivors. Gull Tamat was too valuable to lose.

"We must warn Heaven and the settlers about these things," Tam replied. "They must know that there are dangers in this system."

"What dangers?" Larisha bit out sarcastically. "The only threats I've noticed are those caused by your idiotic pursuit of these balloons! How could these atmospheric creatures be a danger to us on Meridian? Leave them alone and proceed with our mission, as you were supposed to do, if you will recall," she added unnecessarily.

"Two survivors on board," the medical team announced after the rescue ship had recovered the damaged shuttle on board. "They're pretty badly burned, both in shock — may indicate internal injuries. We'll report after we've done a full work-up."

Tam settled back with a sigh of relief. They'd lost no one. Sometimes God smiled on him. Now what was it Larisha was prattling on about? Oh yes, he recalled now.

"They aren't balloons," he answered her. "And they are not creatures that grew somewhere down on Thetti." He spoke slowly, so she would not miss a word. "Gull Tamat suspects that they're artificial." He paused to let that fact sink in. "Larisha, those things are artifacts. They are alien machines!"

"Aliens who can create balloons?" Larisha scoffed. "What a frightening thought," she added dryly. "All right, but even if Gull Tamat's foolish theories are correct, where are these aliens? If they are so intelligent they can build balloons then where the hell are they — down on Thetti where we'll never be able to see them?"

"Gull said that the machines are probably far older than we can imagine — millions and millions of years is his first guess," Tam said, trying to stay calm, trying to simply give her the essence of the frightening concept, and hoping that she would finally begin to understand why he was so concerned.

But Larisha wasn't coöperating. It was obvious from the

expression on her face that she didn't believe a word he'd said. "I suspect that everyone, even Gull, has been heavily influenced by you. I wouldn't doubt that you befuddled their thinking, working so close to it." She laughed mirthlessly, "Aliens, indeed!"

Tam bit his lip and tried to contain the rising anger in his breast. Experience had shown him that giving in to anger was no way to deal with Bul Larisha. Quite the opposite, in fact. "I can show you Gull Tamat's solid evidence. His team all agree that these objects are sophisticated machines; machines that we could not construct with our technology. By God, Larisha, they were able to build machines that fly without using the wind or any method of propulsion that we recognize — doesn't that frighten you?"

"I hope that you aren't saying that there are aliens who have technology superior to Man's, Tam. That . . . that comes very close to heresy." Larisha bit her lip. "If I were you, I wouldn't declare that there are creatures superior to humans in the universe without thinking long and hard on it. Maybe you should have a long talk with Dalgrun before you spread this insane idea. I am certain that she will remind you of the Revelation and the covenant our ancestors received directly from God. We are the people of the Emerging God. It is we who will rule the universe. It is to us that God has given dominion over all lesser creatures of his creation."

Tam was taken aback. When had Larisha become such a rabid believer? For years she had scoffed at his fundamentalism, at his rigid prejudice against the mongrels, against anything less than human. Had she been that influenced by living with the Palm? Perhaps listening to her lectures every evening was starting to have an effect.

"I need no guidance on the mission, nor a reminder of my own humanity," he replied harshly. "But the facts are not in doubt; these are machines. And they were placed on Thetti by aliens for reasons that we have yet to determine."

"You said millions of years ago," Larisha reminded

him. "Doesn't that mean that these theoretical aliens of yours are probably long dead and gone? Whatever reasons they might have had for putting these balloons here are completely irrelevant any more. Forget them, Tam. It isn't our concern. We have a mission to accomplish."

Tam snorted and began to pace. "Gull Tamat suggested the same thing, that whoever, whatever created these machines was no longer a threat, that they were buried somewhere in the ancient past.

"But that isn't what worries me," he went on. "My concern is that we interfered with it. Not only that, but we made this one destroy itself. From all indications it consumed a lot of energy, more than would have been required for a simple explosion. I am worried that it might have used some of that excess to send out a cry for help. I am afraid that there might be something coming to investigate."

"You are insane!" Larisha screamed, backing away from him. "Aliens, machines; this isn't something new, is it? This is something that's been eating at you these past months, isn't it? Now, you are acting as if these mythical dead aliens, these so-called machines, are real instead of a shaky theory based on limited facts gathered by Gull Tamat, who is conveniently unconscious and cannot support or deny your statements!"

Tam slammed his hand on the console. "I told you, the facts are not in doubt. How can you say that this is theory — you must have seen that blast when the machine destroyed itself. Gull could tell you how much mass it was consuming before it finally exploded. He insisted that it had to be doing that for some purpose. I can't believe that you'd deny that."

Larisha made a move toward the hatch, but hesitated. "What is it about Thetti that holds you so, Tam? You've risked our mission, our ship, our very lives in this determination of yours to examine everything about the planet. If the objects that you had brought here had exploded closer to either the ship or the habitat they could have destroyed everything we've built. There was no need for that. You could have left things alone. You could have ignored these damned balloons and concentrated on getting Meridian ready for the settlers. What is it that drives you? What is it that you aren't telling me?"

Tam could not stand her accusing stare. It was the same look she always used to make him feel guilty over some minor oversight, some forgotten anniversary of a half-remembered occasion; like that thing about the bower that had gotten her so upset. He never had understood that.

Now, as then, he could not meet her glance. He turned his head away. "These are alien machines," he muttered, as if repeating it again would make her believe. "There are dangers in this system that we must learn about. There are precautions that we must take."

Larisha softened her voice and stepped toward him. "Oh, Tam, I know that you really do believe everything you're saying. But why do I feel that there is something more? Why do I feel as if you are still lying to me?"

Tam backed away as if she had slapped him. "The possibility of a distress signal from that machine still worries me. We have to stay here and find out the rest of what Thetti has to tell us! Perhaps we can find some clue to what all of this means."

"So, you are still the plotter, the Man with the plan, the Man who knows more than the rest of us," Larisha sneered. "How do you suppose that the explosion would signal some long dead, mythical race? Is that your secret, that you know the lair of these aliens?"

Tam tried to maintain a stone face. She had come so close to the truth that he had to fight not to reveal his thoughts in his expression. "Perhaps they are not so dead," he whispered so softly that she almost missed it.

"You are insane!" Larisha repeated. "Million year-old aliens indeed! You must be absolutely crazy!"

"There are things about this system that we do not understand, even you have to admit that," Tam said reaching out to her once again. "Larisha, I need your support. I need you to help me explain our situation to the crew, to Dalgrun Wofat."

Larisha pulled back to her place near the hatch. "Don't you touch me! I was willing to go along with some of your past foolishness because I thought that you were simply being prudent, but this insane prattling on and on about aliens and machines and distress calls and speaking heresy is too much. I can't help you, Tam. Not the way you want."

Tam hesitated for a moment and then made a decision. Perhaps this time, if he told her the complete truth, she would understand. He prayed that she would hear the honesty in his voice.

"Listen to me, Larisha: I . . . I saw one of the aliens when we arrived — before you all awakened," he said with hesitation, "and — this is hard to believe, I know — it was watching me. I could sense its presence. I could feel its power. Larisha!"

Larisha drew back, obviously horrified.

Tam continued, plowing ahead, seeking some way of reaching her. "Listen, I've been thinking long and hard about this and realize that thing I saw had to be related to these machines we've discovered on Thetti. Gull Tamat is wrong; the aliens who created these machines aren't dead. I believe that they very much alive and aren't that far away."

With a sinking heart, he saw her expression of disbelief intensify. He knew he was losing her trust. He had failed to convince her.

"For the love of God, Larisha, think of the danger: They may already be on the way here!" he pleaded.

Larisha clenched her jaw. Her face had that look of determination that told him that nothing he said would change her mind. Why had he told her of what he had seen? It was a foolish, stupid thing to have done. He reached out, thinking that if he could just take her arms he could somehow shake her until she realized the truth. Larisha's expression turned to one of fear as he moved toward her. She shrank away from his beseeching hands, just as she had in times past.

"Something must have happened when they froze you, Tam," she said gently, her voice pitched to soothe his anger. "You've been acting strangely ever since you were de-iced. It's as if you are fixated on Thetti, and now you tell me that you've had hallucinations. Listen to yourself — you're talking about impossible things; visions that border on heresy or worse."

"It's obvious that you don't believe me," Tam said. "That's why you think that this is all some manifestation of an imbalance, a thing of chemicals and stress, a delusion." She nodded slowly, agreeing with his diagnosis. "Well, you are wrong," he spat. "I know what I've seen. I know what the science team discovered. You cannot deny the facts."

"I don't deny the facts," she shot back. "It's your interpretation that I doubt. If you were in your right mind you wouldn't have given these insane ideas a moment's thought."

She said it so calmly, with so much conviction, that he knew he would never get through to her. He dropped his arms, knowing that he could not hold her, could not touch the inner woman who had shared his life.

He hardened his mind. This had become a dangerous situation. Larisha could use his admission to convince others to move and replace him in the command structure. Were she to tell the Palm of his heresy she could easily create the sort of doubt that would ensure his temporary removal. A period of much needed rest from his responsibilities, they would declare, brought about by the strain of command.

Then they would replace him with Larisha, the second in command. She would not appreciate the situation and would not recognize the dangers they all faced. She would not heed the facts that were so clear to him. Once in command she would stop all of Gull's investigations of Thetti and its surroundings.

He could see her checking the planned mission objectives off as they were accomplished. Once the habitat was finished she would take the ship to Meridian and concentrate on preparing it for settlement. And there everyone would stay, unsuspecting of the alien presence, unknowing of the possible threats the aliens presented. They would be unprepared for the arrival of these things, unprepared to defend themselves! He had to do something to prevent that from happening. But what could he do?

All of this flashed though his mind in a matter of seconds as Larisha left without another speaking another word.

TWELVE

Tam knew that he must act if he was to retain control. Larisha might not act as quickly as she threatened — she'd equivocate for days, as she always had when tough decisions were to be made.

Yes, if his Outriders acted immediately they could, in a few days, have all of Larisha's Halflings and the mongrels moved to the habitat. It took only a few barked instructions, instructions that would not be challenged by his trusted Men.

The remainder of the crew would simply think of the consolidation as a continuation of Larisha's orders to step up the pace of construction. In fact, some of the Halflings were already living on the habitat and putting the final touches on its engines and living quarters. Since the hab could support a larger work force, the movement of workers would not seem unreasonable.

At the same time his Outriders quietly instructed loyal Men to quietly and gradually return to the ship. "They are not to say a word to the others," he cautioned as they crafted seemingly random schedules that would raise no alarms. In a week or less the entire ship would be under his control.

Once the ship was in the hands of his own loyal people, he could safely ignore whatever action Larisha might take to declare him unfit for command. It would be a nervous week, but he could handle that. There were other, time-consuming actions he could take to keep Larisha off-balance and unaware.

Dalgrun worried him. She was a possible enemy, thanks to whatever lies Larisha been feeding her. Perhaps the better part of wisdom, he reasoned, was to convince Dalgrun to move into the habitat. There were ample reasons, the primary one being that she could minister to the Halflings he was shifting to the hab. Yes, there would be a great need for her services. He would bring it up and use that time to speak with her of other matters.

Once he had acted to neutralize Larisha for the immediate future, Tam's thoughts returned to his primary concern. If the alien ship he had seen earlier was the one that would be summoned by the distress call, then it should take at least as long to return as it had been since it left. That gave him a year — maybe a little less, maybe a little more — to prepare for an encounter with the aliens. It would also give him time to prepare measures that would warn the settlers should that not be a friendly encounter.

Neither his faith nor his training — neither God nor the Hand — had prepared him for this eventuality. How foolish they had been — so certain that Man alone held dominion, so absolutely convinced that they were God's favorites. Well, if he was correct about these aliens, then that core belief was about to be tested in the extreme. He could not guess at what that outcome would be. The only certainty was there would be a return of the crystalline ship he had seen earlier, or something far worse.

Tam cast those somber thoughts aside so he could concentrate on convincing the Palm. At this very minute, Larisha was probably telling her everything he had confided. She was no doubt trying to convince the Palm that the Hadir was insane; that Tam Polat was no longer capable of making proper decisions. It was certain that she would embellish his admission, his suppositions, so as to cast them in the worst possible light. She would not miss an opportunity to poison the Palm's mind.

But there was nothing he could do about that, save speak to Dalgrun herself. Perhaps if she heard the facts from his own mouth she would understand that he was not speaking heresy. No, she would agree that he was merely expressing a concern for the safety of them all. Yes, and if he could convince her of that, then she would be a valuable ally. He set up the meeting.

Dalgrun had appeared quite reasonable throughout their little dinner. "I would be very happy to remain on the habitat," she replied after Tam presented the suggestion. "I do feel that I have been neglecting those workers. Perhaps you are right; it would be best for the Halfings, were I to be there."

"Such was my intent," Tam added. "We must pay attention to the spiritual needs of the lesser orders. It is such a comfort to them in these grave times of peril."

Dalgrun raised an eyebrow. "Grave times, Hadir? Is there some danger of which I am not aware? Do you know of something that threatens our mission?"

Tam wondered if Dalgrun was extremely controlled, or if she had not yet heard Larisha's wild accusations. If the latter then he stood a better chance of protecting himself. "Certain information has come to light that indicates that there is some danger to the ship. This danger, I need not add, applies to the en-route settlers."

When she raised a questioning eyebrow, he quickly and concisely explained what Gull Tamat's team had discovered. He carefully introduced as Gull's theory that these might be abandoned, alien artifacts. Finally, after seeing no objections from Dalgrun, he expressed his belief that the disappearance of the object was linked to a signal of some sort.

"So you see," he concluded, "there is a distinct possibility that some protective machine may lurk out in the cometary belt and may, at this moment, be coming to discover what caused the machine destroy itself. Such a reaction is," he tried to appear as sane and reasonable as possible, "a low probability, but one that I must consider. Don't you agree?"

There was a play of emotions on Dalgrun's face that he was uncertain of how to interpret. Was it disbelief, anger, fear, concern, or acceptance?

"I agree, Hadir Tam Polat," she said at last. "The fact that there was some ancient race who had achieved a higher level of technology than humanity's does skirt the bounds of heresy, as you suggest. But, perhaps, God merely created them as a test for us. I agree with Gull Tamat's idea that these creatures, whatever they may have been, are too long gone to threaten us. But even so then there may well be more inimical machines remaining that could trouble us."

"I am glad to hear that you understand." Tam couldn't believe his luck. He'd half expected the Palm to launch into some diatribe about the Revelations, about the Hand, and the Emerging God. But his fears in that regard appeared to have been groundless; Dalgrun was far more intelligent than he suspected. He must have been wrong about her. The Hand had chosen well.

"Best that we do not speak of this to the crew just yet," she cautioned. "I will prepare the way for this in services. Yes, I will prepare them for this news in my homilies. We shall lead them gently into an interpretation that does no violence to their cherished beliefs.

"Now, if you will excuse me, I must make arrangements to move to the habitat. Dear me, there is so much to do, so much to plan. I am glad we had this talk, Hadir. I believe that a frank understanding of positions is essential if we are to retain our control over this enterprise. Don't you agree?"

"Yes," Tam answered with a smile. Yes, and that agreement would give Larisha yet another thing to worry about. It was a benefit he had not expected to come from this little talk.

Tam was observing preparations to move one of the ship's huge drives to the habitat. Once installed, it would propel the habitat into a long orbit that curved around Thetti before skimming and finally circling Meridian. In that orbit it would serve the needs of the settlement group. The habitat's would remain stable for at least a hundred years. By that time the settlers would know for certain whether they needed it as a refuge from some unsuspected danger on Meridian or not. If not, then they could bend its orbit to other uses, perhaps as the vehicle exploit the rest of the system.

"Why did you order everyone over to the habitat without consulting me?" Larisha demanded as she stopped in front of him. "Are you so far gone that you think that I have no voice in how the Halfings are to be used? Damn it, Tam, if you felt that we needed more workers over there you should have talked to me, not the Palm!"

Tam had fully expected his decision about moving the Halfings and Folk to upset Larisha, but he hadn't expected her to be *this* upset. She was probably still wondering about his sanity and that was coloring her thoughts. Yes, he should have consulted her, but she would have probed and asked too many questions. She would have been suspicious of his motives, of his plans.

"We need to finish the habitat as quickly as possible. Listen, Larisha; you've seen the reports. You know how far behind schedule we are. Every worker we put over there means that it will be that much sooner that we'll have the place finished. The Palm agrees that this is a prudent thing to do."

"Yes, you gave her quite a line, didn't you," Larisha answered. "She told me how you managed to make your insane ideas sound so reasonable, so prudent."

"I merely expressed my concerns in terms the Palm understood," Tam answered quietly. "She agrees that all of the Folk should move, including that mongrel assistant you two seem to depend so much upon."

"You mean my personal assistant," Larisha corrected. "I cannot function properly without the boy. What gives her the right to take someone I need so much away?" Larisha's eyes flared with barely suppressed anger.

Why was she so angry, Tam wondered again? It wasn't merely the way he had outflanked her with the Palm, nor was this another manifestation of her suspicions about his sanity. No, he knew her better than that. There was something more, something underneath that he did not understand. "Why are you so concerned about this boy? Are you sleeping with him?" he joked, hoping to wound her pride with the filthy insult and provoke her into revealing whatever was at the root of this anger.

"You filthy-minded bastard!" Larisha said quickly. "There is nothing wrong with me having him in my quarters. After all, the Palm is living there as well. Were anything untoward happening she would be the first to notice."

Tam was taken aback. There was something about her voice, perhaps the smooth way the excuse flowed out, or the apparent lack of conviction, the lack of righteous fire that should have been ignited by his words. Where was the scorching rebuff the insult should have called forth? Where was her justifiable anger?

The sudden realization that his words, intended only to make her angry, had instead struck a target was devastating. "Is it true?" he gasped with shock and amazement as the cold wave of realization spread through his entire being. He felt the bile rising in his throat as the emotional impact of what she had practically admitted began to sink in. "How could you?" he gasped. "That's filthy! Oh God, tell me it isn't true, Larisha! Please? Tell me that you didn't . . ."

Larisha stared at him in cold fury, but didn't deny it. Instead she gave him a humorless smile. "Sin? I doubt that you know what the real sin is where the Folk are concerned, Tam. You treat them the same way you've treated all of us — with that cold, dispassionate calculating mind of yours. I put up with it for longer than I liked, put up with your lack of empathy, your lack of concern for others, and your lack of human emotions! That is the real sin, Tam — that you are a cold, heartless son of a bitch!"

"This is not about me," Tam yelled back, stepping toward her. "This is about you and that damned mongrel. By God, I'll kill it myself, damn it!" He reached for her.

"You will do no such thing," Larisha replied as she danced away. "I won't let you destroy Win the way you did my love for you! I won't let you. I love him!" Larisha put her hand to her mouth as she finally realized that she had admitted far too much, perhaps even to herself.

"You don't know what you are saying," Tam said in a deadly serious voice. He glanced toward the nearby Half-ings to make certain that they hadn't heard her blasphemous remarks. "You're angry, you aren't in your right mind," he hissed. "Come along. Let's go to my quarters and talk about this more reasonably."

Larisha drew herself up. "My right mind! Who are you to question anyone's sanity? If anyone here is out of their mind, it is you, you, you! At least I know how to love. I know what it means to have someone to warm my bed!"

Tam felt as if he were going to throw up. "Get out of here!" he yelled so loudly that the workers glanced over to see what had disturbed him. "Get away from me!" His fists were tightly balled, as hard as the stone that had just replaced his heart. He took a threatening step forward.

With a cry of fear, Larisha vanished into the dark depths of the ship. Tam stood clenching and unclenching his fists, trying to control himself. There was a mixture of both anger and disgust at Larisha's admission boiling inside of him.

Dalgrun! That was his first thought. He must contact Dalgrun and bring Larisha's shameful admission to her attention. They had been quite close of late. If what she'd said were true then the Palm must have noticed some little slip that Larisha and that damned mongrel might have made.

But if she'd noticed nothing, then Larisha's admission was a deliberate lie intended only to mislead him, to wound him. Could she be that subtle?

No, such a lie just wasn't possible. He knew Larisha's mannerisms far too well not to be able to detect a deliberate falsehood. She'd been truthful in her admission, truthful in her statement that she had committed that most grievous of sins. For a moment he wished that he did have some doubt, wished that he wasn't so certain about this terrible, horrible bestiality of hers. How could his Larisha have stooped so low, had become so perverted as to consort with, with a mongrel — a bloody, by damned animal! The very thought disgusted him.

And constantly within his thoughts, so steady that he could not ignore it, was the immediate question of how he could protect her.

He stopped in wonder at that thought. Protect her? Could he have become so addled that he could even consider that possibility after what she had done, after all the arguments, battles, and hateful words that had passed between them? How could he even considering letting Larisha's admission pass without acting? How could he consider forgiving her? No, this was beyond forgiveness.

He sent for Dalgrun Wofat before he changed his mind.

"So that is my dilemma," he said after reporting what Larisha had said. "I am quite certain that Larisha was telling the truth. But I am just as certain that this is something she wouldn't normally do, not her. I swear, in the name of God, she would not have done this were she in her right mind!" He hoped that he could appeal to the Palm's merciful side. Perhaps, he hoped, Dalgrun would see that the preservation of good order within the crew superseded any temporary transgression on Larisha's part.

"At the same time," he continued when Dalgrun's expression did not change. "I cannot permit her to continue this hideous relationship. It is only a matter of time before someone confirms the terrible rumors and then there will be hell to pay! We must do something to protect the Raggi — to protect the command structure. That is why I am bring this to your attention. I want to see if you could suggest a way to save Larisha from herself."

Dalgrun nodded. "You are quite correct, Hadir Tam Polat. Another incident like the unfortunate Jas would raise too many questions about the ship's leadership. This is a serious matter; one that requires that we handle it with the utmost circumspection."

Tam allowed himself to relax slightly. Apparently the

Palm was going to do as he suggested. She would not directly act against Larisha.

Dalgrun pursed her lips. "At the same time I am not as completely convinced as you that Larisha is actually guilty of this sin. I, myself, have seen no evidence of this since I moved in with her. Still," she continued thoughtfully, "it might be possible. Give me some time, and I will see what I can discover, although I doubt that it will prove to be anything so serious as you say she admitted."

"She was unequivocal." Tam protested when he realized where she was heading with that thought. "She admitted what she had been laying with that . . . that . . . !" He could not repeat her words directly, so openly, to the Palm.

Dalgrun smiled at him. "So you say, Hadir Tam Polat. Do you know that she in turn accuses you of being insane, 'quite unbalanced' were her exact words, if memory serves me correctly." She folded her hands in her lap. "I think this matter has more to do with this on-going feud between you two than it does with the truth. Both of your accusations are clearly too fantastic to be believed."

"But she admitted her sins!" Tam said, frustration evident in his voice. "This is not some idle rumor, not some supposition! God, I would not have brought this matter to you had I not been absolutely certain of her guilt!"

"I promised to keep my eyes open," Dalgrun replied. "But that is all I will do. I would also advise you not to mention this to anyone else. A false accusation of this sort against the Raggi would be even more damaging to morale than your belief in these supposedly intelligent aliens." There was no mirth in the toothy smile that accompanied those words.

Tam was crushed. He had hoped that Dalgrun would confirm or deny what Larisha had said. Perhaps he hoped that something otherwise unnoticed would be revealed when he mentioned it. Instead he discovered that the Palm thought his accusations were merely a weapon in the slow war between Hadir and Raggi, between two separated lovers, between two adversaries fighting for control of the mission. The irony of how Larisha's admission had been turned back on him left a bitter taste in his mouth.

Dalgrun smiled. "Perhaps there is something I could do," she said slowly. "Why don't I take this Worker of hers into my quarters on the habitat? If you are right — and I repeat that I doubt your accusations seriously — then leaving him in the dormitories with the other Folk would be tempting fate as much as leaving him to Larisha's devices. Yes, that is what I shall do. I will keep her little pet with me and watch him very, very carefully." Dalgrun smiled again. "I think this will work out very well for everyone. Thank you for seeking my advice, Hadir. We both have an interest in protecting Larisha, don't we."

"Thank you for your guidance," Tam said hollowly. He didn't return her smile.

"I don't understand why you are taking Win," Larisha protested when she finally had a chance to confront Dalgrun's. "You know how much I need him."

"If you hadn't so much as admitted your debauchery to the Hadir then I wouldn't need to!" Dalgrun shot back angrily as she stalked around the room. Her short steps were beating a furious cadence on the floor as she paced faster and faster, as if trying to walk off her obvious anger.

"It perplexes me as to how someone so brilliant, so highly trained, so intelligent, so human, could be so stupid as to admit what you have been doing to the Hadir! What were you thinking about?"

"Tam can see right through me," Larisha replied hotly. "I didn't have to say anything; he knew how I felt about Win."

Dalgrun spun on her heel. "Damn it, Larisha! Quit lying to me. He said you admitted it."

Larisha jerked back as if struck. "I might have said something in the heat of the moment. Tam's attitude made me so angry that I sometimes lose control." The look on Dalgrun face told Larisha that Dalgrun was not accepting the facile lie. "Yes," she finally admitted, shamefaced, "I did tell Tam. I really wanted to hurt him," she explained. "I wanted to hurt him so badly."

Dalgrun wheeled about. "And that was a damn stupid thing to do! If he wasn't so damn protective about you I'd probably be sitting in judgement of you right now. Instead I guided him to an arrangement that will preserve your position and hide the truth of your relationship with the boy. I am certain that Tam suspects nothing of my own involvement — and I want to keep it that way. If you were to keep Win with you, these rumors would surely gain more strength than before I moved in here. If that happened, doubts about your ability to command would form. I am positive Tam would formally charge you if it came to that, regardless of what I might advise."

Larisha shrugged, as if she was immune to anything that Hadir Tam Polat could do to her. "I'd like to see him try!"

"Keep your head, you fool! Take my advice," Dalgrun advised. "You'd better make plans to move over to the habitat in the near future. If Tam is as unbalanced as you seem to think, there is no telling when he might act on his knowledge of your activities. He might even accuse you, in order to preëmpt any accusations of his own insanity."

"He wouldn't dare!" Larisha was appalled. "An accusation like that would require your backing and that," she smiled wickedly, suddenly realizing that she too held knowledge that could be used as a weapon, "would implicate you. No, we are in this together, dear sister. We both survive Tam's ranting or we both go down. It is your choice."

It was clear from the startled expression on Dalgrun's face she hadn't thought this situation all the way through. Of course, any hint of bestiality would clearly show her complicity, if not direct involvement.

The Palm didn't return Larisha's smile. "I fully understand how we are bound together, my dear. Nevertheless, I still intend to take Win with me. That will remove him from the line of fire and remove any suspicions about you. Look on the bright side, Larisha," she continued as her composure returned. "There will be much more room for the three of us on the habitat. The quarters may be sparse, but we'll have so much room that we won't disturb one another. Think about it: We will be less constrained than we have here, where we live practically in each other's armpits. Once we both move over there, we can be much more at ease." Dalgrun made it all sound so easy, so simple.

"That may not be an option," Larisha explained. "Obviously Tam hasn't confided all of his damnable plans to you. It's just another case of forcing everyone else to dance to his damned tune, you as well as me."

Dalgrun looked puzzled. "What are you talking about?"

"Tam wants me to go to Meridian and take command," Larisha replied. "I was planning on taking Win with me."

Dalgrun considered. "I'm afraid that taking the boy along would be impossible, given the situation we find ourselves in. Still, I envy you," she sighed. "I would give a great deal to have a solid planet under my feet, a sky over my head, and to be able to see sunsets once more."

"Then perhaps we should make arrangements to change rôles," Larisha suggested bitterly. "Perhaps we can arrange for you to go to Meridian instead of me. Would that make you happy?"

"Placing my feet on the solid ground of any planet would make me immensely happy," Dalgrun replied. "But it is my lot that such will probably not happen for quite some time. Until then, I believe that discretion is the better part of wisdom. I will keep Win with me, while you and Tam play out your little games."

She took a few steps away before stopping, turned, and said; "By the way, while I do wish you luck with your battle with the Hadir, be warned that, if it looks as if you might try to drag me down with you, I will deny anything you say.

And just to make things perfectly clear," she added in a voice dripping with malice, "I will insist that the boy be put down immediately. A dead mongrel is no threat to either of us. Is that clear, my dear?"

Larisha was shocked that the Palm would go to such lengths. How could she have misjudged the woman so much? She'd never expected this viciousness from someone in her position. She suddenly realized that Dalgrun had been using her, using Win, using the situation, only to satisfy her own needs. Dalgrun obviously didn't care a whit for the boy; he was just a convenience, a toy to fill her needs. How could she have been so naïve to think of her as a friend, a confidant? "Perfectly," Larisha bit out with resignation. "I understand you perfectly, dear Palm."

"Good. Now run along. I have to let the boy know that I have great need of his services." She chuckled. "Ah yes, a great need, indeed."

In that instant, Larisha realized that she had to rescue Win, no matter what the cost.

Larisha preferred the greenhouse in the early morning hours, when the dew was still heavy on the leaves. It was only during the early hours that she could smell the ripe odor of fresh growth, touch the new shoots emerging from the soil, and taste the freshness of fruit brought to ripeness in the heavy night-cycle air. The moist quiet of the early morning gardens made her feel that she was, for a few precious moments, back in the gardens on her estate.

She also loved the evenings, when she could sit as the light faded. In the evenings, the flowers' heavy perfume attracted the pollinators, the nectar drinkers, for one last time before the darkness closed their petals. Sometimes, as the lights faded into semi-darkness, she would watch until everything had settled into the night-cycle.

This bright, lighted day-cycle was time for her workers to tend the stock, mulch the trees, adjust the feed canisters to nourish the rows of crops, maintain the atmosphere's oxygen/carbon-dioxide balance, and trim the unchecked growth that was always trying to thrust foliage into every open space. She'd no desire to see these minor surgeries performed on her precious plants, no desire to see the heaps of limbs and leaves destined for the rotting, redolent mulch pile where the bower had once been. She felt that such needed amputations, while necessary, were too disturbing.

She saw Win as she walked down the rows. He waved briefly at her, a subtle twist of the wrist and a wink, before turning quickly back to his work crew. Larisha swore. She'd told him time and again not to show any sign of undue familiarity. So far as anyone was to know, he was her obedient helper, nothing more.

Larisha stopped in front of him. "Win. Something has happened. You'll need to move over to the habitat immediately."

Win jumped up. "Has something gone wrong in the hab's greenhouse?" He dropped started to move toward the elevator.

Larisha put a hand out to restrain him. "No, nothing has happened to our greenhouse, Win. The move has to do with some things I have to take care of. Listen," she added, leading him away from any prying ears, "I want you to go to the habitat with Dalgrun. Stay there until I come for you. Is that understood?" Win nodded as if he understood. "This is just a temporary separation. I will come along to get you when we are ready to leave for Meridian."

THIRTEEN

Win was puzzled by Larisha's unexpected announcement. "I have to go with Dalgrun?" The thought of not having Larisha around to temper Dalgrun's actions was upsetting. He'd experienced enough of the woman's rather sophisticated tastes to worry about what might happen once she was beyond Larisha's observation.

"Be cautious where Dalgrun is concerned." Larisha warned. "I am not so sure that she is our friend, despite what she says."

Win couldn't understand why the Raggi hadn't realized this long before. The crude way that the other woman treated him said volumes about the Palm's character. But what could he do? He was just Dalgrun's boy, a pet, a plaything! And, once he was alone with her on the habitat, he would be powerless. Larisha must surely realize his vulnerability. To oppose the Palm was to risk death, or worse. "I understand," he replied softly, hoping that she would hear the fear in his voice, hoping his voice alone would express his misgivings. "You will come for me? Soon?"

"I will come for you," Larisha promised. A few moments later they were alone in the descending elevator. Without warning, Larisha threw her arms around him and pulled him close, her lips rose to meet his as she pressed her body tightly against him.

Memories of Amber came immediately to Win's mind. He recalled the many times he had furtively embraced her in this very elevator, the way his heart had jumped whenever that happened, the joy that sprang from each embrace, from the touch of her lips.

But he experienced none of those feelings as Larisha clung desperately to him. For all Larisha's passion, she was simply a warm body, her lips merely a wet, soft pressure on his own, her tongue a seeking, probing intrusion. He dutifully responded. He knew what she liked.

"That's enough," Larisha finally said, pulled away, and

straightened her clothing. She brushed the front to erase any evidence that they had touched, flicking any bit of dirt that might have come from his clothing from the fabric of her own. That done, she faced the doors and ignored him for the rest of the trip, even though no one else entered the car.

Win had never felt so used.

"Come along now," Dalgrun barked as she ordered Win and a dozen other Folk into the shuttle. Win lifted the heavy pack of the Palm's belongings to his shoulder and followed her. One of the girls carried two small parcels — his pitifully few possessions and her own. The girl was slight, smaller than Amber, but just as fair-haired. Opal, that was her name. Her quick movements were another reminder; the way she glanced at him out of the side of her eyes, those darting hands, so nervous that they moved as if with minds of their own, catching her by surprise when they leaped to her face. She stayed close to Win as they moved forward.

Crew members occupied every seat. One leaped up to make a place for the Palm as soon as she set foot inside the hatch. Dalgrun accepted the offer without so much as a nod of acknowledgement as Win and the Folk moved to the back and leaned against the aft bulkhead. They put their parcels and baggage on the deck between their legs.

In a few moments the shuttle's engines fired. The acceleration pressure on Win's back lasted only for a moment before they were in free flight. He kept one foot on Dalgrun's pack to keep it from floating away as he held onto a holding strap. The other Folk scrambled to secure their own parcels. None of the Men would appreciate their luggage floating about the cabin.

After a stomach-turning ten minutes the shuttle's engines fired again. Win glanced out of the port. They were floating just above the unfinished surface of the habitat. Large portions of the hab's skin still lacked the protective overlay of rock-crete. Two shuttles maneuvered a huge slab of foamy rock-crete into position while space-suited workers swarmed over its surface as they guided it into place.

The shuttle entered a long tunnel, drifted for a moment, then came to an abrupt halt that brought Opal and other Folk tumbling awkwardly to the floor. Some of the seated Men laughed.

The hatch opened, and the habitat's air poured in. The warm breeze carried many strange smells. Ah yes, Win thought as he took another deep breath, the habitat is quite different than the ship.

The Folk waited until all of the Men filed out before lifting their burdens and following. There was a Halfing boss waiting outside of the hatch. As the Folk announced their names, he assigned each to a work party with quick jabs of his finger. The Halfing's face was haggard, with bags under his eyes and frown lines at the corners. The hectic pace of work here was taking its toll. He was about to speak to Win when Dalgrun called.

"Over here," she ordered and pointed at a waiting cart. Win hadn't even noticed it in the confusion of the crowded shuttle bay. The Palm waited for him; and, no sooner than he was aboard with his load, the driver started the cart. They moved off rapidly, barely avoiding people who scattered before them.

Far behind, Win saw Opal waving his small parcel over her head. He had a moment of panic. How would he ever find her in this confusion and regain his possessions? But it was too late to worry about that now. He just had to hope his belongings would catch up to him later. He'd never be able to find his way back, so many were the turns and twists the driver took as they drove deeper and deeper into the huge habitat.

The Palm's new quarters were immense. Win's room alone was nearly the size of Larisha's quarters, or so it seemed. Someone had already placed a bed — a bed, not a bunk — inside. There was even a fold-down desk against one wall, but no chair. He'd have to get one, he thought. With a real desk, he would no longer have to sit on the floor and use his bed as a writing desk. Here, in this huge, well-equipped room, he could be more civilized.

"Rather barren," Dalgrun glanced around at Win's few pieces of furniture. "We'll have to make your room a little more livable, won't we. A larger bed, perhaps would be a good choice," she added with a chuckle and a leer. "One with a very hard mattress. But that's for later," she sighed, dismissing the subject with a toss of her head. "You can take care of getting this place more comfortable later. Before we do anything else I want you to see what you can make of the greenhouse. Make certain that they haven't deviated from Larisha's plans in the mad rush to get this place in order. I will see you back here this evening. Now, go. I have more important things to do than see to your needs. Go!"

The interior of the habitat had grown considerably more complex since Win's previous visit. At that time he could see across the entire width of the spherical enclosure on a few decks. Now he could barely see a few hundred meters down any hallway. The vast, open decks had been broken into hallways, divided into room after room.

He could feel the throb and vibration of heavy machinery through the soles of his feet. Somewhere below, the manufacturing sections were using the materials scavenged from Thetti to produce everything from machine parts to furniture. In other places, workers were setting up clothing factories and food-processing facilities. Somewhere out of his sight people were probably building machines to fill every need that the habitat and its inhabitants might conceivably have.

All of this activity was fueled by the steady arrival of the scoops, which deposited their burdens into the habitat's storage tanks. From those tanks Thetti's gases were pumped to the processors, which converted them into more readily useable materials. These latter materials were machined, formed, stamped, injected, molded, or otherwise manipulated into finished products. Somewhere inside the hab, Win thought, someone could make his chair. And that damned hard mattress for his bed, he added ruefully.

The corridors were a maze. What is more, the signage was so limited that he often found himself returning to the place he'd left only moments earlier. If he found himself in a cul-de-sac, which was often, he had to backtrack to wherever the hallway had branched and try the other way. It was terribly confusing.

Sometimes, a helpful Halfing or a passing Folk would direct him on the proper route, and he would resume his journey. The habitat was becoming a world in itself, far more complex than the ship, and enormously larger.

Win walked though several areas that had long tables extending from the walls and benches of soft plastic beneath them. Dining areas, he assumed as he passed. The nearby kitchen areas were bare, however, which made him doubt his guess about the rooms' purpose.

Once he stumbled into some Folk erecting a huge platform in a wide, open area. He could see nearly three decks up to a dome, which was softly illuminated. There were verandas projecting from the upper decks, no doubt places where people could look out into this huge space. It would be impressive when finished.

From the shouts and gestures of the workers he quickly realized that the swinging slabs of rock-crete and heavy equipment that filled the space made it no place for gawkers. The supervisor quickly escorted him out and sent him down a long, dark corridor. The hallway ended at an unmarked door which opened on a stairway, which he climbed. Nine floors up, the supervisor had said; that's where he would find the greenhouse.

The stairway's doors on the first four levels were unmarked. Finally, several decks later, he found a sign. As soon as he read it he realized that he'd just climbed four decks right beside a perfectly functional elevator. He used the small lift to ascend five decks more.

The greenhouse appeared more complete than he'd expected. The last time he was here the plants had only covered one quarter of this level, with construction equipment and building materials filling the remainder. Now plants occupied the entire space, filling the entire volume with a breathtaking expanse of greenery.

Rows of verdant foliage disappeared into a haze of mist in the far reaches of the greenhouse, each aisle fading into indistinct lines. That mist told him that he'd arrived during a rainstorm. Many of the species they'd installed were native to the coastal regions of Heaven and thrived only when a steady supply of moisture drenched their leaves.

Once he oriented himself, Win began walking down an aisle toward the barrier curtain. Beads of moisture clung to his tunic and dampened his hair. He remembered that the more arid plant life was supposed to have been set somewhere to the left. In that area the heavy mist should be less. When he came to the barrier curtain, he pushed through and came upon the first person he had seen since he came out of the elevator. It was Tug, one of the Folk who'd helped him put in the first sets of troughs.

"Win!" Tug said in surprise, "I had no idea that the Raggi was coming today." He put down his trimmers and rushed to take Win's hands in his own. "It's been a long time since you were here. Glad to see you."

Win smiled in reply and gripped the other's hands tightly. "The Raggi isn't coming. There's just me." Seeing the look of puzzlement on the other's face he explained. "All of the Folk have been moved to the hab. Something about getting the place finished ahead of schedule."

"That's strange," Tug replied. "I thought that only minor work — furnishings and the like — remained to be done. At least that's what the crew down on the manufacturing levels are saying — just interior structural units are being made. From everything I've heard, the habitat is practically finished."

"I don't think that can be right," Win said. "What about the engines and the flight gear? I heard the Raggi say that the Hadir declared those as our top priority — the rest of what you mentioned is just for comfort."

Tug removed one of his gloves and scratched his head. "That can't be right either. The engines were checked out more than a week ago."

"Then why is the Hadir sending nearly everyone over here if not to get the place operational?"

"Sending everyone over here? Don't be ridiculous," Tug scratched his head again. "We've seen as many going back as coming over."

Win wondered about that. He had listened carefully to the discussions between Dalgrun and Larisha. He was certain that the Hadir had instructed them to finish the habitat at any cost. Hadn't Larisha herself told him that they were to dedicate all resources to that end? What is more, there was no way that Palm Dalgrun would be mistaken about such orders. He resolved to ask the Palm about this mystery.

"Perhaps we don't know as much as we think, Tug," he suggested to end his friend's speculation. "Now, how about taking me on a tour and showing me what we've accomplished?"

Win spent the rest of the day examining the wonders of the greenhouse, row by row, biome by biome, level by level. For a while he forgot his concerns about the ship, his relationship with Dalgrun and Larisha, and the mystery of the exploding objects that still occupied so much of the ship's conversations.

One thing he didn't forget, not for a moment, was Amber.

Dalgrun appeared preoccupied as he serviced her that night. She barked her commands in short grunts and slapped him hard whenever he displeased her. She came with a jerk, her breath exploded momentarily as she arched her back and pushed down against him.

She usually asked him to hold her afterwards, but tonight was different. No sooner than she was satisfied she got up and left his room, leaving him unfulfilled. Win wondered if she would return or whether he could safely ease his frustration.

Dalgrun's voice carried into his room. It sounded as if she were holding a heated conversation with someone. He moved to the doorway and listened.

"I don't give a damn what Tam says," he overheard her shouting. "There's nothing left to do over here except hang some pictures and roll out the rugs. The hab is fully operational! Even the drives are checked out. The hab is ready to launch whenever the Hadir instructs."

She listened silently for a few moment.

"Yes, Larisha," she continued after the pause. "I know what Tam and your reports have been saying, and I am telling you that they are wrong. Someone has obviously been doctoring the reports to indicate that the hab is far less ready. You need to identify the traitors and find out why they have been misleading you."

Win sucked in his breath. So it was true! Tug's statements about the habitat and the drives must have been right. He was glad he'd told Dalgrun, glad that he'd proven to be of more value to her than a handy pair of hands, tongue, and poker, as she so charmingly called it.

But from what he had been hearing, Larisha must have been misled as well. This was confirmed by Dalgrun's next statement.

"Yes, I know it is hard to believe, and perhaps this is, as you so colorfully suggest, another element of Tam's plans. I don't understand what he could hope to accomplish, though. He must have known that I would discover the subterfuge as soon as I took a look around." She went silent again, grunting an occasional response to whatever Larisha was saying.

"See to it," she finally said. "I don't like the smell of this. There are far too many Halfings and Folk over here for the work available. By the way, I haven't seen any of Tam's

Men. All of his Outriders are back at the ship." She was silent for moments more and then said; "Yes, I agree. He is definitely planning something. Get back to me when you find out more." There was a click as she closed the connection.

Win retreated to his bed and thought about what he had heard. That there was some conflict among the Men was a revelation, something that he never would have expected. He knew that Larisha and Dalgrun disliked the Hadir. They'd certainly made no secret of that in their conversations. Yes, and once or twice Larisha had made comparisons between himself and the Hadir while they lay abed. None of her remarks had been favorable about Tam, as she called the Hadir.

He decided to speak to Tug about this. Maybe he could shed some light on whatever was happening. With that resolution, he fell asleep and dreamed of Amber through the night.

His pillow was wet when he awoke.

Late the next day Tug came over to where Win was adjusting some of the nutrient balances. He'd discovered that the overhead light panels were slightly more intense in the higher frequencies than those on the ship and, as a consequence, the foliage was not so lush. By cutting back on the light levels he could force the leafy plants to produce more oxygen.

"What is it?" he asked, curious as to why Tug was so far from the area he'd told him to work that morning.

"Would it be possible for you to attend services this evening?" Tug whispered.

"Services?" Win asked with surprise. All the time he'd been on the ship, at least after Larisha had taken him under her care, not one of the Folk had asked such a question. What made it so different now that he was on habitat?

"Most of the Folk haven't had a chance to greet you properly, Win," Tug answered. "They want to know you better."

What was going on? From the way most of the Folk had avoided him on the ship he'd thought that his status with the Raggi and the Palm made them distrust him. Well, perhaps things would change now. At least he hoped so.

Dalgrun had returned to the ship to conduct services. At least, that was her excuse for returning. The real reason, Win suspected, was to discover if Larisha had confirmed her suspicions. Since she would not be back until the next day he should have no problems being absent from his room. "I will be there," he promised.

Tug smiled. "We meet at 1900 hours, in the Number 12 dormitory dining room. Here is how you reach it." He quickly sketched out the route Win was to follow.

The Folk service was much the same as back on the ship. The homily and prayers were modifications of the service the Palm conducted every eighteen days. There seemed to be no special reason for Win to be there, no message of faith aimed directly at him as he'd halfway expected. He began to wonder why Tug wanted him to come.

After the services Rex, the administrator who had conducted the service, came over to speak with him. "You are looking well, Win."

"The Raggi and the Palm take excellent care of me," Win replied evenly.

Rex smiled. "So I understand. Tell me, Win, what is your relationship to the two of them?"

Win panicked. Did Rex suspect anything? What had he done to raise suspicions and cause such a question? Oh lord, he could practically feel the rough cord of the garrote tightening around his neck. Sweat began to form on his brow. "I . . . I," he stuttered.

Rex looked alarmed and put up his hands in protest. "Forgive me, Win. I didn't mean to insult you. I merely wanted to know if they mistreated you in any way. That is all I intended. I apologize if I gave you the wrong impression."

Somehow the administrator's words didn't sound quite

as sincere as they should have. So, Win thought rapidly, the Man's apologetic words reflected that there were still lingering suspicions about Larisha, but only suspicions. That was a relief.

"As I said, they treat me very well," he continued without pause. "I have my own room, and," he added, boasting, "sometimes they let me share meals with them."

Rex smiled widely. "Well, that is an honor. I imagine that you are privy to their conversations as well, being present so much of the time."

Win brightened now that any further probing into the relationship subject had been averted. "Oh yes, they speak quite freely when I am about. I think it shows how much they trust me," he added proudly.

"Tell me, Win," Rex asked. "Have they said anything about, oh, what is going to happen to the habitat, now that it is finished? Not that we expect you to betray a confidence," he added quickly, "but many of us are curious about what is to come. We thought that you might be able to tell us something."

For the first time Win noticed that they were surrounded by a dozen or more, all paying rapt attention to their conversation. Not all wore friendly expressions.

Win debated telling them what he'd recently overheard. Dalgrun hadn't said anything specifically about keeping her conversations to himself. After all, she had just repeated what he had said when he disclosed what Tug had reported. There should be no harm in telling these acquaintances. It would just confirm what they already knew, wouldn't it?

"Here is what I heard the Palm say," he began, and told them of Dalgrun's discussion with Larisha.

When he was done Rex threw an arm about his shoulders and led him to the table where some food and drink had been laid out. Once he had taken a few morsels and a cup they sat down and began to talk.

Over the next few hours Rex and his cohorts spoke of a

great many things. Rex told him about how life in the dormitories had changed now that they were away from the ship's confines. They spoke of how the creature comforts were improving, how the fresh food from the greenhouse was such a welcome addition to their diet, and how the day-to-day life of the Folk, now that the harried pace of construction had ceased, seemed to be improving.

Then Rex speculated as to what place the Workers' would have on Meridian, how the Men would use them, and what their ultimate destiny might be. As they philosophized into the evening Rex asked many questions about Win's beliefs. He kept coming back to Win's feelings about the Men. "Surely," he observed, "the Palm has given you some insights into the way they think and act when they are away from us."

Win wondered if he should mention the Palm's hypocrisy, her lies, and the privileges she denied others but had no problem taking for herself? But he said nothing of those matters. "The Palm does not share such intimacies," he replied lamely.

"Well, if she were to do so, you would let me know, wouldn't you?" Rex suggested, ever so gently. "I am very curious about these things." Win nodded agreement. "Excellent. You know, Win, we need to see you down here more often, among your friends. We enjoy hearing about the happenings among the humans, especially those so highly placed."

"I will try to come often." It was so nice to be among those that he trusted, back among friends and family. Win hadn't realized how much he'd missed the Folk's warm friendship. "I will be back," he promised.

Tam was upset. Somehow, despite all of the precautions he had taken to prevent Larisha and the Palm from discovering the true status of the habitat's status, they had found out. He'd known from the beginning that it would only be a matter of time before his deceit was revealed. Well, there was not much they could do about it now, he thought. All of the Men who were loyal to Larisha had been stationed on the habitat while his own Men were totally in control of the ship.

In a few weeks, he would permit carefully selected members of the Halfings' crew, the ones Larisha needed for the first landing on Meridian, to return to the ship. Once the scoops had filled the habitat's storage tanks with all of the raw materials they could hold he could launch the habitat on its fifty-year orbit. That orbit would, he prayed, keep it safe from whatever dangers might come from Thetti. Or beyond.

After the habitat was launched he would take the ship to Meridian. Larisha would be happy about that, about finally letting her begin preparing the planet for the settlers. Getting them in place and self-sufficient would only take about a year — a minimum of nine months if he pushed everyone as hard as he had on building the habitat. Yes, nine months would be the target he would set. Even Larisha couldn't object with that plan. Wasn't that what she had been insisting that he do anyway?

What she wouldn't know was that, after he had her safely on Meridian and out of the way, he was going to bring the ship back to Thetti. Then he could dedicate all of his resources to uncover the mystery of these damned crystalline objects and the aliens who were behind them. If his estimate about the timing for the alien's return had been correct; the ship would arrive at Thetti just in time to greet whatever was coming to investigate the destruction of the balloons.

With the habitat on the other side of the sun at that time and one-third of the crew and Folk on Meridian, only the ship, with just a small fraction of all the people who had come to this system, would be at risk when they greeted the visitors. It was a prudent strategy. It was a safe way to proceed. It was the only way, God help him, that he could protect the mission.

FOURTEEN

Larisha had obviously learned of his alteration of the habitat's status reports. "Why?" she demanded hotly, "Why did you deceive me like this? Are you now as paranoid as you are deluded?"

Instead of answering, Tam gave her the schedule for their movement to Meridian. "Make all necessary preparations," he ordered. "We will leave as soon as the hab is launched." The schedule omitted that the ship would return to Thetti.

Larisha was in no mood to listen to reason. Although she went about the Meridian preparations she continued demanding explanations for every command. These persist questions were starting to spread seeds of doubt about his recent decisions. She used every chance she had to raise questions — a constant, harping pest, continually buzzing at his ear.

To her credit, not once did she breathe a word of his belief in the aliens and their crystalline ship. He knew that Larisha was far too clever to accuse him without more proof than her word. Besides, everyone knew of her enmity toward him and would think that was the real reason for any accusation. He merely had to deny saying any such thing and his Men would believe him, especially now that he had the Palm's backing.

Tam thought her pesky questions were a subtle strategy, and one that he had no way of directly countering. To acknowledge her carping criticisms would give her credibility, and he had no desire to do that. He was Hadir, the leader of the ship, whose word should not be questioned. Even if a question were raised, he could supply ample justification within the mission charter for everything he had done. Prudence dictated that he investigate anything that might threaten the collection operations. Prudence dictated that he build the habitat and place all hands aboard to speed its completion. There was nothing that he had done that could not be easily explained within the scope of the mission plans laid down by the Hand. There was nothing for which he could be directly criticized.

Unless he mentioned his real reason.

He began to notice that he'd had to be slightly more forceful when giving orders. The Men required that he provide reasons in more detail than usual before they would act. The slight change from their former, nearly unquestioning obedience was nothing he could identify specifically, but it was a sign that they had nagging doubts. Larisha's innuendoes were starting to nibble at their confidence in his leadership. Her bickering was slowly starting to erode his authority.

Perhaps he'd been wrong not to confront her criticisms directly, for not presenting his reasons for all to see. There were no fools among his Men. All of them had solid family profiles; and every single individual was a proven, evolutionary stepping-stone along the path that would some day bring forth the Emerging God. Despite their obvious misgivings, he was certain that they would support him if a choice had to be made. He was, after all, acting in everyone's best interests.

On the other hand, what evidence did he really have about the threat? Gull Tamat's theory about the alien machines still had little or no support. Fewer yet would agree, if given the chance, with Tam's belief that these machines represented a threat. Fewer still would give credence to his expectation of an alien ship's arrival.

For all he knew, the objects from Thetti could be nothing more than natural growths, products of some unknown geologic processes. Gull Tamat had been wrong before — he was no different than any other scientist when it came to interpreting new phenomena. Of what value was theory, when they had no baseline save a single-point examination of an object that no longer existed? No, there was no proof that he could offer from that quarter except the equivocal records Gull Tamat had kept of his examination.

Tam certainly could not tell the Men what he had seen with his own eyes. If he did, they would doubt his sanity. There was no way he could ever make them believe his brief glimpse of the crystalline creature/ship/God. There was no record of its visit save his own memory.

Had it really been an hallucination, as Larisha had insisted? Was it merely a vision brought about by the stress of being de-iced? Had something gone wrong and unbalanced his fine mind? If so, then he must surely step down from command. He had no right to make decisions if he was even slightly deranged. For a long moment, Tam debated the possibility that he should, for the good of the ship, surrender command.

"No," he exclaimed aloud and then looked around to see if anyone had noticed his outburst. He knew that he had been quite clear-headed, quite in possession of his faculties, when that crystal ship had examined him. He was absolutely certain of what he had seen, what he had felt as that awesome thing dismissed him. There was nothing wrong with his memory or his mind, not a thing.

He worried that, eventually, she would bring her accusations about his sanity to the fore. Perhaps he should eliminate that problem by accusing Larisha of bestiality — the most heinous of sins. Deep inside he knew that he could never bring himself to accuse her. He could never reveal what she had admitted, no matter what the provocation.

On the other hand Larisha would not be certain that he would not do so. She wouldn't know that he would never use that knowledge. She couldn't know that he would never turn his hand against her. So, he concluded, the situation between them was at an impasse. Neither of them could reveal the other's secret for fear of damaging themselves.

He wondered if he should he use the same tactics of subtle innuendo to offset what she said? Even if he decided to do such a thing he had no idea of how to go about it. Such games of feint and riposte were Larisha's skill, not his. No, he would have to stick to the strategy he had planned. He would simply reiterate his well-documented reasons for choosing the options and leave others to suppose what they would about his reasons. It was a prudent course.

A week later the habitat's storage tanks were nearly full and all systems had been checked out. Tam ordered the cumbersome positioning of the habitat for launch into its long orbit. He knew that by the time they got the hab oriented correctly, the tanks would be full. It was about time that things started to go right.

His thoughts were interrupted by an urgent a call from Gull Tamat, recently returned from the Medical.

"Welcome back to duty," Tam greeted him. "Do you have any new ideas about those objects?"

Gull Tamat grimaced. For the past months he had been slowly healing from the extensive burns he had suffered when his shuttle had nearly been destroyed from the explosion of the alien machine. "No, I do not have anything new, Hadir. However, I am more convinced than ever that my suppositions were correct now that I've had a chance to study in depth the data we collected. I am completely convinced that this was an alien machine of incredible complexity. Is there any way I can have another to study?"

Tam smiled to himself. "You're a glutton for punishment, Outrider. I would imagine that the last thing you would want was to get close to a machine that nearly killed you. But it doesn't matter," he added, "We haven't detected any since that explosion. You'd think they'd heard the blast and it scared them away."

"Yes, I heard that." Gull chuckled. "But since it took us such a long time to find and capture the first one, I don't give much credence to that idea. After all, I understand that you've hardly put any serious emphasis on seeking them." Gull's tone sounded faintly accusatory.

"I'd have a mutiny if I were to order the scoops to find

another one. Those two explosions were enough to spook everyone on the ship. The pilots are especially wary."

"Speaking of explosions," Gull Tamat went on, "I've been wondering why the object would have converted so much mass into energy. The small amount of heat that explosion produced hardly accounts for all of the mass that was consumed."

"I wonder about your term — 'small amount' of heat. It was enough to nearly destroy your ship."

"A relative term, Hadir. Conversion of that much mass could have destroyed us all — ship and habitat!"

Tam thought about that for a moment. "Could it have used the extra energy to send a signal,"

"An interesting idea, Hadir. Hmmm, yes, perhaps a broadcast of some sort would be one way of accounting for the missing energy. That would explain why we haven't detected any more of them. A warning shout, as it were; is that what you suggest?"

Gull's interpretation, differed significantly from Tam's own belief. While the chief scientist thought the recipients of the signal were the other machines down on Thetti, Tam believed that the targets were aliens lurking among the stars.

"I have to study another of these machines, Hadir," Gull Tamat insisted. "I could examine the object at long range, a distance that would not present a danger to the ship or the habitat. I beg you to order the scoops to find another for me."

What was the Man thinking about? Hadn't he listened to Tam's earlier statement about the morale of the crew, the sensitivity everyone had to any more attempts to deal with the balloons? "I cannot do that, Gull. It just isn't possible."

Gull Tamat fumed. "Then I must speak to the Raggi about this, Hadir. Perhaps she will see the wisdom of my request." The scientist abruptly cut the connection.

With some amusement, Tam tried to picture the encounter between Larisha and his intensely focused scientist.

Then, on reflection, he realized what a stroke of fortune such an encounter would be: Gull Tamat would protest that Tam had denied what he considered to be a perfectly reasonable request. Larisha would, he hoped, interpret that refusal to be that Tam was back on track: giving up on the balloons; launching the habitat; and proceeding to Meridian. Yes indeed, he thought happily, Gull's complaint would support his plans very nicely.

He was surprised a few days later when an urgent call came in from Gull. He wondered what the Man wanted this time.

"Have you been paying attention to the surveillance reports?" the scientist barked the instant Tam opened the link.

"What about them?" Tam said impatiently. He wondered why the scientist was so excited.

"Something strange happened earlier today," Gull Tamat continued hurriedly. "One of our orbital monitors seems to have failed."

"So? Send one of the maintenance shuttles out to put a new power pack in it," Tam wondered why Gull thought the failure of one of the orbiting monitoring stations was important enough to interrupt him? "Now, is there some important matter you wanted to discuss?" he asked.

The sarcasm in Tam's voice was lost on Gull. "Yes, I most definitely think so. The monitor that failed is the one on the opposite side of Thetti from our location. Judging from the reports I've seen, I don't think it's a simple power failure."

"I don't understand. How can you make such a statement?"

"Usually we see some sort of signal degradation long before there is any actual failure. This one died suddenly. There was no advance warning, no degradation — only a brief burst of white noise. It was as if its circuits were being overloaded just before the signal stopped."

An icicle of concern started to form at the back of Tam's mind. An abnormal failure was highly unusual. The orbiting monitors were so basic, so simple that almost nothing that could go wrong with them save power failure or a direct hit by some kind of flying junk. "That is strange," Tam said.

"I thought so too," the scientist's voice grew more excited. "So I repositioned one of the adjacent monitors to look sidewise at where the failed monitor should have been."

"Should have been," Tam repeated. Gull's words sounded ominous.

"Right: we didn't 'see' a bright spot where it should have been. Which could only mean that the monitor isn't where it should be, even if it failed. I can't be completely certain, however. As you know we only have fixed-focus optical capability on these monitors so we couldn't get a clear picture."

"Did you see anything at all," prompted Tam. He was getting impatient at Gull's drawn-out explanations.

"When we boosted the optical sensitivity we discovered a big patch of haze surrounding the monitor's position."

"Haze?" Tam asked. "An explosion?"

Gull hesitated for a moment. "Yes. That haze must be residue. The monitor must have exploded."

"There's nothing on a monitor to explode," Tam argued. He wondered how long it would take Gull Tamat to reach whatever conclusion he was trying to make. "It's just a mass of metal and circuits. There's no fuel, nothing that could feed an explosion!"

"Exactly, and the amount of particles comprising the haze far exceeds what I might have expected even if there had been such volatiles in place. To fill the volume indicated by the cloud of debris, the monitor would have had to been reduced to extremely tiny fragments, each practically microscopic in size."

"Get a shuttle over there to examine the site," Tam barked. "Immediately. And while they're doing that, I want you to check your records for anything else that might have happened at that time. Call me if you discover anything out of the ordinary I want a complete picture of what is going on!"

Gull Tamat called back less than an hour later. "One of the scoop pilots reported a brief flash that illuminated the adjacent monitors and Thetti's nearest satellite around the same time the monitor failed. I think it might have been the explosion that destroyed the monitor."

"I still don't understand how the hell an inert object like the monitor could explode."

"It wasn't the monitor that exploded," Gull explained. "It had to be something else. Triangulation says that whatever it was must have originated well above the top of the atmosphere. Only there was nothing there to explode! It's as if it happened in empty space."

Something has started, Tam realized with alarm. *Something that we cannot understand has begun!*

"Have you gotten an shuttle over there yet?" he shouted, wondering why there had been any delay in dispatching someone to investigate. "I want to know what we are dealing with. Patch all the transmissions to my link. I want them to send us constant reports the whole way out and back."

"One is already on the way, Hadir. I shall do as you ask."

Shortly afterwards the pilot's voice murmured laconically through the link; "We should see the haze rising over the horizon in a minute."

"Look at that! It's huge!" another voice, probably the co-pilot's, shouted suddenly. "What is that? I've never seen anything like it."

"What do you see?" Tam demanded. "Give me the visual!"

A few moments later he watched in horror as an image built up on his screen. There was no haze of a fractured monitor, the image gave a lie to that supposition. Instead the blurred image they'd received earlier was now seen to be a vast, asymmetrical mass of glittering angles, an object too complex to grasp at a single glance.

Tam let out a low whistle. If this was what responded to the call of the exploding object it certainly wasn't anything like his crystalline ship. This object was covered with a vast array of projecting spires. There were rhombic and tetrahedral forms. There were crystalline shapes tumbled against one another without apparent logic. The object was a vast iceberg of shining surfaces and flat facets. It had a weirdly fractured appearance to its surface, yet seemed quite organized, quite like a crystal grown without bounds.

"We can detect no signals being emitted," Gull reported. "I'm checking every radio frequency I can. There's nothing but background noise."

"Keep checking," Tam barked. "Start transmitting a mulitband signal, maybe we'll get lucky and get its attention."

Gull chuckled without humor. "I've been doing that since we sighted it, but I doubt that this machine has the intelligence to respond. I believe that this is just another artifact, although it is a bit larger."

"Quite a bit," Tam agreed. "Let's pray that it is just an artifact."

As the huge structure slowly rotated it reflected the ruddy glow of Thetti from the flat faces of its facets on one side and of the starry heavens on the other. The image grew larger as the shuttle approached closer.

"How close are you?" Tam asked. The object nearly filled the screen. Apparently they had the telephoto mode in operation.

"I can't tell, Hadir. The radar ranging shows a complete hash." The shuttle pilot paused. "I'd estimate our range at fifty kilometers, Hadir," he replied.

"Take it off telephoto. I want to get a true estimate of its size."

"It isn't on telephoto. That's the apparent size from where we are!"

"Be careful," Tam warned as the shuttle continued to approach. If the pilot's estimate of range was correct this object must be at least five to ten kilometers across. How the hell could something that large managed to orbit without being detected?

"We're still getting no response to our transmissions," Gull injected. "We're recording everything the shuttle's sending."

Thank God for Gull's presence of mind. Tam was glad someone like Gull was in the right place when this happened.

Tam whistled as the strange image on the screen continued to grow. Its size went beyond the bounds of reason. Beside this structure, the huge habitat they had built would be dwarfed.

Tam began to notice small details that sat like dew drops nestling among the stems of glittering beauty within the interstices of the crystal-like outgrowths. But, instead of finally resolving into something he could understand, he saw only an increasingly confused jumble of crystalline forms, tumbled on each other. By the measure of the pilot's distance estimate the smaller forms were probably the size of one of their shuttles.

"How close are you," he asked.

"Estimate seven thousand meters," the pilot answered. "Braking."

God on Heaven, Tam thought, as he upgraded his already fantastic estimate of the structure's size.

This alien machine was monstrous, a nightmare of chemistry gone wild! What fierce revelation had God sent to greet them?

"Now estimating six thousand meters and still decelerating," the pilot reported. "Say, look at that!"

The shuttle's optics suddenly focused on a bright light glowing deep between two spires within the crystalline forest. The glow intensified. Suddenly it glared blindingly bright, washing out everything on the screen.

"Watch out," he heard the pilot's shouted warning, but it was already too late. The audio and visual link went crazy in a hash of white noise.

"We've lost the shuttle's signal," Gull Tamat was obviously panicked.

"We've lost far more than that," Tam said, and added. "I'm afraid that my worst nightmares have finally become a reality."

Tam lost no time preparing to react to this strange apparition. He called for his advisors, including Larisha, to discuss actions. Since most had been monitoring the fatal approach of the shuttle, he doubted he would have much trouble convincing them of danger. They had seen the face of his nightmares for themselves.

"What is it?" Larisha asked when the first image flashed on the screen. "Is it another one of those things from Thetti?"

The tone of her voice showed that she hadn't been monitoring the encounter. *Damn, someone should have told her about what had happened before the meeting!*

"I think this one came from somewhere else," Tam replied as Gull's quick review of the episode with the shuttle flashed on the big screen. "I don't believe that this ship is native to this system."

"Are you saying that this is an alien ship?" Larisha said incredulously. She started to laugh, but it came out as a nervous giggle. Tam was gratified to see that even she could appreciate the immensity of the object sitting on the opposite side of the planet.

"I fail to see how you manage to reach your conclusions, Hadir," Larisha continued once she regained her composure. "We certainly would have detected a ship that large, wouldn't we? Don't you think that's evidence that it came from Thetti?" she sneered.

Tam looked around the room. Of his four Outriders, two nodded as if they placed some credence on Larisha's remarks. The other two had more neutral expressions on their faces, indicating that they might be awaiting further proof.

"You are quite correct, Raggi," Gull Tamat said when Tam hesitated. "We have no evidence of an approach from anywhere else. No one noticed anything until the monitor failed."

"So it had to come from Thetti while we were on the other side of the planet," Larisha crowed. "This object, large that it might be, must have come up from below. I fail to see what other conclusion you can draw."

"There was a sudden gravitational perturbation, as if some new moon were added to the system just a few moments before the monitor exploded," Gull Tamat said. "I don't think we would have seen a ripple like that if it originated on the planet. My conclusion is that this object just wasn't there before that."

"Are you trying to make us believe that it just popped up out of nowhere?" Larisha scoffed. "What next? Are you now insisting that we have an alien machine that's able to jump across space?" Her ridicule was obvious in every word.

"While fantastic, it nevertheless is a possibility," Gull Tamat said coldly. "We do not have sufficient evidence to reach any concrete conclusions."

Tam rapped the table. "Regardless of its origin it is still something we must deal with. The disappearance of the monitor and the destruction of the shuttle we sent to examine it are testimony to that."

"Perhaps you will tell us what do you think this could be, Hadir," Larisha said nastily. "Perhaps you have an understanding that we do not."

Tam didn't respond directly. This was just her way of teasing out his admission so that she could accuse him. Instead he asked Gull to present the facts, facts that could be confirmed instead of theories. That was safer grounds for discussion.

"So, what are your ideas, Hadir?" Larisha said when Gull Tamat finished. "You must have some theory as to what we are facing."

Tam hesitated. It was clear that Larisha had chosen this emergency to challenge his position. This was the time for caution. He had to be careful not to fuel the doubts about his ability to command. He must sound reasonable. Only he could steer them through this dangerous time — only he knew what they faced.

"I agree with the chief scientist. Somehow, in a way we do not yet understand, this object entered orbit. It is clearly moving purposefully and has defended itself. At least that is how I choose to interpret its destruction of the shuttle." He took a deep breath before proceeding. "I support Gull's original theory." He spoke slowly so that his words would sink in. "This object is indeed an alien artifact." He paused for effect. "I think we have evidence of another star-faring race. That," he pointed at the screen, "has to be an alien machine."

Consternation raged around the table. "Now I know that you're insane," Larisha screamed, coming to her feet and pointing at him. "Tell them about your visions! Speak your heresy. There is no one above Man. No other race but Man has God's blessing. To declare otherwise is to refute the Revelations. To deny God's words is blasphemy!

"You are not fit to command," Larisha continued. "By your own words you show that you are no longer fit to command this mission. Aliens, indeed," she mocked his words.

Who are you to talk of fitness for command, Tam thought bitterly. *You, who has committed the most vile perversion.* But he said nothing. The evidence of the alien ship was irrefutable.

"There it is," he thundered and pointed at the image on the screen. "You cannot doubt the evidence before your eyes! You must see that it cannot be otherwise."

"There's some simpler explanation," Larisha protested hotly. "These aliens are merely something your unbalanced mind has created. Until I see some proof otherwise, I will contend that this thing, whatever else it is, could only have come from Thetti."

The meeting erupted into a shouting match, with Tam, Gull Tamat, and three of the Outriders on one side, and Larisha and a lone loyalist on the other.

"Just look at it. It's just a larger version of those things we found down in the clouds," Larisha contended. "I will admit that I don't understand how something that large could get out of the atmosphere without our monitors detecting it, but I refuse to believe that these things use some mystical, magical transportation method. Aliens, machines, artifacts, teleportation: those are just too many impossible things to believe!"

Gull glanced at Tam and then at Larisha, clearly upset by the disruption of the meeting. "Hadir, I'm afraid that I must agree with the Raggi. We have long known that such a method of transport would violate every known law of nature. There can be no such thing as instantaneous transport."

"Perhaps it has some sort of disguise, some method of hiding its approach from us," someone suggested.

Gull Tamat dismissed the idea immediately. "There is no way it could have done that. Even a perfect black body would radiate. I've gone over every instrument record for the past month and all show nothing, not even a trace. Besides, there is that gravitational fluctuation that coincides with the destruction of the monitor." He looked perplexed as he realized that he was arguing against himself.

"But you still contend that this is an alien ship?" Larisha had trace of menace in her voice.

As Gull replied, it was obvious to Tam that Gull was torn between the conclusions of his training and the religious beliefs that had been instilled since birth. "As I said earlier, Raggi, this may be yet another artifact that has survived for millions of years. It may simply be another, larger alien machine, not necessarily an alien ship."

Tam had to admire the scientist's logic. Somehow he had managed to deflect Larisha's threatened accusations of heresy while preserving the possibility of alien provence for the object. Well, perhaps he is right, in which case all of Tam's concerns were for naught.

"Even so," Tam injected to put a stop to the bickering, "this artifact is undoubtedly a formidable machine. As such it poses a danger to our holy work. I suggest that we proceed under that possibility and let these arguments about theology wait until we acquire further evidence."

In the discussions of proof against belief, where supposition faced theory, none in the meeting had been converted to the other side. It was clear that at least one of his Outriders had been strongly swayed by the Larisha's arguments.

"We must decide on what we must do. It is pointless to wait for more information. Besides, I doubt if more data will convince anyone who chooses not to believe."

"A mess of supposition and poorly interpreted data," Larisha sniffed as she dropped into her seat. "Your theories go against God's word." But she sat quietly as they began to plan.

"Yes, an excellent idea, Hadir," Gull Tamat, at least, supported him.

"We have to get the habitat fully launched as soon as possible," Tam declared. "Getting that away from this object has to be our first priority."

"I agree," Larisha said. "And once we get the habitat on its way we should immediately take the ship to Meridian. I, for one, will be glad to leave this cursed planet and its mysteries behind!"

"What makes you think that thing won't follow us?" Tam shot back, wondering how she could still persist in thinking that this object would pose no danger once they moved away from Thetti. "I think we need to stay here to learn more about it."

"You would use any excuse you can find to delay my

settlement, wouldn't you!" It was clear that Larisha disagreed strongly with his suggestion. "What is it about these things that draws you so, Tam? Why are you trying to delay us?" she pleaded.

Tam felt as if he had been slapped. It was a measure of the stress that she had used his personal name instead of his title in the presence of his subordinates. In all of the time he had known her, she had never, not once, forgotten the proper protocols.

"We cannot just leave this thing behind us," he explained. "It might be dangerous to the settlers. It could imperil the scoops the next time they mine the planet. We have to discover why it came and what it intends to do."

"There you go again, insisting that this is some . . . some alien ship. As I said before, that is very close to heresy, Hadir."

"I have to assume the worst until we have evidence to the contrary," Tam insisted. He turned to Gull Tamat. "Place some shuttles in position to watch this thing all of the time. Tell them not to get too close to it. We don't want a repeat of the earlier episode." He thought for a moment and then added. "Put pilots from the Halfings on the shuttles. No sense taking chances with losing more Men."

A second scoop disappeared a few days later as it passed beneath the intruder. They'd detected a burst of light on the object seconds before. Two observers saw the flash and a third confirmed the ship's sudden disappearance. There no wreckage, no confirmation that anything out of the ordinary had happened. But the scoop did not return.

Tam was infuriated. "Make certain that everything keeps well away from the thing. No one is to mine Thetti in direct sight of that damned monster. We can't afford to lose any more people!" Tam was so tired, so damned tired. He'd been up for nearly thirty hours, dealing with a thousand decisions about launching the hab and hounding Gull's crew to calculate a path that would not use the gravity sling around Thetti. If they went with their original plan it would bring the hab dangerously near the alien ship.

This new plan was an incredibly complex game, made more difficult by lack of information. Who knew, Tam felt sick, a gnawing fear in his belly, what other crystalline ships might lurk in the dark, invisible to their instruments, waiting like spiders in their lairs for the habitat to pass within their destructive range?

But they had no alternative. They had to get the habitat and at least some of the people away from this danger. They certainly couldn't, as had been suggested and discarded, travel onwards to another star. The ship had neither the facilities nor the expertise to ice everyone — they would lose too many should they attempt something so foolhardy. Besides, they didn't know which star to aim for, much less have the fuel needed. Tam might as well push everyone out the airlock as attempt flight from this cursed system. No, whatever else he might do, it was certain that they had to remain in this system and deal with these things, whatever they were. He had no other choice.

Then there were the approaching settlers, the cream of Heaven's Men, the people for whom they were the pathfinders. To leave this system would leave the unsuspecting settlers vulnerable to these inimical aliens. He had to protect them, whatever the cost.

He looked at the calls on his link. Reports on progress of moving the people between ship and hab, another of the hourly update on surveillance of the objects, and a hundred decsions that he had to make on this or that problem. When would he ever have a chance to get some sleep?

FIFTEEN

It had been six weeks since the object's appearance, and Tam was frustrated at the lack of solid evidence regarding the mysterious, inimical object. Gull had used those six weeks to study every aspect of the structure but, in all that time, had discovered nothing further. No matter what they tried, Gull Tamat could get no probe closer than six thousand meters. Anything coming closer was immediately destroyed.

He had watched the recordings of Gull's sacrificial probes, sent deliberately so they could observe how the ship reacted. Its weapon consisted of neither projectiles nor radiation. One moment the probe was closing on the object and the next it was torn apart as if a bomb had been placed on board. Was the mysterious flash of light a weapon or merely some sort of ranging mechanism?

Gull's scientists couldn't answer that question, try as they might. It was highly perplexing, they declared, but no more so than the rest of the object's structure. Gull had tried every means at his disposal to examine it with little success. He'd even sent a probe to the opposite side, exploded it and measured the diffraction patterns as the particles sleeted through the alien ship. This revealed only that there were voids within the structure, voids that could be living spaces. But there were no apparent connecting passages, nor were there any means of access. Other than these empty spaces the object was a more or less homogeneous solid block, with domains of more or less dense material clumped here and there. "These lumps in the internal structure are like raisins in porridge," someone on Gull's staff had quipped. Tam hadn't laughed.

Aside from the destruction of their probes they detected no other activity. Surely, Tam thought, the ship must have some purpose in appearing at this time, in this place. It wouldn't have returned just to sit in orbit about Thetti. He stared at the image for hours as he tried to puzzle it out — friend or foe, rival or slave, Man or God?

"There is no way anything can live inside a solid structure," Gull had theorized, "which implies that it must be completely automated." Tam swore. Gull stubbornly clung to the idea that this was another machine; merely a vast artifact. But why, Tam debated with himself, why would they build such devices, employ such advanced technologies, only to abandon them? Gull's theories, and his own questions, were constantly in his thoughts, subordinate only to what this ship could portend for them, for the mission, for Men.

Could its immediate purpose be only to observe, to watch Thetti, to discover what had destroyed two of its children? No, not children. Tam dismissed that thought quickly. He was absolutely certain that was that this object was not a natural growth, not something brewed in the depths of space nor on the surface of Thetti.

A chill went through him as he pondered an alien civilization that could create such an artifact and launch it to the stars. Did that mastery of technologies make them the equal of Man? Could they have made their own covenant with some horrid, obscene, inferior god? And had that alien god set them here to challenge Man and his Emerging God?

But what purpose would that serve if the Emerging God were supreme? Was this God's test of Tam's resolve in carrying out their holy mission? If so, then he must be equal to the challenge. He, Hadir Tam Polat, was the Emerging God's emissary. He alone had been chosen to confront this obscene device and demonstrate the supremacy of Man. He was destined to demonstrate that Man cannot be denied his rightful dominion over the universe!

He stared at the ungainly thing as its image rotated. The ship's design had a certain logic, a pattern that dangled just beyond the edges of comprehension. He was certain that whatever had created this object had a long history of design and construction behind them. There was a depth of complexity, an investment of resources that went beyond anything Men had ever contemplated. Sometimes he thought he started to see the way the various elements of the design fit together; but when he tried to grasp the pattern, it slipped away. Gull had reported the same intuitive feeling. Was there an alien logic here, or was it simply an accident of chemistry and crystalline growth?

Gull couldn't find anything resembling engines, or exhausts, or any orifice that would allow mass to be ejected and permit flight. How had it maneuvered itself into orbit — whether from Thetti or elsewhere — that was the question.

Naturally Gull had a theory. "It is those seemingly empty spaces," he explained. "Perhaps they are simply filled with something we cannot detect."

"Some sort of stealth material?" Tam suggested. But if that was the case then why would it be applied inside of the ship?

"Not exactly," Gull continued. "It may be that this object has found a way to harness a different form of matter — something we have long theorized. Dark matter, we call it."

Tam was about to ask for a more detailed explanation when the link opened. Someone was shouting.

"The object," a voice shouted in panic. "It's shifting orbit!" Tam checked; it was a call from one of the observers.

"Which way is it moving?" Tam demanded, wishing he could be out there with them, watching this thing.

"Away from Thetti, Hadir," the reply came back. That meant it was moving to a higher orbit. "No sign of exhaust," came another voice. "I'm moving out of its way."

This was the first uninitiated move it had made. All of the others were reactions to their probes. What did this alteration of its orbit mean? "Keep station on it," he directed, and then grinned ruefully; his order was unnecessary, his Men would have already given those instructions, as well as dozens of others he hadn't thought about as they responded to keep the ship and hab out of danger.

He called for his Outriders. They must decide on what was to be done, and quickly.

Tam looked around the table. "I'm grateful that Gull completed his orbital calculations. Now we can send the habitat on its way. I've ordered the habitat to schedule the departure for a week hence. That will take it safely away from Thetti and this mysterious ship."

"We're not ready yet!" Larisha angrily came to her feet. "The habitat still has eighty percent of my Meridian crew on board. Besides, you haven't allowed me to move my Men, Halfings, and the Folk back to the ship! How do you expect me to prepare for our departure to Meridian?"

"They will remain on the habitat until it is safely away. We can rendezvous later if we have to. Meanwhile, if the object makes any move to follow, I will throw everything we have to stop it."

"This isn't a warship and you aren't a warrior," Larisha shot back. "We only settlers, explorers for God's sake!"

Tam smiled bitterly. "The engines of this ship are still functional. If necessary I will use the ship itself to destroy this thing."

Larisha leaned over and whispered harshly. "You are absolutely, totally, unquestionably insane!"

"I must do what I feel is right," he calmly replied.

"Right?" she pulled away. Her voice was no longer a whisper, but a shout. "What is right about ignoring the settlement while we languish out here in the cold, preventing the Halfings and Folk from work, and bending our purpose to your obsession with these — these things? You can't tell the difference between your personal demons and the holy orders of the Hand. You've put yourself above the needs of the ship. You have overstepped your authority!"

The others in the room shuffled uncomfortably. "Raggi, I don't think —" Gull Tamat began.

"My interests are the mission's interest!" Tam shouted back, ignoring the interruption. "The preservation and protection of Heaven's settlers is my concern, no matter what you might believe. It is we who are expendable. It is our duty to make this system safe and to protect those who follow." He glared at them. "Who believes otherwise?" he demanded with the whip of authority in his voice.

"I am with you, Hadir," Gull shouted immediately, seconds before the other Outriders declared the same. But one stood with Larisha. It was a sure sign of the deterioration of his authority. No one should question the Hadir.

"Now, let us get on with the business of preparing the habitat for launch." His words were cold as ice.

Of late Dalgrun had become preoccupied with the situation between the Hadir and the Raggi. She'd become distracted as she busied herself in the organization of the habitat and relied less and less on Win's services outside of her bed.

Win noticed that, although Larisha was still nominally in charge of the hab, it was Dalgrun the Men consulted when serious decisions needed to be made. It was Dalgrun who was increasingly providing mundane as well as spiritual guidance. "I only do it to save the Raggi from these petty details," she'd remarked on more than one occasion.

As her preoccupation grew, she'd become even less considerate than before. Win knew he'd become just a useful appliance, of no more importance than the Palm than her other furniture. He was ignored until her needs demanded his attention.

At the same time that preoccupation gave him more freedom. Larisha's greenhouse had been so well conceived and implemented that its management now required only a fraction of the time it had taken when he first arrived.

The caretakers, which included many of the Folk for whom no other work was available, tended the crops with an enthusiasm and skill that he admired. Many of them worked on Larisha's estate before the launch and knew their craft. All he had to do was to walk through to check that nothing out of the ordinary had arisen, check the nutrients' settings, and prepare a list of tasks for the next day. That completed, he decided to explore.

After leaving the greenhouse Win visited the deck immediately below. It was the habitat's lungs and kidneys Most of the volume was filled with life support equipment: banks of atmospheric converters; huge scrubbers humming overhead; and, linking them together, more pipes and hoses than he could count. He was both fascinated and baffled by the mysterious throbbing tubes and hissing machines. A pervasive hum filled his ears. The scent of ozone tingled his nose as, all around him, the air was replenished, the water purified, and the habitat's wastes processed. He wandered around for nearly an hour and encountered no one. This didn't mean that the machines were ignored, but merely that the complex was so extensive.

There was a stairwell near the center of the deck. He descended. Four identical hallways led off from the stairwell's base. Win chose one at random which, just like all the others, was lined with widely-spaced doors.

Following the corridor he came to a small open space. It was bathed in warm light from glowing panels and, in the very center, stood a pedestal on which was posted a map. He studied it for a few moments and learned that most of this deck had been set aside for the spare parts used for the life support machinery on the deck above.

Once oriented, Win found the next stairwell easily and descended. This level was disappointingly identical to the one he had just left: the same dull set of hallways and storage space.

Four decks lower he finally found people working and then, following his nose, found a their dining area. It had been hours since breakfast.

As Win was finishing a bowl of porridge there was a cry from behind. He turned around and saw the girl — Opal — who had taken his baggage. "I still have your things." She smiled as she slid onto the bench. "They wouldn't let me on the command level to bring them to you." She hesitated as she spoke, as if slightly fearful. Win wondered about that — was this another manifestation of how his relationship with the Men had distanced him from the other Folk?

"Thanks." He smiled to put her fears to rest. "I was wondering if I would ever find them. This place has gotten so confusing. There are so many corridors now. You know, it took me days to find my way from my room to the greenhouse and back."

Opal laughed. "I know what you mean, I had to memorize the layout of four decks above and below before I was allowed to go anywhere alone! But I haven't had time to do much exploration. They've had me outfitting the new quarters ever since I got here — putting together furniture, for Heaven's sake. I wish I didn't have to do it, but it seems that they won't have a need for a lathe jockey until another machine shop is set up."

"You're a mechanic?" Win was surprised. "I would think there would be a terrible need for you in the manufacturing spaces."

As Opal opened her mouth to answer the floor shifted under them and sent everything crashing across the deck. For an instant it seemed as if 'down' had become sideways.

"What the hell?" Win said and tried to keep himself from following his bowl. He was immediately thrown back onto the bench by another gravitational shift that restored the deck as 'down.' His stomach did flip-flops as another small shift in the direction of 'down' occurred.

"Win!" Opal cried from beneath the slipping table. She put her hand out to him. "What's happening?"

"I don't know," he replied honestly as 'down' shifted again.

Everyone was crying and shouting. Alarms were shrieking from every direction. Somewhere far off something huge slammed against ringing metal. Those who had managed to regain their balance stumbled toward the doorways, crashing sideways into tables and walls as 'down' shifted without warning.

"It's not safe in here," Win yelled after ducking to avoid a bench that was sliding by. He dropped to his knees. "Follow me." He crept along the wall toward the closest hallway as 'down' shifted again. This time it made the formerly level deck appear to be a steep incline that he must struggle up. Maybe, he hoped, he could find somewhere to hide until whatever was happening was over — someplace where they wouldn't be hit by flying debris.

Opal followed so close that she occasionally rammed her head into his butt. If he hadn't been so damned scared he might have found this funny.

The closest hallway was empty. About ten meters along he saw an open door. "Come on," he yelled above the yammering alarms and started crawling faster.

Progress became easier. The corridor's deck was stippled, and he could get traction whenever the tilt became too steep. He braced himself against the wall when it suddenly became the floor and concentrated on reaching the open doorway, which was now a yawing hole. It could be an opening to a possible refuge where they could wait out this disaster.

"Win!" Opal screamed when 'down' shifted again — this time sending him crashing against the far wall. Opal was flat on the deck, which had as quickly more become 'down.' She clutched her right arm and groaned. Why did she have to stop now? The yawning doorway was only a few meters further. He pushed himself backwards to reach her.

"What's the matter?" he said as soon as he saw her grimace at the pain He couldn't hear her reply. "Damn, won't that stupid alarm ever stop?"

"I think it's broken," Opal said through clenched teeth. Win noted the reddened swelling around her wrist. She must have broken it when she fell, or maybe she'd just sprained it. Either way they still had to protect themselves against whatever had the habitat in its grip.

He took her left arm and draped it over his shoulder.

"Hold tight," he said and began to crab walk down the hall, bracing himself against the shifting orientation, which, thankfully appeared to grow less and less violent. He prayed that 'down' would not shift disastrously, not for the precious few seconds it would take to get Opal into that room.

Finally they were at the doorway. He helped Opal sit against the back wall before he looked around the small space. It was scarcely large enough to hold the two of them. There was no furniture, no accommodations whatsoever. Then, as he was bracing Opal, the hab shuddered once again. There was increased pressure, as if gravity was increasing. "The hab's moving," he said and then, a moment later; "Damn. We're in an elevator!" He spotted the control panel. At the top of the panel was the button for the greenhouse.

The greenhouse! Thoughts of what these abrupt gravitational shifts might have done to Larisha's precious plants flashed through his mind. How could the saplings that they'd not had time to pot stand against this sort of punishment? Had the nutrient tanks been secured or were they now shattered and broken, spreading their precious stores across the deck? He could imagine the destruction taking place. He had to get up there and make things right! It was his duty; the greenhouse was his responsibility!

He prayed that the elevator was still working and, taking great care to brace himself, pressed the greenhouse button.

Win couldn't believe his eyes when the door opened. The place was a mess. There was an ankle-deep wash of water on the deck, carrying rafts of leaf, root, and limb as it sloshed among the wreckage. He put Opal beside the elevator, wedged between pallets to hold her fast. He struggled to maintain his balance as he fought his way to check the nutrient valves. If no one had shut them there would be nothing left to feed the plants that remained intact.

He found Tug several troughs away. He had a reel of

cord in one hand and a knife in the other. He was lashing the trees to each other, and then tying them to any solid object he could get a loop of cord around. "What's happening?" Tug yelled as soon as he saw Win.

"I don't know!" Win yelled back. "Where are the rest of the workers? What's been done so far?"

Quickly, without stopping for an instant, Tug spat out what he'd been doing. "Shut the valves first, then grabbed this cord. Tie this to that hose, would you?" Win helped as best he could.

"What's that?" Tug said after he was tying the last of the knots.

"We've stopped shifting." Win felt momentary relief, and then noticed something else. "Do you feel that? There's a vibration that wasn't there before."

"It's the engines!" Tug exclaimed. "They must be firing."

"But why would they . . ." Win began and then stopped. Was the habitat being sent into the planned orbit? But that wasn't supposed to happen for weeks. What could have happened?

Tam was jolted out of a sound sleep when the link cried for attention. "There's been another change in the thing's orbit," someone reported calmly. "It's moving toward you." Tam was out of his bunk and halfway to the command module before the alarms started ringing.

"Coming over the horizon now," one of the observers reported. Tam looked along the edge of Thetti. There, just at the edge, a brilliant point of light appeared. It was rising, rising. "Estimate that it will overtake the ship in two hours," the observer reported.

"Keep our distance," Tam said and felt the ship shudder as the engines belched. That kick would lower them to the same orbit as the other and increase their velocity. The combination should keep a constant distance between them, unless the alien ship — and he had no doubts any longer that it was anything but — broke orbit. He could play this orbital game for days, if need be.

But the alien ship didn't coöperate. Instead it continued to rise, closing the separation between them hour by hour.

Gull was frowning. "It appears that the object continues to accelerate. There is no evidence of any exhaust."

Tam felt panic. "Keep us ahead of it! Gull, see if you can figure out where it is going." This was direct evidence that this alien ship was using an advanced, unknown technology. His assessment that this was God's test of his resolve wavered. There was no doubt that this ship was superior to their own. No doubt that this was a challenge to Man's dominion.

"I have calculated what will happen if the object continues to accelerate at the present rate," Gull reported. "If it continues its path will eventually strike the habitat."

"Calculate how long before that happens," Tam ordered and thought furiously. The possibility that the alien ship could reach the habitat would imperil everyone on board. He didn't hesitate to act. "Launch the habitat immediately! We must keep that thing away from them!"

Tam worried about the command structure on the habitat. He wished for a moment that there had been time for a more orderly launch — time to get the Meridian crew back on the ship, at least. Well, too late for such thoughts now. He wondered what Larisha would now think of his 'insane' ideas when she saw the alien ship flying toward her? That certainly ought to convince her of his sanity! Just the same he wished that he could have done so in some other, less dramatic way. But that was only one of too many things that he wished he could have done. There were still too damn many things undone that should have been done had he any foresight. Well, no time for remorse now. He had to neutralize this alien threat.

When Tam called, Larisha was already on her way to the control center, careening from one side of the passageway to the other as the hab twisted and broke orbit. She found the center in a near panic. Technicals were trying to deal with a dozen alarms from every section of the habitat. Others were busy trying to keep the hab stable as it continued to accelerate. A quick glance showed her that they were on the very edge of going out of control as the Con struggled to keep them from tumbling erratically. Sweat glistened on the brows of the Men who were managing the engines. She knew better than to interrupt them.

"Why did we launch? What is the Hadir doing?" she demanded as she looked over at the technical who was tracking the situation. He pointed out two dots that were the object and the ship. They were just disappearing behind Thetti's disk. It appeared to her that the ship was about to overtake the object, but that might have been an illusion from the angle, she thought.

"Won't see them until they emerge on the other side, Raggi," the operator said calmly, "in seventy minutes."

"What's happening?" Larisha demanded when she had Tam on the link. "You're too close to that thing."

"That's my intent," Tam replied. "I'm going to try to stay as close to it as possible."

Larisha didn't understand. "But why are you doing this? Why have you launched the habitat? Don't you realize how dangerous it is? We're not prepared for launch!"

"I had no choice," Tam shot back. "When the alien ship started moving I thought it best that the habitat get out of the way. If the threat turns out to be nothing then we can rendezvous later."

Larisha sighed. "This is stupid. I'm certain that thing's only returning to the planet. There's no need for you to panic so easily. It makes no sense."

"I can't assume that it's descending into the atmosphere," Tam cautioned. "It could be using the gravity well of Thetti to launch itself. Gull suggests it has chosen to attack you."

Larisha felt a chill. "That . . . that's impossible. Are you saying that rock, that accretion, is under some sort of intelligent control? That's preposterous." She was almost screaming.

Dalgrun had come into the room and, after a quick assessment, joined Larisha. "Lower your voice, Larisha. You are not helping matters." Larisha looked around at the shocked faces of her Men and as quickly composed herself.

Dalgrun continued. "Gull apprised me of the situation, Raggi," she said in carefully measured tones. "Perhaps it is time to reassess your opinion of Hadir Tam Polat. It appears that he has been correct, while it is we who have been in error. That thing, whatever it is, is decidedly dangerous. It also — astoundingly, I must admit — appears be somewhat intelligent!"

"I don't care what evidence Tam provides. I still refuse to believe such heresy." Larisha balled her fists. She wished that Tam were here so she could strike him. "Wait and see. That thing will return to Thetti and we will have wasted all our fuel on nothing, nothing at all!"

When a bright speck appeared at the far edge of Thetti's disk and rose quickly above the atmosphere, Larisha was no longer so certain of her conviction. The spot resolved into two separate points of light a few moments later.

Dalgrun touched the display with the tip of her index finger. "It appears that the Hadir is correct once again. The object is indeed leaving the planet, as he suggested; and it is in pursuit of our little habitat. What do you suggest that we do about that, dear Raggi?"

Larisha thought furiously. "I am certain that you are mistaken. It's merely some natural process that makes the object appear to be following us. We merely have to move aside as it hurdles past. Alter our path," she ordered. "Get us out of the way."

"We cannot maneuver quickly, Raggi," the Con reminded her. "The hab's far too massive."

"Try, just the same," Larisha said with an imperious tone, as if her will alone could overcome physics' realities.

Larisha glanced quickly at the display and then out the port. The ship and object were closing rapidly.

Dalgrun pointed at the display where a bright spark flashed between the ship and object. "It appears that Tam has decided to attack."

"Excellent. Once Tam forces this thing into a different path, we have time to discuss options," Larisha mused and then added, under her breath; "And once we rid ourselves of this problem we can finally settle the question of command. That will end this meddling with things not of our concern."

But apparently not quietly enough. "Need I say," Dalgrun said evenly, "that since the Hadir has proven quite correct in his earlier estimate of the danger, the Men would find it very difficult to support your position, Raggi."

"Well, you'd better support me!" Larisha snarled. She kept her voice low so the others would not overhear. "Need I remind you of what Tam knows and what that could mean for you were he to accuse me. Best you think of your own skin, dear sister. Support me for your own sake!"

At that moment the habitat shuddered. "Apparently the Con is attempting your slight course change. Let us hope that it is enough to move us out of the way."

A few moments later the navigator informed them that the object had slightly altered its course to follow their new vector. It would still hit them.

"What were you saying about natural processes and the coincidence of our path?" Dalgrun asked calmly. "Certainly you can no longer dispute that this thing is under control — and intelligent control at that!"

Larisha was appalled at the Palm's admission. "How can you say that, Dalgrun? You say yourself that Man is the only intelligent creature in the universe. What about God's word, the Revelations, everything that humanity has believed for generations? What about our holy mission?"

Dalgrun waved her hand in dismissal. "Just because some extinct alien animals built space ships is no reason to believe that they are Man's superior. I am certain that this is a test of our resolve, much as God tested the Prophet on the mountainside." Suddenly she smiled. "Perhaps these things are another gift from God; a lesser race that will serve us in this new home, just as the Halfings and Folk did back on Heaven. We need only show them the strength of our faith in order to master them." She folded her hands across her lap in smug certainty. "The Hadir will stop them. He will make them submit."

Larisha was not convinced. "I do not for a moment give any credence to your suggestion, dear Palm. But consider this for a moment — what if Tam fails? What if this thing does not willingly accept our supposed superiority?"

Dalgrun frowned and drummed her fingers on the console. It sounded eerily like the roll of funereal drums.

"Careful, my dear, that comes very close to blasphemy." Then she brightened. "But have no fear, Raggi. You will see. We shall overcome. Nothing can oppose the Hadir. He is the Hand of God."

"The alien ship appears intent on pursuing the hab," Tam reported in his next transmission to Larisha. "We're making continual course changes so we can stay ahead of it."

"We dare not make any further alterations ourselves," the Con advised. "We've used nearly all of our fuel. We may not have the reserves we need adjust our orbit when we reach Meridian."

"I've thrown everything I have at it," Tam said. "But it's destroyed whatever we set in its path. We need a good-sized asteroid to throw at it."

"How about one of the scoop ships?" Larisha suggested, putting her doubts aside in the press of this emergency. "They are quite heavy. If you launched one of them, it might do some damage."

Tam said something to the side. "That's a good idea.

From our leading position we should be able to impart considerable delta vee. I doubt if that ship would be able to avoid a direct impact. Maybe whatever it used to destroy those probes won't be able to handle something that massive and moving at a high relative speed."

"You won't know until you try," Larisha responded. "We could launch something from here as well and time it to hit at the same time."

"Gull agrees that might work," he said a few moments later. "Have your Men work with Gull to coördinate the launch. I pray that this will work."

"Have no fear, Hadir Tam Polat," Dalgrun said. "You have the blessings of the Hand of Heaven. You are the agent of the Emerging God in Man. You are the Hand of God! You will overcome this thing!"

"I wish that I had your faith in my abilities," Tam replied. "I fear that this thing is something we don't understand, something that could prove our superior."

"Our superior? Surely you have no such doubts, Hadir." It was not a question.

Tam hesitated. "But what if that were so?" he asked. "What would that make the Revelation? What about Gods compact? Give me some insight, dear Palm. Tell me something that will still my fears."

Tam knew that he was not alone. He could feel the undercurrent of doubt all about him as the Men began to wonder at what these events could portend. The very underpinnings of their presence in this system, God's prod that had spread humanity, the promise that Man had dominion over the universe, all were being proven false. Their belief in a just and supportive God was being challenged. As he waited for Dalgrun's reply his thoughts continued to race, unable to leave the question alone. "What if the Revelations are false? What then of His commandments and our society? Are we as blessed as we believe?"

"No!" Dalgrun shouted back. "God is absolute! God has chosen humanity to command the universe. God had chosen Man as the vessel through which the Emerging God will arise! There can be no doubt, Hadir; no reservations about His word. The Revelation is fact! There is the blessed Emerging God in our blood, waiting in our genes, waiting for Men to achieve perfection. There can be no rivals to the Emerging God. There could be no superior beings!"

"So you say, dear Palm. So you say."

Larisha watched the two increasingly brilliant points of light grow closer. She worried about the brief firing of the engines she'd ordered and concerned about how far this would take them out of the long elliptical course they'd planned. Their original path would loop around the primary, well beyond the orbit of Thetti. Eventually they'd descend to the warmer regions, close to where Meridian awaited, but maybe not close enough. It was worrisome. She would check, once this other matter was out of the way.

The Men had thrown an unmanned shuttle at the pursuing object after coördinating the timing of its impact with Gull Tamat. The shuttle's engines had burned furiously to accelerate it toward their pursuer. She still couldn't bring herself to think of it as a ship, nor as something under conscious control, no matter how much Tam and Gull insisted otherwise.

She watched the ship and the object. They were both so close that she could discern their shapes — the wide disk of the ship and the glistening facets of the crystal. What was going through Tam's mind, she wondered as the final moment of impact approached? Was he coldly calculating yet another stratagem in case this attempt failed or praying as fervently as Dalgrun beside her? It would be just like Tam to have yet another plan, she thought. He was always plotting, always planning.

A flare of light bloomed from the crystal. "That would be the impact of the ship's scoop," she said unnecessarily. If Gull had calculated correctly, the habitat's shuttle would hit a fraction of a second later, driving through the damage done by the ship's scoop. The momentum of the shuttle was so great that it would certainly overcome whatever defenses it had.

But moments after glare died down, she saw that the crystal continued to advance. There appeared to be no change in its appearance.

"There was only a slight decrease in its motion," Tam reported grimly. "Apparently the speed and mass of the shuttle affected it. I think we have to throw something even heavier and faster to stop it."

Larisha considered their options. They had launched the biggest vessel on board. All they had left were smaller craft, hardly worth using. "We don't have anything more massive! What else can we do? Surely you've planned something!"

"Gull has been running options based on what we saw," Tam replied. "He thinks we need something about fifty times as massive to completely stop this thing. I think we have something at least a hundred times that size."

"Where would you . . . ?" Larisha stopped as she realized the enormity of what he was suggesting. "Oh God, you aren't thinking about . . ."

"The ship has more than enough mass, and with the additional velocity the engines will impart we can certainly gain enough momentum to stop it."

"You are insane! Don't do this, Tam. There has to be another way! You can't sacrifice the ship."

"I have no choice," Tam replied. "The God's Hand has been placed on my head. The Hadir cannot avoid doing what he must."

Larisha wondered for a moment if Tam was referring to Dalgrun, but dismissed that thought as unworthy.

"Are you serious about using the ship as a weapon?" Gull and the others asked.

Tam replied with frost in his voice. "Do any of you doubt that something as massive as this ship could stop that abomination? If so, speak now."

The crew remained silent as the enormity of the Hadir's words sank in. Gull was the first to recover his composure.

"I understand," he said slowly. "Will you inform the rest of the ship or should I?"

"It is the Hadir's duty," Tam replied. "You heard the Palm. I am the instrument of God's will. I must show these intruders that Man will not be denied its rightful dominion over this system." He hoped that the rest of the Men agreed. There could be no faithless doubters on God's ship.

Not even himself.

Larisha looked out the port. She saw a bright flare from the rear of the ship as its great engines fired.

"No!" she shouted, beating on the communications panel with her fists. "You cannot sacrifice the people on the ship. Let it go! Save yourselves and let it do whatever it wants with us. The loss of the Halfings and a few Folk won't matter nearly so much as loss of all those Men!"

"The Men are with me in this," Tam replied sadly. "If we are truly God's favorites then we shall prevail in this confrontation. If not, then you must survive long enough to warn the settlers of what awaits them." He paused and then softly added, "and I did love you, Bul Larisha. I really did."

Larisha watched in horror as the two points moved closer together. "No," she screamed. "Stop this!"

"Goodbye." Larisha was stunned that Tam, even at this moment, should insist on having the last word.

There was an intense flare, followed quickly by an even greater eruption of light as the ship and crystal collided.

The lingering light from the destruction faded long minutes later, before Larisha recovered from shock at what she had seen.

"There is no debris," someone behind her reported with awe in their voice. "The Hadir has destroyed the object."

Larisha spun about. "No debris? How is that possible? Certainly the explosion could not be so great as to leave no trace!"

"Nevertheless, it appears that both the object and this ship have vanished. Perhaps it is a sign of God's hand in this — to vanquish the foe so completely! God has saved us."

"Saved us?" Larisha said desolately when she heard Dalgrun's words. "We have lost everything save a handful of Men on the habitat, most of the Halfings, and the Folk. What sort of salvation is that?"

"Have faith," Dalgrun said. "I told you that God would not desert us. He has shown that his protection still holds. He has demonstrated Man's superiority over these alien creations. Man has proven victorious. This is a glorious victory!"

Larisha looked at her with an empty feeling in her heart. The Hadir was gone, dead in the explosion, as were most of the Men. How could the Palm say that this was a victory? How could anyone say that they had shown that Man was dominant? A growing certainty that this might not be the end of their encounters with these strange objects grew in her breast. She feared that this might be only the first skirmish.

"Men shall prevail," Dalgrun went on, growing more cheerful moment by moment as she danced around the control room. "It was God's will that we would persevere. Now come, Larisha we must make plans on how we will survive until the settlers arrive. After all, we are now the leaders of this holy mission."

"Oh my God, the mission!" Larisha was appalled. In the tragedy of the past few moments, she'd nearly forgotten their ultimate purpose, the reason Tam had sacrificed himself. "Yes, we must see to our own survival," she admitted sadly.

Only their survival could redeem the ship's sacrifice.

SIXTEEN

Larisha was appalled to discover how few Men had been spared from Tam's suicidal sacrifice. When she gathered them together to divide up the work that must be done to save them all she realized no more than a dozen were left.

There was some opposition to her assumption of leadership. Many were staunchly loyal and accepted her rôle as Hadir, even though she had not yet been blessed as such by the Hand. Several others, those of Tam's crowd who hadn't had time to get back to the ship, were less willing to be led. Some said they had to seek Dalgrun's advice, although there was none among them who would stand forward to challenge her leadership. Two others seemed ambivalent.

Larisha suspected that more than a few blamed her for the loss of the ship — as if she had called the unholy monster from Thetti's depths! As if she had forced the ship to its incandescent end. Even, she suspected, they suspected this was retribution for her supposed sins, sins that though never voiced, were nevertheless of constant concern. Could they be right, she wondered — could this be God's vengeance on her, on Dalgrun, on them all?

But perhaps there was no religious aspect to this at all. Hadn't Tam insisted that the thing was an alien ship? Strange to be thinking this way when, just a few hours earlier, she had thought him insane. But the way that crystal monster pursued them and the way it followed their moves were nibbling away her doubt. Even she had to admit that an inanimate object could not have behaved in that way. Yes, and hadn't Dalgrun admitted that the thing might be of alien manufacture? It was a short leap of logic to think of it as both alien and intelligent enough to track them. But she still could not bring herself to admit that Tam could have been right, that he proved with his death. Yet, if it were less, what would that make of his sacrifice? Did it diminish the loss and disgrace Tam Polat's memory? She had to think on this more deeply, but later, after the more pressing matters were settled.

"We must spread ourselves thin to lead the Halfings," she concluded after running down the inventory of all that must be done to bring the habitat to full operation — things that she had thought they had months to complete. Even if each of her Men took responsibility for a major system, that still left dozens of lesser ones that must be run by unsupervised Halfings.

But the Men appeared more concerned about what else might come after them. "Are there more of those things?" one of the young women — Jut, that was her name — said, her anxiety evident in every syllable. She'd been one of the first ones married just a few months earlier. She might have been pregnant, judging from the bulge at her waist, but Larisha couldn't be certain. For a moment she wondered if her husband been with Tam. Then, when a young Man put his arm gently about her shoulders, Larisha realized that one couple, at least, had been spared.

Larisha debated how she should answer and decided that honesty was probably the best policy. "I don't know," she admitted quickly. "That thing appeared rather suddenly. Tam and Gull thought that it was a repair ship and was responding to the balloons' destruction. My own belief is that it was simply a much larger one, no different."

"What if something even bigger comes in response to this one's destruction," Jut shot back. "What can we do then?" Han, one of the undecided ones, repeated the question. There was a mumble of discussion on courses of action, past and future among the group as Larisha fielded one question after another.

Dalgrun stepped forward. She raised her hand as if she were about to invoke a prayer. Everyone in the room went silent and turned their eyes to her. "We should not trouble ourselves over questions of what might lie ahead. Be assured that the Emerging God is on our side. Have we Men not demonstrated our superiority over these lesser creatures by destroying the mightiest of them? Put your fears to rest. You need not be concerned so long as your faith remains strong. You have nothing to fear if you remain pure in mind and body."

Larisha winced at how closely that charge came to her own thoughts. Had Dalgrun said that deliberately or was it just another palliative phrase? Before everyone could ponder on that remark she regained the floor.

"Thank you for your reassuring words, Palm Dalgrun. However, while I think it reassuring to have God protecting us from some reappearance of these apparitions we must still concern ourselves with survival. Unless we see to the habitat's systems immediately we will surely die from lack of air, starve to death, or become dehydrated. We all need to get to work, and that means organizing the Halfings who have to manage what we cannot." Without waiting for their assent, she asked for volunteers for each of the systems and processes that needed attention. The meeting went on for hours before the last of them departed. There were still many things to be done, but who could organize the Halfings to do them? She tried to think of those she could trust with the responsibility.

"A true Hadir would have told them what to do, not treated them as equals," Dalgrun criticized. "Nor would the Hadir have volunteered to do some of the work himself. Do not forget, Larisha, it is your responsibility to be a strong leader. You denigrate yourself by putting yourself on their level."

"I notice that you managed to retain your exalted position," Larisha shot back. "You could have volunteered to take control of food distribution, or shift management or . . ."

Dalgrun raised her voice. "I am the representative of the Hand, the religious leader of what remains of our expedition. I must minister to the needs of the Men and the Halfings."

"That didn't stop you from becoming involved before I arrived on the hab, did it? Don't think I haven't noticed how you have been taking control from my hands."

Dalgrun sniffed. "I did so only to spare your valuable time, Raggi. My, do you so distrust me? But, now that you are here, I can resume my proper rôle and not be distracted with mundane matters that compromise my position! Everyone is in great need of my prayers."

Larisha sighed. "Then you had better pray doubly hard for the rest of us because I doubt that your position will protect you from starvation or lack of oxygen."

Dalgrun raised an eyebrow. "Is that a threat, dear Raggi? And I thought that we were such friends, too." She gathered her clothing around her, turned, and left without waiting for a response.

Larisha realized that those crystal things weren't her only enemies.

The greenhouse was swelteringly hot. Sweat rolled down Win's back as he helped his crew upright one of the larger trays. This was the last one for the row and, once in place, they could begin replanting some of the rapid growth crops. They desperately needed as much greenery as possible since over half had been lost. The sudden alterations of orientation the week before had wrecked havoc with the long rows of planting trays, tumbling them onto the deck, crushing the carefully tended plants, spilling their precious nutrient baths, and ripping the irrigation systems loose from their foundations.

There was no magic or technical skill to get the greenhouse back into production. There was only the back-breaking work of saving the surviving plants, getting as many of the feeding systems back into operation as quickly as possible, and making do with the limited supplies on hand. Half of the nutrients had been wasted by the spills. From what he had heard, their fertilizer couldn't be replaced for quite a while, so he'd have to make do with whatever was on hand. That meant triage for the surviving plants — selecting those of greatest benefit and sacrificing the rest. He sighed. Larisha's flowers were first on the list of those that he'd have to compost.

Win had acted quickly to recover as many of the plantings as possible as soon as they could move about safely. Thanks to Tug's fast thinking, they had saved most of the saplings so they only had to keep the roots wet. After saving those they turned their attention to the other plants, leaving those that could stand a brief spell of dryness for last.

Repairing the broken irrigation system had been Win's first priority. By working around the clock he and Tug had managed to re-route the nutrient flow to those trays that had escaped damage and shut off the damaged sections. While Tug had the workers shift the surviving plants to the working trays, Win had the rest assemble a makeshift maze of pipes to deliver water to the undamaged trays that otherwise couldn't be reached.

Win and the greenhouse crew worked around the clock, snatching sleep only when they could no longer stand. Someone had put a sling on Opal's arm and, Win hoped, set the break. She had appointed herself as their provisioner, producing food and drink around the clock from some unknown source.

A burly Halfing named Joshua had wandered in once to see how they were doing. When he mentioned the alien object, Win's ears perked up. "Alien object?" he asked. "Was that the reason for the sudden movement of the hab, for all this damage?" he waved his arm to encompass the shambles around them.

Joshua looked surprised. "Didn't you know that the Hadir destroyed the alien monster? Well, to God's glory he threw the ship against it and destroyed it utterly and completely. It is now we few who must ensure the survival of the remaining Men, or so says the Raggi."

Win looked up, startled. "The Raggi — she wasn't on the ship? She is here, on the habitat?" Despite his fatigue he felt a sudden surge of excitement, of relief.

Joshua stepped back. "Calm down, boy. Yes, the Raggi now acts as if she were Hadir. The Palm, I'm told, don't think it proper, her being a woman and all." Quickly he briefed Win on what was taking place elsewhere in the hab.

But Win wasn't listening: Larisha was safe! Larisha was here, on the hab. Larisha had come for him, just as she'd said she would.

"I said, what does this arrangement do?" Joshua asked as he pointed at the maze of irrigation pipes Win had rigged the previous day. It was clear from this and later questions that he had neither knowledge nor understanding of the greenhouse systems. When Win provided a cursory explanation Joshua nodded. "You'll be needing more help then," he said quickly and disappeared. Shortly thereafter a dozen Folk arrived to relieve them of some of the workload. Apparently Joshua, though only a Halfing, had some power.

"I hoped that you'd be here," Larisha said.

Win hadn't heard her approach and jumped up from the row of lettuce he'd been tending. He shook the dirt from his hands and reached out as if to grasp her. At the last minute he recalled where they were, who they were, and how many of his crew were standing nearby staring at this demi-God who had appeared in their midst. He dropped his hands and let them hang limply at his side.

"Good day, Raggi Larisha," Win let his eyes express his joy at seeing her. "I am so glad to see you," he added politely.

Larisha took a half step backwards and raised her hand to her lips. "And I to see you, Win." From the look about her eyes, the way she held herself, and the weariness in her voice Win could tell that she was as tired as he.

"You look like hell," Larisha smiled. "And I imagine that I must look the same. No," she held up a hand, "You don't have to answer that. I fear that I am too good a judge of my own condition."

"You look as beautiful as ever, Raggi Larisha," Win lied. He motioned to an upturned tray, one of the damaged ones they were patching. "Won't you be seated?"

Larisha brushed away some dried leaves and sat down.

"I can't stay long, dear Win. And don't worry. I'm only here because I need someone to talk to, someone I can trust." She spoke softly, barely above a whisper. Her words would not carry to the nearby workers' ears.

"Surely one of the Men . . ." he began, speaking as softly as she.

Larisha laughed hollowly. "I hardly ever see any of the few who are left. We are all so damned busy that all I have time for is to give orders, coördinate actions, and scream at some Halfing who's done something incredibly stupid! Besides, my Win, there is no one that I trust so much as you — we have each other's lives in our hands, do we not?" Win nodded to show that he understood.

"But let us not dwell on that," Larisha continued. "Tell me, how are things going here? Did you managed to save my flowers, my favorites?"

Win hesitated. "There was so much damage that I had to make choices about which were most important. I . . . I had to rip all of the flowering plants out so we could have space for more productive crops. We lost more than a few trays, you know. Space will be limited until we can get the rest of the damage repaired."

Larisha's eyes filled. "Those flowers were my link to home, to Heaven, to a life I left far behind." She looked away, as if she could see Heaven and all of its glory on the pitifully few plants around her. Then she took a deep breath. "So, tell me, have you managed to get enough in production to take care of the air, to provide some food for our tables?"

"Barely enough," he answered quickly. "Half of the greenhouse was badly damaged, but we've salvaged what we could. I do not think we will lack for food during the next six months." He bit off his words, trying to keep the frustration from his voice.

Larisha tilted her head. "What happens after that six months — is something wrong with forcing the productive crops?"

Obviously he had not managed to hide his feelings from her. "Not wrong, Raggi — just short-sighted. According to your plans we should have one third of the crops ready for harvesting or silage, one-third should be productive, and one-third devoted to plantings, seedlings and grafts. By concentrating so heavily on production we risk the future!"

Larisha nodded. "But we cannot afford to plan for the long term when we might starve in the short term." She looked around. "From all I've heard you are doing a good job up here, Win, far better than any of my Halfing supervisors. I think I will keep them away from here and let you continue to do what you must." She paused and looked wistfully at the spot where her flowers had bloomed. "See if you can figure out how to balance things better so we can get back on plan. Let me know if you need anything — more workers, supplies, whatever. This greenhouse is very important to me."

Win was dumfounded at the trust she placed in him, a mere Folk. "You honor me, Raggi Larisha. I will do whatever you ask."

Larisha smiled impishly. "If only you could, dear Win, but now is not the time or the place — perhaps later." She reached out and touched his arm, a gently squeeze of fingers against rough fabric that recalled her more intimate caresses. Then she stood. "It is good to see you again, Win. Perhaps we can meet again, later. Don't disappoint me. There are those who doubt the wisdom of my decisions and some who wish only to bring me down." With that, she was gone.

No sooner than she was gone, Opal came to his side. "That was the Raggi, wasn't it?" There was no mistaking the awe in her voice.

"Yes," Win snapped. "She came to find out if we are working hard enough and to ask us to do more. Come along," he shouted to the still staring workers. "Get back to work. There's no time to waste." For a moment he stood and basked in the glory of what she had said. He had a grave responsibility.

And she would be back.

Win noticed that the Palm conducted services much more frequently since the ship's destruction. The entreaties was always the same — that they pray extra hard for the souls of all those brave Men who had sacrificed themselves. She also asked that they pray for poor Larisha, who was working so hard to take the Hadir's place. She spoke of Larisha's bravery at staying with the habitat while other Men sacrificed themselves. She said that Larisha needed all the help they could provide if they were to survive. Larisha, to whom they owed allegiance just as if she were the Hadir himself.

Win stood at the back of one of the services and watched the Palm perform the rituals. Since the departure of the habitat he had seen her only at services. Whenever they did encounter one another she looked away, as if ignoring his very existence. This was just as well; he doubted he'd have the energy to service her, were she as demanding as before. It had been a shock to find that he could not return to his room. He had been relocated from the command level to the Folk quarters along the hab's outer perimeter. Dalgrun was clearly through with him.

Dalgrun's continual demands that they honor Larisha were no surprise. He'd heard that many of the Halfings were blaming the Raggi for their situation. He'd overheard some saying that Larisha had caused the destruction of the ship by arguing with the Hadir and so delayed action until it was too late. The rumors of dissention between her and the Hadir were spoken so much that most assumed they were true. Win wondered about that, having heard some of the arguments between Hadir and Raggi himself. But no, Larisha would not have imperiled the ship — she was not that sort of woman.

Win stopped, shocked to his core. When had he started thinking of Larisha as a woman instead of a Man? When had he started thinking that he, a boy, could even dare to judge someone so far above him? He had to watch himself. He had to be careful. He had to remember his place when they were apart. She'd said that to do otherwise was more dangerous than ever.

Dalgrun's pleas for understanding of Larisha became ever more fervent. The Palm produced excuses for every problem throughout the hab, even those that the Raggi could not possibly have been directly involved in, and asked all to pray ever harder.

At the same time Dalgrun always took time to meet with the Halfings, providing reassurance for their efforts, suggesting what they might do to improve their lot, guiding them in establishing a structure so they could operate without the Men's supervision. So helpful was her guidance that the Halfings began meeting quietly among themselves, sometimes in out-of-the-way places.

One of these was the greenhouse.

Win was working late one night, training the early shoots of peas to a makeshift trellis. These slender shoots would fill the spaces between the rows nicely without blocking the light; and, when mature, their produce would enrich their bland diet.

He was halfway down the aisle, kneeling over the tiny shoots when he heard voices coming from somewhere on the other side of the row of thick kudzu. The voices sounded excited.

"We must do something about this latest outrage," one of the voices declared. "There was no need to them to treat one of ours that way!"

"Still, he failed to do what the Man told him," someone said more calmly. "Had he done so I've no doubt he'd have been amply rewarded."

"But it isn't right that Men should be able to do as they wish with our people. The Hadir never allowed the Men to have this much power over us."

"It is necessary. Didn't the Palm tell us that the Raggi has delegated all authority to the Men. She declares that each of them now has the power of the Hadir over us."

"So Raggi Larisha has abandoned us, while she fumbles around trying to manage the hab. I, for one, am glad that the Palm has not confirmed her as Hadir. She's proven herself too incompetent to lead us."

"Still, there is nothing that we can do but persist until a true Hadir emerges among the Men."

"I hope that it will be one of the nicer ones and not one of those who spend too much time playing with their Folk." There was a ripple of laughter through the group. "Well, it keeps their attention away from us, doesn't it?"

"Maybe," someone said drolly, "things would run better if the Raggi spent more time playing with that boy of hers and less in messing things up for the rest of us!" Win felt his face glow as the crude laughter exploded. He crept away in shame.

"What do you mean, you won't give Rams the people he needs?" Larisha exploded when she heard about the failure of the engine leader to surrender forty of his Halfings to life support.

"Raggi," Han replied smoothly, "you must understand the amount of work we have to do down here. The engines weren't fully secured when they were fired and I need to repair the damage. I need every worker I can get!"

"We won't be using those engines until we get more fuel," Larisha shot back. "Repairs can wait — life support needs those extra hands right now!"

"Perhaps I can provide a half dozen for a week or so," Han replied. "But I refuse to stop working — what if another of those things comes after us? I tell you, Raggi, we need these engines repaired now, not later!"

"There will be no more of those crystal balloons now that we are away from Thetti! You are letting your fears run away with you. You are not acting rationally. Give Rams those people and do it now!"

"As you wish . . . Raggi." There was enough hesitation to make his acquiescence insulting, but Larisha said nothing. Reacting to his slur would only acknowledge it. "Good," she said and turned away.

Resistance to her commands was becoming more and more of a problem, even among her loyalists. Perhaps they'd become so independent because they were all so busy with their own problems. This wasn't good. It was as if the hab had been carved into independent estates, one per Man, with each his own Hadir, his own law.

But she couldn't allow the situation to last. If they were all to survive she couldn't have everyone looking only to their own concerns. Engines were important, but without life support the people who maintained those engines would die. Without the greenhouse, life support would have nothing to eat; and without a thousand and one other systems and subsystems operating in concert the greenhouse, her greenhouse, Win's greenhouse would fail.

Perhaps, she wondered, she could ask Dalgrun to stress the need for all to pull together, to coöperate, to share responsibility in her homilies. But she seldom saw the Palm. Dalgrun was always hustling this way or that, ministering to Men and Halfings alike. She had heard that Dalgrun was spending more than a little time with the Halfings, but that was proper since they had to take up so much of the slack due to the lack of Men supervisors.

"The Hand recognizes the hard work you have been doing," Dalgrun congratulated the Halfings during service. "You bring honor on yourselves by performing Men's work. Indeed, you have proven that you are nearly the equal of Men: applying expertise and intelligence to every task at hand and succeeding beyond the Raggi's expectations. You should be proud of what you have done and, some day, when Men see what you have accomplished, you will be amply rewarded.

"But you should not slacken your efforts. The Men are

so few; and the work so hard, that we all must pray that they have the wisdom and judgement to keep us all together so that one day they can take their rightful places in the rôles you have temporarily assumed.

"What is more we must continue to pray for the Raggi as she struggles to save us all from the demons that killed our Hadir and lost our ship. We should continue to be thankful that she chose to come to the habitat with her Folk instead of staying at the side of her husband.

"And we should pray that the Folk continue to serve us all, Men and Halfing, and keep to their proper rôles."

Five of the Halfing leaders met with her after the service to discuss what they would do about the scandal in Han's area.

"Keeping some of our women in his quarters as servants or worse," Joshua reported. "We aren't supposed to tell, but it's become hard to ignore."

Dalgrun tilted her head. "The Men may use their people as they see fit."

"Sharing his bed is what they do," Joshua spat back. "It's indecent!"

Dalgrun made a tent of her fingers. "That is clearly a sin in the eyes of the Hand. Yet, as the Palm, I can do little except recommend their punishment to the Raggi." The five leaned forward, waiting for her next words.

"But I doubt if she will do anything about it," she added sadly. The five rocked back in shock as she continued. "You see, the Raggi has given Men carte blanche and they, naturally, take her as their guide. I ask you, if the Raggi herself used one of the Folk as a personal servant, how can we expect the Men to do otherwise?"

Joshua fidgeted. "There have been rumors . . ." he began, hesitantly.

Dalgrun stood at once. "No more! I will hear none of these nasty rumors about poor Larisha. She needs to hear none of this grief as she struggles to learn how to command us all. I forbid you to voice this vicious rumor to anyone else, do you hear me?" They all nodded assent.

"Now, I suggest that you all decide among yourselves what we are to do about Han. I will cast out those whose sins can be proved. I will see to it that the maximum punishment is applied for any who transgress against the Revelations.

"But you must first bring me proof, not rumors. Only then can I act!"

The five left after kissing her hand and receiving her blessing. "We are strengthened by your words," Joshua said with a sly smile as he slipped away. "Very strengthened."

"Bring me proof of these rumors," she said in closing.

SEVENTEEN

Gull Tamat was desperate. He'd nearly exhausted his fuel supply and the habitat still appeared to be receding from him. He struggled to recall how he had gotten here. A few memories returned.

"Carry these words to the Raggi," Tam Polat had charged him. "Tell her that these creatures examined us when we first arrived. Tell her that I, myself, felt the might of their presence and was humbled. They are mightier than we, Gull. These creatures could be as beyond us as the Emerging God himself, but I pray that they are not. That is why I must sacrifice us — to vanquish them and prove our superiority or to be destroyed so that I might never again feel the pain of our inferiority."

Gull recalled his astonishment that his Hadir, his friend, his leader all these years, had gone completely insane. But no, that could not be — there would be other signs, other lapses if that were so. Yet, the force of the Hadir's words was unmistakable. True or not, Tam Polat had believed in his own words.

"I cannot do this," Gull recalled protesting. "Use the link and tell the Raggi yourself, if you must. I will remain at your side. I will die at your side."

That was when Tam placed his hand on Gull's shoulder and squeezed. "You have been a loyal follower, dear friend. But it is not only my words that I wish you to carry, but yourself." He held up a hand to forestall the scientist's protests. "You are the only one who may be able to understand these creatures and their ships. You are the only one who shares my understanding of their danger. Old friend, it is you and your knowledge that I wish to preserve. Go! Your Hadir commands that you take this knowledge to the Raggi."

Gull looked out the shuttle's port, his eyes seeking the racing habitat. The air was starting to become stale. He felt as if he'd drunk nothing for days, yet he'd only been gone from the ship for a few hours. His tongue was coated with soft slime and when he tried to lick his cracked lips there was little moisture.

He increased the shuttle's velocity with a final burst that exhausted its remaining fuel and prayed that someone on the habitat would see him. He certainly couldn't brake or match velocities without fuel. They would have to take whatever actions needed to rescue him. The habitat grew slightly larger, but imperceptibly.

He tried to relax so he would not use so much of the remaining air supply. Perhaps it would lengthen his survival time by a few minutes. He had to survive. He could not fail his Hadir now, not after what he had learned. He had to reach the Raggi and warn her. He had to let her know the truth of what awaited them.

Han's behavior was becoming outrageous, according to the rumors she overheard from the Halfings. Larisha wondered why Dalgrun hadn't brought this matter to her attention. She doubted the Palm was unaware of what transpired, since she had so much contact with the Halfings. Still, there were only rumors and Han had denied that anything untoward had occurred. "I use these workers simply to relieve me of routine tasks," he'd explained. "The Halfings are simple folk, Raggi. Most of them are hardly capable of understanding how we Men are able restrain ourselves and responsibly in the face of temptation. It is only the nasty minds of those who have too much idle time and less understanding that think otherwise. Don't you agree Raggi? Weren't there similar rumors about that boy of yours?"

Han's query was like an lance thrust into her heart. Did he suspect that the relationship was more than rumor, or was it a veiled threat that she should cast no blame where she was far from blameless?

"Be discreet," she cautioned. "As you've observed, rumors can grow from our most innocent actions."

"I understand your position," he replied. "And I am as certain that you understand mine." There was no mistaking the menace in his voice.

Larisha wondered what was happening. It seemed that every day her control over the Men and the Halfings grew less and less. Tam's Men had abandoned hiding their disregard, had stopped accepting her commands without question, and, as in Han's case, had directly refused to do her bidding. That would all stop when Dalgrun blessed her as the new Hadir. None of the Men would oppose God's will when she had the blessing of the Hand. But when was Dalgrun going to act? It almost seemed as if she were deliberately avoiding making that commitment.

"I assure you that I will do so when the time is right," Dalgrun explained when Larisha finally tracked her down. "But the entire hab is in such disarray — you have no idea of the problems that the Halfings are having without enough Men to guide them. Scarcely a day goes by that I am not called to counsel them in matters spiritual."

"I understand that you are also providing guidance in organization and procedures as well." Larisha hadn't failed to note the charts and reports that were scattered about the Palm's quarters. Without Win to organize things, Dalgrun had reverted to her normally messy self.

"I hesitate to bother you when such minor matters come up," Dalgrun straightened a pile of reports on the table and placed them atop an already tottering stack. "Most of these matters are easily solved, hardly requiring any thought on my part."

Larisha picked up a sheet. "Organizing the Halfings into cadres is not a trivial matter." She pointed to a pair of boxes on one page. "I note that you've organized them by deck, instead of by major system. Was that your idea or theirs?"

Dalgrun snatched the chart away and tossed it onto the pile. "It seemed easier to let them manage their affairs by where they resided rather than where they worked. After all, work doesn't dictate their social structure."

"So it was your idea."

"I merely helped them organize their thoughts. The poor things were quite disturbed without strong leadership. You must admit that the hab is running much more smoothly now that they've begun managing themselves. But let's not talk of such trivial matters, dear Larisha. How is Win? I haven't seen him for days and days. Have you . . . Well, you know." There was no mistaking the smirk on Dalgrun's face.

Larisha felt the blood rush to her cheeks. How dare this woman, this creature who had used Win so badly, this woman who had violated her trust, this woman who had sinned as grievously as she, bring that up! "I have only seen him during my visits to the greenhouse as part of my inspection," she replied frostily.

Dalgrun continued to grin. "And at night, too. I admire your dedication, dear Raggi. Few of us venture there when no one else is around. Tell me, is the flowers' nectar sweeter in the dark?"

Larisha felt as if she'd been slapped. Did Dalgrun know something or was she merely guessing? She had been so careful not to be seen, so careful that their few stolen moments among the greenery would go unnoticed. But apparently, despite her precautions, someone had seen them and reported what they had seen to the Palm.

"I admire your discretion, dear friend," she replied with ice in her voice. "The Hadir must always have moments of privacy."

"Ah, so we come back to the subject of your leadership. Very well, if we must. I am fully supportive of acknowledging you as Hadir, dear Larisha, but with all these rumors, all this turmoil among the Men, the time is just not right. Give us a few more weeks, when things settle down a little more. Then I will do as you wish and provide the Hand's blessing upon you. Just give me a little more time."

Larisha bristled at the delay. "It takes no more than a few minutes, some hand waving, and a few words to do this. Why do you hesitate? You know the hab needs its Hadir. You must know how everyone is floundering because you have not acted!" She tried to calm herself, to bring her voice back down to a conversational level. It did no good for the Hadir to appear emotional, no matter how great the provocation.

Dalgrun sighed. "Very well, Larisha. I will do as you ask at the Revelation Day service. That date will provide added import to the ceremony and will prove to everyone that you have God's blessing. Will that satisfy you?"

Larisha nodded agreement. She wondered what this concession would cost her. "Sooner would be better, but I'll defer to your judgement. Now, let us discuss another matter; why have you said nothing about the problem in life support. I understand that Han has been misusing the Halfings."

Dalgrun leaned back and put her fingers together before her face, as if she were about to pray. She stared at Larisha for long moments before speaking. "It is possible that we have a problem, dear friend — possible. At present there are only rumors and you know the Palm cannot act on rumors alone. Why, if we did that then you would not be where you are, would you?"

There it was again, that thrust into her heart about Win. *What did she know about their secret meetings?* "I don't understand," she replied, understanding where Dalgrun was going with deadly certainty.

"Oh don't act so dense. You know very well that were I to act against Han on the basis of rumors alone then this business with Win would arise and who knows where that might lead? If you must know, I have asked those who brought this to my attention to gather proof and, once that is at hand, I will act. I assure you, dear Raggi, once I have proof of sin I will act with both force and speed. Of that you can be certain."

Larisha had the uncomfortable feeling that those words had little to do with the Han's problems. She must caution Win to be ever more careful of where he went or what he said.

And there could be no more evening inspection tours of the greenhouse.

Larisha was awakened from a troubled sleep filled with nightmares of undergoing questioning while she and Win were pursued by the Palm and hundreds of Halfings, all armed with lances and knives. She found it hard to move since her feet were so firmly rooted in the soil of the greenhouse. Dalgrun was screaming and screaming louder and louder until the noise was unbearable.

It took her a moment before she realized that the noise wasn't part of the dream. It was the hab's alarms! She leaped from the bed and rushed down the corridor to the command center.

Everyone was rushing about, shouting instructions as, above the confusion, the long range screen showed a growing point of light far to their stern. "What is it?" Larisha demanded, wondering if this was another of Tam's demons. There was no Tam to stop it this time. There was no ship to sacrifice on their behalf. She felt an icicle of fear form in her breast.

"It looks like one of the ship's shuttles," someone shouted at her. "We didn't see it until a few minutes ago."

How could there be a shuttle, Larisha wondered? The ship and all who were upon it were completely destroyed when the object and ship collided. For a moment a brief hope arose that some of the Men had survived and were now hurtling toward them.

But that was impossible. Given the time since the explosion, or whatever it had been, and the capacity of a shuttle there was no way anyone could be alive. She was afraid that they would find only dead bodies aboard, yet another reminder of their loss.

"I assume that you've tried to make contact."

"Yes, Raggi. But we got no response. We know that someone is alive inside because we saw the engines fire. I suspect that there is some damage that has disrupted its communications capability."

So someone was alive after all. Who would it be, Larisha wondered — Man, Halfing, or Folk? She doubted it would be anyone important since Tam likely had all essential Men guiding the ship on its suicidal dive. "I want to see whoever is aboard as soon as we rendezvous with it."

Then there was only the agonizing wait.

Larisha was amazed when Gull Tamat stumbled into her room. The Man looked half dead. He could barely stand. "Your clothing is filthy — haven't they even given you the chance to clean up? By God, I will have them punished for . . ."

Gull struggled to speak, and when he did it came out as a cracked croak. "I had to come straight to you, Raggi. You must hear what I have to say."

Larisha started to protest that there would be ample time, but something about Gull's eyes, a haunted look, a fearsome look, the look of someone who had seen their worst nightmares realized, stopped her.

Before she could inquire as to what personal horror he had seen, Dalgrun arrived. "What is this about some survivors from the ship," she began; and, when she saw Gull, she stopped. Her jaw dropped. "It is not possible," she said in amazement. "How did that devil spare you?"

"It is indeed me, honored Palm," Gull whispered grimly through cracked lips. "But it was the Hadir who spared me, not the alien ship."

"Sit here. Make yourself comfortable. Have something to drink, to eat. Rest a bit." Larisha fluttered about Gull like some Halfing servant welcoming her Man back home. Dalgrun flopped into another chair and fanned herself.

Gull shoved everything Larisha offered away save the

mug of water which he consumed in a single, long swallow. Larisha settled herself and waited until, finally, Gull began.

"The Hadir made me leave the ship. He wanted me to deliver a message to your ears, Raggi Larisha." He looked uncomfortably at the Palm and then continued. "So I took one of the shuttles and left as the Hadir drove toward the oncoming ship."

"You mean that machine we destroyed," Dalgrun corrected him sharply. She glared at him as if defying him to contradict her.

Gull stared at her with those haunted eyes until she looked away. "It was a ship, Palm! I no longer have any doubt of that. No, hear me out before you protest."

He settled back, the effort having drained him. "Hadir Tam Polat told me that he had been examined by the ship when he first awakened. He said that it was as far beyond Man as Men are from the animals. Yes, Palm, I too thought it the utmost heresy. I thought that he was, if not insane, then seriously deluded."

"I never knew why he insisted it was a ship instead of something from Thetti," Larisha whispered. "My God, the freezing must have affected his mind."

"An artifact — a simple machine made by a race long dead!" insisted Dalgrun. "You, yourself, said that it was nothing more than a machine — perhaps a very smart machine, but a simple machine nevertheless!"

Gull shook his head. "Yes. I did say that." He paused for a moment as the haunted look reappeared. "But I had no idea — none whatsoever." He began to sob.

"The shuttle was receding from the habitat as I left. I couldn't produce enough acceleration to escape smashing into the object; and, had the collision not forced both ship and object away, I surely would have done so."

Dalgrun erupted. "The Hadir used the ship to destroy the object. If what you are saying were true then you would have been destroyed as well!"

Gull nodded. "That is what should have happened, but something else occurred. Something terrible!"

According to Gull's observations immediately before he left the Hadir, the object was hurtling forward at nearly two thousand meters per second. At the same time Hadir Tam was accelerating the ship, using all of the ship's fuel to impart the greatest velocity he could achieve in the time he had left.

A shuttle's engine was minimal, capable only of driving the thin-shelled cylinder for short distances as it delivered people to ship or habitat. The highest velocity he could achieve was a few hundred meters per second, hardly enough to escape the collision. It was only after he he'd departed that he realized that he should have chosen one of the vessels parked along the ship's rim rather than the one nearest the command module. From the rim he could have flown perpendicular to the ship's course and avoided the worst effects of the collision. But this was no time to have regrets, his fate had been cast and he was surely doomed. The shuttle would not, could not, accelerate enough to save him.

The immense disk of the ship blocked his view of the oncoming object so he had no sense of how imminent the collision would be. The ship dwindled so slowly behind him that it scarcely seemed he was moving at all. Then, around the edges of the ship, he suddenly glimpsed the edge of the onrushing ship. He prayed fervently to be spared, even as he knew that there was no possibility. The collision was upon them.

"That was when I felt them, it, whatever was operating the object. It was only using a fraction of its mind to drive the ship — the rest was preoccupied with, with . . . other things."

Dalgrun bristled. "This is nonsense! I will hear no more of this madness."

"Let him speak. I want to hear this," Larisha insisted.

*   *   *

He had expected an explosion, perhaps some incredibly complex pattern of shards, of debris, of torn metal and broken crystal, or merely the impact of his own ship on the others and then blessed death.

Instead there was a sudden wave of utter cold as the stars disappeared from view and were replaced by . . .

It was as if a thousand voices were speaking at once. It was as if some huge child was examining him with a magnifying glass. It was as if he were weighed, considered, and discarded as of no consequence.

"I cannot describe what I saw," Gull sobbed. "It was a place of the utmost beauty, of sheer terror, of indescribable color and light — it was like no place I had ever imagined, ever dreamed."

"But the ship? What happened to the ship?" Dalgrun exclaimed.

"The ship was there, as was the object — both were nearby, or so I sensed." Gull fluttered his hands. "I'm not sure that I saw them. Not even certain that it was vision. More a sense of place, of impressions, ideas. I'm not making much sense, am I?"

When both Larisha and Dalgrun shook their heads he continued.

"But those weren't the things that convinced me. After all, teleportation of objects might be theoretically possible, even if we haven't yet discovered how. That we were in a different place was not as upsetting as . . . the Gods." Flecks of spittle flew from the corners of his lips as he started to rise, his clenched hands reaching out to grasp something unseen before him.

Dalgrun leaped to her feet. "I will hear no more of this poppycock! He's deranged from the deprivation of his escape. He's obviously been driven insane by his narrow escape."

"They were Gods, Palm Dalgrun," Gull said through his sobs. "If the object was to the Hadir as he was to the animals, then these Gods were at least that far above the object. I felt a touch, only the merest touch of their presence and knew that they were greater than anything I could imagine. My mind felt seared by the sheer power of their presence. I must have passed out then, for I remember nothing else. I woke adrift in space, somewhere behind you. I've been trying to reach you for hours."

Larisha stared at him. "Hours? Gull, it has been weeks since the ship disappeared. Weeks!"

Dalgrun rustled her robes angrily. "I'll hear no more of this nonsense. Obviously this coward must have left the ship long before the collision. He must have been lurking about, saving his own hide while better Men than he were lost. Come, Larisha, listen to no more of this madness. Gods, indeed." She sniffed. "Next he'll be declaring that God's compact is false — that He has not granted Men dominion!"

Gull sobbed. "But everything we've ever thought of as God-like is nothing compared to the power, the intellect, the genius of these creatures! We are less than nothing, Palm. The Gods already exist; and they are here, in this system!"

"I said that I will listen to no more such heresy!" Dalgrun spat out as she strode toward the door. "You are insane, Gull. You are so crazed by the explosion that you can't separate fact from fantasy. I forbid you to speak of this to anyone. I will eject you from the Hand if you ever say these words to another soul."

Gull looked at Dalgrun with empty eyes, all expression drained from his face. His voice was a monotone, devoid of hope. "What value are your threats, Palm Dalgrun? Other races own the universe and they are now aware of who we are! That is what frightens me. That is what I fear so much!"

He bent his head and began to cry, heart-rending sobs that came from deep within his chest. "We are all lost," he sobbed.

But Dalgrun hadn't heard his final protest. She had already turned her back and departed.

Larisha gently stroked Gull's head as she considered everything he'd said. If it was true then it certainly explained Tam's actions.

Yes, now she understood what must have been driving him. Now she realized why he had acted as he had. For a moment she wished that she had not been so skeptical, so insistent on settling Meridian.

Perhaps if she had not been so estranged from him they could have worked together to save themselves, and to protect the settlers who were already on their way.

At one time she had dreamed of a new world where Men would rule. Now it looked as if it would be the Men would be the servants.

Or less.

EIGHTEEN

Dalgrun heard about Gull again during her private meeting with Joshua, one of the more effective of her Halfing leaders. He was emerging as the spokesman for the council. Joshua managed to be forceful, but respectful whenever he put forth a recommendation. He had a nice sense of humor as well and managed to make her smile with some of his tales of what went on during those meetings she could not attend.

She toyed with the idea of inviting him to her bed. Would he be as considerate of her feelings then, would he be one of those passive ones, like Win, or, perhaps, he would take her forcefully, using the sheer strength of his strong arms. The possibilities were as exciting as they were dangerous — any slip of propriety on her part would undo all of the hard work she had done to establish her power base. No, perhaps after she disposed of Larisha she could afford to be less careful, but not now. She looked wistfully at the cat-like way Joshua moved as he took his seat. It might well be worth the wait, she thought.

"The Hadir's scientist himself declares that there are new Gods," were the first words out of Joshua's mouth. All thoughts of dalliance disappeared at once and were replaced by the terrible glow of anger. How dare that demented soul ignore her command to remain silent! She would damn him to eternal hell from the pulpit, she would see that he was thrown from the airlock, that he die a thousand deaths for . . .

"How far has this heresy spread?" Dalgrun said quickly, trying to keep the anger from showing in her expression or voice. "Is this a rumor or have you heard him yourself?"

Joshua nodded. "He was in the main dining area this morning. Stood on a table, he did, and screamed that we are all as nothing — that we are doomed because we dared believe we could become gods ourselves! I tell you, Palm Dalgrun, it caused some terrible cries. One of the Men led him away before the faithful could get to him. Lucky he did, for I think them most upset would have killed him for the blasphemy of it all."

"You did well to bring this news to my attention, Joshua. That must be why you are my most trusted worker." This was worse than she thought possible. Gull's lies had probably been spread to both Man and Halfings, not to mention whatever Folk might have been working in the dining area. His ravings would be throughout the hab before evening, if not earlier. Damn, how could he be so stupid as to upset her at this critical juncture? She would have to accelerate her plans. She would have to figure out how to turn this disaster to her advantage.

"You will tell everyone that he was mistaken, won't you?" Joshua pleaded. "Most of my mates are upset — they say this Man was the Hadir's — a Tamat no less — and must be telling the truth. They are confused. I hope you can explain this at service. We all need your guidance, you know."

Service! Yes, that was how she would turn this around. But not right away. First she must allow this heresy to grow, to ensure that her message would have the maximum impact. She suppressed a smile. "I shall do just that, Joshua. Yes, but first we must see who among us remains a true believer and who will allow their heads to be turned by these lies. That will show us the strength of the Hand. That will show us who we may trust when our time comes."

Yes, when our time comes, she thought and then turned to the other matters that needed their attention.

The split between the Hand's loyal followers and those who held a less firm grip on their faith came sooner than she expected. The faithless would learn, she thought with relish, that only through obedience to the Emerging God would they be saved. When the time came all those who chose to believe the heretic's words would feel the wrath of the Hand. Woe to those who let their souls be led astray.

She suspected that more than a few Men thought that Gull's position as the Hadir's close advisor gave added credence to his ravings, but was not certain. The few she'd contacted had been less than candid — a fact that showed how far from civilized behaviors they all had slipped. At one time none of them would have failed to disclose their innermost thoughts to the Palm nor to seek her comforting guidance on matters spiritual. Now they spoke in guarded tones, hiding their true feelings behind a mask of congeniality. None asked for her guidance. Clearly they had little use for her.

Little did they know that she could see behind their masks, had unearthed the heinous secrets of what went on behind closed doors, of their petty violations, and of their subtle opposition to the proper order of things. Few of them believed Larisha could become Hadir, and most fancied themselves as more qualified. As far as she could see none of them had a Hadir's ability to manipulate people. She, herself, was far more qualified in that respect — look at what she had done with the disorganized Halfings in such a short time. No, she had no respect for the Men on the habitat. None whatsoever.

Disputes among her Halfings were becoming increasingly fractious. Joshua kept her informed of the fights, the ways that entire families were being torn apart by the raging arguments over Gull's proclamations. Within the carefully controlled groups she had organized, separate alliances formed. It seemed as if, at any moment the entire hab would be plunged into anarchy.

Dalgrun wondered if the Folk were equally puzzled. It would be no wonder. The poor things with their limited minds couldn't possibly understand how there could be higher beings than the Men. She must attend to them more often and reassure them of their continued faith in the proper order of things, just as she would warn them that the Men were abandoning their own beliefs and imperiling them all in the eyes of God.

She wondered how long she should let matters proceed. Every sense she had told her that the time was not yet right to make her move. For one thing she had to transfer some of the Halfings into those areas where the Folk had improperly assumed positions of responsibility. It was unwise of Larisha to give them control of life support. Who knew that they might start thinking that, just because they can operate some machinery, they are the equals of the Halfings. If that happened then some of the Halfings might begin to perceive the Folk differently as well. Society would break down and open the doors of chaos.

She had to see that didn't happen. She had to provide leadership or they would all perish for certain.

Win sat by Larisha's feet as the cool mist of early evening washed over the thick greenery around them. She watched the moisture bead on Win's pale hair and wondered how she could ever have come to have such feelings for one of the Folk. That they were her genetic inferiors, there was no doubt in her mind. That they were less than the Halfings was less so. She had never, not once, thought of any Halfing the way she did about Win. But, if she could feel this way about one of the Folk then wasn't it equally possible that she could have felt like this about a Halfing?

Perhaps Dalgrun had been right back on the ship about her infatuation merely being a manifestation of her body's demands — that Win was merely a convenient tool to provide comfort to her needs.

But no, that wasn't the way she felt. She had faced the truth in that horrible confrontation with Tam when, without thinking, her true feelings had blurted out. She'd said that she loved Win only to wound Tam, to reach down inside him where she knew he would be defenseless, but, as soon as the words were out of her mouth, she knew them to be true. The revelation had shocked her as much as it had Tam.

"Why are you so worried, Larisha," Win asked when he

noticed the frown of concern on her face. "Are things going so badly?"

"Worse than you can imagine, Win. Half the hab wants Gull's head on a platter while the other half want mine or the Palm's. Gull's revelations have created a terrible mess."

"The question among the Folk is whether you believe what he says. Most of them do not understand at all. Most just believe whatever the Halfings tell them. I don't know what is going on in some portions of the ship. Some areas have been completely sealed off to the Folk."

Larisha had wondered about that herself. Was that the action of her Men to halt the circulation of Gull's words, to divide the Halfings and contain the damage, or was there something more sinister that she did not know about? They were vexing questions and could not be easily answered.

"Yes, Win, I think I do believe Gull. He was a trusted member of the Hadir. He has a brilliant mind and was trained by the best scientists Heaven could bring to bear. He is not one to let his imagination run wild, not one to let himself be easily deceived. I have to take what he says at face value — that he ran into something that he did not understand. It is that lack of understanding that worries me most. Are his conclusions valid — are there creatures out there who are so superior, so far beyond us or is there a simpler explanation? I have no choice but to believe Gull until someone proves otherwise.

"But let's not talk about it any more. Let's just have a few quiet moments while we can. Let us talk of nothing of importance, dear Win. Speak of Heaven. Tell me about the way the mountains looked in winter. Tell me of the streams in spring. Tell me about a world we once thought was the center of the universe."

The light dimmed, the mist intensified and she was, for a few stolen moments, at peace.

The Palm's entry was abrupt and unexpected. "Where have

you hidden that damned heretic?" she demanded, ignoring the fact that a meeting was underway. Jut and Laun jumped to their feet to give her their seats while Wil looked defiantly up at her.

Dalgrun chose to ignore the slight and took the nearest chair. "This madman's ravings have inflamed the entire crew. We have near anarchy in every quarter, people are losing faith in general and you in particular, Larisha. They are asking why you've done nothing to stop this Man's horrid proclamations. You sit here, doing nothing to halt his vile heresies. I repeat, Larisha, where have you put this heretic?"

Larisha did not allow herself to be swayed by Dalgrun's anger. She maintained control over her feelings. "Gull Bulgat is being well cared for, I assure you of that, honored Palm."

Dalgrun's jaw dropped. "Bulgat? Surely you jest. How could you take this vicious monster to you after he abandoned you own sweet husband. This is unacceptable, Raggi. Quite unbelievable."

Larisha dared not voice her thoughts. That reference to her "dear sweet husband" was clearly for the benefit of the other Men. Dalgrun knew full well how that particular relationship had gone.

"I do what I must to honor the Hadir," Larisha shot back. Let Dalgrun take exception to that!

"There is no need to allow this insane talk to go on." Dalgrun plowed ahead as if she hadn't heard. "There is no need to upset everyone at this point, now that the object is gone. If Gull truly believes this heresy then we can discuss it in time. As it is everyone is now in a panic, not knowing what to believe — even doubting the Revelations."

"I doubt that the truly faithful can have their beliefs shaken so easily, honored Palm. A few words of reassurance from you would calm most." She paused. "But I do wonder why you continue to mouth nothing but platitudes at service. Why do you remain silent, Palm Dalgrun? Why do you say nothing?"

"I provide what guidance the Hand feels necessary," Dalgrun sniffed. "To speak of these heresies would only give credence to them among the less than faithful. I will speak when I feel it will do the most good."

"As you will provide blessing me as Hadir? Such a simple act would provide considerable reassurance by giving everyone a center. Having a Hadir, fully recognized by the Hand, would go a long way to restoring the social order!" Surely the Palm would not refuse her request now.

"I will do just that, Raggi. I will bless you and pray for the soul of poor Gull at the same time. Perhaps when he hears the words of comfort from the Revelations his mind will clear and he will recant this nonsense about those false Gods of his."

"I will see that he attends," Larisha replied. "I think I will ask him to act as surrogate for Hadir Tam Polat. That way we can indicate the proper passing of command."

"I will not have that Man in my service!"

Larisha leaned forward so that her face was inches from the Palm's. "You must, Dalgrun. The crew needs such symbols to reassure them that all is being done properly."

Dalgrun scowled, clearly disliking the arrangement. Finally she capitulated. "Very well, then. I shall arrange it for the next service." Dalgrun then added; "Why not make this a combined service — Men and Halfings both. That should satisfy your cravings for acknowledgement of your new rôle." The sarcasm was heavy in her voice.

Larisha said nothing. Hadir Larisha. She rolled the sound of it around her mind. She was satisfied that the social order was finally being reestablished.

Larisha had insisted that Win and a few of his friends, Tug and Opal, attend the service. They had to stand near the rear entrance, in an unobtrusive corner, almost out of sight of the crowd. A few in the crowd had glared at them, but no one said anything — probably because they thought the three Folk were there to do help with the setting up of the hall. They probably assumed all three would depart when service began.

Opal was uncomfortable, but equally impressed to be invited and among so many of her superiors. She sucked in her breath whenever one of the Men passed by and had nearly fainted when one of them had actually spoken to Win about arranging a meeting with Larisha.

Tug remained as taciturn as ever, taking everything in and probably memorizing every last detail. Win knew that he would be the center of attention when he spoke of this occasion to the rest of the Folk. Tug was probably relishing the rich fodder this ceremony would provide for his tales.

A hush fell over the crowd as the Palm entered, followed by Larisha and, proudly carrying the Hadir's whip, Gull Bulgat. Larisha took a seat to the right of center and Gull took a place slightly behind. Palm Dalgrun sat on the right side as the opening chords of the service began.

Win allowed himself to be lulled by the reassuring pattern of the service. He mouthed the familiar words of the litany along with everyone else. He prayed as fervently when the Palm asked guidance for the hab and all souls within, allowing the peace of the Emerging God fill his heart. Larisha might have her doubts but he had none. He no longer thought of Men as Gods, as Opal no doubt did, but that did not diminish his belief in something higher and more noble.

The installation of Larisha as Hadir was supposed to follow the homily, the message of reassurance that the Palm had promised. All eyes turned to her as she raised her arms in supplication.

"Hear these words, Emerging God in all of us. Bless the interpretation of your Revelations, enrich us all that you wisdom shines through this servant's poor, insufficient words."

"We await your guidance," the crowd responded as one.

"Hear these words," Dalgrun began. "We have come to

this splendid system, journeying far from Heaven, our home. Not all survived the journey; and I pray nightly for those lost souls, just as I fervently pray for the souls of all those who died so recently. I share the sorrow of all you who lost loved ones in that ill-fated disaster. I cry for the needless loss of life and the situation it has left us in.

"All of you have strived mightily to survive. Everyone in this hall knows the sacrifices that we've had to make to keep the promise we made to the Hand of Heaven: to keep the faith, to do what God wishes us to do in this cold and distant place, and to remain free from sin.

"I know that many of you now doubt that our mission is God's desire. I know that some of you have had your faith shaken by the recent cries that there are fearsome aliens who pursue us, despite the obvious destruction of them by the courageous Hadir Tam Polat. I know that more than a few of you have serious doubts about your faith, about the Hand, about Men, about your rôles. Most of you might wonder why this heavy burden has been placed upon your backs.

"I wondered myself why the Hadir felt that he had to sacrifice himself and have realized that it was because of his wife's sinful acts with one of the Folk."

All color drained from Larisha's face. The Men at the front jerked as if stuck. Cries arose from elsewhere in the crowd. A few shouted "No! No!"

Dalgrun raised her arms. "Yes, the rumors are true, and she continues to sin even now, seeking the boy out in the greenhouse and engaging in her filthy practices. Many have seen this with their own eyes, and I, I will admit, observed this myself not three nights past."

The murmuring in the crowd threatened to drown out Dalgrun's voice. Larisha had come to her feet, as had several of the Men at the front of the hall.

Dalgrun thundered on. "Yes, she and this madman she has adopted drove poor Tam Polat to his needless death. It is she who is to blame bringing God's wrath upon them. He is punishing us all for Larisha's failure to keep her marriage vows, to keep the faith, for ordering the ship to its death!

"It is Bul Larisha who brought this serpent into our bosom and allows him to nibble at the underpinnings of our faith." She turned to face Larisha. "I hereby banish you from the company of Men. I declare you without hope of redemption. I ban you from the comfort of the Hand."

The crowd erupted with shouts of rage and anger as Larisha and Gull started toward the rear exit. Win watched in horror as a group of armed Halfings stepped through the door.

Three things happened at once: Several of the Men, Larisha's loyalists, rushed forward past the screaming Palm; one of the Halfings lowered his weapon to point at Larisha; and Tug threw himself forward seconds before the weapon fired.

Larisha could not believe what was happening. She had trusted Dalgrun to do what was best for them all, not to choose to make this another hypocritical move in her quest for power. She could not believe that the woman had the nerve to pervert the religious service to her own ends. That was her failing, that she had trusted Dalgrun. She had been set up and was now in serious danger.

All this flashed through her mind in the seconds following Dalgrun's curse. She stood stunned for what seemed like hours as the voices of the angry crowd became louder and louder. She barely felt it when Gull pulled her backwards toward the door. "Hurry," he insisted, but she could not move — her legs were like lead, her feet felt as if they were rooted in place. She was aware of Win and some others standing nearby, just as she heard the footsteps running toward her.

Then several armed Halfings appeared from nowhere. It was obvious that Dalgrun had thought of everything, guarding even against her escape. One of the Halfings, a young male had his weapon pointed straight at her. In the time-slowed universe, she seemed to inhabit she could see the way he tightened the muscles around his mouth, the way he hunched his back to lean forward, the way his finger whitened as it tightened on the trigger.

The explosion from the muzzle snapped her back to reality. She saw someone fall to the deck with a bloody hole in his back. But she had no time to see who it might have been for other hands lifted her and carried her through the door and down the corridor. Somebody stooped and picked up the weapon. She glanced right and left, trying to see if they were carrying her to her doom or to temporary safety and realized that they were her own Men, and Win, precious Win followed behind. The sound of shots rang out behind them. Many shots, too many for a single gun. She wondered who of her friends had sacrificed themselves.

Larisha learned that shock lessens as time passes. Now that she'd had time to reflect she knew that she should have read the signs of Dalgrun's deception long before. The lengthy delay in blessing her as Hadir, the subtle control of the Halfings, the failure to reassure the crew. Slowly, secretly Dalgrun must have been plotting this since long before the ship's destruction. She wondered what the Palm would have done to dispose of Hadir and Raggi if the alien ship hadn't appeared.

But such thoughts were fruitless. If Dalgrun's actions, her hypocrisy, had done nothing else it made her lose whatever modicum of faith remained. She had lived a lie, first on Heaven and then in the awakened ship. Like the other Men, she had been so full of herself, so certain in her superiority, so positive that she was genetically blessed to rule and lead. But that had been proven false. Now she realized that she had followed a self-serving religion and trusted a Palm who was rotten to her very center. The Revelations were a lie. There was no Emerging God. There was only an uncaring universe populated by creatures who were equal or greater than Man. The implications of her loss of faith were beyond reckoning, and for hours she could think of nothing else.

Finally she broke the cycle of blame and turned her attention to the struggle that was going on around her as her followers saw to her survival.

Jut, the young woman whose husband had stayed behind to protect their escape, was screaming at someone in life support as the tears rolled down her face. "There's a terrible fight going on in the access corridors," she explained when she saw that she had Larisha's attention. "We've blocked most of the upper levels off from below, but still have to deal with our opposition who were caught inside. Lots of them seem to be loyal to the Palm."

"Doesn't it seem strange that they should be so well organized?" Larisha mused as she studied the situation. "I think this sudden uprising was long planned." That meant that they'd be dealing with this moment by moment while the rebellious Halfings were following a planned campaign. Damn, that would make it doubly difficult to wrest control from them.

Reports continued to flood in as they contacted more parts of the hab. Apparently the Halfings, frustrated by Larisha's escape, were taking their anger and fear out on the Folk. She heard horrifying reports of the slaughter from the many Folk who had used the access corridors and byways to reach the volumes still controlled by Larisha's loyalists. Using their information, several of the Men and even more loyal Halfings led rescue parties to rescue survivors. As the hours went on they saved many, but lost some of their own.

There was no word of what might have happened to Jut's husband. It was only one loss among many, but affected Larisha deeply. She blamed herself for his death, as she was for Tam's and all of the others. It was her responsibility to put a stop to this. She had to make a stand.

Her message was broadcast throughout the hab, although she doubted that those in the portions of the hab outside of her control would hear it. "I, Bul Larisha, declare myself Hadir by virtue of blessing of the Hand of Heaven and the will of my husband, Tam Polat. I reject the false accusations of the Palm and declare void her commission as the spiritual leader of this hab. I ask that all who hear my words swear their loyalty to my name and cease fighting in the name of our mutual survival. I promise further that, once we reach Meridian, I will relinquish command and allow the Men to select their own Hadir by law and right.

"Until that time I wish all people on the hab — Men, Halfing, and Folk — to act as equal partners in bringing us safely to Meridian so that we all might survive. This I ask in the name of the Emerging God."

Gull looked oddly at her. "Why did you use the name of God?" he asked. "I know that you, as I, no longer believe."

"There are many who need assurance," she replied. "I think that those words will give them some comfort." As she said that she wondered if she hadn't become as much of a hypocrite as Dalgrun, using hypothetical beings to lead the sheep around. They were so easy, these smooth lies. It was a trap that she would have to avoid in the future or she would compromise her few remaining ideals.

Reports were that the Folk, while confused by the conflicting accusations, had nevertheless welcomed Larisha's declaration of their humanity. "They will remain loyal to you," Win declared with a smile. "None of us will forget your pledge."

At the same time, she learned, many of the Halfings had been outraged by her attempt to demote their status to that of the Folk. She pleaded with their leaders, tried to bring them to viewpoint, but to no avail. They were adamant they were either the equals of Men — in itself a leap of faith for many — or they were one with the Folk; it was not logical that they could be both. So they thought.

The arguments, pleading, and discussions went on for hours; but, at the end, they remained unconvinced. Slowly, almost unnoticed at first, a few Halfings defected, and then more, until they had lost considerable space to Dalgrun's forces.

Larisha despaired that she could ever make them understand that it was everyone's survival that was at risk? Instead they chose to bring their prejudices, their presumptions to the fore. She worried that the Men felt the same — thinking that she was out to destroy the basis of their society. These were constant worries but were overshadowed when Dalgrun's Halfings seized control of food processing.

"The Council kindly requests that you submit and allow them to take control of the habitat," were Dalgrun's opening remarks when Larisha opened a link to her.

"I recognize no Council," Larisha responded. "I, Hadir Bul Larisha, demand that the Halfing Council be disbanded, that you turn over all control to my people, and that you renounce your vows as Palm."

Dalgrun laughed. "I hardly think that anyone truly believes you are the Hadir, not after your obscene behavior. Besides, you are hardly in a position to make demands now that you are cut off from the food processing centers. Eventually you will get hungry enough to submit. I can afford to wait."

Larisha felt cold fury at the smug, sanctimonious expression on the Palm's face. No doubt there were a few of her trusted Halfings with her, and perhaps some of the Men, out of sight. No, she doubted that the Men trusted the Palm any more than Larisha did after her treachery, no matter how much they might believe Dalgrun's accusations.

"This is not a matter of who is right or wrong, who has sinned or not," Larisha answered. "Even you are not free from sin, dear sister. Would you like to hear your dear Win speak of how he assisted you?"

"I have no desire to hear your pet repeat whatever lies you have trained him to say. You have twelve hours to give the Council an answer."

Dalgrun severed the connection.

Larisha considered Dalgrun's offer. There was no question that they should continue to resist. The Halfing Council was a sham and clearly under Dalgrun's control. She had no doubts that Dalgrun wanted to become Hadir and, once in control, would surely find some way to kill her and her followers. Having the deposed leaders around as living reminders would be terribly inconvenient, not to mention a source of future problems.

The threat of cutting off the food supply was baseless. Since Larisha controlled both life support and command she could retaliate much more quickly and decisively. But she knew that she would not do that. There were too many innocents who would die, too many whose only fault was to believe the lies of their leaders. She couldn't countenance any such wholesale death.

It appeared to be a stalemate and the longer it remained so the greater the risk to the hab's survival. There had to be some solution to this quandary.

She just wished she knew what it was.

Gull Bulgat worked his way through the bin of mung bean sprouts, running his hands through, over and over, to turn and aerate them. "Looks as if this bin is ready for harvesting," Win said as he looked over the scientist's shoulder.

Gull had calmed down considerably since he began working in the greenhouse. Only on rare occasions did he speak of the Gods outside, and less of his own fears. In fact, Gull said very little most of the time, choosing to tend the crops in solitude and silence. "Working with these growing things calms me," he'd declared several days earlier.

Win had thought that Gull had overcome his fears, but that hope was dashed by Gull's next words. "Yes, it is calming to work with things as intellectually primitive as we humans."

Converting the greenhouse to produce food was hard work. But it had to be done just in case Dalgrun carried out her threat to cut off their food supply. Win worried that their diet would become very dull, consisting of nothing but beans, sprouts, and greens. They had converted every square meter of the greenhouse to these new crops so that there was hardly enough space to squeeze through the aisles.

The greenhouse was occupying less and less of his time. More and more he was being drawn into the confidence of Larisha, her Men, and the Halfings. Jut and the other Men seemed to accept Larisha's lead that he spoke for the Folk. At the same time it was obvious that the Halfings resented him, a mere Folk, having such power, and even at being one of her inner circle.

Win knew that it was not his own virtues that conveyed power, but his proximity to the Hadir. So long as she valued his counsel he would remain. She had expressed her admiration for his mind on several occasions, but he had discounted that as nothing more than compliments for the fleeting comfort he had provided. Their furtive meetings had become more and more discussions about the status quo, but there were still moments of surpassing tenderness. "I love you, Win. You are the equal of any Man — never forget that, my love." They were the words he would always remember, always associate with the smell of ripening mung sprouts.

The alarms began halfway through the night cycle. Dalgrun grabbed the first person she saw. "What is happening? Why are the alarms ringing?"

The frightened Halfing looked at her without recognition and shook off her hand. "Another of those things," he panted. "You'd better get to your station!"

Dalgrun suddenly realized that she had forgotten to put her robes over the standard work uniform and probably looked like everyone else. But there was no time to go back and clothe herself properly. She hastened to the makeshift conference room to see what her staff could tell her.

"The Hadir says . . ." Joshua began as she stepped through the door.

"She is not the Hadir!" Dalgrun corrected him sharply. "She isn't even a Man. She's the devil's harlot, less than human!"

Joshua bowed in her direction. "I beg forgiveness, Palm. But the woman says that another of those objects has appeared and is pursuing us! She has asked us to prepare the engines so we can try to evade it."

Dalgrun thought quickly. "Do you have any confirmation of what she says? Has anyone seen this object for themselves?"

One of the Council members coughed. Another shifted uncomfortably in his seat. Joshua looked away.

"I see, you are simply taking her word for this supposed threat, aren't you? Well, I wonder what she hopes to accomplish with this ruse? She certainly can't expect us to believe her." She paused. "Connect me to her. I want to test the truth of this myself."

"Why the hell aren't the engines on line?" were Larisha's first words. "That thing is getting closer with every passing second!"

"My word, Larisha, what has gotten you so excited? Are you so frightened by Gull's ridiculous ravings that you jump at every stray bit of cosmic garbage that comes near?"

"This is no rock — it's another of those crystal ships!" Larisha shot back. "Use the facilities in the aft control room to check these coördinates if you have to see this for yourself."

"We can't do that unless you unlock the controls, Larisha. But I am willing to take a look once you do so." This could be a very fortunate turn of events if she could use this so-called emergency to gain more control over the hab. "I'll send someone down immediately." Joshua went to the door and dispatched a few of his people.

"It's too late now," Larisha screamed. "It is upon us!" The entire hab shook as if it were clenched in a giant's fist.

Dalgrun raced to the port and looked out. At first she could see nothing and then, by looking upwards, toward the command end of the hab, she saw the something reflecting the starlight. For a moment she couldn't understand what she was seeing; had a portion of the hab broken free, had Larisha somehow rigged something to deceive her?

Then the reflection shifted and one glittering facet after another came into sight as the object slowly rolled around the habitat toward her. It could not be! This could not be happening! God had destroyed it utterly. He had shown these lesser creatures the might of Man. She refused to believe that this was happening.

But the others in the room had no such doubts. As one they were screaming. *"The aliens have returned!"*

NINETEEN

Dalgrun couldn't stop shaking as she donned her robes and prepared herself for the service. She attached the sacred emblems, tied the sash, put the purple head covering that was a symbol of her eternal devotion over her head. Of course she'd never normally put on so much regalia all at once. Each piece was for a specific service, each had a specific meaning. But this service was different. For this service she needed every symbol she could muster to provide reassurance to the panicked people who awaited her in the meeting hall. They had come, flocking to her in this grave time of need, screaming for guidance.

But what reassurance could she give that God would protect them? Clearly He had not made His word clear when He vanquished the other one, so what did the appearance of this new object portend? Was this God's way of expressing dissatisfaction that she had not yet rid the hab of its sinners? Was this God's way of punishing her for the failings of her own mortal flesh? No, it was unseemly to think that she was so important that this abomination could be directed at her alone. What was the message that God was sending? What was it?

The question continued to occupy her mind as she fell into the familiar routine of the service, leading the panicked, fearful crowd to hushed silence. She waited as the familiar prayers and music acted as a balm for their troubled souls. As the time for the homily approached, the time when they would expect her to place this horror into a context they could understand, she had no idea of what she would say. She prayed as fervently as the rest for some sign, some indication.

Finally it was time, in the back there was a constant flurry of activity as people came and went. The hab shuddered a time or two as the great engines fired in a futile attempt to break the monster's hold on them.

In the front sat the Men. Their stiff attitudes showed

that their presence was not so much an act of faith as acknowledgement of her power. The Halfing Council members sat immediately behind them and acted more nervous than ever. She cleared her throat to begin, still uncertain of what she could possibly say. The crowd leaned forward expectantly.

"We have been given a sign that God is displeased with us," she began slowly, unsure of where her mouth was taking her. "We have been given a sign that sin still marks our souls. Only through the removal of those who have sinned grievously against God's Revelations can we achieve peace and continue the great work that lies before us."

Yes, now the message was becoming clearer as the words flowed effortlessly forth. "We allowed untruth to gain a foothold in our souls. We allowed Men to sin against God. We allowed Men to destroy all that we hold dear and shake the very foundations of our faith."

At those words the Halfing Council stood and pulled long clubs from their jackets. Joshua lifted his high and swung downwards, shattering the skull of the Man closest to him. The other Council members were swinging their own clubs with equal viciousness. The blood and bits of tooth and bone splattered her robe, dotted her appalled face. Wil leaped up and darted to one side but someone tripped her before she went three steps. She fell forward and was buried under an assault of feet and fists and thudding clubs.

Dalgrun didn't immediately understand what was happening. This was not what she had planned. This was not something that she had told the Council to do.

"Hear me," she cried above the carnage. "I pray to almighty God that He strike these unholy aliens down. That He bring His almighty force to deliver us from this visitation and show these creatures the power and might He has invested in Man."

"Man?" Joshua screamed loudly. "It's you blasted Men who are the cause of all this! It's you that are going to kill us all!" He advanced on her with club held high.

Her last conscious thought was that Joshua was indeed the Man she thought he was. He was going to take her brutally with the force of his powerful arms.

Larisha was curious as to why the object, having made contact with the hab, had done nothing else. Dalgrun's people had fired the engines as she'd asked, but too late. As far as she could tell that attempt hadn't dislodged their attacker.

She wondered how Gull was faring. Surely the arrival of this object would send him completely over the edge. He was probably hiding in some dark place gibbering in fear at this nightmare made real.

One thing differed from what he and Tam had described. She felt no sense of the mighty presence they'd reported. Nor had anyone else reported such feelings. Did that indicate that this was a different object than before or had Tam and Gull been mislead by their own fears?

She tried to appear calm as she considered these questions. Many of her people had lost control and she feared that more would do so soon if something didn't happen. But there was nothing she could do, nothing except pray to a God she no longer believed.

Gull wasn't cowering in a closet as Larisha debated her options. He'd had a moment of cold fear when he first spied the approaching ship; but, when the dreaded contact of a superior intellect failed to materialize, his fear had dissipated, leaving only a desire to learn more of this strange, improbable ship.

That is how he came to be at the very top of the greenhouse, in the airlock through whose port he could see the object that floated less than a hundred meters away. Even from this distance he could see the detail sharp and clear. There was no covering of dust and grime as there had been with those they'd fetched from Thetti's depths. No, this one was as pristine as any shining gemstone, lovely in all its facets, dazzling in its rainbow of color. It was as beautiful as any work of art or nature, yet as organized as the finest crafted machine.

He recalled his earlier theory that the makers of these things had mastered manipulation of dark matter. That would explain the human scientists' inability to detect whatever drove the objects but not their seeming ability to appear and disappear at will. No, there was something else at play, some undiscovered forces that had powers far beyond anything he could imagine. But what could those forces be?

His visual examination of the object's surface revealed nothing save a singular hole that had rotated to a position directly opposite his perch. It appeared to be about two meters by three and looked like nothing so much as a doorway.

What lay within that opening, he wondered? Would it be possible to find out what controlled it were someone to enter? He debated for a long time before coming to a decision that reawakened his earlier fears and sent him into babbling panic. He clawed his way down the ladder to hide beneath the thick vegetation.

Larisha despaired of regaining control over events. Dalgrun's people appeared even more beyond control than her own. Everyone was in a state of panic, running here and there as if they could find refuge somewhere within the hab. There were no hiding places, no refuges, no escape from the huge alien ship that held them in its grasp.

She heard reports of a pogrom in the lower sections as the Folk continued to be killed indiscriminately. Someone mentioned that some Men had been killed as well, but she discounted that — no Halfing would raise a hand against their betters. Then she caught herself; it was so easy to fall into her old patterns of thinking, her own misguided feelings of superiority. How foolish. For a fleeting second she wondered if there was any truth to the report and if, inadvertently, she had contributed to that tragedy by her declaration of the Halfings' temporary equality. She prayed that she had not.

Several shuttles flitted away from the habitat, streaking away into the darkness in a futile effort to escape. "Where do they think they're going?" she asked Jut. "There isn't enough fuel or air on a shuttle to reach Meridian, and that's the only habitable planet in this system."

"Somebody's used some explosives," somebody else reported. "They must be tossing them out of the lower airlock."

"Explosives? My God, how could they imagine that anything we have would be sufficient to damage something that size? It's a waste of resources."

"There's something else they're throwing out the lock. Oh, my God!"

Larisha looked at the image on the screen. There was no mistaking the brightly colored robes of the Palm as she drifted slowly across the intervening space to stick to the surface of the crystal ship. Her arms and legs had spread wide as decompression and cold stiffened her body so that she made a huge "X" marking her landing place. The bodies of others dotted the surface around her but she could not tell if they were Men, Halfing, or Folk. It mattered little; in death all of them were equal.

"It appears that the reports were true. The Halfings are killing Men!" Tears flowed and trickled down Jut's smooth cheeks. "Now we are all lost."

Larisha knew that Jut's tears were for her husband. The sight was a confirmation of Laun's certain death, even if he had miraculously survived the fire-fight during their escape. But perhaps the tears were for Dalgrun as well. Without a Palm, the hab was without a spiritual center, without recourse to faith when all else failed. Flawed though she might be, the Palm provided solace, a comfort to all of them.

She knew she should feel some sorrow at Dalgrun's passing but could not bring herself to do so. In fact, she felt some satisfaction at her death. Didn't the woman deserve to die for her own sins — the lesser one of hypocrisy and the greater one of disservice to the hab by her inflammatory accusations and underhanded plots? Perhaps later she would shed a tear, but only for the Palm, not for the person.

She looked around. Gull, Jut, and a few loyalists were the last Men. No, she corrected herself, that wasn't right — they were all *men* now, all equally frail, pitiful human beings trying to cope with something unexpected, unknowable, unbelievable! Halfing and Folk alike, they must all strive to survive, not because of the settlers, but for their own sakes.

Despite the panic elsewhere Win had managed to organize a band of Folk to take over most of the hab's systems during the rioting. It only took a few hours to reëstablish control of food processing. Now his armed Folk were working their way through the lower decks, locating the moderate Halfings and enlisting their help in expanding control. The intense coördinating effort kept him from thinking of the danger outside. He concentrated only on regaining the hab.

Larisha's Halfings, who were equally busy with other concerns, continued to resent Win. That was evident in the way they spoke to him, telling him what he should do instead of asking his opinion. He ignored them, choosing to follow their instructions only when they agreed with his own efforts. There was little the Halfings could do about the situation. The Folk were more numerous than the Halfings; and, now that the Folk were armed, there was no way control could be wrested from them.

It didn't take long for the reports to come back. Some Folk had embarked on a course of retribution. Fifteen Halfings had been driven into an airlock and then spaced. Their corpses joined those who had preceded them on the surface of the crystal as mute testimony to the horror it had created.

Win pleaded with the Folk to stop the killing. They needed everyone they had to keep the hab operational. Loss of anyone meant that many fewer hands to do the work, that much more knowledge that was forever lost. He didn't know if it was his words or whether the killing fever burned itself out, but the pogrom stopped. A level of calm fell over the hab as people came to their senses. The work of treating the wounded, restoring the damaged portions of the hab, and building a command structure started.

Win knew that it would take months before they realized the true extent of the damage.

Larisha had decided that her presence was more of a liability than a benefit to the hab's recovery. There could be no Hadir without Men, and she seriously doubted that the Halfings would recognize her leadership — there were still so many who had believed Dalgrun's accusations, who still believed that she was the cause of all their woes. Perhaps she was.

The greenhouse was her only refuge, the only place where she could seek consolation, to try to reconcile herself to the changes in her status, her life. She walked through the crowded aisles, flicking the useless, meaningless Hadir's whip at the greenery that blocked her way. She came upon an overturned bucket that she could use as a bench and sat. She picked up a length of cordage and idly turned it in her hands, knotting and untying the rope as her mind wandered over the territory of her failures.

The greenery towered over her head, immersing her in a dim half-light. The smell of the lush growth was all around her but absent of the sweet smell of her flowers.

It was a pity they were all gone, destroyed in the need for more needed plants. She could use the scent of flowers to soothe her troubled soul. Flowers would remind her of Heaven, of the happier life she'd given up to come to this horrid place. And her memories of Heaven recalled her bower, the place that she and Tam had first made love.

She tied a large loop in the rope and pulled the knot tight. Why hadn't she loved Tam enough to believe him? Why hadn't she been true to her vows, her faith, her own principles, and tried to work with him, tried to see the spiritual pain he must have endured. Yes, she was partly to blame for that, certainly.

Then there was the matter of her pride. She had believed herself above criticism, above reproach; and yet she'd violated the trust everyone placed in her by consorting with Win and sin.

But while her mind said this was a sin, her heart that it was untrue. She had come to love Win, to love him with a passion that she had never felt with Tam.

Dalgrun had been right. She was not deserving to be Hadir because she had let her body rule instead of her mind. Because of her the entire enterprise had been lost: Men, Halfling, Folk, and settlers were all doomed. All because of her.

She tossed the end of the rope over an overhanging brace and put the loop around her neck. It would be so easy to pull the end tight and step off the bucket. That would solve a lot of problems and end all of her pain. She closed her eyes.

"Hadir, what are you doing?" the cry startled her so much that she dropped the rope.

"Gull! What are you doing here? I thought that you were lost."

Gull took her hand and helped her down. "I was observing the crystal ship and then I found myself here, under that tray. I think something frightened me. Something I didn't want to do."

"What was it?" Larisha prompted. The scientist appeared quite calm, not at all the quivering mass of fear that she expected.

Gull screwed his face in thought. "I think I was up in the lock. I wanted to get a really good look at it through the port." Larisha waited as he tried to recall more. "Yes, now I remember. There was something on the surface that frightened me."

"You didn't hear any more revelations from the thing, did you?" For a moment she was afraid that he would say that he had and give a lie to all his previous statements. It was impossible that he alone would hear.

"No," Gull said slowly. "This isn't at all like the other one. By the way, I didn't 'hear' it exactly. More like a felt presence, something that reaches deep inside of you. I can't explain it better than that."

"Never mind. Go on. What happened while you were watching it?"

"I was trying to figure out what motivated it when I realized the reason this object is so different. I suspect that perhaps they learned from our earlier encounters and understand how damaging their emanations are to us. I recall wondering if perhaps this wasn't some sort of emissary and . . ." Gull stopped. His eyes grew wide with fear and he started shaking.

Larisha took him by the shoulders and shook him, trying to restore some semblance of calm. "Gull, it's all right. Calm down and tell me what frightened you so."

Gull sucked in a deep breath and closed his eyes. "The doorway! It was the doorway! Oh Hadir, it was so obvious. So terribly, terribly obvious!"

Larisha thought she had missed something. "What are you talking about? What is so obvious?"

But Gull didn't answer. Instead he took her hand and led her to the ladder. "Follow me," he said and started to ascend. Larisha followed, her curiosity growing despite her fear.

Once they were in the lock Gull pointed across the intervening space. "There, see that opening. I suspect that we are supposed to send someone into it."

Larisha looked at the yawning rectangle. "What makes you so certain — it could just as easily be an exhaust vent for the engine that drives this thing."

"I think not, Hadir. The opening is too coincidentally shaped to the same proportions as our hatches — too small for any sort of craft. It is the only opening on the entire crystal, I suspect. Note how it remains aligned with this lock."

Larisha was unconvinced. "Why this lock and not one of the others? What is it about this out of the way place that makes it so singularly attractive?"

Gull was silent for a long time. "It rotated into sight while I was observing it," he replied. "I believe that it senses my presence, understands my interest."

"Because of you earlier contact, you think." Larisha added half to herself. "Well, what are we going to do about it?"

Gull drew in another deep breath. "Someone must go over. Someone must enter the object if we are to learn anything."

Win became alarmed when Larisha was gone for so long. Here in the command center she was protected, but outside there was no guarantee or her safety. Why did she leave and where would she have gone?

The answer came to him at once. There was only one place she would go where she would feel safer than here and that was the greenhouse. He surrendered control to one of his assistants and hastened to the elevator.

Larisha was nearly suited up when he found her. Gull was fastening the air pack on her back as she sealed the front. "What are you doing?" he exclaimed.

"I'm going to try to save the hab," she bit back as one of the fasteners snagged. "Gull thinks that I should go across to examine it."

Gull peeked over her shoulder. "I did not say that. I suggested that someone undertake the examination. You volunteered."

Win saw that the scientist was calm and collected, not the gibbering madman they'd expected. "You are insane. There is nothing you can do against that thing."

Larisha finally succeeded in getting the closure sealed. "Gull believes otherwise, and I intend to see if he is right.

Listen Win, I'm not much use to anyone any more. Half the crew think I'm some sort of monster, while the other half want to kill all the Men. I have nothing to lose; this little visit will kill me or not. It doesn't matter if it does; and, if I succeed, then I will have done something to benefit the rest of you."

Win couldn't believe his ears. "What about us, Larisha? What about our future, our love for each other? Doesn't that count for anything?"

Larisha stared at him for a long time. "Poor innocent Win, I hope that you will understand some day why our love can never be. They'd never allow us any peace, never allow us to survive. Listen to me, my dear; even if we rid ourselves of this visitor, the hab wouldn't survive, not so long as I remain a symbol of the old order. The time of Men is gone, as is our Emerging God and all the burden which that implied.

"We can disguise you as a Halfing," Win protested. "We can hide."

Larisha smiled. "No. My time is over. I must do something so that the rest of you will survive — I owe you all at least that much. If I succeed there is an enormous amount of work ahead of you all." She leaned over quickly, placed a delicate kiss on his wet cheek, and pressed the Hadir's whip into his hand. "Goodbye, sweet boy."

That said, she climbed the ladder.

The chasm yawned before her. Only a hundred meters separated the crystal from the surface of the hab and, once she had climbed out of the lock, she could see the enormity of the thing. She didn't understand how could it hang above her so huge and stationary. She marvelled at the object's beauty, the rich complex of color within its faceted interstices, the angles upon angles. It was complex beyond comprehension. It was beautiful. It was horrifying.

"Whenever you are ready?" Gull said. She took a deep breath and braced herself. "One, two, three," Gull counted as if this were a childhood game. And on 'three' she leaped from the hull with all her strength.

Transition to the crystal wasn't as swift as she thought it would be. Instead time seemed to stretch out as she drifted lazily toward the dark opening that was either her death or a new beginning.

Time seemed to slow for her, as memories of all that had brought her to this time and place flashed through her head. She felt regret for the loss of Heaven's seed, of Jas and Amber, of the death that Dalgrun had undoubtedly brought on herself, at her failure to love and understand Tam Polat, at a thousand and one acts of pettiness and ignorance that marked the steps of her life. She even regretted the troubles she had brought upon Win's head. The one thing that she did not regret was loving Win, loving the very thing that all her society, all her faith, all her beliefs protested was wrong.

And being loved in return.

She felt a momentary chill, as if someone had poured ice into her veins. She tried to move her fingers but they felt sluggish, frozen into claws. She could hear her heart as it struggled to move the slush of fear through her bloodstream. The doorway, if that was what it was, was closer now, her own end ever closer, she thought, and wondered if her life had meant anything, if she had made any difference whatsoever. But it was too late for anything except to enter that icy cave rushing to accept her.

The edges of the opening whipped past on either side and suddenly everything became clear. All blame, all sorrow, all fault, all her petty aspirations and disappointments faded into insignificance as the reality of the object enclosed her.

Immense warmth filled her and, for a brief instant, absolute bliss filled her. All blame, all sorrow, all fault, all her petty aspirations and disappointments faded into insignificance as she surrendered completely to God's embracing, all-encompassing presence.

Win blinked in amazement as the huge crystal disappeared.

His tear-filled eyes had followed Larisha as she slowly floated across the separation and then, just as she disappeared into the hole, the entire crystal had just vanished! He could not understand how that could have happened, how such a thing was possible.

He cried for a long time, sitting in the lock and staring at the tapestry of stars, the emptiness where the visitor had been.

Only there was not empty space. A dimly lit globe floated in the distance. At first he thought it was merely the crystal returning, but after a moment he recognized it — Meridian!

But they could not be at Meridian. Approach to that planet was months in the future, millions and millions of kilometers along the course they were following. How could this be? How could this have happened?

"They are aware of us," Gull said with hushed breath. "I was right! Pray, Win. Pray that our new Gods have delivered us to paradise." The scientist's face was aglow with a holy glory. "Pray, Win. Pray!"

Win drew back as Gull raced into the depths of the greenhouse, an anxious prophet seeking converts, no doubt. Perhaps, he thought as he stared at Meridian's orb, Gull was right; this was the Gods' repayment for Larisha's sacrifice, for offering her life that the hab be safely delivered. Yes, it would be easy for everyone to believe that now, with Meridian, indisputable evidence of God's compassion, so near.

But he could raise no feeling of faith in himself. He had so recently lost his own faith in Men, in their God, his God. Of what value was faith in yet another? Would They disappoint as well, twist his faith to Their own ends? Such arguments were beyond his comprehension, beyond his determination.

Larisha had been right. There were an enormity of difficult tasks ahead. What would the people do without a Hadir, without a leader, without Men, to guide them?

Would they return to the old order or build a new one? Either way, where would he fit into this new society? Where would he find a place?.

Uncertain, without faith, without leadership he picked up the Hadir's whip. He was a Man.

He would survive.

THE END